THEY WERE THE MEN
WHO DROVE LARA
TO THE LIMITS OF ECSTASY. . . .

SAM—A Robert Redford look-alike, a millionaire with impeccable credentials, he was Lara's best friend and lover. The world was their playground . . . but for Sam it wasn't enough.

JAMAL—Lara longed to explore the far reaches of her lust with this consummate seducer, unaware that he was an unpredictable Jekyll and Hyde who would cherish and humiliate her by turns.

EVAN—A brilliant scientist, he offered her his heart with no strings attached. Their consuming, unbridled passion was dark, secret, and selfish . . . and cruelly taken away all too soon.

CHARLES—A mystery man who came into her life when she needed love most, he was richly human and loving, yet sensual. His true identity would prove as shocking as it was inevitable. . . .

* * * *

"[Her books] are solidly about sex, but it is unashamed sex between consenting adults, and if they explore domination and obsession, it is with a light touch and a sense that a bit of connoisseurship does not go amiss in bed. . . . It sets a hell of a standard."
The Sunday Times (London)

THOSE WICKED PLEASURES

Roberta Latow

FAWCETT GOLD MEDAL • NEW YORK

A Fawcett Gold Medal Book
Published by Ballantine Books
Copyright © 1992 by Roberta Latow

All rights reserved under International and Pan-American Copyright Conventions. Published in the United States by Ballantine Books, a division of Random House, Inc., New York, and simultaneously in Canada by Random House of Canada Limited, Toronto.

Library of Congress Catalog Card Number: 91-92402

ISBN 0-449-14788-6

Manufactured in the United States of America

First Edition: July 1992

In memory of
a friend
who also loved Lara

I didn't restrain myself. I gave in completely and went,
went to those pleasures that were half real,
half wrought by my own mind,
went into the brilliant night
and drank strong wine,
the way the champions of pleasure drink.

C.P. CAVAFY

1969

LARA

Chapter 1

It was a Cord, a Sedanca de Ville black motor car, long and low and sleek for a model made in 1931. A soundless glide on its huge, white-walled tires eased it into the stream of traffic. Stylish and elegant, it represented to New Yorkers in the know old money, high society, and Emily Dean Stanton, the woman sitting behind the chauffeur's open compartment under the automobile's leather hood.

Every inch the handsome woman of a certain age, she removed a gold powder compact from her purse, released the catch—a small cartouche of diamonds and rubies—lifted the lid, and gazed at herself in the small mirror. She was not displeased with what she saw, but touched her cheek, then the skin at the corner of her eye, with the tips of her fingers. Lowering the mirror, she raised her chin and stroked her neck. She checked her raven-colored hair, swept back off her face in a neat French twist at the nape of her neck. Not a gray hair in sight, not a strand straying from its place. All was perfection.

Emily Dean Stanton was not an impulsive woman, not subject to temperament. Therein lay her strength and her power. She was, too, highly practical. She leaned back against the gray Worcester upholstery, adjusting the jacket of her Mainbocher "little black town suit," and slid her sables off one shoulder to lay them on the seat next to her. It was that practical turn of mind that made her order Rigby, her chauffeur, to stop at Lara's school. They were only a few blocks away. She had checked her watch. The children would be coming out just about now. She would give her daughter a lift home.

Rigby double-parked the Cord behind several other cars. Some minutes passed before the girls, in their school uniforms and carrying books and schoolbags, burst through the heavily carved oak doors into the street. There, some took off swiftly, eager to get away, while others milled around among their friends. Emily rolled the window down. She took note of her own long, slender hand, elegant down to its oval-shaped nails gleaming with ruby-red glossy nail varnish. Hardly the hands of a woman of her years. Emily didn't mind growing old, but meant to keep her good looks and chic. It felt good to be the Stanton matriarch, to be referred to as the American dowager duchess of New York high society. That was her life.

She leaned from the recesses of the backseat to look out of the window. There were the girls, all chattering noisily as they pulled off school ties and stuffed them into jacket pockets, linked arms with their best friends, or walked off by themselves. Irritating creatures. So very inelegant. And what an embarrassment: a woman of her age there to see not her grandchild but her own daughter. The whole thing was just too public. She wished Lara would appear. More girls, and then at last Lara, her best friend Julia two steps behind her. Lara stood out from the bevy of adolescents chattering like a flock of dull gray birds. She had presence; she had a kind of sensual shine that set her apart from the other girls. Emily was quite taken aback. She would have much preferred her daughter simply to fit into the flock. Let her be just another bird, if she had to be there at all.

Two girls raced across the road to climb into the backseat of the Cadillac parked in front of them. Emily felt the Cord purr into life. As Rigby put it into gear, she stopped him through the intercom. "Thank you, Rigby, but let's just stay parked where we are."

"Shall I go and fetch Miss Lara?"

"I think not."

Emily leaned back, safely hidden. With fascination she watched her daughter through the open window. Lara removed her gray felt hat and stuffed it in her schoolbag along with her tie. Her silvery-blond hair shone in the afternoon sunlight. Emily saw Lara reach behind her to undo the bow of gray grosgrain ribbon holding her hair back off her face. The girl shook out a mass of curly tresses. A mischievous glint appeared in her green eyes as, from her pocket, a lipstick appeared in her hand. Without the aid of a mirror she applied a pale peach tint and then passed the tube over to Julia, who did the same. Lara removed her jacket and draped it over her shoulders, then undid the nearly bursting buttons of her white cotton blouse. Transformed before her mother's eyes, from schoolgirl to provocative young woman. The girl's almost sensual good looks were far too apparent. Emily noted the direction of Rigby's gaze. She was not amused.

She had seen hints of Lara's impending womanhood surfacing before, but never on a public street. It was quite sickening. Home was the appropriate place for her daughter's provocative beauty and charm. Let it enchant the men of the family and their friends. Out in the world, Emily sensed there would be peril for Lara—and trouble for all the family because of it. Emily tolerated no trouble. The answer, of course, was Switzerland. You could rely on a good, strict finishing school.

She would speak to her husband Henry that very evening. And David. David, her nephew, had lived with the Henry Garfield Stantons since his parents were killed in an automobile crash when he was five months old. His father had been Henry's brother. David had become like Emily and Henry's son. David, who was ten years older than Lara, had greater influence over her than any of her siblings. He clearly adored her, as Henry and all the children did. They had spoiled her. Only Emily had achieved relative immunity to Lara's charm and her need to be loved.

Lara and Julia hadn't seen the car. Emily watched them walk in the opposite direction. Emily was relieved. She rolled the window up and sat back. From a compartment she took a small silver thermos and a cut-crystal tumbler. About an inch of chilled martini would be right. She drank it down. Must get that girl a new uniform.

Several months later, Lara burst into David's sitting room. "I need to talk to you. All day I've been trying to . . ."

There was no one there. A sound from the bedroom. She flung the door open and barged into the room. ". . . catch you alone."

Her cousin was naked and very evidently not alone. One part of her shocked self took note of the particular beauty of each of

the two sensuous nude women lying with him on the white
sheets. The sight stopped and silenced her. An erotic aura per-
meated the room, like a rich essence, some delectable perfume.

David, with the tousled dirty-blond hair, his nakedness partially covered by Luan astride him in his arms, Myling making
love to him with caressing hands, voluptuous yet delicate kisses:
he seemed even bigger, more joltingly handsome and virile entwined with the women.

Lara had to watch David licking, nibbling the luscious, pale
pink lips exposed between Myling's long, shapely limbs, flung
wide to reveal herself, open and yearning, for the caresses of
his tongue. The pleasure Luan experienced impaled upon him
declared itself in her sighs, her helpless whimpers. Not so
Myling. Pleas mingled with her groans of ecstasy. She wanted
more from David . . . for him to deliver her into the brief oblivion of sex by whatever means, by any act he chose.

And David, Lara's cousin—where did that look come from?
He seemed only half there in his unbridled sexual ardor. She
felt it was a look she could never ask him to explain.

But she also knew she had never seen anything so sensually
exciting. It was somehow desperately intimate and electrifying.
Shocking but utterly beautiful. Scary, because it triggered something new in her, a feeling more intense than she could ever have
imagined possible. Something in her wanted it never to stop.
Retreat was impossible. Her heart raced, the beat drummed
loudly in her ears. She wanted somehow to be magnetized, to
be drawn into the threesome's adventure, to feel their sensations.

In the past, she had felt only vague stirrings of passion. Her
sexual inexperience was torture to her now. She realized she
half wanted a man to take her in the same way her beloved David
was taking his two women. Where would she find a man as
divine as he to deliver her from the burden of her own virginity?
She took a step closer to the bed.

All her life she had known David's love. His friendly kisses,
his gentle hands, the pleasure his touch always gave her, were
as much a part of her life as breathing. But now she saw there
was more, something quite different, to be had from David. Not,
alas, for her. A first for Lara: a stab of jealousy, a hunger. A
twinge of lust. Desire that obliterated all else. Sensations that
confused her. Forbidden excitement.

When, at last, David saw Lara watching his enthralled sexual encounter, he reacted. Embarrassment was not enough. He made the half-angry descent from the throes of an orgasm that had seemed to go on forever. With considered finesse, he unwound the women, limb by limb, from their erotic tryst and relaxed into the disheveled, white linen-covered pillows.

David felt no shame at lying naked in front of Lara, nor, for that matter, at being found entangled in an orgy. She had grown up with four boys in the house, himself and three brothers. Inevitably she had seen them in the nude, even in various stages of erection at one time or another. There had always been open and free discussions about sex between David and Lara. Their bond of love, as close as brother and sister, was strengthened by their physical attraction for each other. Intimate encounters were impossible for them, and although desire was there, at those times David was particularly careful to subordinate his own libido into mild affection.

He had taken on the role of teacher rather than lover, giving Lara knowledge and some insight into the loving sex he sensed she craved. Her questions, the body language she spoke with, were clear indications of that. He preferred that he should send her out into the sexual world prepared to enjoy every experience. Better him to explain the ways of Eros to her than for her to be at the mercy of the horny, unloving university jocks lined up to plunge her into the let's-get-laid syndrome.

But, so far as he knew, Lara had never seen him or her brothers making long, hard, no-holds-barred sexual love. How long had she been there? Just how much had she seen?

No traumas for Lara. That was his prime concern. He would have to make certain she walked away enriched in some way by what she had seen; made to understand that there was nothing ugly or menacing to upset her. He wanted her to know what rich pleasures the erotic had to offer. That unique joy that adventurous sex can deliver. How sublime the descent to the sexual animal in oneself can be.

Always looking to add something valid to Lara's life, David realized she must now be included in the scene she had stumbled upon. How? Instinctively he knew the best way was to behave casually. Her experience as voyeur must not be made to feel like a shameful intrusion. He wanted nothing to damage sex for

Lara. He could only want her to revel in it, love it, enjoy every aspect of it, as he did himself. On her terms, and only when she was ready for it.

The twins, naked Chinese beauties beneath the sheet casually covering their sensuous, silky-smooth mounds, now lay more decoratively erotic than actively pornographic, draped lanquidly against David. It was up to him to ease them all out of the situation. The girl was his adoring seventeen-year-old cousin, not theirs.

David took his time. He studied the pretty flushed face, the smoldering green eyes. He felt a moment of sadness for the loss of the dancing, mischievous twinkle he was used to seeing in them. Instead he read hungry passion in those eyes he loved so much. Suddenly little Lara had revealed the woman within her, and, as such, had all the needs and desires of one. In a moment his feelings for her changed. Now he loved both the child and the woman. He felt closer to her than ever before.

David smiled at Lara. "Hi. Well, since we all had lunch together, at least we're spared awkward introductions." He waited for her reaction.

Lara said not a word, made no move. The stillness seemed only to add to the erotic essence still permeating the room.

Myling, not insensitive to the girl's embarrassment, kissed David on the cheek and smoothly slipped away from him and off the bed. Wearing her long, straight black tresses like a mantle over her nakedness, she moved gazellelike across the carpet. On approaching Lara, she touched the girl's cheek gently with the back of her hand. She kissed her lightly, most sweetly, on the cheek, and stroked Lara's silky blond hair. She showed no re-action to the Chinese woman's advances, except perhaps for the tear lodged in the corner of her eye. Myling, always the sensu-alist, lifted the tear away with the tip of her tongue, and, leaving another tender kiss on the young girl's cheek, walked away from her. She closed the door Lara had left ajar.

Returning, Myling gently, almost cautiously took Lara's hand in hers and coaxed her, while opening the buttons of her blouse, toward the bed. Though David had eyes only for Lara, the sexual excitement he felt now was for all three women in the room—and seemed to expand in spite of his care for his cousin. Myling's teasing and coaxing of Lara, the feel of Luan's long, seductively nippled breasts in his hands, her lips descending upon his once-again erect penis, inflamed him more than he wished. And then Lara was there, as if in a trance, naked to the waist, on her knees next to him. In a moment her ripe breasts could have been in his hands and he could have licked the dark nimbus, sucked hard on the innocent nipples. He heard her pathetic whisper: "I thought you loved me, only me." The tears trickled down her cheeks.

He closed the buttons of her blouse and placed sweet, gentle kisses on her cheeks, the tip of her nose, her eyes, and told her, "I do love you." With sudden unease, he realized Myling had brought Lara to him for sex. It jolted him out of the grip of Eros. He shot a forbidding look at Myling and dismissed her and Luan from the room. Lara was gently pleading: "David, take me, please take me. I want a man's penis inside me, I want to feel what Myling and Luan have with you. Love me, David, the way you love them."

He kissed and caressed her in as innocent a manner as he could, and tried to distract himself from the pleasure he imagined in her hands if he were to slip her blouse over her shoulders and enjoy her breasts. Lara could not take her eyes from David's still-erect penis; she wanted to fondle it. To, for the first time, take that part of a man that she had, always, until that moment, thought somehow ridiculous, slowly, inch by inch, in her mouth. The desire to lick and kiss him came as naturally to Lara as to the babe that finds the mother's nipple. She looked up into his eyes and asked, "What are you going to do? I need you to love me at least as much as those women."

"I love you more, Lara. But I can't have sex with you. Not now, not ever. Not like I have with them and other women. You've always known that."

Before he could say any more, Lara was on her feet and out of the room. Tears of despair streamed down her cheeks. She felt utterly rejected.

David took his time in the shower. He was neither disturbed nor confused about how to deal with her. He tied the gray terry cloth robe, piped in white cotton cord, around his waist. He opened a drawer in the Biedermeier chest in his bathroom and placed a neatly wrapped Cartier package in his pocket. Barefoot, he walked down the corridor to Lara's room. He knocked at the door. No answer. He knocked again and walked into the room.

"I don't think I want to talk to you, David."

"Is that for now or forever?" he asked, with a smile on his lips.

"Maybe not forever. But nothing will be the same for us."

He felt a pang of sadness, for that rang true, and walked over to the four-poster bed. Lara was lying at an angle across it, dressed in a white eyelet cotton robe, ruffled at the wrists and around the neck, and haphazardly buttoned down the front. It made her look young and vulnerable, and hid the voluptuous body so ready for and in need of love and sex.

Her wondrous platinum blond hair spread like a mass of silk threads over the pillows; the sultry, seductive green eyes sent out a single message, her need of a carnal relationship.

David decoded these messages with mixed feelings. He lay down on the bed next to her, gathered her to him, and inched them both back against the pillows, where they half sat, half reclined. Lara was silent while she tried to fend him off. The more she twisted and turned in his arms, the more he tightened his grip.

"This is stupid, Lara. We have to talk," he told her in a whisper. He stroked her hair and kissed her on the cheek. That seemed to soothe her, and slowly she gave up the struggle. Finally she said, "I thought you loved me . . . ?"

"How can you even question that? Surely you must understand that it is because I love you so much that I have always wanted to be the man to help you understand the sexual side of your nature. To tell you how delectable the pleasures of the flesh can be. Love you? I always will, but here, now, this very afternoon, we must come to terms with the lust we feel. We have gone as far as we can together on that road, Lara. You have always known about my womanizing, so blundering in on my sexual activities this afternoon has been no trauma for you. I won't let you pretend that it was."

"Did I say I was shocked? Did I appear to be in distress? Did I run away?"

Her pride was coming into play now. That was a relief for David. The next part was going to be easier than he thought. That petulant pout again! He began buttoning Lara's robe, and gave her that seductive David Stanton smile that endeared him to women and won him whatever he wanted.

"Quite the contrary, wasn't it, David?" The hauteur in her voice, that touch of bravado behind her eyes softened, and she became more hesitant as she added, "I want a sex life like Myling and Luan. I was so jealous of them. I was devastated when you rejected me. Oh, I know all the reasons why. But, David, just that once . . . It would have meant everything to me." Tears welled up in her eyes, but she forged on. "What am I supposed to do with all my sexy feelings? Give them all to some guy I don't care about? Not a very exciting idea when all that I know about sensual good times so far in life has been told to me by someone I love. If you don't take me, who will? Will you choose me a lover? One of your oh-so-sexy friends? Come on! I doubt it."

"You're right. Not one of my sexy friends. But wrong, too, because I *have* chosen someone. I think he is perfect for you— at this time of your life anyway. A man you will be happy with. Someone who loves you, who has always wanted you. Your first sex should be for love, if possible. If you want him, I am certain he is there for the asking. You know, a nod of the head, a provocative kiss . . . Any hint that you are available will do."

Lara began to laugh. There was a note of anxiety in that laugh, and more than a hint of anger.

"What's so funny?"

"Not funny, pathetic."

"Okay, what's so pathetic?"

"You. The very idea that finding me a lover will solve the problem of my wanting you. All it does is get you off the hook. And, of course, safeguard the good old Stanton standard of morality."

She edged away from him and raised a hand, placing it over his lips. "No, not another word about it. I couldn't bear it. One day you will ache for me as I have ached for you, and *I* will find *you* someone else. I guess, till then, you won't ever know the pain I'm feeling now. Oh, God, I don't want to think about us anymore. Let's never talk about this again. Just tell me who this man is who's going to be my first loving fuck? Just who have you chosen to be your surrogate lover-stud?"

She removed her hand so David could speak. He remained

silent, his gaze intent on her. She half expected his determination to deliver her into the arms of another man to dissolve. She held her breath in hope. She knew it was in vain when he finally answered, "Sam Fayne. And he wasn't chosen lightly. He has known you almost all your life. You are the best of friends. He adores you. He's handsome, a kind and loving guy, and you can have a wonderful love affair to go with the sex. I've tried to see that you get it all, Lara. Take him for as long as it lasts."

"I can't believe it! The boy next door. You are more pathetic than I thought. I want an exiting, thrilling adventure. A touch of depravity, like I saw this afternoon. And you set me up with my best friend."

"Don't be a petulant little smartass, Lara. Other women have had him and, believe you me, from what I hear, you may not be exciting enough for him."

The moment David said it he was sorry. The child in this sensuous adolescent surfaced. Tears filled her eyes again. Before they could burst forth he gathered her in his arms, whispering, "I'm sorry, so sorry. It was mean of me to say that. But you're not making this easy for me. You *are* exciting. So exciting that, if I just have you in my arms, I start wanting to take you. My fantasies are full of you. Other women are not enough. You can't imagine how much I want to fuck you, the things I dream of doing to you. The thought of another man introducing you to real sex drives me wild with passion for you." All control gone, he grasped her by the hair and, pulling her head back, told her, "Now I've said it."

The words she wanted to hear. She felt her own power over David and liked the feeling. She had rarely experienced such power over another human being. She liked it, and in that instant Lara Stanton became more of a woman.

David, always alert to any nuance of change in women, especially in moments of grand passion with them, edged his way back to the reality of the moment. He drew away and watched her. She closed her eyes, trembled, and called out softly, "Oh, yes, yes."

When she opened her eyes he was sitting on the end of the bed. All her life Lara could remember that meeting of their eyes as one of the saddest she would ever know. It was over for them, that special illicit something they had always had for each other.

Gone. They both knew it. But neither of them could speak about it. She slid off the bed and walked to her dressing table, found the silver-backed brush, and began brushing her hair. Returning to the bed, she sat down next to him.

"Friends?" he asked.

She did not miss the tension in his voice. She knew they were. She had to answer him. Her own voice almost cracked when she told him, "Best friends."

He took the brush from her hand and replaced it with the slim Cartier box, continuing to brush her hair himself. "Open it. You'll be pleased."

"What's the occasion?"

"Since when do I need an occasion to spoil you with something pretty?"

She smiled and tore open the red wrappings. A bracelet. A cuff of gold elongated links. He clasped it around her wrist. She bubbled with pleasure. "Mother is right, you spoil me. But promise you won't stop. Oh, David, I love it."

He laughed. "No more than Steven, Max, or John will stop. And Elizabeth is the worst of all of us. No, correction, Your Honor, your dad is the worst offender. Aren't you lucky to be the baby of the family?"

"I wonder."

"My advice, Lara, is don't even question it. You're a golden girl, a Stanton golden girl, spoiled and pampered, beautiful and sexy. And the world is all spread out before you. You're intelligent and fun, and have a solid family backing you up. Go out there, Lara, and grab the golden ring. It's what all we Stantons do. Which reminds me, I must do something about the twins."

"You're going back to them?"

"Yes."

"Will you pick up where you left off? Have more sex with them?" she asked—rather more calmly than he might have hoped.

"I'm not going to try to kid you, Lara. Yeah, they still turn me on."

She was surprised she was no longer upset about David and the erotic twins. She had always taken his advice, and it had rarely been wrong for her. Now she would go out and find love, and a sexual mate who would not reject her. She walked to the door and opened it. "Then you had better go, hadn't you?" As he passed in front of her, she stood on tiptoes to kiss him on the cheek, then thanked him for the bracelet.

"Be careful out there. If you ever want to talk, I'm always here for you, just as the others are." He squeezed her hand. He was in some sense leaving her, no matter what he was saying. She could not help the twinge of pain she felt in her heart.

Lara turned back into her room. She lay down on the chaise and covered herself with a white cashmere coverlet trimmed with pink appliqué roses. She held her arm up, better to view her new bracelet. It shone in the afternoon light filtering through the white silk curtains. She adored it. Her mind kept returning to the sex scene in David's room. The excitement took hold. What compulsions of lust were the three pursuing now? Her imagination took flight. And Myling . . . no woman had ever provoked such sexual feelings in her as the Chinese woman had when she offered to make Lara a part of their orgy. Oh, David, you should have allowed me the experience. David . . . Her imagination soared; she conjured up the taste of a man in her mouth and felt again that exquisite yearning to have him deep down within her throat. She longed for a lover in that way, to feel him deep inside her and moving in and out, as she had seen David with the twins.

As she tried to fight her frustration and feelings of rejection and loneliness, Lara felt herself slipping into some dark emotional void. It was pulling her down. An ugly, desperate feeling. She hated it. She wanted to be up, way up. Was David right? Was what she really wanted a man, sex, not him? Now that idea took hold. Half a dozen young men who had pursued her filled her mind. She began to imagine sex with them. It became exciting. She could think of nothing but sex. Her need seemed overwhelming.

Sam? Maybe David was right. She remembered his kisses. Not bad, what his hands had done. Nice enough. She hadn't exactly laughed down his hard-ons, his anguished pleadings to "make it" with her. But, then again, she hadn't taken it all seriously, either. To her it all seemed like kids' stuff, experimentation. She had never thought of it as sex. Certainly not like the exciting sensations that had sometimes stirred her when she thought of David. Or what she had seen that afternoon, or wanted right now.

She made a vow to herself never again to feel rejection and loneliness. That perked her up. She couldn't endure those mental twins any more than she could bear thinking about that human twosome, Myling and Luan, in the throes of sexual ecstasy. She dressed and fled to the tennis courts on the roof of the Fifth Avenue mansion.

Lara joined her father, Henry Garfield Stanton, and her three brothers, Steven, Max, and John, and her father's friend, Mr. Chou Lee. The twins' father was an old friend of theirs from the days when Henry Stanton was an air ace, a Flying Tiger, fighting the Japanese during the Second World War. Now he was one of the wealthiest industrialists in Hong Kong. Why didn't he question where his daughters were? Lara felt a spurt of jealousy again. The twins' absence served to remind her of what she was missing. For a moment she hated David almost as much as she loved him.

There was a fierce match in progress between her mother, Emily Dean Stanton, and her sister Elizabeth, Lady Chester. Elizabeth's husband Jeremy, the Earl of Chester, greeted Lara with, "Seems like that competitive streak in the Stantons means war. At the very least a duel to the death, whether with racquets, golf clubs, or in business. Don't you Stantons ever play for fun?"

"Fun's the only reason to play anything, Jeremy. But with the Stantons, fun and winning are synonymous," interrupted his father-in-law. He placed an arm around his daughter and kissed her on the cheek.

"Oh, Henry, do spare me the Stanton dictum on the will to win. I get enough of that from Elizabeth."

Henry began to laugh. He could afford to: he and his family were famed winners.

Lara relaxed against her father, grateful for his affection, the warmth of his body, his support. She also had the attention of her brothers; their greetings and friendly teasing. John raised her hand and held it. All the while their eyes were riveted on the game being battled out on the court. In the bosom of her family, Lara's spirits began to rise.

Match point, and then it was over, and Emily Stanton was laughing and throwing her racquet up into the air and catching it as it slowly spun down. Elizabeth jumped over the net and hugged her mother, but she wasn't smiling, simply shaking her head from side to side in admiration—and thinking how to win the next game.

Two of her brothers rushed out to kiss their mother and take up the court, eager and ready for battle. That fierce competitiveness was the norm in the Stanton household. It pulsed in every Stanton's blood like adrenaline, and they did everything to cultivate it in themselves.

Elizabeth and her mother joined their audience and accepted tall glasses of Tom Collins, Emily's favorite after-tennis drink, along with praise for their game. It was Lara's mother who was the first to see the change in her. It must have been marked because she commented on it immediately.

"Lara, how very grown-up you have become recently. A young woman, no longer our girl." All eyes were on her. Her father stepped away a few paces. She wanted to run back into his arms. Her mother did not give up. "You seem suddenly to have blossomed into such an attractive young thing. Not our baby anymore. Oh, dear, I suppose we will have to do something about that. Coming out, a summer ball, take you around a bit."

Lara felt resentful at her mother's tone. It made Lara seem like just another of Emily's charities, to be organized and exploited to raise enviable amounts of money through her friends. Only in this case the aim would be to let American high society know there was a second heiress coming up the line after Elizabeth to inherit Emily's title of grande dame of American high society. And the look she bestowed upon her youngest child, love? Well, maybe, but certainly an arm's length kind of love, the sort where nannies and chauffeurs and private schools fill the breach. The kind where brothers and sisters rather than Mama are enrolled to love baby.

Will Mama ever give me the same kind of proud, loving glances she delivers on cue to my brothers, and to Elizabeth, her firstborn and favorite? That same old niggling question. All her life she had heard her mother's: "Baby demands too much attention." "Spoiled with love is our baby." "Too vain. Too self-centered." Well, maybe so, Mama, but I'm not a patch on you. And Lara wondered what her mother's secret was. Every-

one loved or adored or was afraid of Emily Dean Stanton. Even
Lara.

She heard her sister say, "You can count on us for the London
Season, can't she, Jeremy? Oh, what fun."

Now she felt even more like a cause the two women were
taking up. All eyes were on the game again, including Lara's.
Reversion to the family mania: competitive tennis. But the game
could not hold her attention; her sexual need dominated all else.
She went to sit next to her brother Max. They looked at each
other and smiled. "I'm always so happy when you're home,
Max." She gave him a huge hug, and felt tears of relief at having
a man's arms around her, returning her affection, but she held
them back. Max ruffled her hair. "You do seem different, baby.
Mom is right about that."

Albert, the butler, announced tea was served in the rooftop
pavilion. Somehow motherly authority managed to call a halt to
the game in progress. In the pavilion they were treated to a
sumptuous spread of cucumber sandwiches: small squares of
luscious buttered brown bread, cut slim as a leaf, with even
slimmer roundels of cucumber. They melted in the mouth. Bite-
size strips of deviled-ham toast: silver salvers heaped with them.
Baroque French silver baskets, draped in white linen napkins
edged in lace, proffered tea cakes, crumpets, and scones to be
eaten with dollops of Devonshire cream and strawberry jam. A
Madeira and a coconut cake beckoned from pedestal dishes of
antique Galle glass. There were madeleines, florentines, and a
tarte tatin, whose plump, caramelized apple halves lured even
the stern male competitors, outpointed for once on gastronomic
delights.

The butler served tea from a Georgian silver service, a maid
served coffee from another, and a third offered hot chocolate
from a Queen Anne chocolate pot. To Lara, who was not feeling
very happy with herself or her life, everyone seemed to be in an
enviably buoyant mood. Laughter and easy charm seemed to
flow around the tea table. She tried to brace herself and look
objectively at her family and their friends. They were such a
happy, easygoing, handsome, and vibrant group, in their casual
tennis whites and cable-knit V-necked sweaters, exuding health
and energy. She had to admit to herself they were all more
interesting, more vital, than she was, than most of the people

she knew. Lara was suddenly bored with her life. David was right, as usual. Time to go out, take a hold on the world, and find a love of her own, a sex life of her own. Everyone else in that room had done it. At some time in their lives they must have been right where she was now. They had all grown up. So would she. She felt momentarily better. There was scope for a second cup of tea, another cucumber sandwich.

David appeared just in time to take the last slice of tarte tatin and offer a forkful to Lara. She almost choked on it when the twins' father asked, "What have you done with my daughters, David?" Was it her imagination or was it a look of knowing relief she saw in the faces of her brothers when David answered, "I left them in Bergdorf's. They claimed they hadn't anything to wear for this evening."

Everyone but Lara laughed. The twins, both married to Hong Kong millionaires, were famous for their chic. They had arrived with their father and umpteen pieces of Louis Vuitton luggage— and two maids whose sole function was to play as wardrobe mistresses and dressers to the two women. Lara's mind dwelt on Max, Steven, and John, and the look that had passed between them and David. Had they, too, indulged themselves in the arms of Mr. Lee's daughters? Once again, jealousy took a grip on Lara. She despised the feeling, she must not fall victim of it; she tried to shake herself free.

Why did she feel so betrayed? So deserted by the men in her family? So isolated from intimate love? Oh, if only she had not blundered into David's room, had not seen on his face, and those of the twins, the thrill of illicit sexual lust. How naive she had been about sex, its drives, its fantasies. Now she knew for certain they were not confined to her thoughts or steamy movies. They were practiced by men and women as loved and respected as her own family. And amusing, beautiful women, not just hired whores.

It was Henry Stanton who snapped Lara back into the present. "Too bad about the gold cup." He sat down next to her, bent forward and took a scone, placed it on his plate, and broke it open. Lara spooned out clotted cream from the silver bowl for him. He turned to face her and smiled. Ever since she was old enough to do so, it was their habit at teatime for Lara to dress his scone for him. A heaped spoon of strawberry preserve topped off his favorite teatime confection. She watched him bite into the scone. Lara loved her father, his handsomeness, his authority, his genuine kindness. He was the most powerful man she had ever met: she measured all others by him.

"I was damned sure that yachting trophy was going to be yours this year." He replaced his plate on the coffee table. Putting his arm around his daughter, he spoke to the others in the room. "This girl can outsail all the boys in the family and most of the club members, Chou, and I'm surprised that it's not us swilling champagne from the club's gold cup. Well, maybe next year."

Lara could have hugged him for not showing disappointment. Instead she was content to lean against her father. He discreetly removed his arm and drew away from her to take up his cup and saucer. At that moment Henry Garfield Stanton was not offering the affection Lara needed. Often when she looked to him for emotional support he would pull away. Yet, at other times, he could be effusive in his expressions of affection. His pride in his youngest daughter could be blatant. Recently Lara had noted that his reticence always occurred when her mother was in the room with them. It was almost as if he could love no one more than his wife.

"Baby, you had it, you were almost there, dammit. Whatever made you cut sail? There was plenty of time to go in all standing and still not crash into the dock. What made you chicken out?" John's questions were clouded with disappointment.

David shot him a glance of disapproval, but said nothing. Max offered, "Not to worry, La. You'll take that cup next year. But I sure hope you've learned from your mistakes."

It was the critical tone more than their words that hurt Lara. She remained silent but seething. When Steven said, "Horses are my sport, and I've learned in flat racing from getting pipped at the post. A yacht, a horse . . . it's all the same. You have to see losing as just another lesson in how to win next time. Maybe you were just too cocksure of that cup. A touch of complacency or something like that? That's a sure way to lose in anything. You always gotta remember 'It's never over till the fat lady sings,' slim."

Everyone laughed, and Lara fled the room saying, "Very funny. Class humor, Steven. Right now I don't need you to remind me how inadequate I am, less than the best of you Stantons. Thanks a lot, Steve.''

David and Max were the first to arrive in her room, ostensibly to tease her into a better mood. They found her much as they had expected, angry with them and silent. "Okay, why are you so mad at us?'' Max's question deserved ignoring. She went to the armoire and took out a dress and shoes. She pushed past Steven, who blocked her way, insisting on an answer.

"Because I criticized you? Teased you? La, you're being too silly for words.'' David placed a hand on her arm. She pulled away.

She wheeled around to face them. They were now sitting on the four-poster bed. David was casually flipping through one of her glossy magazines, Max untying the ribbon on a box of marrons glacés, a peace offering, her favorite candy. He liked to think he was always spoiling her with them.

"No, it's because you treat me like a child one day, and the next day expect me to be Wonderwoman. Because you desert me when I need your support and make me feel unloved and a failure. And I don't need you to tell me how not to be a loser. And *don't* call me La anymore, or baby. I need you to love me— Lara Victoria Stanton—for *me*. Win, draw, or lose. As of today I want to be treated with respect, like a woman, even though I happen to be your younger sister.''

"Done. You have our word on it.'' That was Steven, who had been standing in the doorway during her tirade. He walked up to her and swept her off her feet and into his arms. Swinging her slowly around in a circle, he added. "Forgive me, and all of us. It's just that your blooming has rather crept up on us. You have to know that we love you. Ever since you were born we've been toting you around because we love you. I know no other sister who has been so loved and spoiled by her brothers as you have, La— Whoops, I mean Lara.''

He gave her his dazzling smile. "Not laughing at you, sweetheart, just getting used to seeing you as a young lady. I can't even remember one of us shunting you off to Nanny if it was possible to include you. Remember the tour of France in Max's little Bugatti? Your weeks in the Mali desert with David and me? When we took you, all of us, on the Nile cruise. And how many girlfriends have all of us dumped because we had you in tow and loved you infinitely more than them? And Elizabeth, she hasn't been an unloving sister. Seems to me it's quite possible we have spoiled you with love. *Now say you love us.*''

Steven would not let her down until she confessed that she did. The family love bond was in place again.

Left alone Lara thought about her day and the coming evening. All the family was assembled in the Manhattan house: Steven from his anthropological expedition in the Solomon Islands; she and her mother and father from the Long Island house, Cannonberry Chase; Elizabeth and Jeremy from London; and her other brothers—Max and John—who divided their time between their corporate and foundation work and the Manhattan and Long Island residences; and David, who air-taxied himself between Manhattan and Long Island when not pursuing his political ambitions or women.

The family was all together. These were the times when Lara was happiest. Dullness was banished. The house filled with guests, friends dashing in and out. Her mother in her element, playing hostess and matriarch. Her father coolly carrying on with his own affairs and sliding everyone and everything into place to suit him.

Suddenly, because something had radically changed in Lara, she saw the events of the coming evening differently. They loomed more important than they had before. A private tour of the Met and dinner, where her family were the honored guests, where she, too, Lara Victoria Stanton, was being feted. A gesture of thanks from the trustees of the museum for the wing to house contemporary art—newly donated by the Henry Garfield Stanton family.

Emily Dean Stanton did not waste love on her daughter Lara. It wasn't so much that she didn't love her, more that the child had always been difficult, demanding, too much trouble. She had come late in Emily's life. Had been a mistake, and an embarrassment, born to her in middle age. A difficult pregnancy, a long and painful birth, and a colicky baby adored by Henry and her other children . . . No, Lara had done nothing to endear herself to her mother. From the time she had become aware of her condition, Emily had made up her mind that Lara would not disrupt her life. So the child had not been allowed to. Emily saw to that with a marvelous nanny and well-trained staff. And the family had removed much of the burden of mother-love by sharing it with her. In fact, she liked Lara, even if she didn't love her. Lara was extremely beautiful and intelligent, and rarely interfered with Emily's busy schedule. Her demands, her needs, were usually answered by someone else in the family. How could a mother not like such a child?

Though child no longer, she thought, as she sat at her dressing table clasping a wide Van Cleef & Arpels diamond-and-emerald bracelet around her wrist. She walked to the wall safe behind a Sargent painting of her grandmother, slid the painting aside, and opened the safe. She found what she was looking for in a gray velvet box. She went to see Lara.

The door was ajar. Emily pushed it open and stood in the doorway. Her daughter was looking in the full-length mirror. "A penny for your thoughts? May I come in?"

"Oh, you do look elegant, Mother." It was said by Lara in genuine admiration. She went to Emily and, taking her hand, led her into her room and offered her a chair. "You will, as always, be the most attractive woman there this evening."

"Thank you, dear. I do like you in that dress. White suits you. It never did me. You look suddenly very grown up. And to think when Elizabeth and I chose that dress for you at Saks, we said you might be too young for it."

Emily stood up and had her daughter turn around. The Oleg Cassini strapless white chiffon dress was wrapped tightly around the bodice and the waist, then eased off the hips, into luscious, soft folds, to several inches above Lara's well-turned ankle. Her feet were shod in burgundy satin ballet slippers.

Emily had to fight the impulse to pull the dress higher up on Lara's bosom. She had not, as she would remark later to Henry, realized Lara had become so "chesty." Nor was she thrilled with the burgundy shoes. She had chosen white satin ones, but could not be bothered to discuss why Lara had rejected them. Her daughter's sometimes flamboyant touches in her dressing were a little too flashy for Emily and her set. She would get one of the boys to say something about the advantages and chic of underdressing. But not tonight. She touched the long, natural silvery-blond hair, so soft and silky, and smiled. Could have been angel's hair with lights behind it at Christmas. It endeared her daughter to her even more. Emily loved Christmas and all its traditions, all that glitter. That smile was certain praise from her mother, and Lara felt loved and beautiful.

"You seemed very thoughtful when I came in. Instead of a penny, these I think. They should be worth your thoughts. They were your great-grandmother's. Have them, Lara, they will suit you. Now lift your hair."

Emily clasped a five-strand choker of perfectly matched pearls, real pearls with a luster rich and luminescent, held together by a long, slim bar of diamonds set to look like lilies. She adjusted the choker so the lilies were set directly under Lara's chin. It accentuated the girl's long, slender neck. Both women looked at Lara's reflection in the mirror and were well pleased. But all Emily said was, "I think we must ask Pa to buy you a pair of diamond studs for your ears. Small, mind you. You will need them now that the Season will be open to you."

Lara was astonished by her mother's extravagant gesture. The dress, and now the pearls, and a suggestion of more. The Season open to her? Could that at last mean an end to her life of Emily's and Elizabeth's hand-me-downs? A dress allowance all her own? What fun. Except, of course, that she had no idea of even how to shop. What a ninny, she thought. You don't know how to fuck or shop.

"Well, Lara?"

"I was thinking, Mother, that I have lived a very blinkered life."

"Self-involved, I think, dear. But then, most children do. What has brought on this revelation?"

Unable to explain, Lara covered herself by telling only half of what she was feeling. "Tonight. All this hullabaloo at the museum— I suddenly see how important it is. How important we must be as a family. I only thought of us as 'just my family' before. I have never thought or cared about what anyone else might think, or for that matter if anyone else thinks about us at all. I have just taken us for granted as being us, if you know what I mean, Mother."

"Well, not exactly. I find it hard to believe that you have been so naive that you had no vision of the Stantons."

"I think that might be true, Mother."

"You surprise me, Lara. But you look lovely, my dear. Downstairs in half an hour at the latest." Emily Stanton turned to leave, and Lara called out: "Thank you for the necklace, Mother. I will return it in the morning."

"Oh, I think not, dear. A gift, shall we say, to mark this occasion."

A note from her arrived a quarter of an hour later.

Only today this was written in the evening paper. Just the sort of attention the family despises. However, under the circumstances, I thought maybe you should read it. We may disapprove, but it is one man's vision of us.

Unbelievably, this was the first thing Lara had ever read about the Henry Garfield Stantons. She was both riveted, and slightly appalled.

WHO IS AMERICAN HIGH SOCIETY?

The Stantons are fortune's children. Many fortunes for a very long time. They are also New York City's high-society elite. That means discretion, secrecy above all, honor, and good manners. They are monument builders who know how to use power. To that end, they wear their disasters like Boy Scout honor badges, know how to appease the gods, and bury their skeletons deep.

Famous for being revered rather than celebrated. Respected rather than admired. A very private family, always living on the edge of becoming too public for their liking, they remain as they have always been for generations, old, heavy money. American quasi-royalty. The saying goes, "When the Stantons close ranks, Newport, Boston, Philadelphia are no more than a step behind them."

Now for the bad news. It's hard to dislike the Stantons. It's even difficult to envy them. They're nice people. An intelligent, interesting family who do things with their riches and behave like the folks next door, good neighbors. Only their houses always have forty-plus rooms and acres of privacy. Next door is a long way off. Because their interests are so varied and their generosity, for the most part, well covered up, and because they never flaunt their riches, there is always that delicious curiosity about how wealthy the Stanton family is in dollars and cents, bonds and shares, property and corporate holdings. A testament to the extent of their power and wealth is that they do not figure in the popular magazine listings of the wealthiest families in America. Not so the Social Register. There, there are the Stantons—and then high society.

Chapter 2

It was one of those very private events that every glossy magazine, whether for the arts or the style-mad public, would kill to have an exclusive on. One of those evenings that is talked about casually among the select few. Kept a hush-hush art establishment occasion, so as not to offend those benefactors who would never be feted in such a manner. Satisfying the family's request for no fanfare had been as much the object of the evening as saying thank you to Henry Garfield Stanton. A glass wing created by one of the world's finest architects at the cost of sixteen million dollars was indeed a gift to challenge gratitude. An exclusive evening walkabout for the family and a few friends, followed by a dinner: it seemed a modest enough show of appreciation. That was what Emily Dean Stanton wanted, and that was what she was getting.

The Indian summer evening was perfect. The city's towers of steel and glass shimmered with lights that shone like diamonds. The sky above was a bruised blue and mauve streaked with pink. There was hardly a breeze, but although warm for September, autumn still loomed in the air. Henry Garfield Stanton, his houseguests and his family, a party of twenty-odd people, walked the several blocks from the Stanton mansion, up Fifth Avenue, to the museum.

At the corner of Seventy-fourth Street they merged with the Faynes, Henry and Emily's lifelong friends, who had decided to walk to the reception from their 1901, English Renaissance, limestone Park Avenue "palace" (often referred to by Sam as

"China House," because his grandfather had brought light to China by way of kerosene and had been one of the major stockholders with John D. Rockefeller).

The attractive group, a gaggle of New York's elite, in a flutter of understated couture evening gowns, summer furs and family jewels, English-tailored dinner jackets and black silk bow ties, walking arm in arm in groups of two and three, crossed the street to walk along the edge of Central Park. When Sam Fayne fell in next to Lara and handed her a cluster of white moth orchids, David whispered under his breath, "Remember, all it takes is a look, a touch of the hand, and he will give you all you're hungry for. Trust me to be right." She swung round to glare at her cheeky, Mephistophelian cousin, but together they simply burst into laughter. Refusing to share the joke, Lara slipped her arm through Sam's, smiling up at him in a new coquettish way. Arms entwined, they approached the Metropolitan Museum of Art, aglow with light against the night sky.

This splendid warehouse of art, a rich and exciting if not confusing mélange: grand and controversial; often elegant; sometimes banal; this palace in the manner of Versailles, that from its beginnings in 1880 had offered regal acres to display the wares within, which are without peer. The flight of stairs up to the entrance seems no more grand than many others, and yet is more effectively impressive than most. The Stanton party now climbed the stairs with enthusiasm for the evening to come.

The main hall is still one of the great spaces of New York, and probably the only place in the city that suggests the visionary neo-Roman spaces of the seventeenth-century Italian draughtsman Piranesi. It is designed to overwhelm, and rarely fails.

The party's voices and footsteps resounded in the hall and barreled through the corridors, accentuating the quiet, the unpeopled stillness imposed upon the museum by the great art treasures. The voluminous space, the magnetic power of real beauty, true perfection, was intoxicating. It consumed the sixty-odd people and the minimal number of museum guards. It dwarfed them, conferred insignificance on them amid all that was timeless, priceless.

The guests dispersed to the various galleries. With maps of the museum to guide them and two hours before dinner in the new Henry Garfield Stanton wing, they began their search like children on a treasure hunt. The party broke up into groups of three and four. Lara with David, Henry, and Emily. Sam with Max, Luan, Mr. Lee, and Elizabeth.

The echoes were now eerie, muffled sounds from different parts of the building. It was mysterious and exciting, scary but thrilling, all those artistic wonders from so many civilizations looming out of the dark. There was no escape from the pervasive sense of timelessness. It generated a schizoid feeling of being and not being, of reeling back through time while rooted in the present. There was something else, a kind of high, an elation, such as Lara had never felt before.

It had to do with the impact of first walking among the stone dignitaries of ancient Mesopotamia in one gallery, then being accosted by life painted in the abstract by a Rothko or de Kooning in the next. Or of being swallowed up as if into the sun by a Matisse, a Picasso that burned into your soul, sent the heart and the feet racing to yet another gallery.

The Etruscan figures in a brooding half light, the Kouros that whispered in the dark, the prancing Han horses, the Ming vases, the Ching paintings, Renaissance portraits . . . rich and vibrant images. Who were those men and women and who painted them, and were the likenesses real? There was always that paradox: not all likenesses are portraits, nor all portraits likenesses. Individuality, idealization, flattery, and generalization—how were they interwoven by the artist to create these masterpieces that had for centuries drawn men and women into their world as they gazed? The old masters, the Giottos and Titians and El Grecos, a feast that grew from a feast. All that and more, like the huge Poussin that enticed you into a landscape as romantic as anything earth could offer heaven.

The museum at night, without the viewing hordes of daytime, captivated its guests with the richness of its wares. And now the small groups broke up and, for the most part, wandered around the acres of galleries alone, enjoying quick, deep flirtations with the art treasures of their choosing. A unique experience, as unexpected by each as it was disturbing.

An hour into the viewing, Lara wandered back down the main staircase. Her footsteps echoed loudly off the marble and resounded against the vaulted ceiling. It was sensuous and exciting to be here, seemingly alone in the half dark, surrounded by such grandeur, hearing footsteps from nearby, echoed whispers that drifted on the air. Each moment promised a crossing of paths with one of the other treasure hunters.

Lara was caught up in the power of perfection and beauty everywhere she looked. She reveled in it. Twice that day she had felt real power, and she liked the feeling. Now, for the first time, she began to understand the compulsion the Stantons had to perfect themselves. Her own striving to be a winner. Excellence and the satisfaction it can give. These works of art, the sex she saw in the afternoon, had shaken her awake.

She gravitated to the Egyptian Gallery. The huge space was in darkness, with only the odd statue and showcase of Pharaonic gold and jewels dramatically lit. The carved figures, whether life-size or towering above her, were monumental. The room . . . dramatic, ethereal. Tomblike, it reached out to impress the power of life and death upon Lara. Ancient Egypt, the pharaohs, their queens and ministers, their gods, their humanity and inhumanity, the netherworld they believed so passionately in, came alive for her. She trembled, as if someone had walked on her grave. A sound from somewhere further on. Stealthily she followed it, lured onward by the exotic and a mystery in the shadows of an ancient kingdom. She stopped and hid behind a gold-encrusted chariot. She had no wish to blunder in on anyone for a second time this day.

Caught by the edge of a shaft of light, and sitting between the feet of a colossus of the god Isis, were Max and the beautiful Luan. There were whispers of affection, of love even. Lara felt betrayed, and alone, and then amazed when Luan said, ''How strange you Stantons are, having to pretend you love. You don't love me, you want me. Admit that, and you can have me, right here and now.''

''You see through me.''

''That'll do as an admission. It gains you admittance to me.''

She stood up, lifting her long, red crepe de chine skirt to above her waist. A seductive, wicked smile broke across her face. Max began to laugh. ''Here? Now? You're mad. What if someone walks in?'' His hands caressed her tantalizingly exposed bottom. ''The danger of being caught—having you right now, at the very moment I want you—that's quite a turn on for me.''

He was already out of his jacket, folding it and placing it on the base, between the gigantic god's feet. "Do you always walk around without panties, ready and waiting for cock?"

"Always. I'm a sexual opportunist, a libertine," Luan said, with a sensual tension now in her voice.

He was quick. He spun her around, had her on her knees, on the jacket, her back to him, arms outstretched, clinging to Isis's limestone legs. In this shadowy and mysterious place she was like a sacrificial offering upon an altar. Roughly he spread her legs as far apart as he could, raised her naked, rounded buttocks to suit him. Long, slim cunt in a shaft of light. With one powerful, deep thrust he burst into her. "You are a glorious whore."

"And don't you love it, Max? Don't all four of you Stantons just love sex with reputable lady whores like me?"

Another thrust and she answered him with a cry of delight. Standing behind her, this big and handsome man, like the god Eros himself, emanated sexual power, a kind of animal lust. He moved slowly, wholly in and out of her. She gripped him with her cunt and released him, and they fucked as one.

"You're delicious, sublime," he told her in a voice husky with passion.

She laughed and begged, "Deeper, faster."

Max, like a modern-day satyr, his rigid cock prizing its way into this woman, looked even more animallike, moving first into the spotlight and then into the shadows. Mounting her from the rear, hands gripping tight on the slender hips, theirs was an erotic encounter made, it seemed, even more vibrant for being enacted between the legs of a forty-foot stone god. The statuesque remnants of a civilization preoccupied with death and the afterlife gave their stony attention to the scene.

They were gone now, lost to their passion. Max clasped a hand over Luan's mouth to silence her blissful protestations and tightened his grip on her as he increased his pace. He would have her as she had never been had before. That was the determination expressed in his actions. Lara caught the wild look in her brother's eyes. His face was pure lust when the light touched it. Muffled moans of ecstasy now from Luan, words of passion laced with filth from Max.

He looked like one of Picasso's lusty men, or one of his beautiful hirsute beasts that fuck luscious, ripe women. She had vi-

sions of the artist's erotic drawings: rampant bulls with their
human faces and great dramatic twisted horns, wielding enormous cocks, that Picasso liked to draw fucking voluptuous,
open-cunted maidens; masterpieces of their kind. Lara's memory of Picasso's blatant erotic pictures peppering the walls of
Max's study in Cannonberry Chase were vivid to her now. They
troubled the awe with which she looked upon her brother's lust.

She was no longer shocked by what she was seeing. Her new
realism about sex and her own needs had mostly stilled all that.
But it could do nothing for the jealousy she felt. She had no
Max. There and then her will to taste the erotic in all its many
phases was confirmed. To drink from it and have her thirst
quenched. To indulge her own appetites and never be hungry
for sex again. That was surely the way to go in this exciting
process of growing up, entering the world of the adult. Her own
libido now flared up, pounding in her ears. To play the voyeur
seemed no role for her.

She slipped out of her shoes and quietly padded back through
the Egyptian Gallery and into the hall. Inflamed for the second
time that day by the sight of such raunchy sex, Lara tried to
compose herself. She felt as if life were swallowing her up, and
to survive she had to stand back and be quiet. She found a haven
in the shadow of a marble pillar. For some minutes, the exquisite
silence of the great hall, the voluminous emptiness of such a
vast place, became as sensuously meaningful to her as the sex
she had just seen and was yearning for.

In those few minutes Lara learned about pockets of quiet—
true quiet, where desire and needs no longer exist, where the
mind becomes empty. And she understood at once here was one
of the great healing powers the world had to offer. There was a
faint sound, voices and footsteps, from somewhere on the balcony high above her, across the hall. Laughter, and then she
saw her father and mother walking together arm in arm.

Lara rarely had the chance to observe them like this, objectively, from a distance. Emily looked her beautiful cool and
stunning self, her father handsome and big and dashing. Clearly
he was still besotted by her mother. Maybe for the first time
Lara understood that. There was something in the way they were
walking together. She watched them go to the marble balustrade, lean over, and look down into the hall. Her father raised

her mother's hand to his lips and kissed her fingers. And Emily—had she never seen her mother lead her father on, play the femme fatale before? Use her powerful, icy beauty to dominate Henry? Emily could use her quiet, introspective character to cast a huge net that caught them all. She could ration her approval and her affection as if they were diamonds.

As Lara watched from below, she could trace similarities between her mother and herself. The proud and sensual, reserved, almost prudish quality that Emily had. That perfect high-society snob beauty, flickerings of which Lara had seen in herself. She recalled what a chum, Garry, had once said about being introduced to Emily, the doyenne of society.

"She's a cross between Marlene Dietrich and an older Grace Kelly. She's so Grace Kellyish she shimmers."

Lara had laughed and said, "You're movie crazy, and quite wrong. And Mother would hate that description of herself—and ban you from ever seeing me again if she heard you. She thinks movie stars are common, no matter how many pairs of white gloves they wear in public." Tonight Lara wasn't so sure Garry had not been spot-on.

She watched Henry and Emily embrace and laugh about something and walk on. Lara had always been envious of her father and mother's relationship. Pangs of envy assailed her now. She wanted them to love her as much—no, *more* than they loved each other. She craved their total love and attention. She knew they loved her, her brothers adored her, her sister doted on her; they all spoiled her. It made no difference. The pangs of envy were more like fangs. They bit hard into her soul. She wanted more, always more, everything. Lara smiled to herself. To the grand and empty room she announced in a whisper, "This is no easy passage, this being an adolescent on the verge of becoming a woman."

The exquisite tinkling sound of Scarlatti played upon a harpsichord shattered the silence. And then a violin, a cello, a flute. A string quartet and a flute playing at the top of the grand staircase. The music, sweet and ethereal, like that of the Pied Piper of Hamlin, drew the guests from everywhere in the building to assemble for dinner.

For several generations the Stantons had been wealthy collectors, conservative masters of impeccable, refined taste. They had always been generous and philanthropic. The museum had been a beneficiary of that generosity from its inception in 1880. Their connection with it was family history. And this evening, in thanks for their constant support, they were dined in a Georgian room, itself the gift of a Stanton, seated around several Chippendale masterpieces, yet another family donation. The collection of chairs, Chinese Chippendale, Hepplewhite, and Adam, were priceless gifts from other Stantons. The Queen Anne silver, Charles I porringers, and priceless Tudor silver pieces were displayed down the center of the table, between arrangements of white roses and peonies. The guests drank from an array of sixteenth-century glasses, Venetian, English, and Dutch. The linen, Edwardian and Irish, all once belonged to Stantons. The silver-gilt candelabra had dazzled the guests at Napoléon and Josephine's banquets.

The trustees and curators involved in designing this extraordinary evening were not displeased at their guests' reactions. Lara sat between Jamal Ben El-Raisuli, one of her cousin David's oldest friends, and Sam Fayne. Through five courses of delectable food, served by waiters dressed in livery and white gloves, she flirted with her dinner companions. Both men, though obliged to behave with impeccable decorum, slid helplessly under her teasing spell. Finally Jamal Ben El-Raisuli whispered in her ear, "Ah, so the little girl I have known for these past thirteen years seems to have flowered into a young lady. If you were not the sweet virgin cousin of my best friend, I might pluck you from this table for my very own. It can be dangerous to flirt with men of oriental sensibilities, you know."

"Ah," she mimicked, and struck quite perfectly the sensual tone, the faint Arab lilt that still remained after an education at Choate and Harvard, and years of living in and out of Morocco. "And suppose I was no longer sweet? Or even a virgin?" she teased. "Would I then allow you to pluck me for your very own?"

A long look from Jamal chilled her. A novice among sexual teasers, she could not cope with that look. It excited, but frightened her. However, pride would not allow her to retreat. She stood her ground and stared back at him, tilting her head, raising her chin. There was a challenge in the look, more explicit than she realized.

"You are ravishingly pretty. For some time now I have seen boys like Sam watching you. Choose one of them soon, girl, or I might have to put my friendship with your family aside and deflower you myself."

She felt the blood rush to her face, a blush that was impossible to hide. Jamal pressed his advantage and stroked her thigh under cover of the table. He added, "Not a sweet virgin? I don't believe it. But *if* you have already been relieved of that particularly delicious burden, all the better. We can play, you and I, with love and lust."

His touch was exciting. She did not pretend to dislike his hand caressing her. Reluctantly Lara removed it and boldly placed it on *his* thigh with a teasing caress of her own. Seduction was a two-way game now, and she was enjoying it. She could afford to be fearless because she knew she was safe, sure to be the winner in this game. Time, place, and the presence of the family ensured that. She laughed and bent closer toward Jamal. She had always thought him the most handsome and sexy man of all David's friends. He had seemed exotic and generous and very foreign. Just above a whisper, she told him, "How presumptuous of you, Jamal. And what makes you think I would have you as a sexual playmate?"

All this with the background of sixty people dining and chatting, the flautist's haunting music, the pomp and circumstance of the dinner. It added a piquancy to the evening for Lara. She had the attention she wanted, and at the same time a chance to wield her newfound feminine power. Then Sam bent forward, reached for her hand, took it in his, and addressed Jamal.

"Okay, go play the old seduction scene on someone else. Lara's with me this evening." Then turning back to her, he squeezed her hand and warned, "You had better be careful. Jamal thinks all women are fair game."

"Well, aren't they?" asked an amused Jamal.

At that moment Sam, distracted by the woman seated on his right, was obliged to turn away. It was then that Jamal whispered in Lara's ear: "In answer to your question, you will have me as playmate because I know how to unleash your libido, how to excite you sexually. That's what you are looking for. You will call me one day, and I will be there for you. And I will make love to you with sex more exciting than your sweet virgin dreams can imagine. That I promise you.''

Shortly after that the guests left the tables to be served coffee in yet another of the splendid showrooms, this time a French salon. This enabled Lara and Sam to effect their exit from what remained of the evening's entertainment. The excuse was Louis Armstrong at the Blue Angel. It worked. Henry, a jazz aficionado, knew that an evening with Louis must take precedence.

But they had other priorities: they allowed themselves to fall in love, declare their feelings, and act upon them. It all happened so fast, that long after the evening was over and they were in their own respective homes, they were unable to believe that such happiness had been theirs.

They had meant to go to the Blue Angel. There was a table waiting for them in the small, chic, East Side nightclub. Sam helped Lara into her burgundy marabou, waist-length jacket, and they walked through the dimly lit museum corridors toward the front door. They were chattering about the spectacular evening when he chanced to remark that the feather down of her jacket sent shivers through him. ''I find it almost sexy, the feel of your jacket.''

''Just the feel of my jacket?'' she teased.

''No, as a matter of fact. I find you incredibly beautiful and sexy tonight, too. Even more than usual.''

It was she who stopped. She took a long look at Sam. He suddenly looked terribly virile to her. Something clicked for them at that moment. He took her arms and slowly pulled her to him. His hold on her was hard and rough, but his kiss was slow and long and easy, filled with love. She felt her body give in to him, her lips eager to return his kiss. They had kissed before, many times, but it had never been like this. He released her and stroked the arms of the maribou jacket.

''Then let's do something about it,'' she suggested.

He took her in his arms again and asked, ''Like make love?''

''Like make love,'' she answered, excited by the prospect. She placed her arms around his neck and pressed herself tight against him, ''I want you to love me, Sam, and make love to me. I want you to fuck me, Sam.''

He knew a place to take her. ''I've been waiting for you for so long. I've had so many dreams of how it would be to take you for the first time, to open you up and bury myself inside you. I want it to be perfect for you. Every woman I have ever had was only there to bring me closer to you. They enabled me to wait for you. They taught me how to love women, how to be a good enough lover for you,'' he told her as they rushed, arm in arm, from the museum, down the stairs. He paused only to kiss her, touch her, love her, and then rush on again.

With every word of love she wanted him more. How had she not seen him before as she saw him now? His sensuality made her tremble.

In the street he hailed a taxi. At the Hotel Pierre he rushed in with her, unwilling to leave her in the taxi alone. Suppose she changed her mind? He spoke to the concierge. Money changed hands and he went to the bank of telephones and made a call.

''Don't you think we're being rather conspicuous?'' she asked, embarrassment in her voice.

He was quite hurt that she should think he would compromise her in the slightest. He let her go, and she wandered away from him while he made his call. He placed an arm around her and they walked to the flower shop. It had been opened for them. He chose forty-inch long-stemmed white roses for her and whispered, ''I love you.'' They were placed in an enormously long, clear cellophane box and tied with a gigantic white satin ribbon. Then he whisked her back into the waiting taxi and off they went to the Sherry Netherland. They walked straight to the elevators. The concierge seemed to know him, several of the porters greeted him.

''Don't look so shocked and nervous. They have known us since we were children. You must have come here to visit my aunt Bidi a hundred times. It's the most natural thing in the world for us to be here. Aunt Bidi is in her house in the Adirondacks, and I have access to her suite.'' Then he whispered in her ear, ''I want this night to be one you will always remember as romantic and beautiful. Not some sleazy sexcapade.''

Lara would never forget that night, or making love and having sex for the first time. She was reminded after it was all over of what she had read earlier: ''The Stantons are fortune's children.'' In Sam's arms, and giving herself up to him and her own lust, she believed that and was grateful for it. Her thoughts were fleetingly of David, and how grateful she was to have had him prime her for sex. Thanks to David, she had been able to enjoy the pleasures of that night with Sam. Her sexual freedom, an adventurous, sensual nature, were all thanks to him. She was magnificent in her lust, a tribute to both teacher and pupil. And she and Sam fell deeply in love.

There was only one sad thing about the evening. No one had been there to tell Lara not to equate romantic love and good sex with true love; that because someone loves you as much as Sam does, and you are so starved for what he has to offer, there is no reason why you have to love him in return. Just a little thing like that might have made all the difference in Lara Victoria Stanton's and Sam Fayne's lives. But no one had told Lara, and because of the events of that day—and Lara's sexual precocity and the unloosing of her desires, her constant hunger for love and more love all the time—new beginnings were mapped out for her.

Chapter 3

It was dawn before Sam brought Lara home. Only Hastings, the night watchman, was around to let her in. Otherwise the house was quiet. She hardly made a sound. The last thing she wanted was to share her first real love affair with anyone. She slipped into the library and slid the large cherrywood doors closed behind her. Embers were still glowing in the fireplace. She fanned them with the bellows and flames shot to life. She placed several logs on the fire. They caught, and she lay down on her side on the old, worn, black leather chesterfield. She stared into the fire, happier than she had ever been in her life.

Sam loved her more than life itself. How had she not seen that before? How had she been so blind to the virile, exciting man in Sam? He had been a generous lover. Eager to bring her to orgasm several times with hands and lips and tongue, nurturing her craving for sexual intercourse.

She had not believed that it could be so blissful, his penis easing slowly deep inside her. And to feel the beat of cock for the first time, to the rhythm of a man's passion for fucking, was to this virgin a taste of the sublime. To feel that first slow penetration quicken to primitive, even crude, animal need, mixed with protestations of love and adoration for her, was a renewal of self. To have her first man come inside her, feel the heat of his sperm, the scent of sex, the flow of his orgasm. Unimagined new sensations. She wanted to suck his come into her womb, her soul, to lose no drop of that special elixir that sent her into spasms of ecstasy.

It was not at all as several of the girls at school who had gone all the way had told her it would be. Yes, she felt a soreness. Sam had a fine control of himself and so their intercourse was long, especially long for a virgin. But she found even her soreness sexually thrilling. That feeling of being riven, stretched open to accommodate Sam, her cunt bursting with cock—not frightening at all, as her smugly deflowered girlfriends had implied. But then she had had years of David being there to answer her sexual queries, to assure her that when she was ready every morsel of sex that was to be hers would be there to add another dimension of joy to her life.

Lara reached for the cashmere car rug, trimmed and lined in beaver, shook it open, and covered herself. The feel of the amazingly soft fur was almost as sensuous as sex. There was no sleep in Lara. She lay there, eyes open, daydreaming of life with Sam.

How painful it had been for both of them to part. She could think only of their date to meet for lunch, to spend the afternoon and evening having sex in Aunt Bidi's suite of rooms at the Sherry Netherland. Her imagination took flight; she wanted to try everything, have Sam teach her how to give as well as receive great sex. What an adventure their life would be. She thought of the white roses she had left in the Lalique vase in Aunt Bidi's bedroom at the Sherry. So romantic of Sam to have rushed her into the Pierre to find them for her.

It surprised her that she herself barely felt romantic. Well, she could improve. Her thoughts jumped to things she and Sam had done together all their life. Now, as lovers, these would be even better. Maybe they would take a year off from college and sail around the world together. She hugged herself, liking the idea of making love wherever in the world she and Sam chose. She began to smile.

Sam, three years older than Lara and in graduate school at Yale, might want to finish his degree first. Well, she could understand that, and wait. Now she began to conjure up a picture of her lover Sam as a man. Handsome, a football jock. Light brown hair and dark, sexy eyes, a face that was big and square, but with a softness to it. The dimples when he smiled . . . Certain expressions of kindness and patience were responsible, she thought, as if he needed defending for looking and being such a nice guy. But then she also knew him to be intelligent, with ambitions for an academic life. His current dream was to teach philosophy at his alma mater. On the other side of his character, he was like his father, a golf-playing social lion, a deb's delight on every mother's in-list.

She sat bolt upright. Women! How many women had he had while waiting for her to grow up and choose him? And did he have a woman other than her now? She slumped back among the cushions, her moment of anxiety gone. It didn't matter. She remembered he had declared himself in love with her—and only her—enough times for it to ring true.

He was there at the breakfast table with the family when she came down at nine o'clock. The moment their eyes met she felt a warmth course through her body. No one seemed to notice the way they looked at each other. They both imagined everyone knew they were in love, seriously in love, that their years of puppy love were over. She at least expected to be teased about the way he kept picking up her hand and kissing it. A new intensity in the way he flirted with her, and suggested that she be his guest for the Yale-Harvard football game around Thanksgiving time, should at least have hinted at their new relationship. The look of surprise on his face when Max and David said they would like to see the game as well, and sure they would bring her, should have told the family, but not even the sexy twins picked up the signals Sam and Lara were sending out. The family, as always, took Sam Fayne and his friendship with Lara for granted. The antennae of her nearest and dearest were not raised at breakfasttime. Lara was almost displeased.

At last Sam had her alone. He closed the yellow sitting-room doors and, taking her in his arms and kissing her passionately, pressed her up against them. "I thought breakfast would never end. I couldn't sleep a wink. Are you all right? Happy?"

She laughed. "Yes, very happy, and I'm fine."

He looked terribly embarrassed. He stroked her hair and hesitated before asking, almost sheepishly, "You're not still hurting, I hope? The bleeding, it's stopped?" She kept nodding her head, reassuring him she was perfectly well. He seemed not to want to believe her. "It will be better this afternoon. The first time is always the most difficult. And you will get even greater pleasure, I promise." He kissed her again, this time hungrily on her still sensitive nipples, bruised and sore from their earlier

encounter. He sucked them so hard, she squirmed with the pleasure and pain. He pulled away and reluctantly covered her naked
breasts, tugging her soft pink cashmere blouse down over them.
He was panting with passion for her and crushed her to him
again. "Tell me you love me. Tell me," he pleaded.

She said nothing. She could only think of how much she
wanted him. She felt moist with desire for him. Her heart raced.
She wanted to feel him inside her. When she had dressed earlier,
she had remembered what Luan had said to Max. To be like
Luan for Sam, she would discard panties. She wanted always,
like Luan, to be ready to receive a man. All through breakfast
she had found it agreeably sexy to be naked under her skirt, to
be open and ready.

Now she raised her skirt and changed her stance, legs wide
apart, her breathing heavy with expectation. She closed her eyes
and tried to control herself. When she opened them she saw the
shock in Sam's eyes. He caressed her hips, grazed her soft blond
mound of pubic hair with the palm of his hand, and quickly
lowered her skirt for her. He gave her a more gentle kiss this
time and tried to cover his embarrassment. But it was too late.
His eyes gave him away. She hardly had time to feel his rejection
because he was so quick to tell her: "I love you. I want you
all the time. But no, not here. Later. Much as I would like not
to, I have to go now." And he asked her to walk him to his car.
Arm in arm, they walked through the house and to his Maserati.

All morning the comings and goings of the family and their
Chinese guests kept the house in a state of bustle. Lara just
rolled along with it, thinking only of her rendezvous with Sam.
Eighteen houseguests were due at Cannonberry Chase for the
weekend, as well as the entire family. It was under cover of all
that activity, of changing houses and making arrangements with
cars, that the lovers had planned to slip away. They felt secure
in the knowledge that Emily and Henry would accept their absence, only too pleased not to have to think about accommo-
dating Lara in the day's busy schedule. All seemed set for their
afternoon of lovemaking.

However, that was in the morning. By midday, it seemed to
Lara that the entire world was conspiring to keep her and Sam
apart. They were still thwarted after every change of plan they
were obliged to make. It was David who found her in Myling's

room, watching every move the Chinese girl made while instructing her maid in the packing of the famous wardrobe. He was amused at Lara's change of attitude toward the lovely libertine. He sat down on the sofa next to her and placed an arm around her. His first inkling of real change in their relationship was when she pulled away ever so slightly. There was nothing hostile in the action, more a case of a cooling of love. The second was the ease with which she accepted the innuendos about how glorious it would have been for Lara to have joined them in their love tryst the day before.

He told her, "Oh, Sam called. He asked me to tell you lunch is impossible, but he will pick you up at three o'clock."

"Why?"

"I don't know why, Lara."

"Did he say anything else?"

"Only that in the excitement of taking you to lunch, he had forgotten he'd promised to lunch with his father at the club, and it was impossible to break the date."

The look of disappointment in her eyes was hard to miss. David understood they were lovers by the way she defended Sam for having to break the date, the softness in her voice when she spoke about him. He was happy for her and teased her about Sam, and her change of attitude toward him. The look that passed between them before he took her in his arms and hugged her told him she was pleased that he knew. She was grateful to him, and grateful that they still loved each other but differently. Their happiness was infectious. Myling suggested that they should go shopping since she was free. Elizabeth, who had been standing at the door, announced she had an hour to spare, and so, with little enthusiasm for the change of plan, Lara went off with the women.

When she arrived home, Sam was waiting for her. Just the sight of him made her heart leap. His arm around her, he kissed her on the cheek in front of Henry and Emily and John, his clear intention to display some heightened involvement with her. Lara could not understand how she could be so happy with Sam and yet somehow feel he was slipping away from her. He gave no outward indication of that. Henry and Emily looked not at all surprised by his behavior. She wondered if they guessed just how intimate the relationship had become. She didn't think that would go down very well. Emily could be the worst prude she had ever met. Her eyes and ears were closed to her sons' reputations as womanizers. No hint of sexual gossip was permitted in her presence.

While musing on that, Lara took Sam down to the kitchen for a raid on the refrigerator. Shopping had been a spree, and more fun than she had expected. Both Myling and Elizabeth were for spoiling her with a new look, which they insinuated she would be needing. It appeared in the form of six beautiful new outfits. For Lara, snack hunting in the refrigerator with her lover kissing the back of her neck, life was fast becoming a wonderful roller-coaster ride. So it came as a great shock to her when he announced, "We have a problem. Aunt Bidi called . . . She's on her way back."

Lara swung around. Sam kissed her eyes and then her lips, ever so gently. "Where can we go?" she asked.

"It's not a matter of where. There are other places we will be able to use. But we can't today, Lara. All we have is an hour. It's too unfair, but that's the way it is. I have to go to the lawyer's with my father this afternoon. I had no idea. He told me at lunch. The trustees are having a meeting and are making over some property to me. I must be there."

"And after?"

"We're leaving directly for the country. But there's the entire weekend. I'm free then, and we can be together. We can make love on your boat, on the beach, in the stables, the boathouse, in my rooms and yours at Cannonberry Chase. It will be wonderful. I love you, Lara. It's only begun for us. We have a lifetime to make love to each other."

Sam did not understand how much she yearned to be taken by him that afternoon, on their own, away from anything that had to do with family or their everyday lives. Yes, fucked. Not just made love to as he was doing now. He simply had no idea how sensual a woman she was. What her needs were. She herself had only confronted her sexuality—and accepted it—in the last twenty-four hours. David knew. Why, even Myling and Luan understood, and yet the man she loved and had wholly given herself to didn't understand. She felt a twinge of sadness. But Sam's protestations of love, like a soothing balm upon a wound, took the sting away. There was, after all, the weekend to look

forward to, and his love and sex then. These were new beginnings for them both. Thus did she rationalize, not for the last
time in her life, as a way to cope with disappointment.

Emily, from the window of her upstairs sitting room, watched
Lara and Sam sitting on a bench in the garden. It was her fondest
dream that they should marry. A merger of the two families
would delight the Faynes as much as the Stantons. Sam had
always been like one of the family. She loved him as much as
her own children already. One less outsider to bring into the
clan. What a lucky girl Lara was, and only a few weeks before
her departure for school. Just enough time for the couple's newfound love to blossom, and not enough time for them to get into
trouble with it. Then home, and Lara's social coming out. After
Smith College—all the Stanton women went to Smith—and a
year at home and in society, a grand wedding. Perfect! Emily
was well pleased with herself. Lara had been slotted into her
plans beautifully.

Emily's tea that afternoon took place without most of the family, who had already departed for Cannonberry Chase. It was
served in the library, in front of the fire, to Emily, Henry, David,
Elizabeth, Jamal Ben El-Raisuli, and his mother, a gloriously
beautiful French woman whom his father had stolen away from
a French Minister of State. She had never been accepted into
the house except at teatime, for scandals were never forgotten
by Emily, no matter how many years of good behavior went into
atoning for them.

It appeared that Jamal's mother had a box at the opera. A
young Spanish-American tenor was making his debut in Ros-
sini, and there was a seat to spare. David declined it, since he
was due for dinner in the country. Emily, of course, declined;
her excuse, that she, too, was bound for the country. She would
never be seen at a social occasion with Jamal's mother. That
would have automatically made the woman socially acceptable,
and in Emily Dean Stanton's eyes she simply was not. Jamal
and his father, well, that was a different thing. One of her relations, Theodore Roosevelt, her mother's great-uncle Teddy, as
president, had sent the troops into Morocco over an incident
involving a relation of Jamal's. An American woman and her
two children had been kidnapped. Politics, power, and black-
mail made for an admirable connection, especially because there

had been a happy solution to the international incident. America
had emerged with honor. Such things were acceptable, they made
a social connection—as history, if nothing else. But a married
woman, once the Parisian mistress of a Russian archduke, who
ran off with an Arab—that, to Emily Dean Stanton, was not
history. That was dirty linen.

During discussion of the weekend, it appeared that all the
cars going to the country would be full, and David's plane fully
occupied. They realized that Lara, who had planned to go with
Sam, had not been taken into account. Now that her plans had
changed, transport to the country had become a problem. The
train was suggested, and rejected. A car and driver would return
for her.

"Not necessary," offered Jamal. "Remember, I'm driving
out late this evening, and I have room for Lara." He gave her
one of his most charming smiles and said, "I'd be pleased for
the company, La," using the family's childish nickname for her.
"And, if you like, I will allow you to practice your most outrageous acts of flirtation on me. Last night at dinner, you hardly
got going."

Lara, rising to the bait, was quick to say, in a sassy retort,
"If that's all you have to offer, Jamal, I'll take the train." Everyone began to laugh. Jamal and Lara had been playing flirtatious games since she was six years old. He was always teasing
her, and claiming that when she was grown up he would elope
with her to show her the world.

"No, you won't, Lara," Emily insisted. "You will accept
Jamal's invitation—and be thankful to him for sparing you that
tiresome train ride."

Emily disliked Lara's traveling alone on the train. Evenings
were the worst. In things like that she was overprotective. And,
never having been allowed to travel on public transport when
she had been a girl, she saw no reason why her children should.
Emily Dean Stanton was of the Lindbergh kidnapping genera-
tion. She remained, even now, as paranoid about kidnapping as
all the wealthy society families became after that episode. Her
paranoia served her well. It allowed her to sidestep yet another
one of life's public unpleasantness: traveling with the masses.
Chauffeur and car were de rigueur for Lara most of the time—
and always when commuting between Cannonberry Chase and

the Manhattan house. It had been that way for all the children until they were adults and able to make their own arrangements. Emily was therefore relieved when Jamal made the gesture. Less so when Jamal's mother mentioned the box at the opera again, suggesting that Lara accept the empty seat, and that she be allowed to attend a supper party afterward. It would be a late night, but more fun than having to wait until midnight for her ride to Oyster Bay.

Emily consented, much relieved that Lara would travel safely with Jamal, and not least because she had not, in any case, expected Lara at Cannonberry Chase that evening for dinner. Her daughter's presence would have upset her seating arrangement. Emily never allowed thirteen or seventeen at her dinner parties. And tonight they were sixteen. So Lara was bound for the opera, and that was the end of it. No one ever opposed Emily's decisions.

However convenient for Emily she resented the invitation extended by Chantal Ben El-Raisuli. The Stantons' box was one of the more coveted spots in the opera house and had been the family box for as long as there had been a Metropolitan Opera House. It was known that Emily and Henry Stanton sat only in their own box at the Met. Had there been such a thing as a royal box and a crowned head among the patrons, the entire opera world in America would have known where the throne was. Emily actually found Chantal's invitation pushy. And pushy was another negative in the Emily Dean Stanton book of etiquette.

Everyone in the house seemed to be on the move, making ready to leave for the country. Emily and Elizabeth, the last to depart, remained only to check Lara's appearance, and for Emily to give a directive: "Jamal is a good friend to the family. But a degree of respectful aloofness toward the mother—essential, Lara."

Lara was annoyed that she had to dress hours early so that her mother and sister could approve her dress. The two women could not agree about the wide, emerald-green satin sash around Lara's waist. They sanctioned everything else. Lara's evening attire was a shocking pink silk taffeta blouse with voluminous short, puffed sleeves and a moderately low oval neckline. It showed off her lovely young shoulders and slender, graceful neck. Elegant and feminine, yet not in the least provocative, was their verdict. Provocation would emanate from within that night, but that lay beyond even Emily's sharp eye. The cobalt-blue taffeta skirt made the evening outfit both sophisticated and youthful, a rare achievement. Its combination of colors seemed stunningly pretty—and right for a young woman to wear for any grand evening out. At last Emily gave in and sided with Elizabeth. The emerald-green sash was indeed right, a stroke of genius. Monsieur St. Laurent was an artist, Emily decided.

With an inward sigh of relief, Lara thought, Thank God for that. Earlier, when the two women had first arrived in her room, she had done a twirl for their inspection. She had been so pleased with the way she looked, only to have her confidence momentarily shaken by their sharp eyes and quibbling. Emily had removed the pearl-and-diamond choker from Lara's neck, saying, "No, dear. Last night, for a private evening, but in public— well, I think not. A low profile, no jewels. Especially when one is first coming out. You must wear your own charm as if it were a jewel. That should suffice."

Lara detected a changed attitude toward her in her mother and sister. It had happened since yesterday, at the tennis courts. In their minds she was no longer a child. They were treating her as a young adult now. Lara accorded due credit to their perceptiveness. She was no longer a child. Having sex for just a few hours with Sam did much more than end what she felt as her overprized virginity. More even than ease her sexual frustrations; it allowed her to open up as a woman. She felt free of that stifling state of not being one thing or another, free of the anxiety of adolescence. She felt able to go forward and explore her own self, her sexuality, be her own person. Explore without guilt or embarrassment her natural erotic needs. It was as if life were beginning for her, really beginning. Like Eve in the garden . . . Until then she had had only inklings of how divine freedom and being a woman could be.

Lara had to swallow a smile when she thought how appalled her mother and sister would be if they knew their pet had been fucking madly for hours with Sam before daylight. That she had actually found a way to be happy without them pulling the strings. Was that mean? Well, maybe so, but it was satisfying. How devastated they would be to know that she had yielded her virginity without their permission and without a wedding band.

Even worse, how shocked they would be to know how much she enjoyed the experience.

The note of annoyance in Elizabeth's voice curtailed Lara's musings. "We are terribly late. The car has been waiting for an hour. We must leave *now*. But you do look very pretty, my dear. And you are a lucky girl to have such a handsome man as Jamal to take you out this evening. But remember what Mother said— a little distance, a degree of aloofness, can be protective. Chantal Ben El-Raisuli is not one of us."

Her sister kissed her on the cheek and told her, "Everyone will wonder who you are. You will be the new fresh face, and that's exciting. You must tell me all about it in the morning." And the two women were gone.

Lara looked in the mirror. They were right, she looked very pretty and very grown up, and much the young lady she was expected to look. And they had, after all, done their best for her. Whatever that was. It had certainly told her nothing about sex and love—or how to behave in a predatory world. Her brothers had been doing that for her all her life. No wonder she loved them so much.

It was five o'clock. Jamal wasn't picking her up until seven. Ravenous, she went down to the kitchen. Cook thought she looked wonderful. While Cherry, the maid, laid a place at the table for her, and Cook prepared an omelette, she tied on one of Cook's great white aprons loosely, so as not to crush her dress. The rest of the staff drifted into the kitchen to see Lara. She had grown up with these people. They had loved, cared for, and spoiled her since she was a child. They were her second family, just as they had been for all the Stanton children. If nothing else, it was their wholehearted recognition of how pretty and grown up she looked that gave her the confidence she needed to go out with Jamal instead of her lover Sam.

She hardly knew where to wait. There must be no wrinkling of her gown, no messing the blush of makeup or the mass of blond, blond hair dressed by her mother's clever maid Whizzy. She had hardly given Jamal and the evening a thought. They had been reserved for herself and Sam, for being in love, and totally one with another human being. And musing on her bad luck that the day had not worked out for them as they had so carefully planned it the night before, and how the world had already intruded on their romance.

Lara wandered through the reception rooms, turning on lights, and in the drawing room found a place for herself. She would give herself a concert. Like a magnificent diamond, there were many facets to this young girl's character and accomplishments. She sparkled with potential. And, though young in years, she brought an innate maturity to what she pursued. Music had been a cherished pleasure for her since childhood. Trained in the classics, she was undoubtedly capable of making a music career for herself. Popular music was easy and amusing to her, pure fun. Like Henry, she had only to hear a song once and she could entertain with it for the rest of her life. There were two Steinway concert grand pianos, lying like two lovers in the curve of their cases, lids raised, where Henry and she, or David or Max, would play marvelous medleys for hours on end to amuse family and friends. She sat down and, with skirts duly arranged, began to play.

Jamal stood for a considerable time at the entrance to the drawing room, listening with Higgins, one of the butlers, to Gershwin, Cole Porter, and Jerome Kern. He had heard her play like this dozens of times: it had always entertained and amused him. But tonight, watching her, listening to the songs in that grand and attractive drawing room, he felt as if he were seeing her and hearing the music for the first time.

And in a way it was. He had never been in that room, so famed for its beauty and its treasures, when it had not had other people in it. When it had not been filled with interesting conversation and powerful men of the world. Never had he been alone in it with Lara.

A hundred feet long by fifty feet wide, two storeys high, with its vast oriel window facing the garden, its four massive marble fireplaces alight, its priceless furniture, exquisite *objets d'art*, its Graeco-Roman antiquities, Impressionist paintings—Gauguins, Renoirs, Monets, four select Van Goghs—were awe inspiring. The draperies blossomed in a fall of thirty feet from the ceiling—luscious red silk damask, trimmed in a thick, egg yolk yellow, and lined in black-and-white silk taffeta stripes. They were elaborately festooned and tied back with huge silk tassels. The silk had a papery, lackluster look to it, a certain elegant patina that comes with age—in this case, several hundred years. They were relics from France in the years when Madame de Pompadour reigned as the doyenne of chic in Louis's court. Brought home in pieces by one of the Stantons, the drawing room of the Manhattan town house had been designed in the late nineteenth century to accommodate them.

The room was alluring. The grand salon of a New York palace? A country house? Softened by the intimate disposition of the furniture, the muted lamplight filtering through ivory silk shades, the many bowls of tulips, daffodils, roses, and bearded iris, all grown in the hothouses of Cannonberry Chase to keep the room always filled with spring flowers. The proliferation of pictures in silver frames supplied images of the family and those otherwise near-invisible power brokers, rarely mentioned and scarcely seen outside their own elite circle.

Jamal loved this room. He had grown up with David and David's cousins here. He took it for granted as much as the Stantons did. They called it the "big room," and it embodied that severe case of parsimony that Emily was famous for, and that added an even greater chic to the room. It had a worn look, bordering on threadbare—notably the chairs and carpets. A look that would later be made famous by several English antique-dealers-cum-decorators. Her parsimony had let in a patina inseparable from class. The Stantons belonged to a stratum of society that doesn't care to be new or extravagant, that eschews labels and glitz, their houses grand, worn, and used for their own pleasure, not show.

Jamal had heard Lara play like this in all the Stanton houses: here, at Cannonberry Chase, the villa in Cap d'Antibes, and Palm Beach, those very private houses where the family lived discreetly, to which strangers yearned to be known to have been invited. The present enchantment lay in being here alone with Lara, the young heiress to this private world and fascinating kingdom.

Slowly he made his way through the room. He stopped to take in the scent of a bowl of white roses, run his hands through a bowl of potpourri. At one point he seated himself on the arm of a sofa and watched Lara. He had been a fool about her. She had been ripe for years. He should have plucked her from childhood long ago. Even as late as last evening. She looked up and saw him. He sighed and smiled at her, and walked to the piano and leaned on it. "No, don't stop."

Lara finished the Gershwin song. He lowered his head and, raising her hand, kissed it. She stood up. He had not let go of her hand. He stepped back, and with a slightly threatening charm, said, "I should have run off with you when you were thirteen, just as I promised you I would. Now you have grown up, and maybe you won't have me. You look very beautiful."

Chapter 4

Coup de foudre, a shattering blow, the thunderbolt of love at first sight. It was crazy, but that was all Lara could think about. *Coup de foudre,* and how her French teacher had given the definition and then added, "Young ladies, you will better understand the power of this expression when love strikes you." How right Mademoiselle had been. It was instant falling in love and being struck senseless at the same time. It happened for her when Jamal held her hand and they gazed into each other's eyes and remained silent, each trying to regain some equilibrium. Impossible and *coup de foudre* kept going through her mind. She tried to block them out and recall what it felt like to be in love with Sam. The absent Sam. Safe, loving, sexy, a friend and lover, completely devoted to her—yet she couldn't even conjure up a picture of him. She had known him always, he was one of their own, but, as if in a puff of smoke, he vanished from her life, dispelled by another man's touch and seductive glance.

Jamal. She had always been drawn to his handsome looks, the dark hair, the bronze skin, the sensuous lips, the large brown eyes, so dark as to seem black, those eyes that smiled and contained such disquietingly smouldering sexual promise. How many times had she teased him about the not-quite-perfect nose? And how many childish crushes had she and her girlfriends had on David's friend. Started and then abandoned for a puppy, a boat, a tennis tournament. But now! This was no child's crush, not even an adolescent one. This was the sexual attraction of a young woman for a man.

She felt a shiver of fear, but he was too quick for her and

dispelled that warning. He drew her slowly into his arms. "It's I who should be shivering. It's I who should be frightened." He placed his hand under her chin, tilted it, and gazed into her eyes. He studied her face. She had known him for so many years, but the way he was with her now, it was as if they were strangers. She felt her senses spiraling out of control, falling for this handsome unknown man.

She actually felt weak when he placed his lips upon hers, ran his tongue so sensuously between them. Her own remained closed. He traced them with his moist tongue and then kissed them with such tenderness that she had to stifle a whimper. Another kiss and another, on the side of her neck, on the lobe of her ear, on her shoulder. Then he raised her hand and placed it over his mouth and kissed the palm, and again, and then he licked it. She was struggling to find something to say. Anything. A tease, a flirt, anything to stop that feeling of falling, of being drawn to him, of wanting him.

He did not let her hand go when he stepped back from her. He reached in his pocket to withdraw a handkerchief, then delicately removed a tiny smudge of pink from her upper lip. He stroked her hair and rearranged a lock of it. She could not be unaware of the passion in his eyes, the emotion in his face, or the way he swallowed hard before he said, "You want me as much as I want you. Tell me I'm not wrong about that, Lara."

She found it difficult and confusing coping with her attraction to Jamal. To confess her desire to be made love to by him was impossible. If only her plans with Sam had not been thwarted, she would be safe in his arms at this very minute. Any further thought of safety and Sam and love completely vanished when Jamal placed his hands on her waist and rocked her gently into his arms. Naively she closed her eyes, hoping to hide the excitement she felt when he caressed the swell of her breasts beneath the silk taffeta. It was in vain.

An accomplished seducer of women, Jamal knew she was hopelessly attracted to him sexually. And that spurred him on. "How lovely . . . You're naked under all this silk." She said nothing, but the blush of pink on her face told him he was right.

"All naked? Not just your breasts?" he asked. There was something about the look in her eyes that touched him deeply. A look of both innocence and carnal desire. He felt an overwhelming hunger to take her sexually, not only for his own pleasure, but for hers as well. He recognized in her a far greater sexual passion than he had thought her capable of at her young, inexperienced age. Who had primed her for this? Certainly not Sam.

Jamal knew about their sexual encounter. He had been in the far corner of the room, in a high-backed wing chair, its back to the doors—where Sam and Lara had been standing. Peeping around the corner of the chair he had seen and heard all. He knew, when Lara had raised her skirt, how ready she was for more sex. He also knew then that he had to have her. He had thought of little else since he had seen her naked from the waist down, except the many things he would like to do to her. Her cunt, hidden under that patch of soft blond pubic hair, became in his mind a beautiful obsession that he would have to satisfy. Fate had delivered her to him, and he was ready to meet it. Now he was thrilled to see that so was she.

This time when he kissed her, her lips parted. He had a first taste of her as their tongues met. He felt her give way in his arms, and he asked again, his own passion rising, "Answer me, Lara."

He could feel her heart pounding, and was astounded when she did answer, "Yes, naked. And I am never going to wear anything under my clothes again. I want to be free and open and ready, and feel like a sexual libertine, even if I can't be one."

It was courageous desire talking, and brave honesty, and female insecurity crying out in all innocence, and Jamal was enchanted by it. "I kiss you for that," he said, and found her to be telling the truth when his hands closed on her nude bottom and slim, naked hips, and his finger toyed with that triangle of blond hair.

This was child's play; he had more than this on his mind. He intended having sex and the thrill of molding Lara into his own sexual delight. He withdrew his hands, enfolded her with one arm, and said, "You've knocked me out. I pray that it is the same for you. I want to make love to you, to have sex with you. I want us to be libertine lovers and to know an excess of love together. Let me make of you an erotic woman who will seduce any man you want into becoming your sexual slave."

Lara's heart skipped a beat when she realized from his own

lips that he, too, was suffering from the shock of love at first
sight. If she had had any hesitation about giving herself to Jamal,
his confession of love for her dissolved it. A double *coupe de
foudre*—irresistible, impossible to run away from. She was already putty in his hands, even before he offered to make her the
sexual enchantress she thought would bring her the love and
attention she craved.

He could see in her eyes that he had gotten to her. She would
be his to do with as he wanted, and he knew that would make
her happy, more content with her sexuality than Sam ever could
make her. How could Sam rival him? Sam loved her too much,
and his love blinded him to the dark side of Lara's sexual fantasies. Jamal had a clear vision of his young sexual protégée and
was anxious to tap into her secret desires, fascinated to see just
how far he could go with her.

"We shall go to the opera. But after that I must be allowed
one night with you. Let me fuck you. Stay with me until I have
made you well and truly mine. There will be no rest for either
of us until we have had each other in that way. Only then will
we know where our love will take us. You must consent."

He gave her his hungriest tortured look, a look few women
had been able to refuse. "Consent," he implored her again.
"Consent."

"David must never know. I couldn't bear it if he were to find
out."

David. Odd she hadn't said: My brothers mustn't know. Had
David been playing sex games with his little cousin? Was it
David who had brought out the sexual side of her nature? The
sly devil! That had to be why she wanted David never to know.
She was right of course. It would end his and David's friendship.
When Jamal recovered from his mild surprise, he asked, "Is
that consent? You must say yes. I need you to want me, want
us."

"Yes." Not a nervous, inexperienced yes. There was passion
and excitement in it. Lara placed her arms around his neck and
kissed him on the cheek, then on his eyes, and, last, his lips.
And now it was Jamal who was aroused by the erotic nature of
this young woman.

In the car on the way to the opera, their feelings for each other
intensified. He was ruthless in leading her on, exciting her to

want him more than she already did. He became more bold: he unzipped his trousers and placed her hand on his penis. He detected none of the anxiety he had expected in imposing such intimacy on her with the cars whizzing down Fifth Avenue on either side of them, rather, a willing submission that made his head spin with fantasies of what might happen.

They agreed on discretion in public. Hers was a cool, somewhat aloof demeanor that went beyond discretion. A performance, or just good breeding? Whatever it was, it unnerved Jamal. He thought he was losing her, that she had been teasing him. He felt insecure about her. This lovely-looking girl had promised herself to him. Now she had him on the run.

She turned more heads than he had expected as they cut a path through the crowds in the lobby. She was that delectable kind of beauty that older roués lust after, and young blades like to conquer in bed and sport on their arms like sexual trophies. She wore that still uncorrupted bloom of girlhood like a delicate dew gleaming on a fresh white rose. No one but himself must have her. He had already discounted Sam. He had been an error of timing, and only just, at that.

Several times during the evening a gaze passed between Lara and Jamal. He saw no flicker of passion for him in those dazzlingly seductive green eyes. During the intermission he took her by the hand and rushed her through the crowds. They paused only to be accosted by a friend, remained only long enough for civil introductions. Then he fled from the opera house with her.

No one had yet possessed Lara. Her cousin might have loved her, toyed with her, but Jamal knew David: he had done no more, if, indeed, he had done that. Sam might have taken her virginity, forestalled him there. But that boy had never possessed her. No man had. He could see that in her eyes. Now he would. He would possess Lara Stanton as no other man had— or probably ever would again. As God was his witness, she would be his, he would mark her with himself. He would make her his in a very special sexual way that few men would ever match. Theirs was already a carnal obsession.

In the lobby she managed to stop him. "No scandal. You promised. Not David, not anyone, must ever know. Promise me again. Not until I want them to. *We* have to be *our* secret."

The urgency of passion. In her eyes, a yearning to place herself in his hands. He adored her candor. She had hidden behind a curtain of reserve. Now she was raising it. Here was another glimpse of her erotic nature. She would be his. He told her what she wanted to hear: "I promise." And they hurried together into the night.

Jamal kept a pied-à-terre, a charming place, where he took women. It was separated by a glass-domed conservatory from the New York family home, a twenty-five-room flat with a staff of ten in the exclusive River House. The entrance to the pied-à-terre, a small brownstone, was on East Fifty-third Street. Once its garden had backed up to River House. Jamal's father had bought the house in order to make the garden part of his River House apartment. At a later date it had been turned into a conservatory. For his eighteenth birthday Jamal had been given the house for sex without scandal. He had responded by having a secret door built into the conservatory wall behind a bubbling fountain.

River House was were Jamal took Lara. The pied-à-terre was where he wanted to take her, but that would come later. For the moment the River House apartment was a better move. She knew the palatial twenty-six-storey cooperative apartment house well. At the River Club, on its lower floors, her brothers played squash, she played tennis, and swam with her best girlfriend, Julia, who lived in the building. They had danced in the ballroom, and Julia's father kept his yacht at the River House dock, where all the best yachts had tied up before the land had been appropriated for the FDR Drive.

The post-opera supper was being given by Jamal's mother, Chantal, in the Ben El-Raisuli River House apartment. They would be expected to attend, but until then the house was quiet, occupied only by the servants. Jamal and Lara would have a few hours before they would be expected to make an appearance. A word to Rafik, the majordomo of the household, and privacy and secrecy was theirs.

The windows overlooked the East River. The panoramic view of lights on the other side of the river was a flickering distraction for Lara from the immediate feeling of excitement—or was it fear?—at being alone with Jamal in his bedroom.

A click of the lock made her jump. She spun around to face him. His sultry, overly handsome features struck her again as more sensual than she ever remembered. Too sensual. She would try and get out of it, with some sort of grace, some sort of dignity. Much as she wanted him to take her, possess her, bend her to his sexual will as he had promised he would, she was afraid of losing herself to this man.

Her instinct was to run back to Sam, where she knew she would always be safe. Run back to Sam? She could hardly remember how he looked, how sex with him had been. Only the overwhelming sensations of sexual intercourse were real to her, nothing else. Not Sam and their love.

She took a step forward and was about to speak. Jamal was too quick for her. His lips closed on hers. There was fire in his kiss. It burned her, but he tempered the kiss with gentle words of welcome, promises of carnal bliss. What reason had she to disbelieve him? But fear of the unknown did its work. She made a feeble attempt to extricate herself. Yet he had only to kiss her hands, caress her breasts, and her fear was quieted.

Jamal sensed the turmoil within her sexual yearnings. It only served to hone his lust. He took command. An arm around her shoulders, he walked her through his room, turning on the lights. Lara had never seen a room like it. There was a sophistication about Jamal's bedroom that made her gasp. The navy blue walls were lined with books and full-length, eighteenth-century Moroccan portraits of handsome desert warriors. They sported flowing white robes and startling white turbans. Jeweled daggers hung at the waist from magnificent gold belts that also crossed their chests. Dark skin and hard, fiercely beautiful masculine faces stared down at her. The carpets were of a great age, patterned in a faded pomegranate color with large silvery-white flowers. One Persian design showed a hunt, fawns and deer and boar being chased by men on horseback. There were deep, comfortable easy chairs in black-and-navy blue silk damask, and a multitude of cushions thrown on the sofa and floor. A panoply of jewellike color, yellow and red and white, gold and silver brocades. Tables of dark rich woods. A mother-of-pearl screen. And the bed—a large four-poster—draped in black-and-navy blue silk damask and lined in a plum-colored silk. It had been turned down to display white linen, pillows of shiny white satin and silk, and a plum-colored cashmere blanket.

There was a dark richness, and yet something slightly sinister

about the room. It was exciting, the most masculine room she
had ever been in. She felt enslaved by it. As if she had stepped
into another world, Jamal's world, and, though she was nervous,
she was seduced by it, by him.

They stood at the foot of the bed. He tilted her chin up, looked
into her eyes, and smiled. His smile warmed her, excited her
imagination. She waited for his first move. To feel his hands
upon her. He made none. Instead he suggested, "You remove
my jacket first." Again the inviting warmth of his smile. She
understood at once and was amused.

She obeyed and walked around behind him to remove the
jacket. She dropped it, almost without thinking, over the back
of a chair. His body scent drew her to him. She kissed his neck,
rested her head against his back, and caressed his shoulders
under the white cotton dress shirt he was wearing. Then she
walked around to face him again. She waited for him to make
his move on her. He didn't. Instead he raised his chin. She
understood, and pulled on the black silk bow tie. It loosened,
and she slid it from around his neck and dropped it on the bed.

"The cuff links next," he demanded, never taking his gaze
from hers. She removed them, and then the sapphire studs holding his shirt together. She opened his shirt and spread her hands
across his chest of dark curly hair. The feel of his skin was like
an electric charge, and unbearably sexy. She wanted his hands
on her breasts, his fingers to bite into her flesh. Nothing. She
thought her knees would buckle with excitement when he undid
the black alligator belt, slid it slowly from his trouser loops, and
snapped it sharply from his waist. It made her flinch. He slipped
it around her neck and let it dangle there. And he waited.

He said not a word. She had to guess what was expected of
her next. She had to invent. Once again she moved behind him
and raised his shirt. She ran her hands over his strong back. He
reached around, grabbed her hand, and pulled her around in
front of him again. He placed her hands on his breast and pressed
them into his flesh. She was quick to pick up his every signal.
Her mouth descended upon his nipple and licked it and sucked
it. The taste of him was exhilarating. She meant to nibble on his
tiny nipples, but passion made her bite hard on them, and he
squirmed under her lips. She reveled in the pleasure that flashed

in his eyes, and felt for the first time the gratification of cajoling delight from another body.

Now he stood naked in front of her, and she actually trembled with desire for him. Until now the two men in her life had been the sexual givers. They had been the ones to take the initiative.

And now, still dressed in her silk taffeta, she was on her knees in a frenzy of lust, taking instructions from Jamal on the giving of fellatio. He was relentless, forceful in his demands. Loveless. Though she did not feel frightened by *him*, she did by his sexual offensive. Yet not enough to retreat. After a short time she lost herself in the act and her own passion took over. She transformed it from what had been, at the beginning, an amateurish and clumsy, gagging performance, into pure pleasure for them both. He took the two ends of his leather belt hanging around her neck and pulled her up from her knees and onto the bed.

She was overwhelmed by his ability to give himself up to her. To lie passively, allowing himself to be made love to. It had never occurred to her that men might like to play that role as well as women. She yearned to be made love to by him. Could she be as sexually bold as Jamal? Legs flung wide, lasciviously offering her cunt, her anus, as he offered her his cock, his balls, his anus, demanding them to be kissed and licked and caressed. She wanted desperately to change places with him. He had her hungry for him.

He was ruthless in holding back. It put her on edge. It made her want to please him more. He was cruel to insinuate upon her sex without romance, when he had seduced her with romance. She was so young, inexperienced. She had expected them to come together. Where was the adoration, the love? She was disconcerted that it wasn't there, but she was unable to pull herself away from him. She sensed love *was* there, somewhere. It was so new this being the giver, obeying his demands, and reaping untold pleasures from them. It didn't bear thinking about, only doing.

He could hold back his orgasm no longer. He demanded, "Lara, swallow. Every drop." And then came, a copious discharge that frightened and excited her. Cock and cum, for a few seconds, took over her whole life. His huge, throbbing penis filled her mouth, was rammed tight down her throat. She pursed her lips tight to its very base and could feel the curl of his black pubic hairs brushing her lips and the salty taste of his sperm as she sucked hard on his cock. She swallowed.

She felt dizzy with wild abandon, emotionally drained from her experience. Slowly he withdrew, and she fell against him exhausted. Only then did he take her in his arms and hold her and tell her how sublime she had been. How beautiful and sexy she was. Her heart swelled with joy for having pleased him, and at the realization she, too, had come, she, too, had enjoyed fellatio.

They lay like that for some time before he unlocked the door and wheeled in a table covered in a crisp, white damask cloth. On it were displayed a silver champagne cooler, glasses, and a bowl of beluga caviar in a crystal dish sunk in a ring of crushed ice. He poured two glasses of champagne and then, taking her by the hand, led her to the bathroom, where he sat her on the edge of the marble bath. He stepped into the shower.

She watched the rivulets of water run down his body, feeling nothing but lust for him. She watched his every movement while he stretched, and bent over, and washed, and the streams of scented suds of balsam-and-pine soap ran down his body. She wanted him—and somehow didn't know what to do about it. That made her nervous.

For the first time since she was struck with love for Jamal she felt awkward. Like some paid whore. It wasn't difficult to figure out why. She had done nothing but service him, he had ignored her own needs. She stood up and looked at herself in the misted wall of mirror. Still dressed in her silk taffeta, looking every inch the innocent young lady. She found it dishonest, quite shocking. More so, even, when she saw him standing dripping wet behind her, watching her. She turned around to face him.

"I need you to tell me you love me," she said.

"I would rather show you," he answered.

He picked up the two glasses and handed hers to her. He drained his and smiled. She watched him slip into a silk dressing gown and tie the black silk sash tight around his waist. Lara drank some of her wine. Together, his arm around her shoulders, they walked back into the bedroom.

He filled a small jade bowl with the black beluga and handed it to her with a lapis lazuli spoon. He smiled. He liked to see greed in Lara only fractionally less than he liked insinuating it upon her. Greed was such a forbidden fruit in the Stanton household. He refilled her glass, prepared a bowl of the Russian delicacy for himself, and together they drank and ate, and, for the first time since they had entered his room, talked.

After several spoonfuls of the caviar, she laughed. "Caviar and lychee nuts—the two sexiest tastes in the world. And you were the first person to offer them to me. Pretty decadent to have acquired a taste for them at the age of ten. And now . . ." She hesitated, and a blush colored her face. He was amused.

"Oh, don't stop now."

But she did. Drained her glass and held it out for more. He filled it. "And now? The taste of my cum. Isn't that what you were going to say? Don't tell me you're going to be a sexual hypocrite, Lara. There is no fun in that. You did have fun, didn't you? You did like the taste of me?"

He took the bowl from her hands. "Go on, confess. You adored sucking cock, swallowing cum."

"Yours was the first time."

"I didn't ask you that. I asked how much you liked it."

There was a look in his eye that discomforted her. She answered him. "I liked it."

"Liar," he said. "You loved it."

She jumped up. He sprang from the sofa with her. He grabbed her hard by the hair and kissed her passionately. That kiss scorched her. When he released her it was only for a moment, to tell her, "Now I'm going to show you just how much I love you." He kissed her wildly, with a roughness and urgency he had not shown before. He released her and threw off his robe. He was hard; his penis looked to her even more handsome, the circumcised knob crimson with desire.

"I don't want to be a sexual hypocrite. You're right, damn you, Jamal. I love your cock. Having it in my mouth was fantastic. Your cum trickling down my throat was very sexy. I'm new to all this. Remember that, give me a break. Promise me you love me so we can have great sex and try it all. I want to be like Myling and Luan. Sexually free. So don't attack me, don't call me a hypocrite."

He liked the anger he saw in her eyes. He liked her talking about sex and the adventurous sexual spirit she showed. It was part of his sexual power over her. He would delight in reducing her to her basic sexual self. Delight? He was obsessed with the idea of doing that, because he sensed how much she would enjoy it. He took her in his arms and kissed her again, and then again on the neck. "You have to believe that whatever we do sexually, you will always be safe with me. Then an erotic world will open up for you that will set you free. I will never let you come to any harm. You can believe that, can't you?" If there were doubts, he sealed them with another kiss.

Ever since Jamal had seen Lara and Sam together and learned about their sexual encounter, he had known she would be his. Nothing spurred him on more than the vision of her offering herself to Sam and being turned down. He wanted her to do more than just offer herself to him: he wanted her hungry for him, willing to submit to all things sexual for him. And it was for that reason he had plotted his seduction of her in the manner he had done.

Now she stood in front of him in high-heeled sandals, a criss-crossing of slim, navy blue satin straps, naked except for sheer navy blue silk stockings and a lacy belt of long garters, stretching down over sensuous thighs of creamy white flesh, to pinch the tops of her stockings. Her bushy mound of silky pubic hair was absolutely tantalizing, framed by the raunchiness of the shapely, silk-encased legs, strips of taut lace and elastic. Exciting, yes, but what surprised him was the body, a sensual contrast to the clean, elegant face and demeanor of this seventeen-year-old beauty. The sensuous, bee-stung lips might have given a hint, but he had hardly expected such erotic bodily beauty. The breasts, tantalizingly large and firm, shaped as if bursting with milk, large aureole of a dark plummy brown against the creamy white skin. The fleshy, erect nipples promised depravity and stirred within him a violence of passion. He held back, taking in the slimness of the waist, the narrowness of the hips. He walked slowly around her and was enchanted by her bottom, high and round and beckoning. He could not hold back. He caressed the cheeks, separated them and ran a finger, tinglingly provocative, between them, bent to lick a spot on one of them and kissed it. A sensuous love bite.

Lara thought she would swoon. She felt strange standing there while he examined her with eyes she thought to be critical. She took a nervous step away from him, thinking to cover herself. He stopped her with a hand on her shoulder.

"No one has ever looked at me this way, Jamal."

"What about Sam?"

"We did it in the dark."

He was suddenly jealous, and said, "Sam is more stupid than I thought. You have one of the most erotic bodies I have ever seen. You were made for sex, and me, and we are going to have a wonderful time."

He picked her up in his arms and carried her to the bed. The dark allure of her nipples and their nimbus drew his hands and mouth to her breasts. He could not repress his urge to devour them. Hungrily he fondled them, sucked and bit hard into them, desisting only to tell her, "You are magnificent. More, much more than I imagined." He alternated between kissing her breasts and slapping them. And, disturbingly, her own violence surfaced. She bit into his shoulder and scratched long welts down his back, and then came in several small orgasms.

He saw in her eyes the little shudders of ecstasy. Urgently he piled pillows beneath her so as to raise her to an angle that he knew would give him a deeper penetration. Then, unceremoniously, he threw her legs wide apart and took her with a violence she had never known before. It was as if he wanted half to kill her with his lust. He was rough with his fucking and his kisses—they tore at her flesh—and it was new and thrilling because it tapped into her own sexual violence, and she was able, after several minutes, to curtail her begging him to stop, not merely to submit to him, but to join him. Her reaction was instinctive. She used her cunt and fucked him with it, squeezing every muscle to give that succulent, tight sensation. Viselike she clung to his cock and eased off and on again, Lara's own form of fucking him. They came together and then, afterward, as they lay in each other's arms, he rhapsodized for her upon the various ways they would make love.

Jamal told her about this pied-à-terre. He tantalized her with stories of the erotic world he had created there. Of the men who were there to service his women friends, of the women who made love to women. The sexual toys he had to show, the scented oils and creams he wanted to tease her body with. He was savage in his seduction of Lara. His explicit descriptions of how he

wanted to have her with two other men at the same time shocked
. . . but excited her. The forbidden. A taste? Maybe just once.
He made a phone call to the house on Fifty-third Street. There
was no turning back. It never even occurred to her. The sexual
animal in Lara Stanton was on the prowl, not to be leashed again
till satisfied.

Before they dressed he prepared several lines of cocaine. He
rolled up a twenty-dollar bill and handed it to her. She began to
laugh.

"I don't do drugs."

"You will tonight. For me. Because I want you to have the
greatest pleasure later, in the pied-à-terre."

"I don't need it. I'm high as a kite on sex already."

"It's that little bit higher that counts."

She took the cocaine.

"It makes ladies very sexy. Later I will rub it on your clitoris—it will make you crazy sexy—and in your cunt. In fact, lie
down."

He was right. Her insatiability with this man began to worry
her. She seemed unable to say no to anything he suggested. And
now, as she dressed, the tingling sensation of the coke acting
upon her genitals filled her with desire to experience the erotic
promise the pied-à-terre had to offer.

Jamal made certain she looked impeccable before they left
his room. There was a party going on downstairs. This intimate
evening of theirs must remain an absolute secret. She looked, if
not the picture of innocence, certainly not the erotic woman he
now knew her to be. Her icy, aristocratic beauty, those mischievous green eyes of hers, had always attracted him; more so
now since he had had her. He had only to think of those strangely
sensuous, plummy-colored nipples to want her again. He had
received much more than he had bargained for with Lara, and
he guessed that, by the time he returned her to Cannonberry
Chase, theirs would be a *liasion dangereuse* that might last all
their lives.

They slipped into the party, made their appearance, and stayed
for a respectable time before they passed, unnoticed, from the
conservatory into the house on Fifty-third Street.

Chapter 5

The open car swerved off the main road and through the massive gates. Their iron frames hung from stone piers topped with spheres covered in lichen. A field mouse scampered around one side, dropped to the ledge it balanced on, and disappeared into some ivy.

A pearly mist clung to the undulating meadow. The sun was already high in the sky. Between the Chase and the sun, puffs of fog rolled in from the bay, half a mile away on one side, and the ocean, about the same distance away on the other. Layers of luminescence and frosty colors. A band of blue, a streak of low-lying, silvery-white clouds, a slab of sun-yellow, and a wafer of milky-gray mist hung ethereally, culminating in a slash of bright green, the grass and trees of the parkland. Multilayered nature encompassing earth and sky. A kind of magic. Cannonberry Chase.

The car sped up the three-mile avenue of huge, hundred-year-old elms. The odd cock pheasant paraded its glorious plumage nonchalantly along the edge of the drive, having abandoned the huge wood that teemed with game birds further on. The estate was on a twenty-five-mile peninsula jutting out into Long Island Sound.

"Slow down," Lara demanded.

Jamal slowed, and they cruised up the drive, listening. The forlorn boom of a foghorn was just audible. The twitter of a bird. From the patches of tall grass and wildflowers came the rustle of some furry animal on the hunt for food. She hardly needed to ask. A mile or so up the drive, the enchantment of early morning, the peace and tranquillity of Cannonberry Chase, worked their magic on Jamal. He stopped the car.

Neither of them said anything. They watched the sun rise higher in the sky and slowly burn off the mist. He opened the car door and disposed of the leather jacket he had been wearing over his dress suit to counter the cold. He walked around to open the car door for her. "A glorious morning. Let's walk together, become part of it. I think we should talk, settle a few things about what happened last night. We should get our story straight for the family, maybe establish some ground rules, before we reach the house."

She didn't move. He removed the chiffon scarf from around her hair and kissed the top of her head. She pulled away. "We have no future, Jamal. I thought I made that clear last night."

"It's too late to behave like a silly child now, Lara. Let's walk." There was a note of sternness in his voice.

He took her hand and kissed it, helped her out of the white Ferrari, removing the lynx car robe she was wrapped in. She gave a slight shiver. He took off his jacket and placed it around her bare shoulders. They walked from the road into the long grass and across the meadow. The rustle of her silk taffeta gown became part of the sounds of the morning, the vivid colors of her dress part of the landscape. She ran her fingers through her long blond hair, and he marveled at the effect the place was having on her. She seemed to respond to the beauty, the peace, and tranquillity of the newborn day. Here was the old Lara he had known as a child, lovely and provocative, an aristocratic maiden in the kingdom of Cannonberry Chase.

Only hours before, he had tapped into her darkest—most secret—sexual core, he had led her into sexual excess, and she had allowed it to take control of her. Lara had reveled in the erotic fantasies of Jamal and the two other men he had provided for her. But now the coke and the hashish, the champagne and the sex, had worn off, and it was time to come to terms with the reality of the night she and Jamal had spent together. He had handled her then in order to possess her. He had no problems about how to handle her now, to keep her as his *liaison dangereuse*, as he had every intention of doing.

And Lara? She had found sexual ecstasy. She had submitted to acts she had before considered impossibly decadent, and had found erotic love. Sexual bliss. But now, as she walked through the tall grass and wildflowers, the morning dew still glistening on them, in her beloved Cannonberry Chase, all life waking around her, such extremes seemed to the young woman too dark and murky to contemplate as anything other than sexual desire gone mad. Desire that must be suppressed.

She began to walk faster and faster and then, flinging the coat from her shoulders, began to run. Jamal caught it and chased after her. He grasped her by the waist and tackled her to the ground. He liked the fury he saw in her face, it excited him.

"How could you? How could you let me be dragged into such an orgy as last night's? A part of me will always hate you for that, Jamal."

"Don't be ridiculous. A part of you will love me all your life, my dear, for what you had last night. For what we will always have together."

"Never again."

He laughed at her. She tried to raise herself, but he had her pinned down. She struggled. "I thought you learned your lesson last night about struggling with me." She became very still.

"That's better. Now behave, and I will let you sit up." She made another, but more feeble attempt. He laughed and pulled her head back down to the ground by her hair. Then he kissed her quiet. It hadn't been his intention, but when he felt her relax into his kisses and then take them over, he found an unbearable need to tame her one last time with his cock. And that was what he kept telling her while he fucked her. Afterward they lay there, replete in their lust for each other, until Lara rose from the ground and offered her hand to Jamal. Together, now as friends, they walked toward the stables, he brushing the grass and leaves and seeds and broken twigs from her dress, and plucking bits from her hair.

"We can't go on, Jamal."

"Of course we can."

"I'm frightened. Where will this intense kind of sex life lead me? I know I can't go where you want to take me, even though I might want to take on that adventure and go. Promise me you will leave me alone to get on with life at a pace I can handle. If you love me, then you will."

Jamal didn't answer. He had had what he wanted. He had

possessed Lara. He had reached down into the sexual side of her nature and had awakened it for himself. She had given him great sex, enormous pleasure, and he knew that for the moment he had to cool it. David, if he were to find out, would never forgive him. The Stantons, as a family, would ruin him in society, and their power could destroy his reputation in the Western world. There was something else: in time, when she was ready again, as she had been last night, he knew Lara would be his again in secret. No other man would ever get where he had been with her sexually. That was the bond that would hold them together, until, if ever, she found some sexual virtuoso superior to himself. But first he would have to seem to let her go, though he had no intention of doing that, ever. Not completely, anyway.

"I can't leave you alone, not forever. Leave you to what? Sam?"

"He loves me. I'll be safe with Sam. He's a good lover, he'll make me happy."

"So, seventeen years old and two lovers, and you think you're an authority on love, sex, and happiness. Not yet, dear. Sam, the Sams of your tiny world—forget them. They won't last. I can offer you much more, the occasional glimpse of another world. Wonderful as life is for you, Cannonberry Chase is not the world. Nor are you Stantons and your exclusive circle of friends. This will never be enough for you. Your brothers know that. They live within the exclusive milieu of the Stanton name and all that it entails. And, with due discretion, out of it. And so must you, if you don't want to wind up with a walk-on role in life. Do you want to turn into some bumbling philistine of an adult? Some passive beauty who knows nothing about what really moves the world—sex, the fear of death, hidden desires, compulsive perversions. A safe and marginally happy lady like Elizabeth—too frightened to do anything to improve herself beyond your mother's design for life. You're letting this world repress you. You think if you don't succumb to that repression you will become some sort of pervert. You silly girl! Exciting sex has nothing to do with perversion, as long as no one gets hurt. Get those two things mixed up, and you'll wind up a frustrated, wasted shell of a woman. Is that what you want?"

"Of course that's not what I want. Give me time to think

about what I want. Please, we have to put last night out of our
minds.''

"You may have to. I don't.''

"Do you love me, Jamal?''

"Love?''

The puzzled look on his face told it all. Until that moment
she actually had it in her mind that he did love her. She had
taken him at his word during his seduction of her. If Jamal's
love for her had not spurred her on to give herself to two strangers
and revel in sexual licentiousness with three men, then what
had? She looked into that handsome, sensual face and could not
deny to herself how exciting and fulfilling sex had been with
him. It had been like dying to all else in the world except that
moment of bliss. But coming out of orgasm was like being born
again. And to be in the arms of a man who loved you seemed,
at that moment, as she stood in the meadow of Cannonberry
Chase, an essential element of life.

"Well, yes . . . Let's maybe not talk about love, or us, or a
future. I think let's just go home.''

Lara found the look of relief on his face embarrassing. Only
then did David's words come to mind. He had often said about
Jamal, "He is one of my best friends, but it's as well to remember that underneath all that charm there lurks an often sadistic
cad.''

Walking back toward the car, Jamal felt an unpleasant stirring
of unease. It had to do with something he saw in Lara's face,
that tilt of the head, a touch of arrogance in the way she looked
at him. That American high-society haughtiness that sparked off
her. He felt his power over her diminishing, and he couldn't
stand that. He cast a line of fear, hoping to reel her back to him,
if only to prove to them both that he still had her on the hook.

"You can't just 'go home.' It's not as easy as that, Lara. You
have secrets to hide. Explanations to make. I will, of course,
support any story you tell. No one will ever know about what
really went on last night. That will always be our own special
secret.'' He looked at his watch and continued, "It's nearly six-
fifteen, somebody's bound to be up and about the house. We
had better create a good cover-up for being out all night.''

Lara listened to him and was appalled. Lies, deceit. She hated
that conspiratorial tone in his voice. These were aspects of life

she knew little about, and her immediate reaction was to reject the very idea of them. She would almost rather confess to her night of sexual indulgence. That was impossible, of course. She was in a trap.

They were standing by the car now, looking at each other. Her feelings were confused. She felt herself drawn to Jamal, maybe even held in some kind of a grip by him, but not enough to be reduced to becoming a liar, a cheat. What he felt showed in his eyes: satisfaction at holding the trump card in his game of seduction.

The tone of his voice changed. It suddenly took on warmth, sincerity. "La, who knows when we will be able to talk openly like this together again? It will never do, our sneaking into corners to whisper something intimate to each other. You have to know that we will be together again, in spite of what you say or may think now. I will plan a way for us to spend some time together without the family finding out. Last night was only the beginning for us. All our sex is going to have to be secret, at least for a few years. Tell me you accept that as a possibility. I ask no more of you than that. Our relationship can be as it has always been in front of the family. And not only the family: between us as well."

In later years, Lara would always recall that moment with Jamal, standing in the sunshine at Cannonberry Chase, as the time that she really grew up and faced herself—and took her first action as a woman. It was as if she had blanked out, but had now regained consciousness. She felt a coldness, a determination never to be a sexual victim, not of Jamal's or any man's. She would master the art of erotic love for her own pleasure, and share it with Sam, or Jamal, or any man who loved her enough to win her to him. One night, one day, a lifetime. She would prefer one man, one lifetime. Jamal didn't send out any signals that he could be that kind of man for her. But Sam? Dear, safe Sam was something else. But for the moment there were other things to cope with: the most pressing, how to handle her arrival home.

"Let's go," she said.

He grabbed her by the elbow as she made an attempt to get into the Ferrari. "Answer me, goddammit! You do accept what we are together? You will not deny us? A yes will do for now."

She suddenly felt in control of herself. Home on the safe ground of Cannonberry Chase, she felt strong enough to admit to her erotic love for Jamal and Sam, yet not to feel compelled to do anything about it until she was ready, if ever. Who was to know? Maybe Jamal was the great romantic love of her life. Maybe Sam was. What was romantic love anyway? Jamal was quite shrewd, while she was no authority on the subject. But she vowed that one day, whatever it was, she would have it. All options open, it was like going for the Yacht Club's gold cup. But for the moment, galvanized by the changes in herself and her life, Lara gathered her strength. Gazing into Jamal's eyes she answered him.

"Yes, yes, yes. Clandestine sex—by what one experience of it can prove—is for us. Yes, when I am away at school it is a possibility. Yes, you win, you win. Now drive us to the stables, and don't ever try and turn me into a liar with the family again. I will handle them, and our being out all night. I have managed to handle my short, shocking introduction into the big, wide world of sex and love. I've still come out of it happier to be there than not. So I think I had better behave like an adult. I've got to take responsibility for my actions, and I mean to do that without compromising anyone—least of all myself."

The stables, like all else on Cannonberry Chase, were impressive. Here you would find some of the best horseflesh in the country. Racing stock, a stud, hunters, an indoor as well as outdoor riding ring. The grooms, already at work, saddled up for Jamal and Lara. They grinned when she rejected any offers of riding clothes and insisted she and Jamal would ride as they were.

She rode Biscuit, a frisky seventeen-hands white stallion, and Jamal rode his favorite, a midnight-black Arabian mare called Cora. They galloped across Cannonberry Chase at a reckless pace. The Chase, the Stantons unenclosed tract of land reserved for breeding and hunting wild animals, was particularly attractive. The terrain challenged a horseman. It included woods and meadows, high and low ground, beaches with sand dunes on one side and cliffs and rougher water on the other.

David and Max were leaving the manor house with Myling and Luan for the stables and an early morning ride when they saw, in the far distance, a pair of horses racing across a field toward the deer wood. Then flashes of vivid color, Lara's silk evening dress streaming out behind her and her long, silvery-blond hair dancing wildly in the wind as she courageously rode Biscuit flat out. They saw her take a three-foot-deep hedge, only to swing the powerful white stallion around and take it again, passing feet away from Jamal as he made the hurdle.

The two couples ran across the terrace to catch a better view of the riders. "She's fucking mad, that girl. More horse *courage* than horse *sense*. But she sure has got Biscuit on the go. Watch her, she'll go for that fence again. She's playing with Biscuit and Jamal. My guess is twice more before Jamal gets ahead in that race." Max was enthusiastic.

David began to laugh. "Jamal must be furious. She would have taken the lead right from the start to get Biscuit all out. That horse is a great ride if you give him full rein. Lara's troubles begin when Jamal catches up and passes Biscuit. She'll have a job controlling that horse then. He's strong and he's crazy. He doesn't like other horses around him and he really hates to be passed. She may be in for a hard fall."

She took the fence, as Max had predicted, twice more, and then Jamal had her. They jumped the next turn together, and Jamal raced ahead toward the wood. The brothers and the two women were clapping and shouting, it was such an exciting performance. And then they held their breath for several moments when, as David had said, Biscuit reared up and fought Lara's control. He raced ahead and reared again, and she was in serious trouble. They saw her thrown forward. She clung to the reins and hung on to his mane, then slipped out of the saddle. David started running toward the field, the others following. Somehow Lara hung on. Jamal must have looked back and seen she was in difficulty. They saw him charge out of the wood toward her. Suddenly Lara was in the saddle again. The magnificent white beast reared up once more and tried to unseat her, and then she had him, somehow pulled him in and raced ahead, passing Cora, being ridden hell-for-leather by Jamal to her rescue. They all laughed when he was left seated on his horse, watching Lara bring Biscuit down to an easy trot. She disappeared into the wood.

They rode together, Jamal on Cora, careful to stay always slightly behind Biscuit. Neither of them spoke. Jamal wanted to shout at her, What the fuck was that all about? What do you think you're trying to prove? He stifled the impulse, but he was seething. It was Lara who finally spoke, and then in a whisper, sometime after they were deep into the wood.

"If we are very quiet and keep to a steady pace, we will be able to watch the deer, over there, down in that little valley where the stream is. They're always there at this time in the morning."

The horses' hooves, muffled by a blanket of brightly colored autumn leaves, dusted up the patches of mist still over the ground that the sun, filtering in angled rays down through the branches of the trees, was fast burning off. The atmosphere was thick with a rainbow of greens and yellows, spatterings of other muted colors in pearly hues. It was like riding through an enchanted forest, but Jamal was too unnerved by Lara to appreciate it. He sidled close to her and took the reins from her hands. Never mind the deer for today. Taking her by the waist, he lifted her off Biscuit and sat her down in front of him on Cora. Biscuit seemed unaware of the change: he led them on through the wood.

"I don't know what you were trying to prove back there, Lara, and I don't want to know. I tamed you last night. I rode you as hard sexually as you rode that horse today." Lara began to squirm. She took the reins of the stallion from Jamal. He held her more firmly. "Last night was only a beginning for us. You would do well to remember that and appreciate it. I am not a stallion you will ever be able to control. I do the controlling. But, remember, for us there is not just sex and control, there is also a kind of affectionate love that has grown over the years. All you have to remember is that they don't overlap, and that is part of the passion and romance of our relationship. If you don't understand that today, you will another day. I don't mind you competing, trying to diminish me in some way, as long as you know you will be hard-pressed to succeed."

With that he removed the reins from her hands again and, lifting her by the waist, helped her to remount. He passed the reins back to her once she was seated. She directed the horse away from the wood, and they rode peacefully for some time before she spoke.

"There were some people watching us. I was hoping there

would be. It will make it easier that they know we were out all night and rode as part of that night. Now I'm leading us to the beach and we'll go for a sail. If we are open about being out all night, there will be no need for lies.''

Sometime around eleven Lara and Jamal returned from their sail and tied up at the dock, where they found Sam waiting for them. Sam kissed her and placed a proprietorial arm around her. ''Thanks, Jamal. I hope he remained a gentleman, Lara? . . . Or is to be pistols at dawn?''

The joke fell a little flat with her. She tried to put aside her irritation with the two men, and so, linking arms with them, walked up the cliff to the manor house. Lara and Jamal were still dressed in their evening clothes. The family and their guests were sitting out on the lawn. It was midmorning coffee time. Everyone already knew about their ride and their sail. The only question about the most momentous night of Lara Stanton's life was asked by her mother. And even *it* was hardly a question. ''Lara, dear, out all night should not be made a habit of. Remember, there is something to be said for beauty sleep.''

Life at Cannonberry Chase, her family, their friends, the guests, staff—nothing had changed, only Lara. She felt at once the same person she had always been, and yet someone else. Lara, grown up? She hardly questioned it, but accepted her sexuality and Sam's love as facts of life. Even her fear of losing herself in sex as she had with Jamal. Even the excitement, the physical ecstasy, her utter submission to lust.

More than once during the weekend, memories of sexual sensations intruded. Not just those she experienced with Jamal and the two strangers, but those she had had with Sam. They excited a desire for more, and yet she could not bring herself to accept any sexual overtures made by Sam. She led him on rather than letting him down, more to distance herself from her sexual encounter with Jamal than for any other reason. For, whatever had passed between them, however she was feeling about Jamal, inconvenient as it was even in its diminished intensity, a *coup de foudre* such as she had experienced with him was not so easily forgotten.

It surprised Lara that with all her lusty thoughts, all the changes she was experiencing in herself, she managed to enjoy her weekend. There was much to be said for the way Jamal behaved. It had been just as he said it would be: they were friends and having fun. Not a hint, not a tease, no innuendo as to what had happened in the house on Fifty-third Street. She drew closer to Sam.

Two weeks later, they made love again. Their sexual intercourse was, as Sam had kept promising it would be, even more exciting than when he had taken her at Aunt Bidi's. They confessed yet again how much they loved each other. How great the sex was. They were happy. And, pleased as Emily was when she saw Lara wearing Sam's fraternity pin, she was relieved when the following week she kissed Lara good-bye and sent her off to Smith College. Lara's life was proceeding along Emily Dean Stanton's plan.

1974

NEW YORK

Chapter 6

Five years is a long time in the life of an overachiever. It can wreak extraordinary changes. With a family of overachievers as strongly bound together as the Stantons, those individual changes were accepted as a matter of course. Remarkably, the wealthy American landed gentry, powerful and loyal families such as the Stantons, give largely unconditional support to each of their members. Approval or disapproval rarely enters into it. With the foundations of the family so firmly underpinned, and a retinue of trustees and advisers at their disposal, there was not much any of Henry and Emily's children could not or would not attempt—and for the most part, succeed in.

At work or at play, the family always moved in the fast lane. Though the world was only rarely made aware of what they were doing, the Henry Stanton family was making its mark. And as their children pursued their various interests around the world, Emily and Henry and Cannonberry Chase became more and more the powerful axis from which they radiated and to which they returned.

In many ways it was Cannonberry Chase, rather than Henry or Emily, that wielded the greatest power over them all. One needs to understand the American country house in the manner of, say George Washington Vanderbilt's Biltmore in North Carolina, Kykuit at Pocantico Hills, New York, John D. Rockefeller's retreat, or Caumsett, the Field estate on Long Island: their English parks, their country houses as stately homes, and their Marie Antoinette–style farms that made their owners appear to be self-sufficient. They were not the celluloid Tara of *Gone with the Wind*, but the real thing, where the lives of their owners seemed to be lived more completely than anywhere else. At least that was the pattern at Cannonberry Chase.

The house there was on the grand scale, but it was not just another grand manor house set down in acres of wilderness. A host of sports and leisure pursuits formed a shared and familiar world for the limited few lucky enough to afford it. Magnificent stable blocks of serious architectural value, and indoor riding rings, were no less impressive than indoor and outdoor tennis courts and swimming pools, landscaped as part of their architecture. Gymnasiums and basement shooting ranges and bowling alleys were paneled in French walnut. Billiard rooms were as magnificently turned out as libraries. Hunting rooms, game lodges, and motor houses or garages were also designed in the grand manner. Boathouses were not in name only. They were one of the most attractive and impressive features of the American country house. The one at Cannonberry Chase was a fine example of its kind, elaborate and large, slung half over the water, and capable of housing half a dozen of the Stantons' larger boats, several of which were used to cruise into New York when Henry was commuting. The airplane hangar and small grass airfield had always been de rigueur for the American country house that had enough land to carve them decoratively into the landscape, as was the eighteen-hole golf course. The hangar on the Stanton estate housed several vintage aircraft as well as a Cessna and a small jet. And Cannonberry Chase boasted an excellent polo field, a maze, and a grotto where Emily entertained her guests with mini-operas.

The American country house weekend had been a major part of these people's lives ever since the 1920s. The generations, able still to live in the grand style, were a product of time and environment. They knew no other way of life.

Cannonberry Chase did have a kinship with the grand country houses in England and France. But was it the same thing? Not at all. The mansion stood on its own land, twenty square miles of it, beyond the suburbs and any possible site of planned housing. It radiated self-sufficiency. A landed life, even though the money that sustained it never came from the land.

What underpinned the costly creations of Cannonberry Chase was its status as a palatial residence kept largely for sport. It

satisfied a desire for the wholesome rural life. Like many other
such houses, it maintained a large, complex farm. The mid-
eighteen hundreds until the nineteen forties had been the heyday
of magnificent country estates in America, but for Cannonberry
Chase there had never been a decline. It thrived with the passing
years.

Henry, his father, and that father's father, inherited one crucial characteristic: they were powerful and influential citizens
who knew how to insinuate their personal thinking into the minds
of the great men of their nation. But they also kept them as
personal friends. The ultimate diplomats, astute politicians, they
contrived to remain nonpolitical and evade the inhibitions of
holding office, accepting nothing more than personal power at
a friend's side. Until now.

David had political ambitions. In the four years that had passed
since they had all been together for the private viewing of the
Stanton wing at the museum, he had taken substantial strides
toward the White House. Cannonberry Chase had always been
a haven of leisure, a very private meeting place for the powers
that ran the country. In the past, Roosevelt, a frequent guest,
had entertained Churchill there. Eisenhower met Eden for in-
formal talks there. Heads of state from various countries had
been received by Henry and Emily at Cannonberry Chase as
unofficial guests of the White House. They were brilliant hosts,
knowing how to put their guests sufficiently at ease to mingle
with the family. Guests were made to feel, for a short time, a
part of Cannonberry Chase. Powerful politicians and men and
women of the world, fascinating minds, promoters of conversation that at times moved like a chess game and at other times
amused, had influenced all the children. But it was David more
than the others who had been stirred by political power. David,
who, as far back as Henry could remember, had been more
interested in life at the Capitol and geopolitics than the other
children, with the exception of Max. Max had been fascinated,
but not interested in a political career for himself.

Cannonberry Chase inculcated home, security, the notion of
life lived to the fullest in an atmosphere of elegance and beauty.
The scent of success, glimpses of the best of all worlds. It impressed anyone fortunate enough to be a part of it even for a

short time. And it gave every one of the Stantons a solid base from which to launch them.

John married and produced two children during those four years. A grand, high-society wedding at St. Thomas's on Park Avenue, two christenings, and four family Christmases at Cannonberry Chase were hardly enough to compensate Lara for the loss of his doting love. Those first years away from home and her brothers were hardly years of separation from them. Phone calls, three or four times a week, endless quick visits, and extended holidays with John, David, and Steven, and even longer ones with Max, remained the heart of Lara's life, in spite of the attentions of Sam.

What Lara perceived as loss—John's lack of attention and love for her (which, of course, it was not, just an alteration)—was compounded by Steven's running off with a Texas beauty Emily disapproved of. Lynette seemed to have Lara's once-adoring brother completely besotted not only with herself but with Texas. As with everything, Emily and Henry took Steven's mistake in their stride, and the family rallied round in support. They waited for Steven to come to his senses and return to them and Cannonberry Chase, with or without Lynette.

Elizabeth kept having children during those four years, returning to Cannonberry Chase for her confinements, to England for the births, and always to Cannonberry Chase for the Stanton family Christmas. It seemed to Lara as if these new wives and Jeremy, Elizabeth's husband, and their babies, had always been a part of the family and the Chase. It was as if she had grown up with them. They became Stantons, and as such only made the house and the Chase come more alive than ever.

Much as Lara might feel she belonged to the family, she also felt somehow apart from them. She attributed her feelings of apartness to the real and deep loss she felt of that special love and attention they had always showered upon her before the Stantons started multiplying. She never let her loss show, and fought hard to overcome her feelings. Once she spoke to Steven, not about her personal feelings, but the family and the power it seemed to wield over her. Ever the anthropologist, he suggested to her that she should envisage their immediate family as an expanding, close-knit tribe. The Stantons as the most exclusive club in the world. Therein lay their happiness, that was where their aspirations would always be nourished, support be found for their dreams and needs.

Without even mentioning Lynette's name, Steven had made Lara understand that, besotted as he might be with his wife, he had not lost track. In time Lynette would understand what a privilege it was to be taken into the family, to have become a Stanton. She would one day comprehend the importance of the tribe to her life and cease fighting it. He hoped she would embrace it, realize not what she had given up but what she had gained by joining it. He had shown Lara that it was no different for Lynette than it was for Jeremy, or anyone who married into the family. Lara should try to make the man she eventually chose understand that.

She had been amused when Steven had said, ''You can only tell them the truth. Now, in our case, Lynette has a problem about accepting the truth. She fights it. So she irritates Mother, and it's all a waste. Lynette, after all, is quite selfish. She's self-centered and, I guess, a bit stupid. She's gonna create her scandals, cause us embarrassment, and finally lose. Then either she'll leave me or I'll throw her out, or we'll settle down and be happy. Those are the facts. Plus one more: There is no accounting for whom or what you fall in love with. You'll find that out soon enough, La.''

She gave Steven a big hug and a kiss and for a moment she was as close as she had ever been to him. She loved him as in the old days, before he had loved someone else more. No matter how she rationalized it, it still hurt, her brother loving someone else more than her.

In those four years Max had taken tremendous strides forward in his life, and had absorbed Lara into it whenever he could. He, like David, had a fascination with geopolitics. Had he not been a dedicated doctor of medicine, a diagnostician of exceptional merit, he would surely have given his cousin a run for the White House. Instead he had made medicine in the Third World his life and world politics his hobby. He was more like David than any of his other brothers. They were close, sharing many interests, not least womanizing. Though Max was no less a lady's man than David, he was a more complex one. His love affairs tended to be serious but short. His usually bitter, discarded women claimed that in sex he was a romantic, imaginative, virile lover, but ruthless in dumping them. He broke hearts and thrived on new conquests. Max had a dynamism about him that influenced on a grand scale. It gave him the power to achieve wonders where others failed. He divided his energies between the Stanton medical research foundations in Manhattan and his medical practice, and having a very good time.

In the last four years Lara had been much influenced by Max and David. She often remembered what Jamal had said about David that first night they had been together: that he had learned to live in the Stanton world and, discreetly, out of it. She now understood what Jamal had meant. She was learning from David and Max how to be a rebel with and without a cause, and win. How to use the world and add to it. How to play the world and people and win. How to keep secrets, skeletons even, well hidden. How to handle admiration, adulation, and not be trapped by it.

Between college, breaks with the family in the villa at Cap d'Antibes, travels with her brothers and with friends she had met at Smith, a year at the Sorbonne in Paris, a final year back at Smith again, returns to Cannonberry Chase whenever possible to recharge the batteries, Lara had fast found new worlds to experience. She was voracious in gobbling them up.

Sustained by the family and Sam's undeniable love for her, the security and pleasure she felt in their intimate relationship, the Stanton golden girl became in those years the rebel in the conservative Stanton family. More spoiled and adored by them than ever for her achievements: valedictorian of her class, winner of yachting trophies any of them would have been proud to take, skiing championships that had eluded all but John in the past, she matured into a ravishing beauty with an undeniable charm of her own that was original and provocative. Yet the family remained critical, always expecting more, as the over-achieving family is prone to do, without overtly asking anything of her.

During those years Lara had managed to sidestep Emily's greater plans for her coming out, her year in society in New York and London, with a promise that she would give herself up to Emily as soon as she had finished school. She had gotten away with that because Emily was satisfied that Sam was still on line as future husband. And Lara and Sam had duly performed as the beautiful couple several dozen times at the more important of the Season's events during the last four years.

Lara's brothers and her father were, however, not so sure that she would settle into the place Emily had envisioned for her and be happy. The men of the family were less concerned with Lara's sometimes rebellious nature than with the vulnerable submissiveness beneath that superficial rebellion. This worried them more. They were all thankful for Sam, certain she was safe there.

But how safe was she? Henry had lost count of the times he had asked himself that about his favorite child. He had always to counter his own favoritism toward Lara. He would find himself doting upon her, showing his love for her openly, then pulling back abruptly. It had always been that way for father and daughter, ever since Lara was a baby. He loved her more—more even than Emily; more than his mistress of twenty years, Janine; more even than the twenty-three-year-old girl he also kept in Paris. Only Emily knew that, and that was why he was so cautious with Lara in her presence.

Emily and Henry had an arrangement. He could stray just so long as he was discreet, and she—but no one else—knew anything about it. Then she would never leave him. It had always been that way. Those were the conditions she made before she married him. That was the hold she had over Henry: sexual freedom within her rules for their marriage. It worked for them. They were devoted to each other as husband and wife, as partners in a family, and until Lara was born he loved and adored Emily more than anyone or anything on earth. But, from then on, conceal it as Henry might, Emily was only second best.

Lara was a constant reminder to Henry of the night she was conceived. The night that Emily and he had a frightful row that culminated in his rape of her. For the first time in his married life, he forced Emily into sex against her will. Her husband's near rape of her had continued until she submitted to him in a frenzy of lust such as she had never allowed herself to enjoy before. It had been the most disturbing sexual night of their married lives, and Lara had been the fruit of it. Emily's disapproval of such extreme sexual pleasure precluded the luxury of such lust again. Lara was no less a reminder of that night for her mother than for Henry.

Henry was having a prelunch vodka Gibson with Max and David in the library when he saw through the oriel window the two Range Rovers circling the white marble Oceanus Fountain, a copy of Giovanni da Bologna's masterpiece in the Boboli Gardens in Florence. It had been playing its watery tune, there in the main courtyard, for nearly a hundred years. The three men smiled. She was home. Glasses still in hand, they went out to meet her. Only to find that she had not ridden home with the drivers who brought home the worldly goods of her Smith College years.

"I am not pleased, George. Where is my daughter?"

"I told her you wouldn't like it, sir, but you know Miss Lara. She insisted. So we came in convoy. She said you would understand because you would have done it yourself, sir."

"You mean she came all the way from Northampton on that blasted Harley-Davidson I gave her?" Henry shook his head in disapproval, but could not hide the smile on his lips. The minx— he could hardly say more about it: Lara was right, he would have done the same.

They heard the sound of the motorbike before they saw her, because of the rise in the road as it approached the house. The men drained their glasses and left them on the stone balustrade. They started down the white marble stairs as they saw her come over the rise. It was Henry who spoke first.

"Boys, you do spoil that girl."

The two men began to laugh and protest at the same time.

"Dad! Look who's talking! Who bought her the Harley?" cried David.

"I stand corrected. *We* spoil her. It's a miracle she has come out as well as she has."

Their joy at her return was evident, no matter how she arrived. Lara still had that quality of bringing an extra verve into the lives of everyone in the family.

She wore no helmet. That had been discarded as soon as she entered the gates of Cannonberry Chase. She sported a camel-hair jacket with wide revers, belted at the waist and worn over a matching pair of trousers. They tucked into brown leather boots buckled tight across her calves. Her long, silvery-blond hair flying in the wind, she rose out of the seat and waved as she rode at full throttle toward them.

She cut the Harley's motor, secured the cycle, and tore off her gloves, dropping them as she swung herself off the bike and into her father's arms for an enormous hug. She felt her father's hand caress her hair for an instant, before he held her away from him and said, not unkindly, "How is it possible for me to have a daughter who looks like a glorious angel, behaves as if the term 'free spirit' was a label especially designed for her, and has a devilish will of her own? I thought I bought this bike for you to get around Northampton. I was obviously wrong. Welcome home, La." He kissed her, first on one cheek, then the other, and a third time on the forehead. He tossed a "See you later, children," and then climbed onto the Harley. After a quick turn around the fountain, he took off on it down the avenue of trees.

His children watched him disappear. Then Max and David greeted Lara with their usual enthusiasm and teasing, and the three walked arm in arm up the stairs and into the house. The two chauffeurs spirited the Range Rovers around to the side door to unload them there.

In the library, Lara discarded her jacket. With David taking one leg and Max the other, they helped to pull her boots off. She had been riding flat out for hours with her convoy to get to Cannonberry Chase in time for lunch, so now she was stiff and sore and just a little weary, and her legs seemed to have swelled tight into her boots. But she had been even more exhausted from her ride before she came through the gates of Cannonberry Chase. There a wave of renewed energy flooded over her—and something more: a diminished dread of the year she had promised Emily and Henry in which she would rest and relax and take her place in society, their society.

She braced herself, holding tight to the arms of the chair, and watched the two men struggling with her boots. A surge of affection for them rolled over her. For the last few years she had seen much of the world, had participated in several conscience marches, had lived a happy-go-lucky existence. And they had been fun years, a sexy, preppy life with Sam. A free-spirited time of travel with college chums that had nothing to do with family, and life at Cannonberry Chase, and being a Stanton.

Oh, she had had those, too, but they had been something separate from her new experiences.

Her cousin David's obvious affection for her, returning home, and being in that grand room of books and maps, with its whiff of leather and spring flowers, triggered in her a sense of belonging. That formidable yet almost cosy library had always been a haven for her for as long as she could remember. Until that very moment, she had thought the last four years were to be the pattern of her life, her future. They seemed like the backbone of everything she would ever be or do. Suddenly, and for no reason at all, she was not so sure. Doubt took hold. Had she been fooling herself? Was she or was she not the liberated lady she thought she was? Cannonberry Chase, the family, her need for their love . . . five minutes in their enveloping embrace—and everything else in the world seemed questionable.

That bastard Jamal, was he right? The last time, nearly a year ago, when he had tricked her into three days of off-piste skiing on a Swiss mountaintop and sex: he had lulled her back into believing that he loved her obsessively. That the erotic passion of his life was herself. She had almost believed him. Until he had gone too far in his urge to enslave her sexually. He was so certain he had her. Yet she had slipped away from his depraved demands as easy as quicksilver running through his fingers. Enraged that she had foiled him yet again, he had shouted, "You silly, spoiled bitch! You think you're a liberated lady of the seventies. You're no more liberated than a frivolous, fantailed goldfish in a tank of water."

Chapter 7

The party of the season was not one but three. All given by Henry and Emily Stanton to launch Lara Victoria into society. The tribes of the New York 400 mingled with the Boston nobs, the Philadelphia mainliners, the more select of the uppercrust San Franciscans, and the odd guest from St. Louis and Chicago. Not a penny of new money was to be found disgracing the pockets or purses of any at the events. No Texan, either (with the exception of Lynette). Emily had screened the guest list.

Only days after Lara's homecoming, Emily and her social secretary, Missy Manners, trapped Lara in the library. It was the first of what appeared to be an endless stream of meetings on the events of the looming '74–'75 social season. Instructions on protocol, some sprucing up of social etiquette, outlines of her own coming-out parties, were meticulously recorded in a set of beige ostrich-covered books of blank paper. A large desk diary and a smaller matching one for the handbag were also included. Emily was assembling Lara's bibles.

No surprise when Lara casually thumbed through the desk diary to find dozens of dates already filled with events she knew nothing about, and cared even less for. She knew well the map of Emily's world. Here were the beginnings of her translation from the margin to the center of the Stanton world, the family, its wealth and social position, and all that was expected of it.

Clashes of temperament between mother and daughter, embarrassing double bookings, social gaffes of all kinds, crucial decisions about which invitations one accepted, which (with devastating sadness) one rejected, were all avoided by the loan of Missy from Emily to Lara from 9:00 to 9:45 A.M. every morning. This was also judged the best time for Lara to dispose of the necessary correspondence that went with the position of Number One Deb of the Season.

Missy would, of course, have a duplicate of Lara's diary: Emily must be *au fait* with what was going on. Not to interfere, just to advise. Through all this, Henry, who stood off to one side listening and saying little, watched his daughter. He was not displeased by her attitude. She seemed to take it all well enough. Henry had been summoned by Emily for support, yet had not had to participate in any of the unpleasantness Emily had suggested might occur. Relieved that there had been no negative scenes between the women, Henry decided to reward his wife and his daughter. He would sail them across the bay for fresh lobsters.

He was about to make his offer when he heard Emily say, "Lara, as you can see in your diary, wardrobe day is tomorrow. Oleg Cassini will be here at ten. Elizabeth Arden at twelve, Mary McFadden at two, and the Bergdorf people at four. No shops—much better, don't you think?"

"Fine. The only better thing would have been to do it over the telephone."

"Too chancy. But a fashion show in the ballroom, privacy, and we can see everything, and you can try things on at your leisure— Don't make a face, Lara. I know it's a bore, but there it is. Must be done. May I come and look over what wardrobe you do have? What we might make do with? No need to over-spend."

Henry interrupted, "Emily, in this particular instance I think we can dispense with the 'make do,' don't you?"

There was an unmistakable firmness in his voice. They had all heard that tone before: the women knew what it meant. Especially Emily. It didn't sound often, but when it did, she obeyed, just like everyone else from the boardroom to the bedroom. As a husband, he appreciated Emily's parsimony. But toward his youngest child? Some extravagance could be permitted there surely. He made up his mind then and there to go into New York and buy her a piece of fine jewelry. Something special for her graduation from Smith, her coming home, coming out. Soon, with school behind her and fun ahead of her, she would be swept along on a tide of men, and slowly Henry would lose his daughter to them. That appealed to him even less than the idea that she would one day settle down and marry and he would lose her forever. The only thing that reassured him was that it would be to Sam.

Emily answered him, "Yes, if you say so, Henry." She walked over to where Lara was sitting and sat down on the arm of the girl's chair. She added, "You heard your father. We can splurge tomorrow, Lara. You are indeed fortune's child." She brushed a piece of lint from Lara's sleeve and smiled at her. From Emily that amounted to a gesture of affection.

Henry was not insensitive to the warmth in Emily's voice. He sensed that she was relieved that all was going to plan. There had been none of the bucking she had expected from Lara. Henry looked at his two women with some pride. They were beautiful, and he could respond positively to beautiful women, especially those who gave him what he wanted without trouble. Not that trouble ever posed a problem for Henry Garfield Stanton. He marveled at his luck: he both liked and loved his wife and daughter.

For days the family had been assembling at Cannonberry Chase for the first of Lara's parties, a late summer ball. The winter cottage, a charming, eight-bedroom stone house, covered in pink climbing roses and set in a field on the edge of a cliff overlooking the Atlantic Ocean, was where Elizabeth and her brood, and John, his wife Ann and their two children, were staying. Steven and Lynette remained in the main house, as did Max and David. Every day someone was arriving and was accorded one of the remaining fourteen bedrooms. The beach bungalow was reserved for Jamal, who had managed to infiltrate the guest list. Emily still considered him just about suitable and an old and trusted friend of the family. And she was not immune to his dark good looks and drawing room charm. There had been years of subtle attentions and respect toward her. He was instructed by Emily to play host to the other houseguests staying in the beach bungalow. The remainder of the cottages scattered over Cannonberry Chase would all be filled to capacity with friends by the evening of the ball.

Just the mention of Jamal's name and Lara looked forward to seeing him again. And yet? . . . she wondered. Would there

ever be a time when his name would mean nothing to her? She
could only hope so. She disliked her sexual enslavement to him.
He provoked an erotic excitement in her that disturbed the equilibrium of her life. She displayed no reaction to the news that
he would be there, but just the mention of his name set her
emotionally on edge. Since she had walked out on him in Gstaad
there had been no contact, direct or indirect. There were moments when Lara actually despised her own voluptuous nature.
Maybe not so much despised as *feared* it. She banished Jamal
from her thoughts.

It was dusk, and the first veil of gauzy mist could be seen
rolling low over the water, several hundred yards behind the
boat, toward Cannonberry Chase. Henry steered the *Justina*
smoothly in, close to the dock. He threw the towline to Bill, the
boatman. The sloop was secured. They were gathering their
things together and making ready to leave when David's plane
swept down out of the sky and buzzed them. He and Julia waved
from the six-seater seaplane. It made another low pass over the
sailboat. The three Stanton sailors waved back. Lara was delighted.

Julia Van Fleet had been Lara's best friend since childhood
and until Lara went to Smith and Julia to England to study at
Oxford. Time and distance, new friends and different interests,
had caused a drifting away from each other. New worlds other
than the one they had always known had opened for them and
partly swallowed them. But the bonds were still there. The
friendship survived. Now both girls were home, returning to
New York and the life-style from which they had taken a four-
year sabbatical.

Julia Van Fleet was special, but not lucky. She was almost as
American an aristocrat as Lara. A Van Fleet was there when the
Dutch settlers paid the Indians twenty-four dollars for New York.
Her ancestors fought in the Revolutionary War, took part in the
battle of Bunker Hill, and one of them, an artillery officer, helped
outwit General Burgoyne at Saratoga.

The Van Fleets were especially sweet and kind people, in
spite of the tragedy in their lives. Their friends, the Stantons
and the Faynes, and many of the other New York 400 (the magic
number of people who could fit into Mrs. Astor's ballroom and

ever after set the numerical limit on "old" New York society),
closed ranks and supported them through their periodic bad
times. Those periods when Julia's mother, who suffered from
severe depression, would have to be sent away to the Stock-
bridge Clinic in the Berkshire Mountains of Massachusetts,
sometimes for months.

The Van Fleets had been the beautiful, romantic, and glamorous couple of their set. The Scott Fitzgeralds of another era.
Their house in Newport could have modeled for Gatsby's. The
effect of her mother's illness on Julia and her father was to ensure
they took full advantage of the periods when Betsy Van Fleet
was well. They traveled together, and were valued wherever they
went for their charm, wit, and amazing joie de vivre. But those
other times, the dark times, were a heavy burden that they bore
with a quiet stoicism, while their hearts were sore. Each time
they worried that maybe this would be the one when Betsy would
not emerge from her dark and lonely pit. Maybe this time she
would slip over the edge into the vortex of madness.

Her mother's illness made Julia's father overprotective of her.
It was really he who brought her up. He and sundry nannies and
tutors, and the wives of their close friends. When Betsy was
well enough, they summered in the house in Newport, or they
traveled. When she was not, it was as if a part of themselves
had died. They carried on. That constant shunting about between people and places created in Julia an ability to fit in easily.
It instilled in her a sense of compassion that some might mistake
for weakness, but it was her strength. Julia had a calm, loving,
and loyal nature. She was like a breath of freshness among the
competitive Stantons. When any members of the family walked
onto a tennis court, they were like gladiators entering the Col-
osseum. When Julia played doubles with them, there was no
hint of aggression, no flash of the killer instinct about her. Like
some disciple of Zen (which she was not), she quietly locked
herself into the game. Not infrequently she walked off the court
the winner. Slow, quiet, and rational was her way. She wore her
calm self-possession like a coat of silk gauze.

When the moment arrived both girls had reluctantly donned
vestal white from bosom to toe, and clutched snowy roses in
kid-gloved hands. To the fanfare of a band, a melodious horn
woven into a drum roll, they had descended the sweeping stair-

case, each on the arm of her father, to the Debutantes' Ball. They had duly dropped two deep curtsies to their social peers in unison with twenty-two seventeen- and eighteen-year-olds. It was tradition, and Emily, the old stickler, was holding out for every ounce of it that evening. A lump bulged in many a maternal throat as that bevy of top-notch teenagers crossed the threshold into eligible adulthood. Though the girls relished the spotlight and had been properly launched, were officially "out," they never sailed through the social scene quite as their contemporaries had. But here they both were, belatedly agreeing to make it up to Emily by spending the year she felt a girl needed in order to find her place in society.

For all her snobbery, Emily did have the ability to create for her family homes that were not only grand and elegant, but also attracted people and music and laughter. The atmosphere was always charged with hospitality, whether for two or twenty or two hundred, which was to be the quota for Lara's ball. Emily appeared to manage it effortlessly, or to have trained her staff meticulously both behind and on the scene. She ran her houses and her family with éclat. Hers was a powerful presence that ruled and sustained her unshakably as the doyenne of New York's old-guard high society.

Julia had been given the room next to Lara's. After a delicious dinner and several hours with the family and guests, the girls retired. It was not long before Lara arrived at Julia's room with two large bowls of homemade peach ice cream and a box of Belgian chocolate truffles. Lara sat cross-legged on the bed facing Julia, who had propped herself up against the pillows in readiness for the sugary orgy.

"You know this is wicked."

"Sure. But nice," answered Lara, with a big smile. "It's so long since we've done this."

"Four years? Nearly five?"

"You don't think we've matured beyond this sort of preppy gourmandizing?"

"Not a chance, I'm glad to say." And Julia reached out for her portion of calories.

They fell silent while they tucked into their ice cream. It was an awkward silence.

Lara buried her faint unease in a champagne truffle. The succulent soft chocolate stuck to the roof of her mouth. She sucked on it with her tongue. It prompted that instant chocolate high that makes you reach for the next round blob of addiction. But before she succumbed, she bent forward and said, "Try this. I think I've died and gone to chocolate heaven." Both girls began to laugh, and Lara popped the remaining half of the truffle into Julia's mouth. She closed her eyes and sighed. The truffle was delicious. Lara's declaration seemed to have broken the ice between the two girls. The years of separation vanished.

They talked for hours about their lives and loves, their aspirations and their friends. Half a dozen times Lara was on the verge of telling Julia about her relationship with Jamal. Half a dozen times she thought better of it. Was it too dark, too murky a relationship to expose to scrutiny? Or, she wondered, was it simply too sexual, too loveless, too peculiarly private to share with anyone else? Could it be that she didn't want Julia to know her sensual nature governed her life? She allowed no more than hints of this to her friend.

What did come out of the frank talk between the girls was the revelation that Lara and Sam had not been faithful to each other. That they had come to an arrangement that suited them both. They were in love, and believed that they would one day settle down with each other. But, until then, they allowed each other freedom to date others. Date, yes, sex, no: that was the tacit agreement.

In those four years, Lara had taken up with several young men: a Princeton boy, an Amherst guy, a French charmer. Nothing more than a fun time had ever come of those affairs. Maybe a spurt of falling in love, a little preppy sex, a *soupçon* of French romance, a stint of Peace Corps passion—even a fling with a biker—but always she returned to Sam. She discussed with Julia how strange it was that she and Sam knew there were others, but not once did they confess to each other that they had been unfaithful.

"And now?" Julia asked.

"And now," Lara answered, "we are the same as we have always been. The love is great, the security of that love even greater. The sex has always been very good, maybe even a little more than very good, the best, even—with the exception of one other. And I am not in love with anyone else. We are happy, and in love, and free. We like it that way, and the parents have accepted that's the way it's going to be until we marry.''

''Then you are sure about marrying him?''

''I'm not sure of anything, except I can't imagine marrying anyone else.''

Lara felt uneasy talking about marriage. She quickly changed the subject from herself and Sam to Julia and David. And so the girls had had their heart-to-heart.

One advantage that Julia had was that all the Stantons loved her. She had had her girlhood crushes on each of the boys, but only Max had given her a tumble. He gave her her first kiss, had been the first man to see her naked, to kiss her breasts. Then he went away somewhere, and her crush on him eventually petered out. Julia's being back in the Stanton fold reminded them how much they had missed seeing her around. They showered attention on her, none more so than Emily and Henry.

Emily had always found a softer spot in her heart for Julia than she ever had for Lara. Lara had rarely minded in the past, and she certainly didn't mind now. If anything, she was grateful. So it was no surprise when, at the fashion show, she consulted more with Elizabeth and Julia about Lara's new wardrobe than she did with Lara herself. Lara felt more than ever like one of Emily's causes.

The women sat together in comfortable, sixteenth-century French chairs. Their concentration was sustained with refreshments served from a table. Emily allowed them breaks between the end of one designer's show and the start of another. They were in the Cannonberry Chase ballroom, supposedly one of the prettiest of such rooms in the country, renowned not only for its dances, but for the private concerts and operas Emily sponsored for her friends. The Stantons' private Tanglewood, their very own Glyndebourne.

The room was dazzling: a huge rectangle with a vaulted ceiling. One of the wings of the manor house, it tucked into the architecture of the building and the landscape of the gardens with a grace and elegance that muted its obvious grandeur. One entered the ballroom either from an oval reception room in the house, a yellow, ochre, and white music room of which the family made great use, or from any of the French windows, of which there were twelve, on each side of the thirty-foot-high walls. The windows were fifteen feet high and curved at the top; in effect, pairs of glass-paned doors that opened onto lawns and marble fountains and lily ponds. They had overdoors and side panels of sixteenth-century tapestries. A framework of mauves and peach, ochre, plum, lime, and rusty rose, stitched into garlands of flowers and fruit framing the shades of green: the grass and enchanting topiary that one saw through the glass panes.

The inlaid floor, a masterpiece of parquetry, shone like a mirror, reflecting the five crystal chandeliers. These were still used, not with electricity but slender, handmade ivory candles. The ceiling was of the palest sky blue, with subtly soft white clouds behind which bursts of faint pink and shimmering pallid yellow broke out, just as Whistler might have painted.

At the far end of the ballroom, pairs of doors led into a rectangular room of glass, the official reception room. Here the buffet suppers were set up; the champagne tables of crystal flutes and vintage Krug in huge silver coolers set among the palm trees. Today, instead, the designers prepared their shows here for the four women waiting in the center of the ballroom.

Lara had expected to be bored in the first half hour, but not so. Mr. Cassini joined them to charm and amuse while the pretty models strutted their stuff. They minced and used their shoulders, swung their hips, and struck poses. And there were dresses for every occasion: day wear and sports wear, evening wear, and even tea wear, if you had time to wear it. Oleg Cassini charmed and kissed hands, flattered and charmed again. In its own tinsely way, it had been fun.

The hopping in and out of the clothes was sheer hard work, only lightened by the dressers and Cassini's over-the-top flattery. Then, when Lara did her own little imaginary catwalk, and she saw Emily trying hard not to laugh, she realized the occasion had its own dotty uniqueness. She decided to relax into it and have a good time. It was, after all, a new experience, this whole sartorial fanfare just for her. By the end of the day she had enjoyed herself. Still, she hoped that it didn't happen too often in the life of a Number One Deb-type.

If Oleg Cassini dripped charm, Elizabeth Arden's top vendeuse and her staff oozed the importance of being earnest about clothes and hair and nails. They displayed a refined, if not grande-dameish style. Whereas Cassini made Lara feel the greatest beauty of all time, and the only woman in the world who was still able to up his heartbeat, the ladies from the red door on Fifth Avenue left her to fall apart unless she gave herself, body and soul, to Elizabeth Arden at least twice weekly throughout the Season. Once past their potted face cream and beauty pitch, she found their clothes very pretty and wearable and, if not fun, lovely and feminine.

Lara remained easygoing about Emily and Elizabeth and their selection of clothes for her. It was not difficult: they chose nothing she really disliked. She managed to win, though, on one or two things they disapproved of, but only when Julia stepped in for her. The two women then seemed quite resigned to her right to choose her own things at least as much as they did.

When Mary McFadden arrived with her models and clothes, everything changed for Lara. She became an instant clothes hanger. There was not a gown that she didn't want, not a jacket, not a pair of trousers. The fabrics were luscious—the only word for them—handpainted and printed, or accordion-pleated or embroidered. They were modern and not modern, ethnic and not ethnic. They were pretty and inspired. Lara didn't listen to Emily or anyone else; she bought almost the whole collection. So inspired was she by them that it became infectious. The other women conceded that Lara, as Emily put it, had "come a long way in her ability to choose well."

Lara answered, "That's such high praise, Mother. I am so flattered and exhausted from all this. I give you Bergdorf's. I will wear anything you choose." And choose was exactly what Emily and Elizabeth now did. They mulled over all the day's purchases and filled in the gaps of the wardrobe; Lara was certain they would last her a lifetime. She'd be unable to justify entering a shop ever again.

But nature asserts itself: shopping would soon become part of her new life-style, being chic a priority in her life.

Chapter 8

It was during a particularly amusing dinner party of family and many guests that evening that a phone call had come through for Lara. A friend from Smith, one of the girls she had gone on several protest marches with.

"Sorry if I took you from dinner, Lara, but I need as many supporters to rally to the cause as I can get. We have got to do something fast. I have just heard that in three days' time the Santos Dupuis Chemical Company is going to close a secret deal to build a huge plant on that tract of magnificent rain forest—the one we've been trying to get the government to buy and turn into a national park. Hawaii will end up nothing but concrete and chemicals."

Lara listened and suddenly, after four years of supporting Marcy Gialombo, she felt so removed from her old Smith College roommate and her protests that it embarrassed her. Though she still wanted to support Marcy and her causes, the reality was that all those marches she had made with her, in the final analysis, had not done very much.

"Marcy, it sounds too late for a protest."

"It's never too late for a protest."

"I think we need stronger action and a swifter result than another march."

"You sound as if you are not interested in a march."

Lara took her courage in hand. "I don't think I can be interested. I have other commitments."

"I never thought *you* would let me down."

"I won't. I will do what I can to help. Just tell me what you know about the sale and I will call you back in the morning."

This from Lara, the Lara who always followed? Suddenly a leader? A takeover lady? What a joke. A spoiled beauty who was just learning that there was a world out there that didn't revolve around her. A joke, or a cop-out? Marcy could not make up her mind. Disappointment muddled her. "You won't call back. I can tell. It's in your voice."

"Marcy, I won't let you down. You have to let me try it my way. If you don't believe I will call, then you call me at noon tomorrow."

"Lara, we've lost you," said a disheartened Marcy. "We have, haven't we?"

"I don't know, Marcy. Just give me the details."

Marcy gave the information she had and hung up. Lara had been such a staunch supporter of Marcy's conscience marches. Could her interest have been only superficial? But who, what, was influencing Lara now?

Lara returned to the dinner table, no less troubled about Marcy than Marcy was about her. How Marcy would have loathed the day Lara had just spent having a binge on clothes. Was she letting her friend and the cause down? Such a short time back at Cannonberry Chase and into the Stanton world, and yet her perspective of Marcy and her causes had shifted radically. She looked at the paper crunched in her hand. She must make an effort to help Marcy in some way—but how? Lara knew that she could do better than another march. At least she hoped so. She looked at the faces around the table. Marcy would have loathed those faces, too. Her Socialist heart would have demanded it. If Marcy were to see Lara sitting at that table she would most certainly be furious. She would hang a label on Lara that would read: "Right-wing liberal with a capitalist's heart." God, she thought, how I hate labels.

As the guests filed out of the dining room, Emily caught her attention. "Something wrong, Lara?"

"A friend in need."

"Then you must, of course, help, dear."

"Yes."

"David, I think. If you need to talk about it to someone. He's always so good when people have problems."

Lara's estimation of her mother rose. She suddenly became aware of the positive side of Emily Dean Stanton, which she usually had trouble seeing. She reached for her mother's hand and squeezed it, "Of course. David. Thanks, Mother." Emily slid her hand from her daughter's and looked embarrassed as she joined her other guests walking to the drawing room.

Lara tried to get David's attention for several minutes. In vain.

"Settle for me?" From a smiling Jamal.

"Now what am I supposed to say to that?"

"Anything that's flattering will do. How are you? I've missed you, and I'm really pleased to be here for your party."

He was his usual handsome and charming self. As always, he behaved in public as if there had never been a sexual liaison between them. Ever grateful for that, she smiled at him, and tried to calm her twinge of attraction to him. A look passed between them, nothing that anyone in the room could recognize as intimate. But they both knew how very intimate it was. She watched Jamal swing into action. He never merely spoke to women, he always seduced. He raised Emily's hand, gave it the perfect continental kiss, and asked, "Madam Stanton, will you grant me permission to take Lara away for a few minutes? I have a gift I would like to give her. Something to mark the occasion." He bent close to Emily and whispered in her ear. She gave him a thin smile and a nod of consent.

He placed an arm around Lara's shoulder. They were barely halfway across the room when Lara, who was feeling nervous about being alone with Jamal, said, "Jamal."

He saw the fear in her eyes. He knew her so well. She wanted him, she needed him, but this was neither the time nor the place. Her fear of his putting her into a compromising situation made her tremble. He stopped, was about to say something, changed his mind, and instead told her, "Rest easy. Have I ever put us in an embarrassing situation?"

"No."

"And I never will. I have always told you we have two relationships. And this one never intrudes on the sexual one." She visibly relaxed. She even sighed, and kissed him on the cheek and whispered, "Thank you."

In the hall, she asked him, "Jamal, have you ever heard of a

company''—she unfolded the crumpled paper still in her hand—
''the Santos Dupuis Chemical Company?''

''It's actually Santos Dupuis Chemical International. Yes, I
have. The second largest company of its kind in the world.''

''You don't know what bad news that is.''

''I wouldn't look so dejected if I were you. But never mind
that now.'' He opened the front door.

His name was Azziz. A black Arab steed as high-spirited as
Biscuit. A magnificent beast whose mane had been plaited with
narrow silver-and-gold ribbons that shimmered against his silky
dark beauty. Lara thought him the finest horse she had ever seen.
He reared up once when she approached him, but his groom,
Nick, a blond, curly-headed young man, settled him down. The
second time she patted his neck, caressed his flanks, he remained calm. She ran her hands down his leg, walked around
him and spoke to him, caressed his head, toyed with the stream-
ers hanging from the braided mane. When she turned around to
tell Jamal how much she liked him, she was greeted by the entire
house party walking down the stairs to have a look at her gift.

Jamal climbed into the saddle. David clasped Lara by the
waist and gave her a lift. She sat sidesaddle, and Jamal held her
by one arm, the reins by his free hand, while everyone milled
around admiring the horse. Lara bent forward to grab one of
the horse's ears and give it an affectionate tug. The necklace
sparkled, a slim, platinum band of square-cut diamonds. It hung
over Azziz's ear. She slid it up, off the horse's ear, and held it
toward the light of the cast-iron lanterns on the terrace.

''For me?'' She was obviously quite overwhelmed by his generosity.

''Well, it's no use to Azziz.''

Everyone began to laugh, including Lara. Everyone with the
exception of Sam. He looked quite put out. Jamal handed the
reins to Lara, unclasped the choker, and encircled her neck with
it. She was wearing one of the Mary McFadden evening dresses.
An aubergine-colored long skirt of crepe de chine and a bodice-
hugging, off-the-shoulder blouse of silver lamé that showed off
the ripe beauty of her breasts. They were made even more evident by the contrast of the huge puffed sleeves of the blouse in
the same fabric but accordion-pleated. With her silvery-blond
hair crimped and worn long and loose, she seemed the perfect

setting for the slim band, now clasped snugly around her long, slim neck.

Such extravagant gifts from Jamal to Lara did not seem at all unusual. He had always been extravagant and generous to the family, and been berated by them for it. No one criticized him tonight. It was impossible. They had all been too charmed by Azziz. Jamal strutted the horse before them, back and forth several times. They were horse-loving people, yet had seen few more proud and noble than Azziz. With Lara still sitting in his arms upon the horse, Jamal now swung Azziz around to face the guests, who used the stairs to the terrace as a viewing stand. His dressage performance, though brief, was brilliant—and culminated in a bow by Azziz that drew spontaneous applause from the onlookers.

Lara insisted she wanted to ride Azziz back to the stables. Finally she was talked out of it and settled for walking part of the way with the horse, his groom, Jamal, David, and Julia. On the way down the drive all the talk was of Azziz, who had come from Jamal's father's stables in Morocco. After watching the horse, ridden by Nick, disappear into the blackness of the night, the foursome turned to go back to the house.

The manor, aglow with light, looked impressive. Every bit the rural American palace, even though everyone pretended it was just an American country house. The night was one of those perfect end-of-summer evenings, still very warm, a slight breeze coming off the ocean, a sky of black velvet perforated with stars, and an almost full moon. A marvelous day, a marvelous night. It all seemed so extravagant and glamorous to Lara, and fun. She could see what a good time her mother's life-style delivered. Until this day she had largely discounted it as a boring, unimaginative existence. She was beginning to wonder why she had rejected the idea of coming out into their social whirl for so long.

Jamal handed her the crumpled piece of paper she had given him to hold when she had mounted Azziz. "Here, you had better take this now. I might forget to give it to you."

The Marcy details she had hastily scribbled out on the paper now in her hand intruded upon her good time. Walking four abreast, she had David linked on one arm, Jamal on the other. Julia and David were softly intoning songs from old Broadway musicals. Jamal, remembering the occasional phrase, would chime in. Lara tugged at Jamal's arm. "Jamal, why shouldn't I feel dejected about the Santos Dupuis Chemical Company?"

"Chemical International," he corrected.

She ignored that. "I have good reason. They are going to buy a piece of land that I'd rather they didn't."

"Then stop them. Do that, and there is nothing for you to feel dejected about. Much the best solution." They were close to the fountain in the courtyard now. The light from the terrace fell across her face. Jamal tapped the tip of her nose with his index finger.

The gesture irritated her. It felt as if he were merely tapping in a full stop to the end of a final sentence. "Easier said than done," she snapped back at him, more than a little annoyed with him for acting in so cavalier a fashion about something that really troubled her.

"Not for you."

"And why not especially for me? You make it sound as if all I have to do is raise my magic wand, and, hey, presto, the land is mine."

"That is just about the way it is. Only, you are the magic wand."

"Oh, I don't know what you are going on about. I have three days to stop the sale of that land. This is important to me, and all you do is make cryptic remarks." Now not only Jamal, but "The Surrey with the Fringe on Top," sung slightly out of key by David and Julia, was an irritant. She wheeled around to face Jamal. "Unless you have anything really constructive to say about my problem, then just forget it."

He pulled her away from the others and rushed her up the stairs, onto the terrace. "I hate it when you pout. It always makes me want to beat you. You have two options. One is to buy the land yourself. The other is to tell Santos Dupuis you don't want them to buy it."

"How can I buy it? It will cost millions."

"Talk to Harland Brent. He can handle the whole thing for you. He is your trustee, isn't he?"

"Jamal, you are crazy. I haven't that kind of money."

Jamal began to laugh. He hoisted her by the waist and sat her on the balustrade that encircled the terrace.

"Nor the clout to stop a company purchase," she added.

"You do, you know. Maybe not all the corporations in the world, but certainly Santos Dupuis."

"I do?"

"Ask David."

"Ask David what?" chimed David, joining them and hoisting Julia onto the balustrade to sit next to Lara.

It was beginning to dawn on Lara. She felt the adrenaline pump, an excitement that hadn't been there only seconds before. "David, do you happen to know who owns Santos Dupuis Chemical International?"

"Sure. The family. Now don't tell me you didn't know that?"

The look of surprise on Lara's face told him that she didn't. "Don't you even look at your dividend sheets?"

"No, but I think I will from now on. David, am I very wealthy? I mean, do I have enough money to buy something that cost millions?"

"Lara, you should be asking Harland these questions, not me. I have no idea what you are worth. And what's this all about, anyway?"

Lara finally told them, then showed them the information she had on the paper. "Well?" she asked.

David began to laugh. "La, besides the dances and partying this year, I think you should get acquainted with your assets. If you want to stop the sale of that land to Santos Dupuis, talk to Harland. He can register your objection to the purchase with the board. I have never known the board to go against the wishes of a member, and you are a member, proxied by Harland. Santos Dupuis will be furious. They will have to find an alternative piece of land for expansion. That will cost them, and leave them disappointed."

"That only half solves the problem. If Santos Dupuis doesn't buy it, someone else may. Then where are we?" Lara asked.

The men remained silent, eyes on Lara. Lara tapped her head, a quick, sharp gesture. "Of course, how stupid of me. I will get Harland to buy it for me."

"Right," the three agreed in one voice.

"The correct terminology to win your trustees round to agreeing to the purchase would be, 'I want to buy this property as a long-term investment for my portfolio.' They'll never say no to that. They will know that, if Santos Dupuis wanted it, it's valuable and has potential. It's in the bag,'' David added.

"What if Santos Dupuis won't agree to pull out in my favor?"

"They will, baby. They won't oppose the family," David assured her.

"But what if they do?" Lara insisted.

"Then tell them you will bid against them in the sale. That would only raise the price of the land and do none of you any good," Jamal suggested.

"Right, I'm going to see Harland right now. Wow, today has been some eye-opener. If I add the purchase of Hawaiahoo to the day's events, this will have to go down as a major turning point in my life."

She held her arms out to David to help her off the balustrade. He swung her down and gave her a hug. A look of love passed between them, and Lara was thankful for the cover of darkness, relieved Jamal and Julia had not seen it. . . . She had been wrong. Jamal saw it. One day, he vowed, she would emit stolen glances radiating love for him just as she had for her cousin. Eyes that had nothing to do with being loving cousins—and everything to do with passion between a man and a woman.

Harland had not been easy to convince. He had irritated her when he suggested that she call him at nine o'clock the following morning, if she still felt she wanted him to try to purchase the land. Harland was a man in his mid-fifties, and it embarrassed her to tell him off. It did not, however, impede her. They were both shocked by the tone of authority she took with Harland. The threats to call a family meeting, if necessary.

Now it was a few minutes to noon on the following day, and she had heard nothing from Harland. He knew that it was essential that she have a progress report on the matter, from him, before twelve o'clock. The clock in the hall chimed twelve, the telephone remained mute. No Marcy, no Harland.

The call came at twelve-twenty. The land was hers. Papers were being drawn up. It would be finalized in three days' time. But the land was indisputably hers. The money, nine million dollars, was already in escrow in the seller's bank. She had only to put a name to the holding company. She was too overwhelmed to think of a name, and left it to Harland Brent.

Lara dialed Marcy's number. She did not complete the call.

What was she to say to Marcy? She could hardly boast, I bought it. Marcy would hate that, no matter how relieved she might be that the land was safe from a chemical plant. It could only sound crass. How do you tell a lefty liberal you have just raised nine million dollars to save a piece of the earth in one breath, and your family owns the chemical plant that wanted to pollute a piece of paradise in the next? Of course, the answer is you don't. Now she simply could not call her friend, and she prayed Marcy would not call her—not, at least, until she worked it out.

Lara went to see David. He was with Max and her father in the latter's study. She told them her dilemma. It was Henry who suggested, "You must begin right now to learn how to handle your wealth and your position, Lara. Harland was going to brief you on these matters sometime in the near future, when he acquainted you with your holdings, but you rather jumped the gun. You talk with him. He's your financial adviser, the man who you should listen to. But I am always here for you, ready to listen, and, if possible, to suggest on any problems you might have.

"In this instance, you have a classic problem with Marcy. We have all had it in one form or another. Discretion, privacy, about your personal means, your holdings, the influence you might have and use—that's what must guide you. I know Marcy is a trusted friend. Just the same, you tell her nothing of how you pulled this off. She should be happy you did it, and that's enough for her. Rule number one: Never deal direct in financial transactions or deals. Not when you can get your advisers to do it. Get yourself out of the firing line. Let me tell you, you can accomplish more with less ill-feeling that way. We pay the best people to stand in for us. They know better than we do how to sidestep awkward questions, manipulate us into better positions. That is, after all, what they are trained to do. We are trained to delegate so we get what we want. It's our job to direct our affairs from behind closed doors.

"Marcy is a charming girl, passionate for causes. I like and respect and approve of most of what she supports. But I don't know that she will appreciate this new ability you have shown to thrust and cut, and get the job done. Although I can appreciate it, I can't say that in this particular instance I am thrilled about it. You have cost Santos Dupuis several millions in forcing them to drop out, and probably as much again to find another site."

A stony look came across Lara's face. She was tough with her father—as she had never been before—when she blurted, "Dad, Santos Dupuis and the board should see to it they find a barren volcanic island next time, and have concern for the earth." The three men began to laugh. The joke was lost on Lara.

"For a rather submissive girl, you have certainly taken the lead in this little affair, Lara. In the two years that you girls were roommates I have not been unaware of how Marcy always likes to take the lead. Take my advice, stay silent—or be as evasive as you can be about your role in this piece of ecological white-knighting. Save the friendship."

"I had to do something more than march, Dad."

"It's to your credit, Lara, that you moved on this so promptly. But, my advice is, step back. Let Harland handle Marcy."

"I can't do that, Dad. It seems much too mean. And I am thrilled that the land is saved. I want to share that with Marcy."

"That's the thing about suggestions. You can only make them. I am sure you will work it out, dear."

David offered, "Dad knows what he is talking about, La. Think it over."

Lara went for a walk. She was anxious because Marcy had not called. She knew what that meant: Marcy was knocking herself out trying to arrange the march, which was now virtually unnecessary. It was too cruel not to call her and tell her the fantastically good news. Lara broke into a run. In the house she took the stairs two at a time and burst into her bedroom and swooped upon the telephone. Marcy's line was busy, and busy, and busy. She knew Marcy well. When Marcy had the bit between her teeth she would charge forward, blinkered to all else but her cause. Lara would never be able to get her on the line.

Lara declared it an emergency and had the operator break into the line.

"I've been trying to get through to you, Marcy."

"You've changed your mind? You will support the march? I knew you wouldn't let me down."

"Marcy, I have good news. Santos Dupuis Chemical International has pulled out of the deal. You can call off your protest."

"Lara, that's fantastic. When did you hear that? Are you sure?"

"At about half past twelve, and yes, I am sure. Marcy, we've won. There will be no plant built on that land, not ever."

"How can you be so sure? The sellers are ruthless, only interested in the buck. How do we know they won't sell it to someone as bad, or worse?"

Lara was about to tell Marcy, I can guarantee that, but Henry's advice was in her ears. She hesitated, and then she told her former roommate, "Marcy, the man who gave me the information is a man called Harland Brent. It seems he purchased the land for an anonymous buyer who intends to keep it as a wildlife and fauna sanctuary. That's all he would tell me. If you want more information than that, then take this telephone number down and call him."

Marcy took the telephone number. "It's still not the same as the government buying it and turning it into a nature reserve."

"No, Marcy, it isn't. But maybe it's even better than that."

There was some hesitation on the line before Marcy spoke. "Lara, how did you find this guy, Harland Brent?"

Father had been right. Lara surprised even herself with her new alacrity in backing off from Marcy and her questions. "Marcy, I'm over the moon that Hawaiahoo is safe, and I know you are—and so will all those people ready to fight to save it be when they hear the news. I have done my bit. Now, if you want to know any more, or want to pursue the idea of the government buying it, you do it your own way. I'm satisfied the place is safe. I must go, Marcy. Talk to you soon. And see you when you come to New York. Lots of love." And Lara hung up before Marcy could say another word.

Lara felt both guilty and puzzled about the Marcy-Hawaiahoo affair. She had done something for a friend, but without being able to come clean on how she had operated. And she had found herself using the leverage that her family's wealth granted her. She had gone about it with hardness and decision. There was iron in her soul.

And now she came out of the affair as owner of a small slice of paradise. . . . Her very own paradise. She knew she would never let it go. How Marcy would have hated her possessiveness.

Chapter 9

Samuel Penn Fayne had the family talent for being a nice guy. Fayne had several generations of niceness to look back on. It could have bred weakness and dullness by now, but in Sam it hadn't. The debs and their mothers thought of him as the 400s' Robert Redford. And what mother would not cast a line to catch a Robert Redford lookalike with millions *and* impeccable high-society credentials for their daughter? No matter that a fact of life was that Lara Stanton and he had been an item for years, or that it could only end in marriage. It was a merger the families meant to bring off.

Hopes rose and fell among the eligible beauties, depending on whether Sam Fayne was on the scene or off. Off meant that he was traveling to exciting, remote parts of the world with one of the Stanton boys or some other friend. His absence then was more acceptable than when he disappeared into some university: Cairo, Istanbul, Athens, Moscow, as a visiting lecturer. Or, worse, if he were sighted alongside Lara Stanton. The love for "the Stanton girl" that brightened his young eyes was, for the young beauties and their mamas, a disagreeable glare.

The Stanton girl had, until now, left them hope. Not only might she not get to keep Sam Fayne: she might not catch anyone else on the most-eligible-bachelor list. Had she not, after one prim curtsy at the ball at seventeen, gone decidedly off the rails? "Bohemian!" snorted the mothers. The daughters dubbed her "women's-libbish, sort of," "liberal maybe." But no one could really figure her out. Her behavior was so alien to her contemporaries. She had rarely appeared in society. She had chosen college and travel, horses, sports, and friends outside their narrow world—people that no one had ever known or would want to know. She was quite obviously not mesmerized by the eligible catches other society daughters aimed to land. So Lara Stanton had been considered a doubtful runner in the deb stakes, in spite of her name, wealth, and beauty.

But that was then, and this was now. And many a high-society heart not so much fluttered as twitched with anxiety as invitations were handed over and names announced at the threshold of the yellow and ocher oval room. There the Henry Garfield Stantons lined up: the men, big and dynamic, all charm and toothy smiles, each more handsome than the other; the women, as regal as they were beautiful. The most powerful family of what was left of the 400s. And in the center of the receiving line, Lara Victoria Stanton, standing between Henry and Emily. The Stanton rebel, who had decided, at last, to step into their world. They were a picture for posterity, the Stantons in the prime of life, bright and handsome with health, with worlds to conquer.

There were smiles and introductions, and hearts sank. "The Stanton girl" was exactly as they had feared. The looks, the charm, the wealth—and a name to open any door. And she was coming out, seriously out, to occupy their world.

They would, of course, embrace Lara, accept her in their homes, invite her to their parties, inveigle her into participating in their charitable endeavors for the less fortunate. They had committed themselves to nothing less the moment they had looked into Emily's eyes and put in plain sight their enthusiasm for having been invited to this ball.

There was Sam Fayne, hovering in the oval room, distracting Lara with meaningful glances and tapping his watch. He felt less anxious about not being with her when she smiled back at him, or when she sent warning signals: a flash of the eyes, an unsubtle gesture of the hand. She would be with him as soon as possible. Or he was spotted in the ballroom, staying close to the entrance so he might catch Lara the moment she passed through the doorway, an antique Lalique champagne *coupe* in his hand, several debs and cloned deb's delights such as himself constantly converging upon him.

There were few strangers in the ballroom. No press, no gate-

crashers. It was strictly a private affair. Most everyone knew
everyone else. There were catchings-up on friendships, and delicious exchanges of gossip that spiced the party with cheerness.

A dozen violinists, playing romantic Russian ballads, wandered among the two hundred guests, who were bathed in the
soft, voluptuous light of a thousand tapering ivory candles cradled in crystal chandeliers and wall sconces. A perfect setting
for the prettiest women in their luscious silks and satins, the
men in white tie and tails, whose suave presence complemented
the festive ambience of the room. All doors to the lantern-lit
gardens lay open, and the fifty-odd waiters, in red hussar-style
jackets and white ties, filtering among the guests with magnums
of vintage Krug, ensured a steady flow of the chilled wine that
warmed the encounters.

At last the receiving line dissolved, and the family flowed into
the ballroom. Sam caught Lara by the arm. The twenty-strong
orchestra struck up the first waltz of the evening.

"You promised. The first dance is mine."

"Not quite, Sam. A father's prerogative." And it was Henry
who twirled Lara to the center of the floor.

The guests had been waiting for this moment, the commence-
ment of the ball. Milling around the edges of the room, they
watched Lara's voluminous skirts of ivory silk, each layer fine
as a spider's web, flare to the rhythm of the dancing feet. Not a
man in the room could keep his eyes off the bodice of her gown:
a provocative off-the-shoulder affair of black-and-ivory, candy-
striped silk taffeta. Less because it clung to her breasts like a
second skin and expressed sensuality, than because there was a
cheekiness, a teasing quality about the gown, that was mature
and seductive, yet innocent and young. Its play of materials:
large puffy bows of the same black and white taffeta, in tiny
checks that contrasted at the shoulder with the stripes of the
bodice; and, around the waist, a two-inch-wide belt of tangerine
glass bugle beads. Not a woman in the room could take her eyes
from Lara's pearl-and-diamond earrings, the only jewelry she
wore: Henry's gift to her. Champagne *coupes* were drained and
placed on the silver trays, and ladies chosen. Couples drifted
out from the fringes of the room to swell the dance.

Sam thought: Lara has never looked lovelier, or happier. There
was something different about her now. What was it? He danced

close to her, but with *mère* Emily in his arms. Why resist his impulse? He tapped Henry on the shoulder. With no more than a broad smile he exchanged Emily for the girl he loved and waltzed her away.

"Marry me?"

Lara began to laugh.

"We can announce it right now."

"You're serious!"

Now he began to laugh. It had just popped out. He had not intended to ask Lara to marry him. Well, not then and there. "Yes, I guess I am. So will you?"

"No. And what a moment to ask me!"

"Oh! Should we fuck instead?"

They were all smiles. "Now you're talking. Right here? Now?" she answered, with just a slight worry that he might accept.

"Wrong music. But whenever we can slip away from the ball. Just give the signal and we're off."

A few seconds later, he said. "You didn't even say maybe. Should I be worried?"

"Why should I say maybe if I meant yes? I would have thought a yes to a fuck was better than a maybe. And why, Sam, should you worry because I want you?"

He smiled down at her and said, "You're being evasive. You know I mean about marrying me."

"Oh, Sam. What I should have said was, Choose another time."

"So I don't have to abandon hope?"

"Well, there's no hope for anyone else."

There was a look more of hunger than relief in both their faces. They were sexually ravenous for each other. It was difficult for Lara to hide her feelings. The very thought of Sam going down on her, his searching tongue, his raging penis pumping passion and love into her . . . She blushed, and felt the rush of a light, sweet orgasm for him.

He understood at once, and could do nothing about it. What could he do without offending the Stantons and their guests? He felt his own need rising, and was dismayed at how much he wanted her. He quickly danced Lara into the Palm Court, where they greeted some people and accepted a *coupe* of champagne.

They partly quenched their thirst for each other with the wine. And promptly replaced the empty glasses with fresh ones.

Aware of many eyes on them, he bent forward and whispered in her ear, ''I love you. I have always loved you, and I want you. I will wait for you.''

She sipped from her glass and then returned a whisper in his ear. ''Ask me again sometime. I can't imagine marrying anyone else.'' She squeezed his hand, emptied her glass, and drifted away among her guests.

Sam was happy. She would be his one day. He felt secure in his love for Lara. And she was right: to commit himself to her in marriage now was not good timing for either of them. She had some living as a top deb yet to do. And as for himself, he was enjoying his freedom. Bachelorhood suited his life-style. Sam was not a man who questioned his actions, or analyzed things to death. But for one fleeting moment, he did wonder what had possessed him to spring a proposal of marriage on Lara that way. Was he really interested in settling down? He had several different lives going for him that did not include Lara or marriage to her—and all it might entail. They were lives he'd be reluctant to abandon.

He had put it down to love. He had simply never adored any other woman as he did Lara. His being in love with her had overwhelmed him. Knowing that it was mutual only enhanced his feelings for her. *They* were in love, and safe together. They both knew and appreciated that. The unshakable security it gave them was enough for them to go their separate ways for a few more years. Well, at least, for the remainder of the evening. They were both swept up by the party and other people. They had scarcely another moment together until the following afternoon.

At midnight a buffet supper was served in the Palm Court behind the ballroom. Tables were set up and draped with white damask cloths, and ivory candles in silver candelabra were festooned with honeysuckle. Full-blown garden roses, summer's last, spread a romantic glow. People glided in to supper, from the ballroom and the grotto, where raging, provocative rock music—Chuck Berry, Eric Clapton, and Phil Collins—was being played.

Oysters were proffered from mounds of crushed ice; precarious pyramids of giant prawns. A huge crystal-clear ice bowl had frozen flowers embedded in it—baby white roses, ferns, and lilacs—and was lined with a thin, golden crust of filo pastry encasing several pounds of golden caviar. There were other choices on the long, white marble table. Silver chafing dishes simmered gently with lobster Newburg, Rock Cornish game birds in a cream sauce, chicken livers and tiny green grapes, and wild mushrooms sautéed in a Mouton Rothschild wine, pampered with the faintest hint of cinnamon and nutmeg. The roasts: lamb and rib of beef, boned and rolled and roasted *en croute*, and a pair of prettily decorated suckling pigs, with collars of daisies and ripe, red apples in their mouths. There were whole poached salmon lying on beds of seaweed. Fresh foie gras, and green salads, and Russian salads, and white asparagus served with a vinaigrette dressing, and fresh endive. Tall Baccarat celery glasses offered crunchy stalks, and a huge French rococo silver bowl of crudités looked as fresh as a garden. No palate needed to languish untickled.

A squadron of chefs was busy behind the table serving, with waiters to shadow each group of guests and carry for them their Napoleonic dinner plates, see that they were seated, and supply their choice of wines. The champagne was Louis Roederer Cristal; there was a Montrachet the gods themselves would have downed, and for claret, Château Petrus of several different vintages.

With a mixed guest list of the young, the middle-aged, and the elderly, the party was elegant and yet still buzzy. Drink rather than drugs was the stimulant. Fear of Emily's power to ostracize anyone from the exclusive high-society A-list banished any snort of cocaine or puff of grass. No one dared cherish hopes of a long, deep drag on a joint. But the WASP's drug has always been alcohol, ever acceptable, ever reliable. The party was as high and as much fun as if they had drugged. You thought otherwise at your peril on Emily's territory.

There were flirtations, lots of them, always discreet. Couples wandered between the grotto and the ballroom, in and out of the garden pavilions, all through the house, and in and out of bedrooms, even aboard some of the guests' boats that had sailed in for the party. And fucking? You assumed so, but it would have been prurient to attempt confirmation.

The hosts had been lucky with the weather. It had held: the night had stayed unusually warm. Dawn arrived with the party, if not in full swing then certainly still swinging. It broke slowly. A gray dawn that slid into a pink haze and rose to a soft light the color of maize. It lit up Cannonberry Chase, and hardly a guest was unaware of the beauty of the day that was dawning. The party seemed to go quiet for a short time while the light spread over the gardens and haloed the people wandering around them. The ladies in their ball gowns, the men in their tails, added a human dimension to the gardens. Never had they looked more romantic, with the colors, the silks and the satins, and the beautiful people.

It was as if dawn had played the last waltz. The party was over. Those couples who remained meandered back into the ballroom in search of their hosts. There Lara and Henry were playing their Jerome Kern and Cole Porter medleys. Three-quarters of the guests were still partying. They stood around the pair of concert grand pianos singing, or danced or drifted to the round tables, dressed prettily with crisp, white organza cloths and bowls of full-blown yellow and white roses that had been set up around the ballroom. Magnificent, period silver coffeepots, creamers, and sugar pots, and white and yellow Limoges porcelain plates, cups, and saucers, Baccarat goblets of fresh mango juice, sparkled in the sun's leisurely rise in the sky that spilt light through the open French windows. Chairs of chinoiserie red lacquer encircled the tables, where a chef attended each, ready to make omelettes to accompany the sausages and bacon, thin buckwheat pancakes, and clear, golden maple syrup. Breakfast was greeting the sunshine.

They met at three, and made love till five. Lara returned to Cannonberry Chase. Sam went back to New York and the waiting Nancy Kaplan.

From the beginning of his dating days there had usually been a Nancy Kaplan in Sam Fayne's life. The names changed, as did the ethnic backgrounds: Italian, Jewish, dusky Southern black girls. He favored the Jewish-American Princess-type, who attended Bennington, Vassar, Mount Holyoke and were ''WASPified'' to some extent by the ivy-covered walls of their schools, exposure to an academic life that excluded a Jewish mother, and fucking with the likes of a Sam Fayne. They were dazzled by his handsome White Anglo-Saxon Protestant looks, the cool, uncomplicated personality, his lusty lovemaking. The confidence he exuded, the sense of guilt that simply hadn't gotten started.

He was fascinated by their middle-class values, their dark hair, and sultry brown eyes. They were invariably beautiful, extremely sexy, intelligent, and with academic aspirations. And they were heavily into sex, wanting to please, eager for passion and emotion. They were to each other exotic creatures, alien to their own worlds.

He liked their sexual hunger. He liked all their hungers. They were the most voracious shoppers, husband hunters, degree collectors. They played at nesting. The chicken soup might have changed to consommé, the gefilte fish to prawns, canelloni been replaced by *blini*, black-eyed peas and greens for lentils and a green salad, but the end result was the same: they were all girls who nurtured Sam Fayne. And he loved it . . . until they wanted a return on playing the whore in bed and the lady in the kitchen: love, entry into Samuel Penn Fayne's life on any basis, preferably a full-time basis.

Impossible. Sam was already deeply in love. He could envisage no other wife for himself than Lara. A bracelet from Tiffany's and, reluctantly, Sam moved on.

He found it curious that the Nancy Kaplans of this world usually made the same mistakes. They got hooked by the "nice guy" in men like him. They saw him as easy prey and went for it. Relationship with a big *R*. They gave everything they had and more, and they never read the signs given them. Only heard what they wanted to hear. And the more they gave, the more they fell in love. Mostly with love itself. They rarely learned from their experience of giving too much, too soon. But Sam did. Every time. He walked away from his little flings always the wiser man, and more in love with the lady of his choice than ever.

The second of Lara's coming-out parties took place in Manhattan. It was an even grander event, boasting the Stantons aristocratic European friends who had not appeared at Cannonberry Chase. The third was hosted by Elizabeth at Claridge's in London, and that was a very English affair—with Lara and the family as old-guard American society—several of whose ancestors, wealthy heiresses, had married into the aristocracy and so were accepted among the English upper classes. With such connections—a sister, Lady Elizabeth, whose husband, the Earl of Chester, was a well-respected and likable man who sat in the House of Lords; and an eccentric octogenarian distant cousin living in a disintegrating Tudor manor house, set in a parkland and fifteen thousand acres, pleasingly adjacent to a royal in Gloucestershire—all avenues opened for the beautiful young deb from America. Lara took to the English as much as they took to her. She was swept away on a tide of adoration and fun.

Wherever she appeared she gathered around her eligible men, of all ages and various nationalities, who were besotted with her. Her telephone never stopped ringing, her date book was filled for months in advance. She became not just *the* deb of the season, but *the* international jet-set deb. Lara was having the best time of her life.

She became, almost overnight, the gossip columns' favorite item, the paparazzis' target, the glossies' most sought-after deb for their snob feature articles. And none of them got very far. She remained elusive, discreet. She smiled prettily and gave no interviews. All of which made her more interesting, mysterious even. It was sound, if unconscious, marketing of her personality.

The family watched and enjoyed her success, and paid no attention to the names linked with hers. They were all of them acceptable, but meant nothing. The family knew better where her heart would finally settle. Emily advised when necessary.

Sam was not amused. He hardly saw anything of her, and when he did, they were too preoccupied with sex and the joy they felt at being together to talk about the others in their lives. But, in the months that had passed since the party at Cannonberry Chase, he sensed a change in their relationship, an intensity in their sexual encounters that drove them both toward depravity and away from love. He was not so much shocked by the road they were traveling as unable to continue with Lara on it. He loved her too much. He adored her. He could not bear to let her climb down off the pedestal he had placed her on, to have the shadow of sex envelop her. He had any number of Nancy Kaplans, or a thousand-dollar-a-night prostitute he called on frequently, to play those sexual games with. He indulged Lara because he wanted to please her, and when he could forget that she was his adored, he delighted in their sexual excesses. But . . . he would rather their excesses had been in love.

Lara, far from being a mere sensualist, was not unaware of the problem slowly emerging in their relationship. She loved being loved by Sam. She wanted to have him love her not less but more. She was giving herself up to Eros in Sam's arms, but, great as that might be, it was not what he wanted. Sam was in love with being in love with her even more than loving her, or actually making love to oblivion with her. If they wanted their love to flourish, she would have to consent to stop cock-teasing her many suitors and sleep with them. Or go back to her secret liaison with Jamal. Both were interesting prospects to Lara, but fraught with danger.

She never spoke to Sam about it, but, the next time they met, after a crazy partying evening at a private disco club they ended up in bed. Sam had been particularly sexy and exciting, and she more the erotic aggressor that evening. They were lying in each other's arms, sexually replete, when she found the moment she had been waiting for. He had said, "There's a fine line between being the top jet-set deb and a party girl."

"Are you saying I've slipped over the line?"

He rolled her into his arms and kissed her breasts, and he smiled at her as he said, "Yeah, but I'm not complaining. I like party girls."

"Mother would hate it if I have."

"I'm not your mother."

"I have noticed that, Sam."

"So long as you're having a good time, Lara. That's what this year is supposed to be about."

"I'm having the best time of my life. I like being a playgirl. And who says it has to stop after a year?"

"It doesn't have to stop at all. You can be anything you want to be, Lara."

"Do you mean that?"

"Of course. I love you."

"You mean I can have this wonderful playgirl life *and* be your wife?"

He sat up against the pillows and pulled her up with him. "I promise. All you have to do is name the day."

"Sam"—she kissed him—"someday, I told you. I can't see myself married to any other man."

That was all he ever wanted from her, to love him enough to marry him and bear their children. He reacted to her love for him as he always did. Overwhelmed with desire for her, fully erect, he lifted her by the waist and impaled her on his cock. She called out in delight, and placed her legs on his shoulders. He sucked on her nipples as he cupped her buttocks in his hands and raised and lowered her on his pulsating penis several times with a slow and exquisite rhythm. A penetration so deep as to make her bite deep into her hand to refrain from calling out in a frenzy of passion.

Finally she brought herself under control enough to ask breathlessly, "Stop. Let me rest sitting here like this."

She lowered her legs, tucking them under her, and rocked forward to kiss him lovingly. They held each other, and she said, "Sam, you know that I love you."

"Why do I think I'm about to hear something I don't want to hear?"

"You do know that?"

"Yes, of course."

"I don't want us, either one of us, ever to love each other less. But I want us to be free until we decide to make it official that we intend to marry. Sam, I want us to be able to have other affairs. They can never be a threat to what we feel for each other."

He placed his hands on her waist and slowly lifted her off him. She closed her eyes, sad not to have him inside her. She bent down to lick his still-erect penis, to kiss him. He stopped her. Gathered her in his arms. They gazed into each other's eyes. Suddenly she wanted to cry and didn't understand why.

He asked, "What's this all about, Lara?"

"It's about never having been in love with any other person. About each of us dating other people but never really being with them. It's about the secret affairs I imagine you have that I turn a blind eye to—and we never talk about—because they don't matter—any more than the dates I have. It's about giving ourselves a chance to make sure that we can make each other happier than anyone else can.''

''You have doubts?''

''No, I have no doubts. I just want to be a real playgirl, free to go for a while with anyone I choose. And I want the same for you, Sam. The only doubt I have is that we're so in love we have never had a chance to give ourselves to anyone else. I may never want to. Maybe you won't, either. Let's find out. That's all I think we should do. We owe it to ourselves.''

''For how long?''

''For however long it takes for us to want to give it all up and live together.''

''And what if I refuse?''

''Then you refuse.''

''What will you do?''

''I don't know.''

''You have posed us a problem, Lara.''

''I know.''

They were silent for some time. Sam kissed her on the cheek and said, ''Don't look so sad. It's not the end of the world. We'll work it out. But it's a hell of a test you're putting us through.'' And he went into the bathroom.

Lara heard the sound of water. She reached for her glass on the table at the side of the bed. The champagne was flat, but she didn't care. She needed that drink, a kind of after-the-fact, Dutch courage. Her eyes settled on a large, silver-framed photograph of her and Sam. She picked it up. He looked so handsome, they looked so in love. Her heart skipped a beat. She did love him. It showed in the photograph. He loved her, that showed, too. The perfect couple. Had she been a fool? Would they lose each other? She placed the picture frame back on the table, and was reassured she had done the right thing when Jamal's words came to mind. ''You had better sort out your libido, Lara darling, before you settle down with Sam. The guy is great, but he'll never understand your basic sexual needs and cater to them like I do. I don't know if he loves you too much—or not enough— to get down there in the sexual dirt with you.'' Was that their basic problem? Jamal seemed to think that it was. She could not be so sure. She was certain only that she did have to sort out her blasted libido.

They spoke almost every day. But they gave each other space. Within weeks every deb's mother's hopes were up. Rumor had it the Fayne-Stanton relationship was on the rocks. They appeared with other partners among their social set, and, incredibly, so secure were they in their feelings for each other, were able to dance together, dine at the same table, go to the same weekend house parties. If they did not feel embarrassed by the situation, their new partners did. They saw the furtive looks of love that still lingered in Sam and Lara's eyes and resented them. Finally Sam and Lara agreed: if they wanted to give this little experiment a real chance to work, they must not see each other for six months.

That decision worked wonders for them both. They put their love for each other on the back burner of their lives and then hit the "I'm dating and available circuit" with a vengeance.

Chapter 10

In the midst of the hectic social whirl, Lara suddenly felt impelled to see David, if for no other reason than that she still loved him and had been neglecting him. She called him and asked him to take her to dinner. He didn't hesitate, saying only that he would have to cancel other arrangements. She was suddenly very happy—with that special kind of happiness that transcends ordinary joy—and decided to get him a very special gift.

She strode briskly down Fifth Avenue to Tiffany's glass door. They knew her there. The well-turned-out salesman on "gold bracelets" gave her a broad, indulgent smile. "Good afternoon, Miss Stanton. Are we well this afternoon, Miss Stanton?"

"Good afternoon, Mr. Ripley. Yes, I am well, and you are, too, I hope?" she intoned.

She looked around Tiffany's vast, glittering ground floor. She liked the cool unpretentiousness, the hushed way people shopped here. Most of them whispered, as if worried that their preferences might somehow be amplified for all to hear. She tapped her foot, impatient for inspiration. She was looking for something to show him she still loved him as she could never love any other man. A bauble to keep with him always. So that no matter what, he would have it to remind him of what they really meant to each other. She felt terribly sentimental about David. Her eyes roved around the room. A watch, cuff links . . . it all seemed so wrong, so banal.

"Mr. Ripley," she called. "Could you find something special? For my cousin David."

"What did you have in mind, Miss Stanton?"

"Something unique. Small. Something he can carry around with him always. A keepsake? Is there such a thing as a keepsake with a purpose?"

"A period piece, perhaps?"

"Could be."

The salesman glowed with pleasure.

"In that case, Miss Stanton, I think I might have one or two things to interest you. They are on exhibit in one of the galleries upstairs. Just give me a few minutes."

He came back with a black velvet tray, a black silk cloth over it, looking like a magician.

Lara chose for David a sixteenth-century Japanese ornament the size of a walnut, a lump of clear, honey-colored amber, magnificently carved. The netsuke, a voluptuous, tiny reclining figure filled with luminescence, seemed to have a magic about it. Fondled for centuries, it was irresistibly sensuous. The tiny object, so nearly alive, cried out to be touched, stroked, loved. Cleverly conceived to depict a reclining lady draped in an open kimono that revealed a naked breast, raised hip, bare leg, and elegant foot, the netsuke was as round as a walnut as well. Held in the palm of the hand and rolled around with the fingers, the amber lady was warm to the touch and silky-smooth. The mere feel of her fired the senses, a magnetic little treasure.

At two o'clock in the morning, calvados was their nightcap. They lay on cushions thrown on the floor in front of the library fire. David held the netsuke in the palm of his hand. It caught the light from the flames. Mesmerizing. He kept rolling it between his fingers and then letting it drop into the palm of his hand. Then he would display it in his palm, his fingers flat, enchanted by the reclining lady.

Lara rolled on to her side and leaned on her elbow, her back to the fire. She faced David, watching him, thrilled that she had chosen something so special.

She had had the most wonderful evening: David all to herself. They had dined at a small, out-of-the-way restaurant in Little Italy, the kind of family place hardly to be found any more in the New York Lara frequented. They seemed to know David well there. Certainly they had fed them both well. Afterward he had taken her to an off-Broadway production that had delighted them both. Then, avoiding a disco or nightclub, he had whisked her up to Harlem and a seedy jazz place, redolent of stale beer and fabulous music. They seemed to know David very well there, too.

They had talked and laughed with scant anxiety and deeper feelings than they had had for each other in a long time. Once or twice Lara had to fight off her desire to flirt with him, to try to seduce him. That isn't too difficult when you know the man you are with is giving you everything he can and loves you. Only her greed for more love from David could have ruined the evening for them both, and she wasn't having that.

Light from the fire cast shadows across his handsome face. She smiled, and he caught her.

"A penny for your smile?"

"It's a very ordinary smile. Just a smile because I'm happy."

"That's good enough for me. Be happy all your life, Lara."

"You, too, David. Promise me, if we are ever in trouble, we can be there for each other."

"I thought you always understood that, Lara. I will always be here for you. And always, darling girl, is forever." And he resumed his ecstatic scrutiny of the amber lady.

"I wasn't saying that so much for me as for you, David. I want you to promise me that, if ever you want me, if ever you need me for any reason, you'll . . ." Suddenly she felt over-whelmingly sad. She swallowed hard to forestall a tear. With a forced smile, she made light of what she was saying. "Send me your amber mistress and I will come to you, wherever you are."

"It's a wonderful present, La. I will carry it with me always."

"Promise?"

"Yes, I promise. If ever I am in trouble, I will send it to you, and you can come to my rescue." He flipped the netsuke up into the air and let it bounce into his palm, then closed his fingers over it. He bent forward and kissed Lara on the forehead, and then on the cheek. She put her arms around his neck and kissed him on the lips, a quick, sisterly kiss, then announced, "I'm off to bed. I have had the most wonderful evening, David. Thanks. I sort of needed to be with you tonight."

He remained in front of the fire for some minutes, fondling the netsuke. He, too, had had an excellent evening. Lara was the enchantress; she always had been, but even more so now.

David knew about her love affairs, her sexual liaisons. Even her strange, erotic relationship with Jamal. They had no idea that he knew, and he intended to keep it that way. He was not unhappy about her affairs. After all, he knew how much she needed them.

Still high on the evening, unable to sleep, Lara was standing in her darkened bedroom, looking from the window into the courtyard. She was not surprised when the front light came on. She watched David fling a white silk scarf around his neck and toss a coat into his car. Just before he slipped behind the wheel, she saw him look up at her bedroom windows. She quickly moved to one side, not wanting him to see her. She saw him bounce the netsuke up into the air, catch it, and place it in his trouser pocket. The door slammed, the headlights went on, and he was gone. Several minutes passed. Where was he going? Who would he be making love to? She imagined him naked in a woman's arms, his penis hard and sliding into a luscious, moistening cunt. In and out, deeper, faster. She agonized that she was not that woman. The pain of her loss was too much for Lara. She wanted it to stop.

Impulsively she dialed Jamal's private number at the house on Fifty-third Street. No answer. It did not occur to her to call Sam. She blanked her sexual longings for David and Jamal out of her mind and fell into a restless sleep.

Chapter 11

" "You have the kind of life that dreams are made of."

"You trying to tell me something, Marcy?"

"Just that."

"Just what, Marcy? That my life is all walking on air? Do I spot an insult in there somewhere? Had you meant to be insulting?"

Marcy was alone with Lara. The other two lunch guests, girl-friends of Lara's, had left for appointments, one to an afternoon at Elizabeth Arden's, the other for a fitting at Halston's.

The women had been lunching at the Russian Tea Room on Fifty-seventh Street, at Lara's invitation. In the two years since Lara left her preppy life at Smith behind her for a fun life in society, Lara and Marcy had, several times, made an effort to meet. The effort showed, and they were aware of it, and that made them tetchy. They had drifted apart and were no longer close friends. Neither of them wanted to admit to that, so they kept trying.

Maybe Marcy could claim some credit now for looking embarrassed. She had not meant to say anything. But there had been two hours of listening to Lara and her friends talk little more than inconsequential gossip. Fretting about horse trials. Bitching about their clothes allowances. Marcy had been ready to walk out on them halfway through the meal. What had pushed her over the edge was the pouting and whining from the two beautiful debs, who had not been asked to some house party. It was hosted by one of the so-called "great catches." Someone called Willy. Who was he, for crissakes, when he recovered from his own name? Marcy detested the way Lara was almost apologizing. And why? Because she'd not only been invited, but was to be Willy's date. Trite, trite, trite. Marcy found Lara, from in among the caviar *blinis* and white wine, too superficial to take. At least she could blame the debs. She'd eaten through a whole lunch without their acknowledging her existence. Now the words had just tumbled out of her mouth. She was not sorry.

"No insult intended. Maybe what I should have said was, your life is what millions of girls dream their lives should be. You've got it all, and in spades. As if the looks, the money, the right family name, the intelligence were not enough. The world is your cupcake. A playgirl with a French count and an English earl chasing after you. A great guy like Sam waiting in the wings to marry you. And nothing to bother your pretty head but parties, hairdressers, and clothes—and winning trophies and men. You behave as if you have nothing to live for but being loved and adored. And the more you are, the less you give of yourself."

"All quite true, Marcy. *But so what?* Why so judgmental about it? Next thing you'll be telling me I should be doing something with my privileges. Not just having the best time of my life. What's your problem about me, Marcy? Is it because our lives have led us in different directions? We have grown out of *my* adoration of *your* ideals? Maybe I have some ideals of my own on the back burner of my life. You don't know that I don't. Who told you you can't have ideals and be a playgirl at the same time?"

Their outbursts silenced both girls. Lara poured more espresso in the tiny white cups. Pouring replaced the need to talk. Marcy floundered for an answer. She had been told off by Lara in a way that had left her feeling foolish. And Marcy hated feeling foolish, almost more than being wrong. The silence that lay between them was not an angry silence, nor was it awkward or embarrassing. Just silence. Lara selected a sliver of lemon rind from a saucer, gave it a twist, and dropped it into Marcy's cup. Another plopped into her own cup. Marcy pushed her chair back and placed the white napkin on the table. She started to rise from the chair. Lara grabbed her by the wrist and suggested, in what could have been a calm, sweet manner, "Marcy, you may have a problem. I was never aware of it when we were at school, but I am now. I happen to like who I am and where I come from, Marcy, my superficial, good-time life. When I stop liking it, I will move on. And that may never happen. If I can accept that, then why can't you? It will be a sad comment on our friendship, if all we ever liked about each other was that we marched well together. But, then again, maybe that's enough.''

"Clearly it isn't.''

Lara let go of her friend's wrist, and Marcy stood up. "My dear, Marcy, you are a snob.''

"Yes, I guess I am. I guess that surprises us both. I don't suppose we will meet again, except at class reunions. When I did know you, Lara, it was great.''

"Yes, it was, Marcy.''

Lara sipped her coffee. Why, she wondered, had she not put Marcy out of her misery and saved their friendship? It would not have taken much. Tell her about the hundred-thousand-acre cooperative-farm program she had invested in. How she had come to the aid of Hawaiahoo. Because she didn't mind playing the white knight, but was not prepared to get embroiled in working projects. More to the point, it was none of Marcy's business, or anyone else's, how she lived, what she did with her life.

Lara paid the bill and spoke to several people at another table before she left the restaurant. She was not the least bit sad that Marcy and she had perhaps let their friendship die. Relieved, rather. It had been dying for too long.

Well, at least now I know that some friendships, like some loves, die. How can I be sad over a fact of life? And I do believe that that is a fact of life. Growing up, maturity, learning the old life lessons, is interesting, *but painful*, only because ignorance is *such bliss,* she thought, walking down the street.

Two days later Lara made ready to attend the annual family meeting, her second appearance. She was too distracted to look forward to it, by men—three interesting men, and that was not counting Sam. She liked them, more than liked them, and all three were giving her a wonderfully good time. Keeping them on a string and at bay was a full-time job. It took lots of plotting, and organization, and looking good. There was fun in all that. Having a good flirt, playing the hard-to-get seductress, with several men on the chase, gave her a high, did wonders for the ego. With little space left in her life to think of anything else, the annual meeting was a drag. Drag or not, though, she dressed for it and tried to forget her latest admirers. She must focus on the family meeting.

Halfway through the morning session of the meeting (an all-day affair, with an hour for lunch), Lara began to perk up. She was understanding more about the family's holdings, their wealth, her own, and how really powerful the Henry Garfield Stanton family was, than she had a year before. Two more trust funds had matured and been made over to her. She had inherited, upon the death of her eccentric English cousin, a Tudor manor house, nine hundred acres of parkland, and thousands of acres of farmland that she had never seen. The realization that she was rocketing toward becoming one of the wealthiest of the Stantons was a surprise.

Henry topped the list, followed by Emily and then David, who as Henry and Emily's adopted son had his real father's estate. It meant he jumped a place or two on the list of family holdings. Steven was next. Then came Lara, who had risen above Elizabeth and Max and John. She had learned to take her wealth, not exactly for granted, but in a relaxed manner. Today, however, having been made aware just how far up the list she had risen in so short a time, she had to remind herself that one day, in years to come, she would have to take a more active interest in her affairs. "In years to come" seemed to be the operative phrase as far as Lara was concerned. What she did take for granted, however, was that the family would remain, as they always had, silent about her private affairs. That had been a mistake.

The high point of the annual meeting for Lara was dinner. The trustees and advisers gave the dinner in honor of the family. It had been policy for twenty years that it should be a semiformal affair and a mystery: after a tense and sometimes tedious day, a degree of levity and surprise was needed. Surprise and levity had been the recipe ever since.

The family left the boardroom of the Stanton building on Park Avenue and Fifty-third Street in the two family Rolls-Royces. At their town house they bathed, changed, and met for drinks in the drawing room. At eight o'clock exactly they returned to the cars and were swept away to a gastronomic destination, not to be revealed until their arrival. The trustees could boast that the family had never been disappointed.

Chinatown was this year's location and the surprise lay in their own incongruity there. Transported to one of the seedier-looking Chinese restaurants on one of the busier, neon-lit streets, the Stantons were indeed a sight in their elegant evening clothes: the men in black tie, the women in floor-length gowns and furs, Emily in emeralds, and Elizabeth in sapphires. They glided past pyramids of smelly trash in cardboard boxes, piled against the restaurant's plate-glass window which was hung with grimy Chinese lace curtains. As they passed into and through the restaurant. Harland Brent met them. He led them past large round tables, crowded with Chinese families, rapturously eating off paper tablecloths under the cold fluorescent lighting. They filed up the narrow staircase, for two flights, to the private dining room. The trustees waiting there were gratified by the relieved and approving smiles as each family member arrived. Another successful surprise, this year at any rate.

The room was a magnificent piece-by-piece transplant from an eighteenth-century palace in Hang Chow. The furniture matched the period. Certain objects, fifteenth- and sixteenth-century pieces of breathtaking beauty, were as fine as any museum could boast. The view absorbed the rooftops of Chinatown. The chef had been jetted in from Hong Kong to prepare this meal, and with him had come the waiters, while Chinese peonies—masses of them, now the centerpieces of the long dinner table—had filled most of the rest of the place.

The food was delectable, and they dined from white jade plates and pale lavender jade bowls, manipulating ivory chopsticks and sipping tea from sixteenth-century celadon porcelain cups. During dinner they were entertained by a young Chinese girl playing a harp, and after dinner were given a miniconcert by the harpist and a flautist. With them was a brilliant Chinese boy whose Stradivarius had been bought for him by the Stantons.

At home again, before the family retired for the night, they had a nightcap together and reviewed the day. They were all well pleased by the evening.

Henry refilled Lara's glass with her latest discovery. Tia Maria was sniggered at by her father and brothers: for them it was

"Deb's Brandy." He then interrupted her conversation with Max, who was sitting on Lara's other side.

"What would you like to do with your life, Lara?"

She was flummoxed. "What a question, Dad. I don't know. Pretty much what I am doing, I suppose. As it happens, I'm having a very good time."

"I am glad to hear it, dear. You do look happy. You are certainly busy enough."

Her father sounded quite satisfied, and Lara heaved an inward sigh of relief. But what had prompted him to ask such a question? His persistence unsettled her when he asked again, "Would you like to take a job of some sort? There is an opening on the acquisitions committee of our art fund. You would, of course, have to have some work experience. As, maybe, an assistant to one of the curators for a year. Does that appeal?"

"I don't think I'm ready for that, Dad; or that the art world interests me all that much, just now. Maybe later on."

"You could do some charity work, Lara. I have been rather surprised that, in these two years you have been out, you have taken no step in that direction," said Emily.

"Oh, Mother," interceded Elizabeth, "leave off. Lara's having the big rush on several continents. Let her enjoy it."

Nice of Elizabeth to come to her rescue. Could that be the end of it? It wasn't.

"Maybe there's a project of your own you would like to take an active interest in? Is that it, Lara?"

"No, Dad."

"Is there anything that interests you, other than the life you are living?"

"La wants to sail around the world one day, Dad. Don't you, La?"

Lara sensed that John was trying to distract her father, to preempt other suggestions. Henry picked that up almost as if he had been thrown a lifesaver.

"I know you do, dear. Something I have always meant to do myself. You know we approve and will give you all the support you need. Help you plan it, if you like. I suppose you will want to do that before you marry?"

"Marry?"

"Well, you are going to marry one day, aren't you?"

"Well, yes, of course I am. One day."

"Well, Sam won't wait forever, Lara."

"Don't be so sure of that, Dad," chimed in David. "He sure is in love with our La."

Smiles of approval on the family's faces. Not Lara's: she had had enough. She rose to stand next to her father, who was leaning against the fireplace, glass in hand. She faced the family, lazily sprawled out in deep, comfortable, worn-leather chesterfields and chairs. Each of them was silent, but inwardly admiring the girl whom many hailed as the most beautiful deb high society had recently produced—on either side of the Atlantic. Her hair, tied back in a large red chiffon bow, added a touch of innocence to her creamy complexion, set off by provocative red lips. Khaki-colored eye shadow made her emerald-green eyes and dark lashes seductive. Her chiffon evening dress was also red. Its plum-colored, beaded bolero jacket sparkled in the firelight and showed off her figure, no longer a girl's, but that of a voluptuous young woman. And the still fresh and feisty spirit she exuded also proclaimed her a woman.

Her beauty and her charm had always harvested their love for her. All along, she had been able to wind each of them—if maybe not always Emily—around her little finger. Not just by the superficial elements like beauty, but the happy, incredibly loving qualities she possessed as well. They expected more, always more, from Lara, and she had never disappointed them. She was, or would be one day, a credit to them all. The seeds were there.

"Dad, marriage is not in this season's appointment book for me. Nor is it in Sam's. We aren't ready to settle down, together or with anyone else. And I certainly don't want the responsibility of work. I haven't the time for it. I'm too busy having a carefree, irresponsible good time just living. I like what Mother has molded me into. I'm having a wonderful life. I was reminded only a few days ago—by a friend—that I have the life every girl dreams of having. I just hope it goes on and on. At least until I am bored."

This sort of announcement was unlikely to surprise or disturb Henry or anyone else. They took it as the Stantons always took such things. They had a sort of code: live and let live. And, with family, the code also entailed support and loyalty.

"So be it, Lara. It seems all of my children have a flair for playing hard. They have also, with time, understood how lucky they are. They have found the concept of 'duty' has meant something to them. And all of them, without exception, have felt they have to put something back in, with no prodding from either their mother or myself. I have no doubt that when you are bored—if, indeed, you ever are—you won't be an exception. Just out of curiosity: What would you do if you were bored?"

She placed an arm around her father and smiled at him. In a teasing manner, coyly even, she kissed him on the cheek and said, "Leave my frivolous life behind me." Then, more seriously, she added, after going to sit on the arm of Max's chair, "I might want to work as an agronomist in the Third World. The science of farming has always fascinated me. Or I might buy a large estate somewhere near the sea, then farm it on a grand scale. I mean, a really grand scale. Some place in Italy or Spain, or France even. Yes, maybe on the coast of France, so no more summer resorts can pollute the area any more than it already is."

Emily's laughter drew all eyes. "What's so funny, Mother?" A note of annoyance crept into Lara's voice.

"You, darling."

"Well, it's a gift, to be able to make people laugh."

"Oh, Lara, there's no need for you to get all huffy. I simply find it amusing that you should see yourself as some sort of earth mother. Darling, you may have what it takes to be a class-A student, a scholar. That is, if you pursued the intellectual life, which you have so far clearly proven you have no interest in. A scholar and a beautiful deb, yes. But, really, darling, you lack what it takes to be in command of that kind of project. The Third World!"

Already angered by her mother, Lara got to her feet to hide her feelings. She went to the fireplace again and rammed another log onto the fire. Henry placed a hand on her shoulder. If it was meant to reassure her, it didn't, because he added, "What Mother means, Lara, is that to be successful with the poor of the Third World, or with less well-to-do country people, you have to be able to adapt to them. Then maybe you can draw the best out of them. And you, my dear, may be good with the groom and the maid, but you are better with polite society:

competing in yachts, riding Biscuit and Azizz, and being the belle of the ball. It's there you were made to shine. It's been a long time since you have taken a holiday in the real world, and you have never lived in it.''

"I take offense at that, Dad."

David went to her. "La . . .'' But she shrugged away from him.

Elizabeth came to her father's defense. "Don't carry on so, baby. Dad is only trying to show you the way things are."

Rage stiffened her, but Lara controlled herself. She raised her chin and, in a calm, icy voice, quite slowly said, "Elizabeth, fuck the way things are,'' and stormed out through the library door.

It was a fairly comprehensive blasphemy, so the boys allowed Lara her exit before they burst into peals of laughter. Then one of them called out after her, "Right on, Lara!" Emily looked very dour.

"That expletive may be fashionable, but we can do without it in the library. The sooner Sam Fayne marries Lara the better, Henry. You spoiled that girl. All you men have. She has ruined a very nice evening for me. I am going to bed. Don't be too long, Henry."

He was unruffled but saddened to see, once again, his daughter make a minor scene because she was challenged by the reality of a situation. And she had shown him once more that edge of vulnerability he worried about.

By morning it had mostly been forgotten. Missy was there as usual to check Lara's diary and answer letters. The phone never stopped ringing, and she was going for her pilot's license. Only David knew about the lessons. He had arranged them for her, and would be waiting to hear the result. Life was sweet, and she was happy. While she was dressing, Cherry, the maid, arrived with four dozen long-stemmed white roses. No card.

Lara buried her face among the open blossoms and was deliciously enveloped in their scent. Sam? Who else could the mysterious man be who courted her with flowers and anonymity? If she were to mention receiving flowers from someone who preferred not to make himself known, he would never admit to having sent them. Jamal? Possibly. He would never sign a card

for fear the family might find out. She and Jamal had not spoken
in more than a year, nor seen each other since her coming-out
party. He had been abroad, out of the New York social whirl,
except for several fleeting visits, during which their paths had
not crossed. The only news of him came from David. They
remained friends and stayed in close contact. No, Jamal was an
unlikely source. A stranger, more likely. She had so many admirers that to spot the culprit was nearly impossible. So she
chose to think that they had come from Sam. Had he not given
her white roses in exchange for her virginity?

Summer moved in fast on Lara's life. And it was one of those
idyllic summers: long, hot days and nights broken by just enough
showers and rainstorms to green and freshen and keep everything interesting. The summer of 1976 at Cannonberry Chase
was one long house party, peopled by glittering youth, distinc-
tive men and women, enlivened with races and tournaments,
and discreetly peppered with charity concerts.

Lara drifted in and out of the house with her friends, dividing
her time between Cannonberry Chase, Newport, Rhode Island,
and the Hamptons. There was a race around Martha's Vineyard,
another around Nantucket. By midsummer she had brought
home racing cups from Newport and both the islands off Cape
Cod. Somewhere along the way she resumed her sexual relationship with Sam. They began to date. Love was still there,
and friendship; it was as easy as it had always been. Too easy.
They continued to date other people as well.

She heard the news before he reappeared in the swirl of New
York society: Jamal was returning to live once again in New
York. She tried to keep him out of her mind, but it was difficult.
His name kept cropping up. Lara was surprised to detect many
of her new friends, girls who had never met him, surreptitiously
seeking ways of meeting him. It seemed his reputation as an
exciting, extravagant man-about-town, sexually irresistible to
women, had hit the city before he had.

Once, in a powder room at the Plaza, during a charity ball,
she heard two women, much older than herself—beautiful, elegant, sophisticated women, the sort of dazzling beauties that she
and her friends would like to emulate—talking about him.

"Jane, dear, it's too much. The thought of that gorgeous cad
being here in New York again, and my not being with him. Bed

with him, was . . . well, I can't really explain. I was like his slave . . . and did I love it! Me! Can you imagine? Me, who always wound any man I ever wanted round my little finger. And now I can't land Jamal. He made me feel I was the only woman in the world he really wanted, the only one to make him the man he always wanted to be. What a joke! And the laugh was on me. I feel such a fool still wanting him. But what am I telling you all this for? I can guess that you know the pain. Still in love with him?''

A closed door and the blessed blur of drink left the two women unaware of Lara. Sometimes it is better not to hear things. She was left conjuring visions of her own relationship with Jamal. She had one of the more furtive gods to thank that they had at least kept their sexual liaison secret. Exposure as just another sexual conquest would have rankled, to the point of acute shame. She sat in the marble-lined booth, trying to banish vivid pictures of Jamal from her memory. His weighty penis, erect and cupped in one hand, while experienced fingers probed her cunt's lips to find and excite her clitoris, to tease her into begging him to plunge himself deep inside her. She actually whimpered, remembering the exquisite, slow, tantalizing pressure of him. She could almost feel that divine sensation of being slowly rent open to be filled with cock.

Lara covered her face with her hands. She took a deep breath. Then she was all right again. There was a chance she might gain control of her emotions, stand up and compose herself enough to face the women who shared her very own desire to be enslaved by Jamal. She tried to put aside her feelings of self-loathing for being unable to off-load her sexual attraction to him. Her desperate need to be able to give herself sexually, her passion for the brief voyage to oblivion with him, was still there. Why did he have to return? She had managed nicely without him. She thought he had been replaced by other lovers. She had talked herself into believing her passion for sex with him was yesterday's whim.

That night, fired up with sexual passion gone crazy, she and Sam had sex—sex that had little to do with love . . . and everything to do with need and the unleashing of desire. The joy of sex unbounded.

Chapter 12

Naked under gray terry-cloth robes, Sam and Lara were walking barefoot and arm in arm along the deserted beach where he had a house. Fayne Island, just off the mainland, near the tip of Long Island. His launch had brought them here the night before. A romantic inspiration, prompted at Lara's return from the powder room, to their table in the ballroom, by a whisper in his ear. "I want you to whisk me away from all this—to the most quiet place on earth—and then make love to me like it was for always." Three hours later, he was carrying her in his arms, under a full white moon, from the dock, up the sandy path that wound between scrubby pines and blueberry bushes.

His was the only house on Fayne Island, except for a lighthouse that had been made over for the caretaker to live in. But that was on the other side of the dunes. Sam's large, unpretentious, weather-worn shack lay like a heap of driftwood between sand and a dwarfed, windswept wood. It was his private hideaway, and Lara his first guest. It had water, but no electricity. Everything had to be hauled over from the mainland by the caretaker or Sam.

A romantic inspiration? He could not but wonder, as he walked with Lara under a hot sun and the soft breeze coming off the Atlantic Ocean: how had it come about that the romance died the moment he had closed the door behind him and lit the fire and the kerosene lamps? The lust of two sexually hungry people had snuffed out love and romance like a candle in the wind.

Debauchery, depravity with Lara of a kind hitherto confined

138

to the imagination, had been thrilling. Even now, walking with her in the sun, with the rippling foam of once-crashing waves running up on to the shore and over their toes, he could not recollect what had tipped them from romance into lust without love. They had not just wandered into a world of sensation and release. They had both been steeped in it, wanting it never to stop. And Sam was somehow lost in it. But when morning came and he found himself, he detested the memory of having used Lara as he had rarely used even a whore.

He was forced to offset his feelings of detestation with the fact that Lara had seemed to revel in such usage. Sexually sadistic! That he could do what he had done when sexually uninhibited had not been part of his profile of himself. Such heightened pleasure for them both—but was that reward enough for perverting his soul? For allowing Lara to descend from the pedestal of adoration he had placed her on? He could not rest easy with their corrupting influence on each other. Where had love gone? It had hardly been part of that wild sexual ride toward oblivion.

Awake before Lara, he raised himself against the pillows and watched her sleeping. Who was this woman he had loved so well? The woman he had chosen to be his wife. Only with difficulty could he equate her with the Lara of the night before. Sam had to ask himself if he was one of those men who couldn't love the women they slept with, and couldn't sleep with the women they loved. He had friends like that, but had always prided himself on the belief that that was no problem for him. And yet . . .

He watched her for an hour before she opened her eyes. In that time he came to know he was not one of those men. That he loved Lara, on or off her pedestal. She had said "Good morning" to him so sweetly, he thought his heart would break. He had bent down and kissed her. It had blocked out the night before.

He made them bacon and eggs for breakfast, and they ate with ravenous appetites. The aroma of hot black coffee was the scent of their fresh new day. Their caffeine high had pumped life back into their exhausted bodies. It blew away the cobwebs from their minds.

On the beach next to her now, Sam realized that they had

hardly said a word to each other since she had opened her eyes.
They had smiled and touched each other in a loving fashion, but
there simply had been nothing for them to talk about. Anything
about the night before seemed superfluous to where they had
gone together in their quest for bliss through sex. The present
appeared to demand silence, both of them needing a space of
their own to live with themselves. And yet they were secure in
the knowledge that they were together.

He could not easily keep his mind off the night before. Sexuality seemed to have been dominating both of them. He admitted to himself that it dominated him—made him fall in love
with unsuitable women all the time until now. But was Lara
really any different from those women he lazily dubbed unsuitable? They had controlled his libido in an unfathomable way,
and so did she. And what about Lara? Perhaps she, too, was
controlled by her sexuality. If the night before had been some
indication, now he had to know the answer. What had they been
doing last night—beyond the sex? he wondered. He chose to
think that their rabid exploitations had been a kind of courtship
display. Or did that simply insult the animals of the bush?

He bent down to pick up a shell and dusted the sand off it.
He washed it in the surf, dried it with the belt of his robe, then
handed it to Lara. She held it up to the light before placing it in
her pocket. Her arm found its way through his once more, and
they resumed their walk. He understood her silence, and that he
could hardly exaggerate the importance of sexuality. For now,
it governed their lives.

Sometime later they dropped their robes in the sand, ran naked into the surf, and swam a good distance out into the ocean.
The water was icy cold, and they floated for a while and let the
hot sun warm their bodies as they drifted back toward shore.
When Lara's feet touched sand she stood up. The water lapped
around her chin. She threw her head back and shook her hair so
that it shimmered on the surface of the water like a fine golden
net. Sam ran his fingers through it. She dipped her head below
the water, came up again, and smoothed the silky wet hair from
her face. Hand in hand they walked toward the beach. A large
wave slapped into them, and Lara lost her balance. Sam caught
her by the waist. Their eyes met, but they didn't speak: they,
too, seemed mute as the sea and the sand around them.

He lifted her high above him, from her shoulders a waterfall.
She threw her head back and looked at the sky, stretched her
arms out as if to embrace the heavens, and laughed. Once again
he plunged her under the water and raised her high above him.
''Glorious,'' he heard himself say.

He wrapped her legs around his waist, and she lay back on
the surface of the water, swishing her hair from side to side. He
caressed her breasts and her shoulders, and, slipping his arms
under hers and around her back, pulled her to him for a great,
loving hug. They could feel each other, sex rubbing against sex,
his erect and hers craving. Yet neither of them felt compelled to
seek release. The ocean, without warning, turned rough. A huge
wave rolled over them and they were thrown off-balance. Their
hands still joined, their feet found the ocean bed. Toes digging
into the gritty sand, they pushed forward and were able to wade
into shore. They ran to where they had dropped their robes,
spread them out, and lay naked. Under the lazy heat of the sun,
they soon dozed. Sometime later Lara touched his arm. ''I'm
famished.''

''Me, too.''

They walked back to the shack, stopping to eat blueberries
from bushes warm with the sun. Sweet, juicy berries stained
their lips and fingertips blue. Lara delighted in memories of
when, as children, she and Sam used to fill their tin sand pails
with berries for Cook to make into a pie. She stopped to watch
him holding a handful of the blueberries above her and, in a
stream, letting them fall into her open mouth.

Lara had been surprised more than once by Sam since she
had whispered in his ear at the Plaza. The sex, yes, but still
more the island: how secretive he had been about it. It was a
strange, remote place. Yet there was something amazingly sensuous about it, and about his behavior here. She had enjoyed
the fruits of him and his hideaway, and yet she had discovered
something rather disturbing. Samuel Penn Fayne had a life all
his own that she knew nothing about. A life where, until last
night, he had never admitted her, of which no hint had escaped
him.

Their eyes met. He picked a handful more of the berries and
brought them to Lara. He took her hand in his, opened it, and
transferred the berries. Then he picked them up, one at a time,

and fed them to her. Once, between mouthfuls, he kissed the tip of her nose, then tapped it with his finger.

There was something in the gesture, and in Sam's gaze, that Lara found disturbing. He scooped the remaining berries from her hand. Tilting her chin, he dropped them all at once into her mouth. She made a gesture of delight and said, "I am a pig for blueberries." This was a juicy smile.

"A pig, yeah."

"Swine. You didn't have to agree."

"Lara."

There was a tone in his voice she didn't like. Something akin to a chill ran through her. She suppressed any outward sign of it. The smile left her lips. She stood her ground, facing him. "Just come out with it, Sam."

"I should have told you last night. I'm going away for a while." He placed his arm around her shoulder and they continued to walk toward the shack.

"For long?"

"I don't know."

Lara felt a hollow in the pit of her stomach. He was leaving her. They both knew it. He was not going to tell her outright. She could not bring herself to confront him. She attempted composure, the refuge of silence. But the blow was too hard on her; she was in pain. She wanted him to see she was not stupid. To see she was wise about the way men walked out on you.

"You didn't know last night, Sam." She placed her arm around his waist. They walked on, silent.

Then, before pride could take over, she asked him, "Is there no chance that you might change your mind?" That was the closest Lara could bring herself to asking him not to leave her. His silence confirmed her worst fears. He could not cope with their sexual excesses. She tried to control the panic she felt at losing him. She had used the man she loved as a safe stud. Inevitably Sam had picked that up. She was as certain of that as of anything. And she could think of nothing to say or do that would make it right for him. She had wanted Jamal, and had settled for Sam. Not a crime. But not very honorable, either.

They were walking up the steps of the shack when he grabbed her by the arm and abruptly turned her around to face him. "About last night . . ."

"Forget last night."

"We were two different people last night."

"No, that's the trouble, Sam. We were not two different people last night. Let it go."

She broke away from him. He caught her just inside the screen door, pulled her roughly to him. And again she broke away. He was suddenly very angry with her. He lunged. "You damned well listen to what I have to say!" He tore her robe open and pushed her onto the kitchen table. He swept the breakfast dishes away. They clattered to the floor. He tore off his own robe. And forcing her legs apart he pounced on top of her.

"Don't do this to us, Sam."

She felt him penetrate her, hard and angry, with one fierce thrust. Then, pinning her down by the shoulders, he told her, "We were not the Sam and Lara I know. We used and abused each other sexually. It was fantastic, but I wish I thought it had really been us. Who's the man? How long has it been going on? How could you give yourself up to sex, wallow in it with such abandon, debase yourself for cock—with men who could never love you as I do? You were better than any whore I ever had. You made me do things to you that I cannot reconcile with the image I had of myself. We brought out what's base in each other. We reveled in it. You made me look into myself—and I know I am not the man I was last night. Nor do I think I want to be. I need to go away for a while, to get away from you. Loving you has been my life. But after last night I don't think I know who you are. How can I have spent my life loving someone I don't even know?"

There were tears in his eyes. Lara could see the pain. She wanted to feel sorry for him, but at her expense? No. Much as she might want to, she couldn't. If he has truly loved me so long and so hard, then why doesn't he know me? she asked herself. There was the question. No point in repeating that it had been Lara's *and* Sam's sexual bliss last night, no one else's. If he couldn't face loving her as she was, without imposing his image of what he wanted her to be, that was too sad. And not just for her, but for them both. Two people, friends and lovers for years, with no room for others in their thoughts of the future, destroyed by a glimpse of reality. She could think of nothing to say to Sam.

He was choked up when he whispered, "I don't want to go away without making love to you. And I need you to make love to me."

She placed her arms around his neck and kissed his eyes, then his cheeks. Her lips nibbled at his. Her hands roamed freely down his back, over the flesh of his buttocks. Their lips opened and they kissed deeply. He began to move lovingly in and out of her. They were turned on by love and affection, by good sex, as they had been so often, and they shared an orgasm as intense as any they had experienced the night before. They fucked under the delusion of love, to calm the anxiety of their separation.

Two days later he called to say good-bye. She panicked. It was as if her safety net had collapsed, and she would have to scale the high points of the remainder of her life without it.

"Don't go. I need you."

"Don't make this harder for me than it is, Lara."

A silence that had to be ended. Neither could find the right words. Finally it was Sam. "Friends?"

She hung up.

Lara's anger at Sam for leaving her, combined with her fear of losing him, showed in her blanking him out. No tears. Just one frustrated kick at the bedpost, and a determination to find a man who could love her for herself and not for love's sake. One who would give her what she had hoped for from Sam: a successful relationship that would culminate in a marriage capable of producing a vital, loving family. One as constructive and monumental as her own. Was she destined always to lose the men who loved her and lent her emotional stability? Her father, David, and now Sam.

So far, it looked that way. What to do now to reverse her track record? Cultivate her own emotional stability, her own successes? Not live like some appendage of the men who loved her? She would go for it, but it did seem like the hard way out. Mercifully the heart of her life, the ostrich-covered date book, was completely filled for weeks in advance and partially for months. Sam would be replaced.

The fun times came and went. So did the dates and the suitors. Jamal seemed more than ever the man-about-town, at least in the social circles Lara frequented. She evaded any encounters with him. In her misery she blamed him for Sam's departure.

Had he not been the man to exploit her lusty nature? The man who pretended that men love a woman all the more for her erotic soul? The last thing she wanted was to rekindle their secret relationship. Or so she pretended to him and herself. It became ever more difficult to keep away from him. He and David were inseparable. He was, as always, a welcome guest at Cannon-berry Chase, with an open invitation, a room permanently at his disposal.

He entertained lavishly at the Moroccan Embassy, where he was climbing fast as some minor offical. It was difficult to avoid his invitations, especially when all the family were included. He was dating a variety of glamorous women, all of whom made Lara jealous. Enough to make her aware that she was not as through with Jamal as she wanted to be. She reacted by ignoring him whenever and wherever possible.

He behaved impeccably. Not a pass, not a sexual taunt when they found themselves alone. Only affection, friendship, and flattery, open and for all to see. Her negative reactions to him, no matter how much she tried to disguise them, became obvious enough for the gossips to probe: why did Lara Stanton dislike Jamal Ben El-Raisuli?

Her consistent avoidance of him was fast becoming an issue she was unable to explain to her friends. And that was the reason she decided to accept Jamal's invitation to a party in his River House apartment. Most of her friends were going. She saw it as a chance to scotch the gossip.

It was years now since her first traumatic sexual encounter with him. There had been long gaps between succeeding en-counters. She felt herself mature enough now to deal with Ja-mal, able to fend off her own erotic feelings for him. Yet an encounter with him? With Sam no longer there to catch her on the rebound? She could not help a tremor of fear at the thought. She repelled it with pride and determination to be her own woman, able to deal with her own life. Fighting thoughts.

"It's a party we're going to, not a wake, Lara." Julia reduced both of them to giggles.

"Happy face and all that? I know. I think I have a perverse nature. I have no enthusiasm for this party or Jamal, and yet I'm looking forward to it."

"You do have a perverse streak in you! I have a good feeling about tonight. Buck up, it'll be fun. Jamal's parties are always great. One way or another. Are you sure about this dress, Lara?''

"Julia, stop fidgeting. You look fabulous."

"I still think it's too provocative for me. Are you sure?"

"Trust me."

The matter of outfits for Jamal's party had vexed their ingenuity. The invitation had had engraved on the bottom of the card: "The Lady and the Tart and All the Men Are Studs." David said the line meant Jamal was throwing a party for the prettiest hookers and debs in New York. The two girls had been amused at Jamal's audacity. They questioned David endlessly as to how the girls would dress, what the women would be like. He had answered them, "Most of them, gloriously beautiful and elegant. You know, the sexiest ensembles from the best couture houses in town. The cheaper the hooker, the raunchier she'll look. Some of them are gonna look as much the deb as you girls do. Real stiff competition there for all you 'ladies.' " Lara and Julia gave each other a look and dressed accordingly.

They were in the Van Fleet entrance hall. The elevator would take them down to the Ben El-Raisuli apartment. They had dined earlier with Julia's father. He now stood in the doorway, between the hall and the living room, watching them. He had been amused by the girls as they plotted how they intended to behave at Jamal's party. Lara saw him reflected in the seventeenth-century gilded mirror. Lately, each time Lara saw Julia's father, she thought he looked more frail. Grief seemed to be desiccating him. She turned to him with a broad smile.

"How do we look, Mr. Van Fleet?"

"I tremble for the men at that party. You're both irresistible. You could snatch any man there. They'll be putty in your hands."

The two girls looked delighted. "Oh, Dad! Ever the gallant gentleman."

"Certainly not. Old and doddery I may be at times, but I am not blind or dead. Not yet. You girls constitute a danger to an old man with even a spark of life left in him."

Julia saw a smile on her father's lips, a twinkle in his eye, as if the sight of them had suddenly enlivened him anew. She looked at herself in the mirror and knew that it was the youthful spirit of Lara and herself, masculine response to female sexuality, that had made her father's heart race. She swung round to face him.

"Oh, Pa. Come with us. Jamal would love to have you. It's going to be young and crazy, and maybe a little wild. It will be amusing for you. Could be you'll meet a woman."

He actually laughed. "You girls have been amusing enough for me. The way you look, your exuberance, youth—they can still give a rise to an old fogey like me. Who was it that said an old man is just a platonic Casanova? Some art critic. Confessed it in his diary. Anyway, he certainly got my number: 'a platonic Casanova.' " He went to both girls and kissed them on the cheek. "There is no fool like an old fool." With that he retreated to his living room.

Seeing that extra flicker of life come back into Julia's father was a thrill for the girls. It gave them a feeling of female power, which they liked. The elevator arrived. They accorded themselves one last look of approval in the mirrors on either side of the lift doors.

"Good evening, George," they intoned simultaneously to the elevator man.

He greeted them, a look of surprise on his face, then closed the doors. The elevator began to descend. The girls did it again after yet another look at themselves in the lift mirror: in unison, "God bless Halston."

Julia was dressed in a long-sleeved, see-through blouse of black chiffon. Around her waist, a wide black satin belt. Her skirt, tailored to fit her like a second skin, was heavy black crepe de chine, little more than a miniskirt. Long black stockings, and high-heeled, open sandals with straps of black satin. Sexy, sophisticated, provocative—Julia had never before worn anything like it. Her long hair was combed smoothly off her face and held back by a black satin Alice band, with a small, soft chiffon bow tied to one side. On her wrists were rock-crystal bracelets. She knew she spelled: "Sexy. Come and get me." But she also knew that Halston had made her nakedness more than acceptable, beautiful and desirable. It was the cut of a master: the way the folds in the chiffon fell, teased with a glimpse of the swell of the breasts, yet obscuring the nipples.

The girls had told the designer they wanted to look like ladylike French tarts: very *soignée*, priceless hookers, fit to seduce on a grand scale—and, to his amusement, added, "And get away with it." And lady tarts he had made them, at least with needle and thread. Lady tarts with two-thousand-dollar dresses.

It had been black for Lara as well. Her dress was of fine crepe de chine. A long-sleeved, wraparound dress with a neckline that plunged to the waist, it clung to her ample breasts, revealing their voluptuous swell and the shape of her nipples. The skirt was a sarong, worn a few inches above the knee. It draped skimpily but seductively, and was tied at the waist in a soft bow with long tails. When she walked, it opened to reveal just a sliver of inside leg and thigh, almost to her mound of Venus—a miracle of tailoring and sensuality, with no hint of vulgarity. The soft drape of the neckline revealed the flesh between her breasts down to the waist, and long, shapely limbs that seemed to go on forever were encased in black nylon. Her shoes were black satin, high-heeled pumps adorned with her great-grandmother's diamond shoe buckles. The dress, a most sophisticated sexual come-on, was enhanced by Lara's silver-blond hair, with its mass of long, spiraling curls held off her face by a pair of tortoiseshell combs. The girls had cleverly played down their makeup, letting their bodies tell it all. They looked young and fresh-faced, almost pubescent, bodies primed for fucking.

Jamal had proclaimed, "The debs will come in their slightly—just slightly—provocative silk taffetas, all puffed sleeves and full skirts. Lots of chest and no breast, or demure cleavage-boasting jewelery. An occasional plunging neckline, if Mummy hasn't been around to see it. Maybe even some tit on show. And the hookers will all look like ladies or cheap tarts. And I'll love them all. The variety will be exquisite." David had called him "the lady-game player." And he had answered, "And why not?"

"Why not, indeed?" echoed David.

Never averse to a challenge, Julia and Lara had passed the word on to any deb they knew to be going to the party. There would be few sleeves puffing or silk taffetas rustling this night. Sexy, provocative, cock-teasing clothes would adorn hooker and deb alike.

The surprise on the elevator man's face said it all. The girls gathered all their courage, and the lift bumped to a halt. George, who had known them all their lives, turned before he slid the bronze door open and said, "Miss Julia, Miss Lara, you be careful tonight.'' A smile, a pause, and, shaking his head less in disapproval than in resignation, he opened the elevator door.

On entering the room they got the buzz, the excitement that some parties have. Instantaneous magic. The men all in black tie. The women: it seemed there were any number of beautiful, sexy ladies. They came in all ages, with a rich social and ethnic mix. Lovely as flowers, they adorned the room. The debs were there, but only the odd one had slipped through in silk taffeta. They looked cool and beautiful, but almost dowdy alongside the high flyers in their sexy gear. The guests stood in groups, leaned on pianos, against fireplaces, sat in deep chairs and on elegant settees, or on the stairs leading to the floor above. They drank and smoked, and some swayed to the music of Diana Ross sounding like liquid sex, looking sensuous as a panther draped on top of the grand piano.

The Moroccan servants, in white turbans and kaftans, drifted among the guests with trays of crystal goblets of champagne, mirrors with long, straight lines of cocaine and silver straws, amethyst boxes filled with a variety of slim cigarettes: hashish, Indonesian grass, even Chesterfields. Silver trays proffered mounds of tasty titbits parceled in filo pastry. Servants in pairs walked among the guests with large glass bowls of caviar, which they served on bite-sized pancakes. On demand, they filled the pancakes with the delectable beads and topped them with a slash of sour cream, before rolling them.

Jamal saw Lara and Julia the moment they entered the room. He was the first to get to them. He approached Julia, took her hands in his, and lowered his lips to kiss first one, then the other, hand. His delight in the look of the girls was obvious. Still holding her by one hand, he had her turn around to give him a full view of herself. His eyes beckoned Lara to do the same. The girls had gotten him, and were delighted. Finally detaching himself from Lara, he gave his attention to Julia once again,

''Julia, my dear Julia—I had no idea you were such a sexy lady. How *wonderful* you look, and how brave to wear such a provocative ensemble to my party.'' He adjusted the fold of her blouse to expose the nipple of her small but pert breast. He consumed her with his eyes. She playfully slapped his hand and readjusted the blouse.

''And Lara!'' The way he looked at her made her heart race.

What was so different about him tonight? She had seen him many times since his return: he had rarely affected her as he did now. All barriers between them seemed to fall away.

"Jamal."

"You certainly have risen to the occasion. How delicious you look." He took both her hands in his, as he had Julia's. He had scarcely kissed one before he made up his mind that she was his, that no other man would have Lara Stanton this night. He suddenly realized how much he had missed having sex with her, that his life, if not quite a sexual desert, had not seemed as fertile since last he had had her. He now realized how very thirsty he had been for her. A thirst that demanded quenching before the night was out. He understood why he had not been bothered one way or the other for the last year or so about not bedding her. She hadn't been ready for him, so sexy and available to him, as she seemed tonight. She was as he desired her, bursting to be fucked by him. That was what had originally turned him onto her, and that was all that ever did. He yearned to probe the sexual depravity within this angel of a girl.

He smiled with delight again as he asked, "Is it possible that you girls are playing with me?"

"No more than you are playing with us . . . and every other woman in this room," answered Lara.

"I'm thrilled you have at last accepted an invitation of mine, Lara. You are a great asset to my party. But I had better warn you: this party is not for husband hunting, spoiled debs, but for fun girls. Look around. It's a fast, anything-goes party. A fun party for those who drug and drink, and want sex and music. But nothing that you two girls can't handle, if you want to."

He reached for glasses of champagne from a tray and handed them to the girls. Then, slipping an arm through each of theirs, he led them into a crowded room overlooking the East River. Several people converged on them with evident delight that they had made the party. The girls did not miss, in the eyes of some of the women, envy at their appearance and the lasciviousness they engendered in certain of the men.

Jamal lost no time. Before she was swept away, into the swing of the party, he whispered in Lara's ear: "You look sublime, and I want you almost more than you want me. And you are not as safe as you think. David has been here and gone. He had to leave. A call from Washington; something he has been expecting for weeks has come through. He said to tell you he will be back the day after tomorrow. He won't miss all the fun and sex games, though. He has taken a gorgeous French lady with him.'' He felt Lara stiffen. He had shot an arrow to just where he knew it would wound her. It pierced her jealous heart. He admired the speed with which she recovered herself. She gave him a look so hard it surprised him.

"I don't need David to protect me. Maybe you haven't noticed, I'm a big girl now. All grown up.''

"Oh, I've noticed.''

Bob Flanders, Lara's latest affair, interrupted them. He was one of her on-again, off-again men. His surprise at seeing her there was evident enough for Lara to conclude that her presence would quell all rumors about some secret rift between Jamal and her—the object, after all, of her being there. Bob was a fun guy, and she happily went off with him to join some of her other friends.

Jamal watched her skirt divide, exposing the long, luscious limbs and the provocative walk. He was crazed with desire for her. Julia caught the look in his eye and knew at once there was something between Jamal and Lara, some dark secret so deep that her friend had not been able to confide it even to her. Julia could feel the intensity in Jamal, the heat of his passion for her friend. And there had been something Julia had glimpsed in Lara's eyes when Jamal had touched her, when he spoke to her, that she had never seen before. She was quite shocked, concerned, because she sensed more than passion—something deeply sinister—in the sexual electricity that passed between Jamal and her friend.

A gaze between Julia and Jamal, and he knew that she had guessed. He gave nothing away. Instead he turned his attention on her, unleashing his charm,

"Julia, I have never seen you looking sexier.'' He kissed her gently on the lips. They had known each other for a very long time. He had watched her grow up, just as he had done Lara. She knew he didn't want her, no matter how pretty and sexy she looked. Not really want her the way he wanted Lara. She didn't have that something special deep inside her that Lara had, that men lusted after. That something she had never wanted to investigate too deeply in her best friend. She was thinking about that now, when, suddenly, she was surprised by Jamal's caress of her naked breast under the see-through, black silk. Before she could react, he quickly bent his head to her breast and kissed the nipple. A shiver of delight, and Julia backed a pace away from Jamal. He gave her a sexy laugh.

"Surprised? Don't be. I won't be the only man who will take liberties with you tonight." He placed an arm around her, caressed her naked back, and whispered in her ear, "I won't do it again. Not unless you ask me to. That's my secret: I only like to take women who want me."

He plucked one of the delicacies from a passing tray and fed it to her. Julia watched him. He had eyes only for Lara. Julia tugged at his arm, and he looked at her. She told him, "Great party. Don't spoil it for us, will you?"

He laughed at her. "Spoil it? Hardly. Come with me. The way you girls look tonight, nothing can spoil this evening for you. I predict you will both go home happier than you have been for a very long time, and with the man of your choosing. Or maybe you won't go home at all. It's that kind of party. Full of surprises—even for me, it seems. Come with me; I can't wait for Dan to see you." He grabbed her by the hand and was leading her to the far side of the room.

"Don't do this, Jamal."

"Don't be childish. I might be doing you the best turn of your life. Be brave; it's about time you made a grab for what *you* want, Julia."

Chapter 13

The atmosphere at Jamal's effervescent party was electric, light, buzzy, filled with gaiety. Lara, who had dropped her guard hours before, had danced and flirted. She found the party charged with sensual energy, and that suited her. She felt uplifted, as everyone else seemed to be. She drank without moderation, and did more coke than she had ever done before. But at a party such as this it was the norm, as natural as breathing. Her happiness seemed boundless, and she allowed herself to be worn down by Jamal's advances.

He found her between two men who were making overtures to her. "Not tonight, boys. You've been outflanked by the host." He attempted to whisk her away. She held back.

"Anything, anything you want."

"Anything?" She wanted reassurance.

"That's what I said."

"Can you give me love?"

"Love? Oh, yes, and much more."

She believed him. His intent, anyway. She was tired of flight from sexual bliss with Jamal and allowed herself to be discreetly swept away by him to his bedroom. Once in his room, memories of their first night together flooded back. How passionately in love with him she had been. How anxious she had been to give herself to him. How cruelly tantalizing he had been: he had known how desperately she had wanted him.

On entering the bedroom, Lara was more overcome with emotion than she expected to be. She disengaged herself from Jamal. Outside, across the East River, were the twinkling lights.

In this room he had made a woman of her, as no other man had. Not dear David, or safe Sam. Lara wanted him. But this time she felt mature enough about her sexual passion for Jamal. Strong enough to face her own erotic self and take responsibility for it.

She felt his presence behind her before he even touched her. When he placed his hands caressingly on her shoulders, a tremor of excitement caused her to close her eyes for a moment and sigh. He drew the combs from her hair and it tumbled into his hands. Jamal arranged the blond tresses around her shoulders and down her back. He kissed them with great tenderness, then the side of her neck, and the lobe of her ear.

"I want you. I always want you. I've wanted you terribly, for these many weeks since my return. I hardly dreamed you would come tonight."

Lara felt elated that she had been able to keep him guessing.

"I have never seen you like this—brimming with sensual power for all the world to see. It thrills me to know that no man has ever had you as I have. Tell me how much you want me. Tell me you're not going to pretend that I mean nothing to you. Let me make love to you. And don't be afraid of who you are and what you are. Take courage and trust me, and we can go together to places you have never been before. I want to make all your erotic fantasies come true."

Lara turned around to face him. One pull on a strand of the soft silk bow and her dress seemed to dissolve. He slipped it from her shoulders, and she stood before him in her black satin, spiked-heeled pumps, naked above her black stockings. The dark, plum-colored nimbus round her erect nipples and against the creamy whiteness of her skin triggered the sexual violence in Jamal. The full breasts so ripe for his hands and mouth . . . He swung her up into his arms and carried her to the bed. He placed her against the pillows while kissing her eyes and cheeks, biting passionately into her lips, between mumbling his love for her.

He undressed with an urgency she had not seen in him before, flinging his things away from them, then sliding onto the bed and lying next to her. He pulled her roughly into his arms and rocked her for a while, while licking the dark nimbuses, sucking deeply on her nipples, sometimes slapping the sides of her breasts, wanting her to feel the sting of the passion he had for her. He forced her to say she loved him. And, once she had, she could not stop. She told him more, it all kept tumbling out. How she loved him for his cock, his tongue, those hands of his that searched out every nuance of her erotic nature and steered her toward sexual bliss.

Her honesty and passion affected him. Though he wanted to tell her he loved her more than ever before, he could not find the words. Instead, he showed her in the way that would give her the most pleasure. He placed her on her knees, straddling him. She offered him first one breast, then the other, and he, more calmly now, kissed them, opened his mouth and devoured as much of them as he could, while his hands roamed freely . . . wherever he located a place to excite her passion.

He placed his face between her breasts and smothered himself with them. The thought of dying inside her excited his lust. He parted the breasts, and, as if he fantasized them full of mother's milk, caressed one tit with great tenderness and sucked deeply, half disappointed not to taste her milk. She seemed lost, as if transported to some realm of the god Eros. Searching fingers found her soft, moist slit, open and yearning for him.

Slowly he pulled her down to lie on top of him. His penis probed that soft, warm place oozing with sweet cum. He crushed her in his arms, kissed her with wild passion, with lips and tongue, as he felt the fire rising in her. They made love, she relentlessly impaled by his throbbing penis. He loved her, and at that moment, nothing else in the world mattered to Lara.

Her eyes spoke wordless volumes of her deep need for sexual ecstasy. He had not understood before her desperation to be loved, adored for herself, and her appetite for life. She filled his heart at once and forever. He gave in and confessed.

"I love you."

"You've said that before."

"But do you believe me?" He was kissing her again.

"Yes, I must believe you."

"Why?"

"Because you reach me as no other man has. Because you set me free to explore my passion to live. And you could not do that unless you love. That's the way sex with you has always been, but, until now, I could not accept that. I was too busy suffering guilt feelings about my sensual self and your exploitation of me." She kissed him deeply and bit into the sides of his mouth, dug her fingernails into the flesh on his back, and raised and lowered herself again and again on his penis, riding him with urgency and coming in waves of lust made more powerful by her honesty.

He lost control. This young slip of a girl was in command. She had a seductive power over him that, until now, he had not admitted to. He pulled her head back by the hair and told her, "Give yourself up to me—now and for always—and I'll give myself up to you as I have never done with any other woman in my life. Be my sexual slave, and I'll be yours, and we will love each other for it. It's a fair exchange, Lara, and I promise you will never be happier. A bargain?"

She was tired of running away from Jamal, from her sexuality. She gave herself to him, without fear or conditions. She committed herself to his desire, to do with her whatever he chose. She longed to explore the far reaches of her lust. With him she felt she might be half-safe in doing it.

Jamal, the consummate seducer, believed her, not while she told him, but when he felt her give herself to him, before she even assented. It was as if her heart, body, and soul submitted simultaneously. That was how he loved his women the most: enslaved to him. That was when he sensed real power over them, felt able to mold them to his will. Lara had taken longer than most, but then she had been younger, more spoiled, and better protected than most.

Jamal raised her off him and rolled her over on her back. From the small chest of drawers next to the bed he drew a large pink jade object, a sculpted penis encrusted with raised flowers. Chinese roses. A Han Dynasty piece of art made to be used by men to excite themselves by watching the jade penis violate their women with ecstatic pleasuring. Jamal, like those emperors and noblemen of the past, enjoyed sinking this pornographic *objet d'art* into Lara. She attempted to stifle moans of delight as he twisted and turned the penis, better to impress the flowers, the knob, on her tender inside. In vain. Her ecstasy enraged his lust. And now he stradled her with his face between her legs to watch the thrust and parry between jade dildo and flesh as he manipulated it with such dexterity. She caressed his bottom and fed his engorged penis slowly into her mouth. Filled, to the rhythm of the jade thrusts, she fucked him with her mouth. They were the god and goddess Eros that night.

When Lara woke the following morning, she was in Jamal's bed, enfolded in her lover's arms. He opened his eyes, and they made morning love even before they spoke. They bathed together before breakfast in bed, on white lacquer trays. The sun streaming into the room, two Moroccan servants fussing over the breakfast trays, a recording of Rubinstein playing Chopin—sexual slavery in this case seemed to have a tolerable aftermath.

From long, slender crystal flutes, stuffed with tiny white peaches that had had vintage pink champagne poured over them, they toasted themselves without words, simply the rims of their glasses touching. A sound like the tinkle of a tiny silver bell. Crystal meeting crystal. Lara took a sip, enough to quench her thirst. She watched Jamal empty his glass in one long, slow swallow. His servant filled it at once. He drank again and plucked a white peach from the glass. She watched him eat one, then a second. She followed suit. She felt the succulent flesh as it burst on her tongue. It was sweet, and the juicy texture sensuous. Placing his glass on the tray, Jamal dismissed the men. One arm pulled Lara that little bit closer to him, gently enough to avoid upsetting their trays.

"Why have you been staring at me, my love? Do you think our being here together so unreal? Am I a mirage? Should I vanish in a blink of your eye, a puff of your imagination?" He laughed. That teasing, wicked laugh that she knew so well, and had, until now, feared because of its power to charm, to seduce.

"Is something wrong?" he asked, the smile still on his lips.

"No. Nothing's wrong. Except . . ."

"Ah, with women there is always an 'except.' Except what, my decadent angel?"

"Except I'm surprised to be here having breakfast with you in this room. I have never done that before."

"No, that's true. How do you feel about it?"

"Comfortable."

He gave her a smile and asked. "Just comfortable?"

"Strangely happy. As if my being here has brought us closer together."

They gazed into each other's eyes for some time before he spoke. Then he asked her, "Will I flatter you too much if I tell

you that you are one of just a very few women who have stayed
in this room, awoken in this bed?''

"Does that mean something?"

"Only that I love you more than the women I entertain in the
Fifty-third Street house. You know the form. You've been there."

He raised his glass and drank. Broke off a corner of the warm
croissant and buttered it and popped it into his mouth. He had
said it, he loved her. He was done with talking about it. Without
looking at her, he changed the subject, suggested, "My favorite
egg dish. You must eat it now, before it gets cold."

He placed a forkful in his own mouth, then exclaimed,
"Merveilleux!" He followed it with a sip of champagne, another corner of the croissant, and picked up his fork again. "You
will never find this dish prepared better than my chef does it.
He is a master at fresh oysters and scrambled eggs. First he
shucks the large, plump Belon oysters, flown in from France the
same morning, and pats them dry. Then he places them gently
in a frying pan of hot walnut oil and butter. In seconds, Lara,
seconds, they catch a golden sizzle and he has turned them over,
and is pouring the beaten egg over them. A quick scramble, and
this . . ."

Lara tasted the oyster as it burst, still soft at its center, in her
mouth. Combining with the egg, it was as he said, sheer am-
brosia. Jamal was still talking recipes, but she could hardly concentrate on what he was saying. She was too distracted by the
knowledge that he loved her. She felt dizzy with joy: he loved
her, and he was able to tell her so. The moment she had opened
her eyes and seen the room, she had known. She sensed that,
unless he loved her, he would never have allowed her to stay in
his house.

Suddenly she was ravenous; she ate her sensuous scrambled
eggs, croissant, and brioche with gusto. She drank, as he did,
hot cups of Fortnum & Mason's Royal Blend tea. Then, suddenly, she slumped back against the pillows laughing. She had
no idea what he was talking about; she had lost him seconds
after he had told her he loved her. Her laughter did at last stop
his babbling.

"It never stops with you, Jamal. Even at breakfast. It's always
sex with you. If it's not carnal, it's epicurean. This is the best

breakfast of my life, and I will never forget it. It will always be one of the special experiences that happened to me."

Unable to contain her feelings for him one minute more, she threw her arms around his neck and kissed him. "Breakfast—sexy and delicious, just like you. Oh, I'm so happy. What does it all mean?"

"That we're in love. That we've a larger secret to hide than before. Now finish your eggs before they get cold."

He seemed not very happy about being in love. Or if he was, he was hiding it too well for Lara's liking. His attitude sobered her up. She felt compelled to ask him. "Why does it have to be a secret? Why can't we proclaim it to the world? I will."

"You won't, you know."

"Why?"

Jamal removed their trays to the floor next to the bed. "Now listen to me well, Lara. Things have changed for us since last night, but not a lot. Think about it. You will see I am right."

He took her in his arms and kissed her. She accepted his kisses, but could not agree with him that things had changed so little for them. She protested, "I can't agree with you. Maybe not a lot for you, but I feel my whole life has changed because we are in love. Why, give me one good reason why we should keep our feelings a secret."

"You know too little about love and being in love, Lara. I have loved you since you were a little girl. But not in the way you want me to love you. You were a spoiled child who had everything she ever wanted, got everything her heart desired. You had every advantage in the world. And now you are a woman and nothing in you has changed, and I love you all the more for it. That's the way it is, and that's the way it should be, as far as I am concerned. But the one thing you cannot have is me. Or not the way *you* want me. Lara, take what we have, and enjoy it to the fullest, because that's what I'm going to do. But it can only go as far as *I* will allow it, and that's why it has to remain *our* secret.

"Girls like you, Lara, want monogamy. It will never happen with me. I love women. I love sex, not love. And the greatest pleasure I have in life is to pursue and exploit them both. I live for sexual adventures. And not for you—or any woman—would I give that up. I am telling you now, because I do love you and

want you to know what you are getting into. So long as we keep
our sexual life a secret, our deeper love feelings even *more* secret, then we can see more of each other socially, and no one
will be the wiser. Come with me for as far as you can go, my
way, and I will give you the best time of your life. That's the
only commitment I am prepared to give you.''

Lara listened. There was emotion in Jamal's voice that was
more impressive for a young woman in love than the harsh facts
he was so insistently stating. She banked on the emotion and
asked, ''What if I want more?''

''Lara, listen to me. I can give you no more than what I have
offered. You want more, go elsewhere. It's as simple as that.
Mark my words well, there will be *no* marriage at the end of
this rainbow. It's not in my nature, nor is it what I want. I know
you better than you think, my love. You are exactly the sort of
girl who follows the old, well-tried formula. Find your love,
have a little adventure. Once you have bagged your quarry, it
has to be marriage, and settling down to children and heavy-
duty family life. You are not your mother's daughter for nothing,
Lara, but more like her, I think, than you would admit to. Nor
your father's, either. You will want your rightful place in the
world of the Four Hundred and all it entails. If we do not keep
our sexual liaison secret, I will ruin your reputation and you will
never get that place. Trust me. I know you, and I know me, and
I know us. It's my way or it's over. So don't spoil that.''

''I'll never want any other man but you, Jamal.'' The promise
flowed from her, and she kissed him.

''That's good. That's what I like. You love me better and
longer than anyone else and be happy. But I don't necessarily
think that's true—that you will never want another man. You are
a girl who always wants more. The day I don't give you what
you want, what makes you happy and fulfilled, you will walk
away with the first man who will. And, incidentally, I promise
we will still be friends. I will let you go with my blessing. Until
then be mine, let me feed you a sexual life to satisfy your hunger.
No one else will, and that's a fact for you to live with.''

''You make it sound like I'm making a pact of love with the
devil.''

''Well, maybe you are. A fairly dark angel, certainly.''

''I don't in the least believe that.''

"You had better."

"Is that a warning?"

"You might take it that way. It would be best for you if you did not create an unreal image of me. I want no tears over the other women, and I insist we remain a secret for both our sakes. Can you deal with that reality?"

"You are afraid of the family."

"No, I respect the family. I love them like my own family. You, too. But you have become the object of my sexual affection, and I love you the more for it. Leave it at that."

Lara resisted no longer, but gave herself up to Jamal.

Months passed by as if they were days, with Lara living only for those secret liaisons. She was fast becoming obsessive about sex and her lover. He had, as he promised her, found ways to be with her socially, for all the world to see, and yet for them not to become "an item." Friendship by day, erotic oblivion by night. His attention filled her life. His liberal attitude toward her overactive libido gave her the security she needed to soar. She was happier than she had ever been, but he had been right. She wanted more: she kept that well hidden from him, and tried desperately to rationalize the greed out of her life.

What she had remained thrilling, a sexual adventure few women would ever dare to embark on. It took months for her to realize the perils of her sexual game with Jamal. She naively assumed that because he loved her she was safe. By the time she realized Jamal had an erotic hold over her, her will was powerless to break it. When they were alone, he dominated her sexually. Among the family, he displayed an open admiration for her. It was a double bond that chained her to him.

She suffered the humiliation of knowing there were other women in his life. He pursued them, and would never give them up for her. She began to see a kind of devil at work in him as he made her accept his infidelities by the reward he bestowed upon her: the admission she so cherished that he loved her more than any other woman he had ever made his own. And there were always new sexual experiences created to excite her pleasure. Her life was full of fun and sexual gratification. But it was not enough. She began asking herself why, if her life was so good, she was always feeling empty and alone. Her sexual excesses with Jamal were soured by the fear that ultimately she must leave him, if she was to have all she wanted from a love relationship. Anxiety over her clandestine affair with him finally began to erode her happiness. She loathed her own weakness, the deceptions, her masochistic clinging to a man who undermined her self-esteem.

"Today I leave him." Her near-daily resolution was addressed to the mirror. Every night she went mad with anxiety, awaiting his summons to surrender to their sexual whims. Months passed without the pattern of her life changing. The will to leave him was simply not there. She didn't have a chance. Her youth, her inexperience with men, her pampered, privileged life worked against her. Had she been streetwise, or forced by circumstances to cope at survival level, she might have known better what to do.

Lara suffered more because she was not blind to what was happening to her. She saw it all: the ebbing of the last vestiges of self-esteem, her inability to halt her own decline. In desperation she at last gave a cry for help—but even that cry was self-destructive, and a little mistimed.

"I'm in deep trouble. I want to tell you about it. If I don't talk to someone, I think I'll go mad. But you must promise me you will tell no one, do nothing. Never ever let on that I confided in you. If he should find out, he would leave me and I couldn't bear that. Not now, not ever. It's me. I must be the one to leave him, or I will never recover from this love affair."

Her voice was shaky, and she spoke only just above a whisper. She was terribly pale, pathetically nervous. Julia was aghast.

The organ was playing "O Promise Me" as Julia looked at her friend. She was always beautiful, but at that moment she seemed so fragile. The frailty of her loveliness created a soft vulnerability that one rarely saw in her brand of sensual, provocative good looks. Julia took Lara's white kid-gloved hand in hers.

St. Thomas's was packed to the last flower-bedecked pew. There was a bevy of morning-coated men and well-hatted ladies, all smiles and pretty spring couture. Everyone loves someone else's wedding.

"You're not going to faint are you, Lara?"

"No." But she sounded unsure.

"Well, you certainly picked your place and time; there's no place like church for confessions! I'm here and I'll help, but you must hang on. It will be all right."

Lara tried to calm herself, but seemed more panicked than ever by partly relieving her emotional state. "How can we get out of here, Julia?"

"We can't. If we make a break for the door, everyone will think it's the bride coming down the aisle." As if to prove her right, the organ suddenly blared into the march that launches bridesmaids into churches.

"*Coraggio!* We'll talk as soon as we get out of here."

But they never really did talk. Not that Lara didn't want to, or Julia wouldn't listen and help any way she could. It was more that the moment of truth and pain got lost in the protracted ceremony and elaborate escape from church and people to the seclusion of Julia's apartment.

The room overlooking the East River was muffled in silence. After pouring them both a glass of champagne, Julia sat down next to Lara, feeling such anguish for her friend that she could think of nothing to say. In silence she stroked her arm.

Lara had never looked more the tragic beauty than she did now in her white chiffon pleated skirt. Its jacket was of white raw silk with a large sailor collar piped in silver and gold, and it had a double-breasted set of gold buttons. She still wore the wide-brimmed, white horsehair hat, embroidered with gold stars. A clump of fresh magnolias was pinned to the gold band around the crown. Her beautiful clothes contrasted strangely with her wan look.

"Now what's this all about, Lara? And how can I help?" asked Julia.

"I don't know where to begin, what even to tell you, except that I am at my wits' end. I feel desperate. I don't want to feel so bad, but I don't know how to stop the pain."

Julia's feeling for Lara in her desperation left her shaken and unable to help. This was not the girl she had known for most of her life, and Lara's inability to cope with her own feelings frightened her friend.

"You are obviously having some sort of an emotional breakdown. I can do nothing to help you unless you tell me exactly what has brought you down."

A combination of things—the tone of Julia's voice, her choice of words, the mere fact that someone outside herself was focusing on the state she was in and demanding that she must reveal her secret if she were to receive the help she needed to expel her misery—snapped Lara out of her acute anxiety. She suddenly realized that she could not reveal, even to this loyal and loving friend, the depths of the despair she had fallen into because of her all-consuming sexual attachment to Jamal. She edited the story. She had to spare them both embarrassment.

Half-truths do not make a full confession. Minutes passed in silence, waiting for her to speak. During that time she kept mulling over the idea that evil branded with the light is no longer evil. Bring the darkest secret into the light and it vanishes. But to bring her relationship wholly into the light now seemed impossible to her. Exposure might entail an end to her affair with Jamal. That was a chance she would not hazard yet, no matter how unhappy she was.

She put down her empty glass and, placing her hands over her face, lowered her head and took several deep breaths. After several seconds, she removed her hands from her face to give her friend a reassuring look. She rose from the sofa and walked to the window. When she turned back to face Julia she felt buoyed by the concern visible in her face.

"I'm not having a nervous breakdown. I think I might have if I hadn't poured my heart out to you in the church. What I am having is an affair with Jamal. An intense and very secret affair. Promise me again you will never reveal it to anyone. . . ."

It was at this point that Lara faltered. There was a crack in her voice, a suppressed sob of emotion.

"You're desperately in love with him?"

"Desperately, and that's what I can't bear. Being desperate. I don't want to feel that way over Jamal, or any man—anything, as a matter of fact. Desperation is a destroyer. I wouldn't want it to have any place in my life, and here I am steeped in it. I loathe myself for that. But I just can't crawl out of this dark place I seem to have created for myself."

"Don't be so hard on yourself, Lara. You have a formidable lover who has a longtime reputation for doing the same thing to every woman he has an affair with. Give him up, if you want to be happy."

It was good advice, and bound them closer together. Julia began to understand the more complex side of Lara's nature, and accepted it. She made many attempts to distract Lara from slipping into despair. Some of them worked. But nothing broke the spell of her romance.

Chapter 14

And it was a romance. Maybe even, in its own peculiar way, romance on a grand scale. There was a real bond between Lara and Jamal, a depth to his caring for her. The clandestine quality was confined to the sexual escapades. There were surprise holidays in Rio and Paris, a week in a castle in the Atlas Mountains in Morocco. At those times they were careful that no one should guess their deeper relationship. Only during their secret romantic trips, when no one they knew was likely to appear—a river journey up the Nile, a sneaked break in Spain, another on safari in Africa—did they behave in public as the lovers they were in private. When those secret holidays came to an end and they returned to live apart—she in the world of deception he insisted they maintain—the sense of loss Lara felt was nearly unbearable.

The family watched her drift away from them, but without anxiety: she would drift back again. They labeled it "finding her place in the world." Only Henry was concerned when Lara rejected a holiday with David, or another with Max in India. The old Lara would never have done that. Then she passed up a chance to sail around the world with an ideal crew, one she would have handpicked herself. She still had not undertaken any of the long journeys she had planned to make in her new four-seater plane. She appeared to her father to be happy enough until he caught her off-guard, and then he saw a sadness in her he could not bear. He loved her too much not to do something about that sadness.

He went to Emily. "I don't think Lara is having a very good time of it."

She looked up from her book. "Not for want of trying. The girl never stops; she's invited everywhere. Her problem is she favors the wrong men."

"What exactly does that mean, Emily?"

"What it says, Henry. The sooner she marries Sam the better." Emily went back to her book.

A phase. Every girl went through them en route to maturity. Henry knew his daughter, her good qualities and the bad. But he also knew that she had what all his children had: a core solid as steel to sustain her through any emotional traumas life might inflict upon her. Just one thing worried him. There was a flaw in her the other children never had; a vein of vulnerability that, worked on by the wrong sort of man, might damage her forever. Almost certain that someone was tapping into the need Lara had to be loved, for the next few weeks he watched more closely what his daughter was doing with her life.

There had been so many signals, they became impossible to ignore. She no longer awakened in the River House apartment. The Fifty-third Street house became their sexual playpen. His erotic demands became even more adventurous, and yet their rendezvous less frequent. He flaunted his latest conquest, a leggy French model, in front of her. Actually brought the girl to Cannonberry Chase and taunted Lara with an open show of passion. The humiliation was too great. She knew in her heart that it was the beginning of the end of the affair with Jamal. She was doing her best to deal with it, working herself up to leave him. And when she was feeling at her lowest, with little respect for herself and her behavior in the matter, help materialized. Sam returned. He appeared at Cannonberry Chase one Sunday lunch.

She was never so happy to see someone. His arrival was sunlight in the darkness of her soul. She suddenly felt light and gay. She was the innocent adolescent again. They greeted each other with the same kind of love and affection they had always shared. The family embraced him: it was a reunion that brought home to Lara how much she had missed Sam and all he represented to her.

In the weeks that followed they saw a great deal of each other.

But they were cautious with each other when alone, even though they admitted they still loved each other as they always had. The sexual attraction was still there. But, although Sam plainly desired her, she asked for time. Neither mentioned the island and their last sexual encounter. Jamal was still very much her sexual scene, and she was involved with several other suitors whom she had used to ease herself away from him. Now Sam? Too complicated.

Missy still saw Lara every morning at nine o'clock when she was at home. Their routine rarely varied. Over breakfast they did her correspondence and the diary, and kept Lara generally in line with her busy social schedule. Every day it was their habit to review first that day and then the week ahead. It had become a procedure that kept Lara so distracted from her secret life that for most of the time she lived from day to day, accepting the diary as a life pattern from which she rarely deviated. And so, when she was told she was dining with her father that evening, and going to an auction of old master drawings at Sotheby's afterward, it came as no surprise to her.

It had been many months since she had gone out anywhere alone with Henry. She was quite looking forward to the evening—that is, until the phone call for which she was always waiting. It came around eleven o'clock. Her heart skipped a beat the moment she heard his voice. He had not called for nearly a week.

"I've missed you."

"And you love me," she intoned, a note of sarcasm in the voice.

"Yes, that's true."

"Liar! You only play with me. Bothering to phone means you want sex."

"Is that so bad? You've always known the score. And, admit it, you love the game."

Lara remained silent. He laughed. It was a wicked, teasing laugh. Foolishly she rose to it by maintaining a silence that told him she was pouting. That excited him. He loved her more when she was unable to cope with him. He took a tone with her that she knew he found irresistible and commanded, "Come to me tonight, the Fifty-third Street house."

"Impossible, I have other plans."

"Break them."

"Not this time, Jamal."

"Do I take it you have decided it's over?"

Her voice trembled. "One day I'll leave you Jamal."

"Ah, but not today. Today would not be the moment to choose. I want you too much and, whether you believe it or not, I need you even more, my angel."

"I hate it when you call me angel."

"Why so tetchy today? Think of our coming together, the taste of us on your tongue, the feel of me inside you. Don't be tetchy. Eight o'clock at the Fifty-third Street house, and I will make love to you and let you make love to me. Isn't that, after all, what we are all about?"

"I hate it when you cunt tease me."

He smiled to himself. He always knew how to reach the sensual, rebellious Lara. He enormously enjoyed erasing the refined, spoiled deb in her. *Cunt, cock, fuck*—words she might be shunned for even knowing, never mind using, in her conservative, high-society world. In the throes of their thrusting, he could force from her obscenities fit to excite a hard hat or make a stevedore blush. He was satisfied. The hardness in her voice, a smattering of lewdness: she would be there.

"Well," he snapped. "Over is over for me. You know that. Just say the word, Lara. Is it to be today?"

He could hear fear in the voice that answered him: "Not today, Jamal." There were tears of anxiety in her eyes that he could only visualize.

"I do love you, you know, La." She knew at that moment that he believed he did. His tone was kinder now, it soothed them both.

"I know. But, Jamal, I do have a problem about tonight. I am out this evening with my father. It's dinner, then the auction at Sotheby's."

Never offend the family. Most certainly never Henry. That was something Jamal understood. It did not, however, deter his plan to be with her that night. Jamal was adept at getting what he wanted, a superior manipulator. He was quick to adapt his plan.

"Ah, but I want you more than any other woman tonight. You'll have to make excuses—a late night party, for instance. You can be very convincing with excuses for your absences. Quite a pro when deceiving the family. I've watched you. You are a convincing little madam when you want to be.''

"I may be good *at* it, Jamal, but it doesn't mean that I feel good *about* it.''

He ignored that. "A party, and then staying the night over at Julia's or some other friend's. You know the form.''

"What happened to this past week when it would have been easy for me? The calls I made and you never returned? When I was free and wanting to be with you?''

"Oh, that's what this tetchiness is all about? Don't behave like a spoiled child.''

"Stop pretending I'm a child! I'm acting like a goddammed fool of a woman. Isn't it enough that I let you put me down and pick me up again like some piece of old luggage, for crissakes? What about when I want you?''

"Ah, but I have on many occasion responded to your call. Changed my plans to accommodate your sexual needs. Isn't that true, Lara? Haven't I come running when required?''

"Not of late.''

"Stop whining. We'll be together tonight—and I'll make you tell me how much you love me and how happy I make you. You want me to do that, don't you?''

She capitulated. "Of course that's what I want. That's what this conversation is all about, wanting you and not having you. Waiting for phone calls that never come. I hate it, Jamal. I am at my wits' end about it.''

"Then either leave me, or tell me where to pick you up and what time.''

That harsh voice that she knew only too well. He was calling her bluff. He was stronger than she was; he meant it. She hesitated, but still the willpower wasn't there. "Sotheby's. The auction starts about ten. Dad says it should all be over by midnight, champagne reception and all.''

"Tell him I'll be picking you up and you're joining a party going to Jilly Wainwright's bash. That I invite him on Jilly's behalf to join us. He will, of course, decline and insist that you go. Perfect.''

"Not so perfect. I hate these games you make me play, and especially with my father.''

"I love these games. It puts an edge on things. Excitement, that's what we're all about, Lara. Wear something provocative. I want you looking your most sensual. There's someone I want you to meet. A little surprise. Something to add spice to the night."

"Jamal . . ."

"Enough, Lara. Do it." She was left with the whine of a disconnected phone.

In the living room sat David, Henry, and Emily, drinking double martinis, very dry with a twist of lemon. The men rose from their chairs when Lara entered the room. She noted the look of approval in her father's eyes: he had always liked her in red. She had chosen a cardinal-red silk dress. It had long sleeves and a bodice bloused to the waist, then a straight, slim skirt worn to just above the knee. It was high in the front and backless to the waist. It was young, fresh, and provocative—and she carried it with the swagger and self-confidence of youth. Her legs were clad in silvery silk stockings and her feet shod in silver kid, high-heeled shoes. She wore no jewelery, except for the diamond earrings her father had presented her with for her first coming-out party.

David poured her a drink from the silver shaker. "You look a knockout, La." He presented her with the conical-stemmed glass of crystal-clear liquid. And with it a hug.

"By God, you do a father proud!" Henry smiled.

"Jamal has just called to remind me there's a party tonight. He wants me to go, Dad. Says he will pick me up after the auction and wants you to join us. He says he has a good crowd that you will enjoy in his party. He asked me to find out if you are going, David."

"Can't. Mother and I are having dinner in the country on the way to the Chase."

"I told him I wasn't sure, Dad."

"Good, then we can decide what to do after the auction."

Lara knew what he would do. Send her on with Jamal. He would never deprive her of a good party. He would wave her off and go to his club. That was Henry.

He looked his devastatingly handsome self tonight. Powerful and important, and very elegant in his Savile Row dinner jacket and black tie. Henry possessed the male charisma of certain older men that attracts luscious young ladies. Lara had often noticed longing looks cast in her father's direction. She was proud to be his daughter and to walk out with him.

"A neighborhood night out, that's what I'm offering you tonight, Lara. Depriving some young swain of your company doesn't bother me in the least." And, after picking up the Sotheby's catalogue from the table, he offered her his arm. David draped the matching red silk shawl of her dress around her shoulders.

"Gotham's Little Red Riding Hood," he teased. "I don't suppose I have to warn you about all those wolves lying in wait out there."

Lara detected some irritation in Emily's voice. "Lara, don't let your father go berserk at the auction. When he gets his eye on the goodies, he always buys more than I mean him to."

"Good night, you two," called Lara, savoring her mother's pettiness. She knew better: no one ever steamrollered Henry into anything. She threw her mother and brother a kiss, and slipped her arm through her father's. They left the house together, and they walked down their street, turning the corner onto Madison Avenue. They strolled with a leisurely eye on the shop windows, and watched the Upper East Side poseurs and were watched by them. It felt good to be on Henry's arm.

He always emanated that manly, reassuring charm that goes with the good looks, breeding, and megamoney of a sophisticated older man. Both men and women felt his allure. Lara had always been attracted to him, first as a father and then as a man. He was the role model for the person she could be happy with, yet had never yet encountered.

They passed the famous auction house, whose illumination proclaimed its readiness for one of its more prestigious sales. A few blocks further down and around the corner was a restaurant she had not seen before. She was surprised when Henry led her to the door. It was not like him to dine in a small restaurant which, if not exactly unknown, was unfamiliar to Henry and Lara's social set. She had expected La Cote Basque, the Carlyle, the Oak Room at the Plaza. There was a host of smart restaurants he frequented.

The inside of the restaurant was discreet, with a certain *charme ordinaire*. It was immediately obvious to Lara that the maitre d' knew Henry Stanton. The man ushered them to a table, where Lara was seated on the velvet, horseshoe-shaped, high-backed banquette. It gave an impression of being boothlike and private. Henry faced her from a well-upholstered armchair, across a square table draped in starched white damask.

"Will you let me do the honors? I know the menu. Unless, of course, you fancy something in particular?"

Lara was delighted to let him take over. He ordered Oysters Rockefeller, crabmeat soufflé, salad, Camembert, and large, luscious black grapes.

He smiled at his daughter. "Light, but delicious. We have an auction to sit through. And now to drink. What do you think, Lara?"

"Champagne—Roederer Cristal."

Immediate parental approval.

"This restaurant is rather a find, Dad. Completely unpretentious. I had no idea it was here, yet I must have passed it dozens of times. You surprise me, though. This is not your usual sort of place."

"Well, not ordinarily. I come here on occasions when I am dining with someone and want it to be very private. If I want to talk to someone without being distracted by friends and acquaintances."

"Sounds exciting. Has Mother ever been here?"

"Not to my knowledge. It's not exactly the sort of place to which your mother would accord her custom. The food, by the way, is excellent. Not all of it, and not all the time, but what we have ordered will be very good. I do sometimes come here alone just to eat the Oysters Rockefeller."

"You're full of surprises, Dad."

"And so are you. A girl full of surprises, that is. Actually, we're having dinner together tonight for just that reason—Ah, but more about that later. Here come the oysters."

That remark should have told Lara something, but it didn't. It slipped by her in the enthusiasm Henry displayed for the sizzling crustaceans set before him. She was suddenly ravenous and had to admit that, with the perfectly chilled champagne, they were a gourmet's delight. She pronged the last oyster and its chip of bacon and placed it on her tongue. Afterward she sipped the last drop of juice from the shell and replaced it on the white porcelain oyster plate.

Only then, when she and Henry had exhausted the conversational potential of a plate of oysters and a fine bottle of champagne, did Lara realize there was more to the evening than just father and daughter out together. "What are we doing here besides eating, Dad?"

A waiter arrived at that moment to refill their glasses, another to whisk away the plates. "I think another bottle, Peter." Henry waited for the man to disappear before he answered her.

"We are here, Lara, because of a father's love for his daughter. This evening is happening because I sense an unhappiness in you that disturbs me. Yes, I think that's what this is all about. And because I want to talk to you about it. There is no reason why you should be unhappy—or, more to the point, why you should permit yourself to be unhappy. I love you too much to allow that. Lara, you are going to have to do something about it."

She had prided herself on her ability to maintain the facade of a happy-go-lucky deb while secretly prolonging her not-always-happy romance. She was shattered now to think that Henry had seen through it. How many others knew? She suddenly felt psychologically naked, exposed to the world's gaze. Her deepest, darkest self had been surveyed and evaluated. She hardly knew what to do with herself as she sat opposite her father. She had to take a deep breath to hold back tears. She felt pained to have been revealed as a fraud, yet relieved that she no longer had to be one. But, of all people, her father to broach the subject of the charade of her life! If it had to be, she would have preferred Max or David. She could have handled that. But her father? No one handled Henry. How could she rationalize her life or her unhappiness to him?

She had been listening, eyes lowered to avoid his while she sought her bearings. She was overwhelmed that her father should admit to her that he cared enough about her to see past the surface of her life. That he loved her enough to step out of character, to deal directly with her and whatever her problem was, both surprised and flattered her. This time he was not sending in a trustee, a son, a nanny, or any other family retainer to sort her out. Nor was he offering her the distraction of a new boat, a horse, a plane, a holiday. He was confronting his love for her, his raw need to do the best for her.

Some minutes went by in silence, while both father and daughter composed themselves. When Lara felt calm enough, she took courage and gazed directly into her father's eyes. She was aware at once that Henry, though in control, was himself quite uneasy about the confrontation, but determined to press forward. How much did he really know? Was it no more than a guess that she was unhappy? She knew the way her father worked, he would have had to have had facts. He would never confront her on a mere impression. She was on the hot spot, and began to squirm on the banquette, waiting for him to say something. His changing the subject came as a momentary relief.

"I am quite looking forward to the auction this evening. There are wonderful things coming up. I think my collection of old master drawings might benefit enormously from this night." The glossy catalogue lay open. "I covet this Rembrandt drawing." He spoke at length about his passion for acquiring works of art, and then teased her, "I am quite shocked at how long it takes my children to come to terms with their ignorance, and you are no exception, Lara. I take heart, though. They have all proven late developers, and I have no doubt so will you."

She thumbed through the catalogue and opted for a securely prestigious name or two. "Are you after the Raphael or the Caravaggio? If I were not such an ignoramus, I think I could put up with one of those in my collection. If I had a collection, that is."

"Touché," her father said, not at all displeased to be put in his place. "There is hope for you yet, my girl."

The soufflé arrived. It was delicious. A sliver of crabmeat clung to Lara's bottom lip. Henry leaned forward to remove it with his napkin. Gazing intently into her eyes, he said, "Your mother says you choose the wrong men, and that's why you are unhappy."

"Dad!"

"Don't be irritated. I told you we were here to have a talk about you. And we *are* going to have this conversation. I don't mean to embarrass you, Lara. Let's both of us put embarrassment aside, and maybe we can sort out a few things that might be helpful. Don't look so angry with me. It wasn't me who said men were your problem, your mother did.''

"I do not choose the wrong men! Mother doesn't know what she's talking about.''

"One thing about your mother, Lara: irritating as she can be at times, she is a wily and observant woman. She does not have her head buried in the sand all the time—only when it suits her. And her hunches are not always off-center.''

"Mother can be such a bitch.''

"Yes, we all allow her that. But I doubt she was being merely bitchy in this instance.''

"Forty-two years! Why didn't you leave her? You have so little in common?''

"Lara, I would hardly say five children, four grandchildren, and an often-happy married life add up to nothing in common. Respect, admiration, love even, for the family and the life she has run so well for us all, have something to do with it, as has duty. I understand that and so does your mother. And we have an understanding about the separate lives we lead outside our marriage. You don't just walk away from that, throw away a family. You learn to accommodate your differences with a life that is your own, and live it with discretion. And anyway, your mother remains the most important woman in my life. I should have thought you realized that. Now, more to the point, is your mother right? Have you become involved with a man who is consuming your life? Is that what is confusing you and making you lose your direction?''

Lara remained silent. Her father continued to eat his soufflé and signaled the waiter to refill their glasses. And then very calmly, he said, ''Lara, this conversation is not going to go away. Let me make it easier for you. You are not really having a very good time of it, are you?''

"No.''

"And do you agree that you feel that you have lost direction in your life and are confused as to what to do about it?''

"How did you know, Dad? Is it that obvious?''

"No, darling girl. Now don't fret, it is not that obvious, I promise you. It took me a long time, maybe too long, to realize you were in trouble. Once I'd sensed that you were, I watched you for weeks to make sure I was right, to confirm it. You have a very good cover. Maybe too good for your own well-being.''

"How did you know?''

"We have all been there sometime in our lives, Lara. Even your father.''

"Oh, Dad.''

It was relief that she could talk to him that he detected in her voice, so that he knew he had done well to come to her aid. "Lara, I don't happen to agree with your mother. For the most part I like the sort of men you choose. At least the ones you have brought home to Cannonberry Chase, or the men I have seen you with on occasion. But then I look upon them as men. Your mother looks at every man you are with as a potential husband. And maybe in that she is right.''

"Mother! She always says she disapproves of the men I go with. Then when she meets them, she lays on the charm, and comes on the grande dame with them. She plays the coquette much more than I do, Dad, and then crosses them off her list—unless, of course, they were on it to begin with. She demands all their attention—and gets it, I might add. Finds them utterly charming, takes in the flowers they send—and then damns them behind my back, and me for choosing them. It really is too much. She's always directing the traffic in our lives, and frankly I'm fed up with it. Now, Dad, can we please drop the subject? I know what I must do.''

"But you can't do it.''

She hesitated. He pressed her. "Can you?''

"No.''

"Forget your mother, she has no idea we are having this conversation. This is between you and me, Lara. What is said here tonight will go no further. What is it you must do but can't?''

"Leave the man I am in love with.''

"Ah, in love. In love, or infatuated?''

"I can't tell any more.''

"Let's talk about it, Lara. I don't need to know who your lover is. I am only here to help you out of your situation, if I can. Understood?''

"Understood.''

Henry felt relieved. At least she was resigned to talking about the brute she was involved with. "Let's try again for a clearer picture of what's going on. Is it love, Lara, or infatuation? Or maybe it's just sexual?''

''It's a combination of all those things.''

''And him—what is it for him?''

''The same. Or at least that's what he says.''

''Two people with the same intense feelings for each other? Then why don't we know about it?''

''He demands we keep the affair a deep secret.''

''Ah. And you would prefer it out in the open?''

''Yes. It's a dark—I almost said dirty—affair. And I hate the secrecy. I despise the hypocrisy.''

''What else do you hate about the affair that makes you so unhappy?''

''That I have no control over it, over him, over myself even. And as a result, as you so aptly put it, I have lost direction in my life. I hate that and myself.''

''And you can't do anything about this appalling situation? You can't leave him because you are afraid to lose him?''

''How did you know that?''

''I'm afraid it's not very original. It rather goes with the territory. And you may not believe this, but it is nonetheless true: I've been there myself. Anyone who has been a passionate sensualist has been there one time or another. Only some of us recognize the futility of such an affair sooner than others, and leave because it is not in our nature to remain in an abusive relationship.''

Lara tried to interrupt in defense of herself, but Henry held up his hand to silence her. ''No, please, let me continue. One can be abused in many ways. It doesn't have to be physical, but abuse is abuse . . . and usually does lead to the physical. Beside the sexual attraction.'' He saw a blush color her cheeks and made an attempt to put her at ease. ''No need to feel embarrassed about such a thing, Lara. We are two adults talking about life, and sex is a part of any life. How else can a man hold a beautiful, spirited young girl like you? Sex is a powerful weapon.''

''So is love. He says he loves me, and needs me.''

''And if you add those two things to an exciting, erotic life—and offer them to an impressionable young girl—a man can not only control her but also destroy her. You are in trouble, my dear girl. Perhaps deep trouble.''

''I know. But I will leave him. I just need a little more time.''

''How long have you been telling yourself that?''

She looked away, a tear lodged in the corner of her eye. She sighed. Barely above a whisper, she said, ''I'm afraid of never feeling in my whole life as I feel with him.''

''Oh, my dear girl, that's youth and inexperience speaking. I promise you, you will, and even better. You are only at the beginning of your life and loves, Lara. I do really think you must accept that your time has run out with this man. The longer you remain in this relationship, the longer it is going to take you to get over it. Why not concentrate on that . . . and how much damage has already been done to you?''

Lara looked frightened when she turned back to face her father. ''Dad, promise me you'll do nothing about this. I couldn't bear it if you had to bail me out of this affair. I must work this out myself—or I will never be free of him. I know enough about myself to know that.''

''You are asking a great deal, Lara.''

''Only for you to trust me to do what's right.''

Henry saw the slight tremble in Lara's lower lip, heard the anxiety in her voice, and recognized determination in her eyes. He had not seen that look for a very long time. He was wise enough to know that the decision he made here and now would affect Lara for the rest of her life. He would not ruin his favorite child's chances. He believed that beneath that one small chink of vulnerability was a woman of steel. He believed her to be more like himself than any of his other children, and he loved her for that as much as for any of her other qualities.

''I trust you to deal with it. Just remember, I'm here for you if you need me. You will win through. It's all part of growing up and finding out who you are.''

And, for the first time since returning to Jamal on the night of his party, Lara knew that she would. In an hour's chat over a meal, her father restored the confidence that Jamal had been systematically undermining with his paltry erotic games.

Henry and Lara made no mention of her problem again, not that evening, not ever. Instead, he eased the tension with enticing descriptions of old master drawings and fired her with a sense of the importance of the auction they were about to attend. Between them they gently reanimated the spirit of their meal together.

At Sotheby's they shook the hands of numerous people they knew and exchanged elegant verbal trivia. Just before they took their seats in the auction room, Lara looked at her father and said, ''I am, after all, not that ignorant, Pa.''

Henry smiled. When had his daughter last called him ''Pa''? He sensed something of her former sparkle returning. Perhaps he needn't worry about her problem any longer.

''At the viewing the other day, I fell in love with the Duccio. It's mine; I have made up my mind to that, so please don't bid against me.''

Henry felt more proud of Lara at that moment than he had for a long time. His spoiled, beautiful angel. Fears once briefly entertained that she might be a dark or fallen angel now evaporated. His child was surely going to take her place in the bright, angelic courts. She was the dark horse of all his children, the one that would come from the back of the field to win. He knew that now, for sure, and maybe in his heart he always had.

Chapter 15

A stark, unnatural silence. The hush of several hundred people holding their breath. A tension electric with anticipation. Then the quick, sharp blow of the wooden gavel cracked the quiet. "And again, sold to the lady in red for seven hundred thousand dollars," announced the auctioneer.

The room released its collective breath. Hands came together in applause. There was a buzz of chatter, alive with the excitement of the crowd who were rising from chairs, milling about, attempting to descend from the adrenaline high the sale had induced. Handshakes and whispers among the dealers, the winners and the losers, the curious and the societymongers. The telephonists who had taken bids from around the world slumped back in relief at a job well done for the auction house. They conferred busily, and the auctioneer mouthed thanks to his audience for their participation.

Who is she? Who is she buying for? Never saw her around. How did she crash in on the bidding? Who's her dealer? She some kind of a dealer? The room simmered with questions about the young slip of a thing who had so shrewdly played off the other bidders for what she wanted, until her determination and dollars wore them down. Some said, "She's a ringer for Henry Stanton. I happen to know he wanted that Botticelli. He would never let it go."

"You're kidding. Did you get a look at Stanton's face? He's as surprised at that broad bringing it off as we are."

"She's with Henry, but who is she? Why didn't he bid against her?"

One of the women in the small group began to laugh. "He wouldn't, would he, if she were family?"

That silenced the museum director, who was feeling the loss more than most. He, too, had made a play for the drawing. The woman enjoyed telling them, "That's Lara Stanton. More like Henry, I think, than Emily Stanton. A nice enough girl, and charming, but I heard she was rather frivolous. Not interested in anything but the deb life. But I guess that bit of gossip has been knocked on the head."

By now there was a cluster around Henry and Lara, the big buyers of the sale. There were congratulations and a great deal of fuss over the Stanton purchases, and much discussion of how the auction went. The losers appeared disgruntled, or as Henry suggested to Lara on the way into the reception hall, "Not serious collectors, I think. Fancy approaching me to sell for a profit! Art is big business. Hardly a gentleman's game anymore. Anyone who knows us knows the Stantons buy but never sell. It's a good policy to remember, Lara. Swap, maybe. Donations to the better institutions can be rewarding. But never sell."

"Point taken, Pa." There was a sparkle in her eye as she quipped, "There's nothing like a shopping spree to ease a girl's anxieties."

Henry began to laugh. Lara poked him in the ribs with her elbow, which prolonged his amusement. Then she took him by the hand and whispered, "I am having the best time I've had in ages. The adrenaline is flowing. You never told me what a turn-on an auction can be when you're in the bidding, Pa. That old competitive nature you bred in us Stantons has done its stuff yet again. I knew if I was going to get what I was after I had to stay in there, especially when the heat was on with several people in the bidding. To outbid those guys and acquire a great work of art—it's like winning the America's Cup. I think I could really get into this art game."

"Yes, darling, but can you afford to make a habit of this?"

"I don't know. I'll have to talk to Harland about that, won't I?"

"You will if tonight is anything to go by. A Duccio, the Caravaggio, a Leonardo, and a Botticelli: You don't do things by halves, my girl."

"You, neither, Pa. Mother will be furious. What are you go-ing to tell her?''

They were in the reception hall. He took two glasses of cham-pagne from the tray carried by a red-jacketed waiter and handed Lara one. ''That I have a very clever daughter, with an unex-pectedly good eye, in whom I have every confidence.''

Both knew to what he was referring. They clinked the rims of their glasses together in a toast. Once made, the reference was quickly taken and as quickly forgotten. Lara said, ''No, I mean about your extravagance, not mine.''

''Oh, I know how to silence your mother. She can be bribed with a charity concert. It works every time.'' They both began to laugh again.

They were surrounded by art lovers who insisted on shaking Lara's hand and her father's. Strangers never met before, un-likely to be encountered again, were congratulating them upon owning a masterpiece. Lara found that part of her evening at the auction odd, but fun. Nevertheless she did wonder what it was all about. She had bought the drawings because of some inner desire to continue experiencing the bond she felt with the figures in them. The masterful beauty that they emanated af-fected her so deeply she never wanted to have to let it go. There was a magic and power and timelessness about these great works of art that enveloped her. She felt eternity in them, and love, and could not relinquish the feeling.

Lara sensed Jamal's presence. She felt a shiver of excitement just knowing that he was somewhere in the room. He was watch-ing her. She perceived his admiring glance and her already joy-ful heart knew yet more delight. She glanced at her father, in animated conversation with two men. At that moment she felt no fear, no guilt about the petty lies and deceits she had per-petrated in the name of love. She knew, after the conversation she had had with her father earlier, he would understand what had driven her to use them. Her father's trust, that she had thought lost to her, was now restored—and had renewed a sense of self that could never again be shaken.

She felt an overwhelming desire to be with Jamal, in flagrant sexual communication with him. She made no excuses to herself for her sexual appetite. She knew she would not allow herself to be unhappy over their relationship now. Trust, she thought, is a powerful weapon against defeat. And at that moment she loved Henry more for what he had so generously given her than she ever had before.

It was not at all difficult for Jamal to find Lara in the sea of black ties and expensive dinner jackets, glittering dresses, and hundred-dollar hairdo's. She glowed like some bright star. Her youth, that fetching combination of sensuality and innocent Aryan beauty, shone like neon. Everyone else was consigned to the shadows. There was her provocative red dress: its message that of an aristocrat thumbing its nose at the conservative establishment. Jamal caught in her, once again, that special spark that had flashed in her since childhood. Anxiety that it had been extinguished left him.

He greeted several people distractedly as he struggled through the crowd, never taking his eyes off this girl-woman, the sensualist, the strangely powerful yet vulnerable creature who had the ability to offer him more than most women. How often she seemed to challenge him to force her into total submission. For him she was still a game that he was always on the brink of winning. Tonight perhaps?

He saw Henry, the all-powerful Henry. The gentleman par excellence, manipulator of so many aspects of so many lives. Some close to him, and some he would never see or hear of. Jamal had always loved and respected Henry, as a man and the father of his best friend. And he was not immune to Henry's wealth or his mastery of power and influence. He had always wanted to belong in some way to the Stanton clan, but had never seen Lara as his way into it. Any hint of that would have entailed ostracism by his best friends. Such entree into their society as he enjoyed would have been closed to him. Yet what drove Jamal to pursue his dangerous erotic relationship with Lara? Could he simply neutralize his guilt at deceiving this man he so admired, and his family?

Jamal knew that he was corrupting Henry's most precious possession. From passion, he told himself, his own and Lara's. Yet, she was safer with him than with any other man she might play erotic games with. A fortune hunter might have exploited her sensual nature, exposed it to the world, while Jamal had gone to great lengths to keep it secret. Henry himself could have done no more in Jamal's position, and Henry had earned his reputation as a hard-liner when he wanted something, whether a sporting trophy or a financial triumph, his art collections or his most private affairs.

Jamal saw Henry place an arm around Lara's shoulder. A glance passed between father and daughter. How alike they were; he had never realized that before. And he saw in this vulnerable young woman, who was sexually dependent on him, a strength more fierce than he had imagined. It excited him enormously, knowing that he had a power over her that no other man wielded. She was indeed a prize. He redoubled his efforts to reach her.

He placed the key in the latch and turned it. The door clicked open, then he faced her. His kiss was tender and sweet. He licked her lips with the tip of his tongue and surprised her when he swept her up off the stone step and into his arms, to carry her over the threshold.

He conveyed her into the ground-floor sitting room and set her down in front of the open fire. He walked around the room, putting out all the lights except one in the far corner. Then he returned to Lara and slid the red silk shawl from her shoulders. He raised her hand and lowered his lips to her fingers, kissing them, then licking the palm of her hand. He could feel her dissolving under his touch.

In the semidarkness of a room flickering with firelight, she looked, if possible, even more sensuous. So feminine, so delectable for a man with the sexual appetite of Jamal. He walked around her once, and then a second time. She almost felt her clothes peel away under the penetrating gaze. She imagined the frenzy of his mind, conjuring up sexual delights to please her, and tried to hide the shiver of excitement she felt. He could always prime her with those eyes, the touch of his lips, the very feel of his skin against hers. This was to be *her* night. Everything would be done for *her* sexual pleasure. She could tell that by the way Jamal all but sniffed around her. Like some sleek beast that stalks his prey until she is ready to receive him on his terms, he knew with what looks to transfix her, what things to say and do to prime her for what was to come. And she waited, always holding back, holding back for as long as she could.

He was the shrewdest of seducers. He well knew the longer she held back, the further she slipped under his spell—and the stronger grew her desire to escape into sexual nirvana. Once lost in that outer place, so far from the reality of life and of herself, she would do anything, submit to anything, to remain there for as long as possible. That was where Lara Stanton imagined she felt love and peace, and more excitement for life than anywhere else. At those times, with Jamal, each orgasm was like a little death. She was as if chained to a cycle of death and rebirth in her seemingly endless stream of orgasms.

"Thirsty?"

She could hardly utter, and so nodded assent.

"Good. I have a lovely wine for us." He smiled, and, running his hands down her arms, kissed her once more on the lips. He felt them part, slid his tongue between them and kissed her again. He walked behind her to lavish a kiss on her naked back.

It was by no means a one-sided thing with Lara and Jamal. The taste of her flesh on his lips was like an aphrodisiac. He nibbled at her flesh and slid his hands over the strong, bare back exposed to the waist. His hands reached under the silk and found the swell of her breasts. He cupped them in his hands and felt her yield that little bit more to him. He sensed she was already moist between her legs. But her banded dress, her clinging skirt, prevented his delight in confirming that.

Lara, her eyes closed now, put her hands over his, the red silk separating them. She tried to move his hands to her nipples that ached for his touch. He kissed her on the back of the neck, but instead of responding to her pressure, discreetly avoided it, caressing the swell of the breasts with a teasing tenderness that was simply not enough for her. He skimmed his hands across her flesh, to the silk of her dress, and through it caressed her hips. He pushed tight up against her, allowing her to feel the rigid swelling in his trousers. He pressed it to the cheeks of her bottom, and then whispered in her ear, "The wine."

He brought the glasses, charged with the perfect Margaux, whose color in the firelight was all garnets and rubies. Their eyes met, and he recognized that hunger in hers that so excited him. He stepped back a few paces and held the glass out to her. "Come."

He sat down on the white damask-covered Chippendale settee. Lara didn't move. She couldn't. She stood as if glued to the spot. Her knees felt like jelly, and she had come so copiously she was afraid to take a step for fear she would stain her dress and he would know how much she wanted him. She didn't have to say anything. He knew. They had, after all, been there before, many times. She had confirmed his power over her, and that was all he wanted.

He went to her and handed her the glass. He was aware of the slight trembling of her hand as she raised the glass to her lips. "A Botticelli, a Caravaggio, a Leonardo, and me. I would say you are having quite a night."

That eased the tension. She drank some of the superb wine before answering. "Can you compete?"

"I've only just begun."

"I hope so."

That was another thing he found exciting about her. When it came to sex, she was usually honest, unashamedly so. He lifted the empty glass from her hand, put it beside his on the mantel. Then he took her in his arms, held her and kissed her deeply, with great passion. He whispered in her ear: "How wet are you? How ready are you for me? Tell me how much you want me. I am crazy to take you. To feel you run with pleasure under the influence of my cock, my tongue. To feel, with my fingers deep inside you, the silky-smooth syrup of your lust for me."

He registered the change in her breathing as he unbuttoned the cuff of her sleeve to kiss her waist. He found the fastening at the back of her neck. She watched him, relishing every nuance of his slow, sensuous way of undressing her. She retrieved her glass and finished the wine. He kissed her lips. Her taste mingled with that of vintage claret. He eased her dress off her arms and let the blouse fall down around her waist and over her hips. He stood back, the better to admire the ripeness of Lara.

"You didn't answer me. You don't have to. I know where you are."

He managed the hooks at the waist and let the red dress slip down off her hips to the carpet. She had worn nothing under the red silk, not a stitch. That thin red wrapping apart, she had come undressed, ready to be taken by him where and when he wanted. It had been his sexual demand, made long ago, and she had always answered it. Her stockings were held high up on her thighs by lacy elasticized garters. She stood there, shamelessly ready to submit to this man, seemingly a willing victim, a young

woman sexually molded to please men. She knew better, and
so did Jamal. Willing, yes. Sexually molded to please men, not
wholly true. Molded by sensuous men to enjoy her own sexual
appetites would be more the truth of it.

Jamal could make each seduction of Lara like the first for her.
He could create in her the sense that she pleased him beyond all
else on earth. That she was the most erotic woman he had ever
known. There were his eyes, his words of promise of what was
to come, the overwhelming need he showed to master her sexually. That is erotic power for many women. It was for Lara,
and it generated in her a yearning to be touched by him. No,
much more than touched, to be penetrated, possessed, to be
manhandled by him for the delight of both. Caresses, yes, but
she demanded violent passion, too. The kind where two people
can lose themselves and let the erotic take over and transport
them beyond ecstasy.

And sex with Jamal was to lose herself in orgasm. It was to
float out on a stream of erotic lovemaking that accepted no
bounds. The stream of orgasms this extraordinary lover could
induce in her allowed her a sexual submissiveness that she had
enjoyed with no other lover. The exception had been Sam, that
one night on the island. With Jamal, Lara's body submitted
naturally to anything that would keep her chain of orgasms coming, until she was faint with exhaustion. Only a woman who had
complete trust in her lover, as Lara had in Jamal, could give
herself up to him, and reap from her submission that very special
ecstasy that intense sex promises. Every sexual experience with
Jamal was searing bliss.

It meant becoming merely an open vessel, ready to receive,
or being fine-tuned for the playful touch of such a master. The
reward was nothing more than the perfect bliss of orgasm. What
woman would give that up? Nothing that Jamal offered or demanded for their pleasure surprised her. At times in their sexual
relationship all was geared to giving him pleasure. Those times
featured more bizarre sexual games. But tonight, everything
sexual was for Lara. Everything to induce from her longer, more
violent orgasms. Multiple orgasms. He nourished his lust upon
her comings. Never could she seem to come enough to please
him. He would often tell her how he wished she could swim in
her come, he could drink it as from a fountain, bathe in it. When

it was like that for them, before the night was over he enjoyed
his lust as much as Lara enjoyed hers.

There was a discreet knock at the door. Jamal showed no
disquiet. A man entered. ''I told you I had a surprise for you.
Someone who has admired you for a very long time, who wants
to be with you. I promise you . . . you will not be disappointed.''

Jamal kissed her. Lara, no longer Lara, but a woman well
into the search for some ultimate sexual experience, accepted
the man without a word of protest, only open arms. If it had
been for her own sexual delight that would have been acceptable,
but it wasn't just that. It was the excitement she saw in her lover's
face, the pleasure she knew he derived from sex with her and
another man. The three gave their bodies passionately to their
flagrant intercourse. They sought nothing else but giving the
best sex. It was a joyous encounter.

The blond Russian stranger made himself known to her as
Misha. Within minutes he held her in his arms, kissed and caressed her. He was always touching her, arranging her for Jamal's pleasure, and Jamal entered her and fucked her in long,
slow thrusts, while Misha kissed Lara and whispered blandish-
ments to her. At other times it was Jamal who held Lara in his
arms, while the handsome, virile young Russian, so massively
endowed, took Jamal's place. She came for herself, and for Jamal and Misha, and for Eros and all that god had to offer. For
a few hours sex was an autonomous world where nothing else
existed. There came a point in their erotic tryst when they fucked
as one body, one heart, one soul. The ultimate sexual experience. A point, it seemed, of no return.

When she awakened, the glorious White Russian was gone.
Jamal and she bathed together in his black marble sunken bath.
They lay in each other's arms and sponged each other with the
steaming hot, freesia-scented water. They talked about their
night of sex. He always liked talking about their erotic performances. Lara didn't mind. In some odd way, talking about their
sexual excesses took away the stigma of dirtiness, the depravity
their secret liaisons seemed to imply. It legitimized her sexual
appetite, confirmed its naturalness, which she liked. And there
was no other man in the world she could be so free with. Once
she had thought that about Sam. She had been wrong.

Afterward breakfast with Jamal in the glass cage on the roof terrace of the Fifty-third Street house. The sun streamed in. At that moment life seemed to Lara to be incredibly rich and beautiful. Freshly squeezed peach juice and champagne, omelettes filled with wild mushrooms, hot black coffee and buttered toast, kiwifruit preserve and strawberry jam kindled her palate. Ravenous, she ate with gusto, and was unaware of Jamal watching her, until he said, "You seem different. I sensed it when I picked you up at Sotheby's last night. You were standing with Henry. I saw you from a distance, and knew even then that some subtle change had happened. I have that same feeling now."

"Different *better*, or different *worse*?"

"Oh, most definitely different *better*." He raised her hand and held it, then lowered his lips to kiss it. "You were incredible last night. You always are, but somehow last night, more so." He replaced her hand in her lap and returned to his breakfast. "I don't think I ever thank you enough for being you. And with me. Thanks for last night; you were memorable."

She said it without thinking: "You can thank me by giving up this idea that what we have together has to be kept a deep, dark secret. A trashy, dirty affair. Marry me."

He kissed her on the cheek once more, ignored her suggestion and, still laughing, returned to his omelette.

"God, that was a condescending, shitty reaction to a serious proposal."

He looked at her, and could see in her eyes that this was something more than her customary charming anxiety about their relationship. Surprised, he said, "I told you it would come to this. You know I am not the marrying kind, the very reason we must keep our sex life a secret. The ring on the finger and instant hate, that would be the name of that game." He began to laugh. "One woman in my life? No, never. Not my kind of arithmetic. The very idea is unthinkable. I always warned you that one day you would demand monogamy and all the trimmings. You're that kind of girl. But you have proposed to the wrong guy."

"Then I'll leave you."

"Ah, then this is it?" He laughed at her—and was surprised yet again by how calm she was. She was playing with him. He knew she wasn't serious. There had to be the hint of a smile at the corners of her mouth. And her eyes sparkled in a half-coquettish, half-teasing manner. The tormented Lara of the last few months seemed nowhere in sight. Something had changed, and the change intrigued him.

He leaned in toward her and adjusted her robe, where it fell open to show a hint of breast. "And give up what we had together last night? No, I don't think so. A very childish idea. What we have is irreplaceable, and you are not a girl who deprives herself."

"I will, you know."

"Before or after another cup of coffee?" He refilled her cup.

She leaned back in her chair and thrust her hands into the pockets of his Turnbull & Asser, red-and-white-polka-dot silk robe, which she was wearing. It fell open and showed some naked thigh. She adjusted the robe. He knew she wore nothing under it. The thought of her flesh stirred his lust again. Instead he teased her by opening his own silk moiré robe. And this time it was she who draped the powder blue silk over him to cover his erection. She who tied the belt with a double knot and adjusted the brown velvet lapels. "You're cuntteasing me again, Jamal. And that, at this moment, is a cheap shot."

He found her behavior amusing. But when she tried to continue, he put up his hand to silence her. "One more word about it and I'll sweep these dishes off this table, rip open that robe, and fuck you right here for all the neighbors to see. I'll eat my breakfast from your cunt, Lara, and prove to you, yet again, that you can't give me up."

He broke off a piece of croissant, buttered it and spooned strawberry jam over it, then fed it to her. They both began to laugh, more delighted with the idea than they dared to admit. Lara was serious, but Jamal didn't believe her. She herself was surprised to find herself less disturbed by his reaction than she had expected to be. He was quite right: some fundamental change had taken hold in her that she herself could not understand. She could only think that it had come about because of Henry and their evening together. The very idea that she should have to lie to her father one more time because of a love affair didn't bear thinking about. She knew she could never do that again. Henry's love, his trust in her, would not allow it.

There was a commotion of some sort going on somewhere in

the house. Some minutes later Jamal's manservant Mulai entered the solarium and there was an exchange in Arabic, and then in English. There was a note of annoyance in Jamal's voice when he told the man, "Show her into the second-floor sitting room."

The interruption was timely for Lara. It broke into the intimacy that was developing between her and Jamal, overshadowing what was for her a serious question: their future. It furnished her with a much-needed pause in which to regain her resolve to deal with him on terms other than those he had in mind for them. She rose from her chair.

"I have to be going."

Together, hand in hand, they walked down the winding stairs, from the roof terrace to the guest room, where Lara kept several articles of daytime clothing. To walk through the streets of Manhattan on a bright sunny day in a cardinal-red cocktail dress would not have enhanced her reputation.

Parting after a night such as they had spent together was always a problem for her. She handled it badly most of the time. But today Jamal sensed an indifference in Lara. Where were the trembling lower lip, the tears that usually lodged in the corner of her eyes? The petulant, "You're a *pig* to send me away like this." The *"Cochon!"*? The turn on her heel and the dash from the house? The phone call from the first available booth, the different variety of tears, the "I'm sorry. You're not a pig— forgive me. Tonight? I can make myself free." The reassuring pattern had been disturbed.

Relieved as he was not to have to go through that same old performance, he did wonder what exactly this dramatic change signaled. And what had prompted it?

Lara's lack of curiosity about the commotion in the house and the woman sent to the second-floor sitting room was a surprise. Previously the mere mention of another woman in his life had stirred that streak of jealousy that could take her over and turn her into a harridan.

He sat down on the edge of the bed and watched her choose a pair of jeans, a red polo neck, silk knit sweater, and pair of white sneakers. She looked so young, so fresh in the dappled sunlight dancing through the window behind her. She charmed him with her youth and vulnerability, her letting him mold her into whatever he wanted her to be at any given moment.

She sensed his eyes upon her and turned from the armoire to face him. She felt a slackening of her resolve to change their lives or leave him. She was lucky to be there with him at all. He had caught her off-guard, as he sometimes did, with his physical beauty. She knew no other man who possessed so powerful a male radiance, or who affected her with his looks the way Jamal did. She wanted to touch his hair, thick, black, and silky, always worn a little too long, as if he were due for a haircut that very day. His skin was bursting with health and vigor, bronze and taut over a frame that could have served as a model for any museum sculpture. That wonderful bony head with its high cheekbones, noble nose, and powerful chin. A man's eyes, yet so eloquent, so dark and sultry, with lashes thick and long, perfect for melting down his victims' resistance. The muscled but slender neck and wide shoulders. The strong, perfect torso and slender, athletic body. How could she live without him?

She took a few steps toward him, unable to drag her eyes from the sharp, intelligent face, the sensuous lips that knew how to make love to her as no other man's ever had. And what of his own special male scent that she found irresistible? She felt an impulse to touch him, place her lips upon his, to sit in his lap and be held in his arms. She wanted to be embraced by all that male beauty. Simply to dissolve into him, always, for the rest of her life—was that asking so much?

Jamal could feel her yield to him. The light in her eyes changed. He could see her surrendering to a desperation that was familiar to him now. He had not realized before that he might suffer if he lacked it. It gave an edge to their relationship that excited him. He was tempted to reach out and take her hands in his and kiss them. He resisted. Their time together was over. Instead he handed her the jeans she had placed on the bed next to him.

The pattern was resuming. Dismissal till he next wanted her. She took them from him. "Do I have to beg you? Grovel? Why do you do this to me?" She disrobed.

He liked to watch her. The way she moved while she dressed and undressed. The way she bent over to wiggle her naked young flesh into tight blue jeans. Now she was so close that he could reach out and pull her between his legs by the loops in the waistband. He caressed her flesh with his hands for several seconds before he zipped up the fly. "My touch of Venus!" he quipped. His hands on her hips, he rocked her gently, savoring the movement of her breasts.

"Yes, go ahead, beg." There was a hardness in his voice that had not been present seconds before. She suddenly felt as if she weren't there. Only her body and his lust seemed to have significance. He seemed transfixed by the large, dark nimbuses of her breasts. It excited her, so that her nipples performed, became erect.

"The most depraved thing about you, Lara, is not your cunt and what you can do with it, but your tits and what I can make you do when they respond to me."

He took the nipples between his fingers, rolling and squeezing them. Then he tanalized her with his tongue upon them. He felt her lean in to him.

"Well?"

Lara could say nothing. Her body was already eloquent. She was moving, just perceptibly, from the waist down, back and forth, with slow, sensuous, pelvic gyrations, not wholly conscious of what she was doing.

"You want me? Go on, beg. Tell me how much, what you will do to have me."

She couldn't do it. She wanted to. After doing just that for so long, it should have been easy for her. But it wasn't. She wanted him as much as she ever had. But somehow she felt that she had gone as far as she could. She removed his hands from her breasts, bent forward, and kissed him lovingly on the lips.

When she straightened up and gazed into his eyes, the hardness that had been there, the meanness, the sadistic pleasure he was deriving from her, seemed to have vanished. He rose from the bed and was reaching for her, to take her in his arms, when the door suddenly opened.

Lara jumped back, her arms spontaneously folded across her uncovered breasts. The woman who stood framed in the doorway was clearly stunned by the scene she had burst in upon. A menacing stillness enveloped her.

The mere charm of youth was absent, displaced by a ravishing elegance. Her beauty quite took Lara aback. She reached for the red silk sweater and turned her back, pulled it over her head, and covered herself with it.

"Amanda, not a very clever move. And your timing, my dear, is right out."

"Agreed. But you should have come downstairs, Jamal, instead of provoking me. Can't you see how angry I am? I feel so humiliated by all this. But I'm not going to apologize for the intrusion. I want to talk to you, Jamal, and now. Right now."

Lara caught the note of real anger. She grabbed her sneakers and started for the door without a word, trying not to look at the woman.

"Stay!" Jamal took Lara by the arm and pulled her to him. He then propelled her into the wing chair near the fireplace.

"I want to leave, Jamal."

"Quiet! You might learn something from this."

"Let her go, Jamal. She's only a child."

"Not quite, Amanda." His mocking tone said too much. More than Lara wished. "Now, what do you want, Amanda?"

"Not in front of the girl."

"Only in front of the 'girl,' Amanda." It was more a directive than a suggestion.

Lara began to wonder what she was caught up in. She wanted to be anywhere but where she was. The woman carried herself like a movie goddess, dressed in Ralph Lauren. Her anger was as fiery as her red hair. She managed to maintain a degree of poise that seemed superhuman to Lara. For the woman's situation seemed unpromising.

She threw her handbag down on the chaise. "By god, you're a real shit. You're not going to make this easy for me, are you?" She seemed angry enough to hit him.

"No, why should I? Okay, out with it, Amanda. What do you want?"

The woman nervously tossed her auburn hair back from her face. She paced the floor for several steps in front of Jamal. Her fingers, embellished with gems—a large square emerald, surrounded by diamonds, on one finger, a square-cut diamond on another—were raked through her hair. "You know what I want, you bastard. Take me back."

"Why?"

"Because we were happy together."

"That's no longer a reason."

"I can't live without you."

"Neither is that."

Lara could bear it no longer. She rose from the chair, but Jamal shouted, "Lara, I said stay and I meant it." Stunned by his anger, she sat down.

"You don't know what you're saying! You can't mean that, Jamal!"

"But I do."

"Am I nothing to you?"

"Not quite *nothing*. Everyone is *something* to me. Even my—" He broke off. Whatever he was about to say was too cruel even for Jamal to dish out.

"I don't believe you no longer want me."

"I didn't say that. You're still beautiful. You're not a woman to be thrown out of a man's bed. And I like how you're begging to stay in it. I said I wouldn't take you back. Remember, you left. I didn't send you away."

There was a terrible beaten note of resignation in this beautiful and proud woman's asking, "What must I do?"

"Well, the first thing is to apologize to this young girl. And then we'll take it from there."

That was it for Lara. She broke in. "I'm going to be sick," and fled from the room. Jamal caught up with her on the stairs.

"Lara!"

She sat on a stair and hurriedly put on her sneakers. She was trying to think of something to say to him, but suddenly there seemed no point. All she managed was, "I'm out of here."

He sensed that she meant she was out of there for good.

"You'll be back."

"Not on your life. To wind up like that woman?"

"You will, you know."

"If you think that, you don't know me at all, Jamal."

Chapter 16

Relief predominated. Lara had broken out of a spiraling fall. She would not falsify to herself the nature of her relationship with Jamal. That was not her way. In fact, she did quite the opposite. As she fled Jamal and the house on Fifty-third Street, she reviewed ceaselessly in her mind the depths she had fallen to in the name of erotic love. The vision of the beautiful Amanda groveling for readmission to Jamal's bed was the unflattering mirror of her own pleadings.

"Relief is all I feel, nothing more. Just relief that it's over and I'm out of it," was what she told Julia. She did not elaborate, and never mentioned the love affair to her friend. It was a conscious falsehood to block out her real feelings of despair at having to leave him. The transition from that untruth to self-deception meant that she could lie to herself and her friend in good faith, and would be more readily believed.

Whatever the success of the self-deception, however, the rest of the process did not work out too well.

She could cope with her sense of how much sex with him had meant to her, and the emptiness she encountered in living without their secret liaisons. She blocked out her still-strong sexual desire for him, the erotic fantasies that haunted her night after night. She retreated from any sexual relationship with any of the men who pursued her. Most disturbing was her behavior toward Jamal, who remained, as he had always been, a friend to the Stanton family. She showed not a hint of *angoisse*.

Relief, she kept telling herself, was what she was feeling.

That, and nothing else. But retreat was implicit in everything she was doing. She retreated first to Cannonberry Chase and the family. To the horses, her plane, her sailboat. Even in retreat she fought to carry on as normal. She kept most of her diary engagements. On the surface she was still the beautiful, charming, rather nice girl. Sexy, wealthy, altogether eligible.

She had it in mind that, so long as she could carry on with her life, no emotional damage would result from her escapades with Jamal. She couldn't have been more wrong.

She began seeing a lot of Sam again, and the more they saw each other the happier they seemed to be. The comfort and fun she found in the reawakened relationship was by no means one-sided. Once more their relationship eliminated all others for her.

They were playing romantic roles with each other long before either of them realized it. When Lara and Henry sailed his sloop from Cannonberry Chase to Newport, Sam was already there, on the dock, his arms full of flowers. When Lara made her solo flight across the Atlantic, Sam was there with the family to see her off. And again at Charles de Gaulle Airport with Elizabeth, Henry, David, and Max to see her land, and to pin a pair of angel wings, solid with diamonds, on her flying suit.

More and more Sam and Lara seemed, as in the old days, always to be there for each other. It was Lara who surprised him with a birthday party. She was waiting for Sam in Los Angeles when he arrived at the Polo Club to win a silver cup. Together they had long weekends in exotic places. Everyone but them knew they had once again fallen in love. They rekindled the sexual attraction they had for each other hesitantly, remembering the past and trying to ignore it. They became reluctant lovers.

Like all else in their relationship, the sex was comfortable, satisfying, without trauma. Jamal saw it all. He affected disdain for what Lara had settled for. Only once was he prompted to say something about it to her, something that might induce her to resume their secret sexual life. They were dancing at one of Emily's charity events when he made an attempt to penetrate the invisible wall they had erected. It was meant to keep their sexual past out of their present relationship as lifelong friends. He pulled her that little bit closer into his arms. He knew she still wanted him, for her body, reacting to his intent, went rigid. He could

feel her heart race. She missed a step—the slightest of falters—
and he knew she was still his.

That misstep brought her back to herself, gave her the strength
she needed to resist. "Not a word. Not if you want to remain a
friend. I still value our years of friendship, and I know you do,
too. So not a word."

"And are you a clairvoyant, to know what I was going to
say?" he asked, as they continued dancing.

"That part of us is in the past. Leave it there."

She was so emphatic, he knew she was lying. "Just a word
of caution, then. Beware of the rebound. Yes, that old syndrome. Now come with me for a glass of champagne, and I'll
tell you about a horse race. One I want you and Sam to enter.
It should be exciting. David, Henry, and Max have already accepted. It's down the coast of Morocco. One of the events I'm
putting together in honor of my father's seventieth birthday. I
want you all there as my guests."

Lara should have been warned, but she wasn't. She blocked
out her momentary panic that he might seduce her back to his
bed. She could not deal with the thought that she might even
vaguely want him. Instead she listened to Jamal's plans, accepted his invitation, and showed a genuine enthusiasm for the
race and the week of celebrations he was planning.

Had her abrupt departure from Jamal changed Lara? Always
courageous, now perhaps she appeared even more so. She
seemed constantly to be seeking dangerous and thrilling com-
petitions to test her skills. Big risks, higher stakes. She was
more aggressively competitive. Winning, ever a Stanton obsession, was now more exclusively hers. It was Emily who recognized the change. She suggested to her daughter, "To win at
everything is very commendable, dear. But some of your pursuits
. . . I hope you're not turning into one of those thrill-seekers.
David has a streak of that in him. It throws me somewhat, I must
say. But I'm damned if I've ever been able to do anything about
it."

The San Gennaro fair in Little Italy: all color and Sicilian
music. All very "O sole mio," all cannolis and pizza and pasta.
Garishly painted madonnas and plaster saints in tinsel dresses
and lots of crimpeline ruching. Church brass bands with rolling

drums, and bleeding Christs, crowned, crownless, or crowning themselves with thorns. Christs poised ten deep on purple plastic stands, row upon row, offering their divinity for $39.99.

Garlands of plastic flowers in luminescent pink, yellow, ugly blue, were entwined with real flowers and draped in profusion from every stall, cart, booth, and lamppost. The streets were arched with swirls and stars, circles and bows of colored light bulbs. Under them street vendors hawked sausages from the overhead racks of their stalls. Sausages: fat or skinny, long or short, spiced or garlicked. They were on sale by the pound, but people seemed to be buying them by the yard. Fat, pink mortadella, and Parma ham, and prosciutto hung voluptuously between mysterious white balls of cheese: ricotta and provolone, Parmesan and Gorgonzola. The odor of the San Gennaro fair teased the senses, and mingled with the garlic and cured meats, the oregano and chili and peppers roasting over open fires. Cauldrons of bubbling meatballs in tomato sauce, incense and hot candle wax wafting through the open doors of the church. Just-out-of-the-oven Italian breads, vanilla and chocolate, almond and caramelized sugar, pastries and cookies. Cheap ladies' perfumes—violet and carnation and rose—and men's pungent aftershave.

The crush of people was as much a part of the decorations as anything. People surged up and down the streets. They ate, drank, bought and sold, laughed and sang, shouted and muttered. Sleek, dark, and handsome Italians of all ages, shapes, and sizes. Crying babies and out-of-control children screaming for sweets. Mischievous, sullen teenagers by the hundreds, still half responsive to their mother's pinching thumbs. Horny Italian studs eyeing succulent virgins with lowered lids and innocent smiles, secure in their parents' clasp as they pushed through the fair, seeking the right connections for an Italian wedding.

Every restaurant seemed to be decorated for New Year's Eve and was bustling with trade. Any shop whose owner was not on the street was stuffing shopping bags inside as if famine loomed, or a tax on Italian produce was to be levied any minute. People leaned, comfortably propped on bed pillows, from tenement windows, shouting to their friends in the streets.

Once a fair for the families of Little Italy, it had grown into the most colorful and best-fun street party in the city. Before other street parties got the message, it had for years been New York's Little Italy party. They rushed down from all over the city for a taste of something other than New York, other than chic, a taste of ethnic fun and down-to-earthness. They celebrated the Italians in New York, their saints in heaven, and were out for one of the great free, good-time parties of the year.

The high point was when the multicolored saint, garlanded with plastic roses, crinoline-robed, and draped in jewels, was carried through the streets, under a canopy of silk, and velvet-embroidered flowers, and sequined stars, on devout macho shoulders. The horde frantically crowded in on the statue, their ultimate desire to kiss or touch the figure before its return to the niche in the church. The bells clamored, beckoning the procession home.

One of a party of twenty or more friends, all participating in the crush, Lara was swept along in the stream of people. She, Julia, and Sam, with two other friends, separated from the rest of their party, finally broke away into a less-crowded side street. Beer in one hand, hot pizza in the other, they ate as they walked, following some of the crowd down an alley. Alley led into alley, till they found themselves in one that bristled with a marvelous collection of motorbikes and preening, leather-clad bikers.

The bikers, several Hell's Angels and a dozen or more neighborhood Italian boys, obviously had permission from the fair's organizers to show off their bikes. Lara stood with her party, among the other people who had drifted off the street into the alley. But not for long. She abandoned her alfresco meal for a closer look at the bikes.

"Let's go," Sam suggested. Taking her arm, he tried to lead her back into the street.

She laughed. "And miss this? No way, Sam." Her arm through his, she marched him down the line of motorcycles, eyeing them and their owners alike.

"This," a biker said, with languid disdain, slowly, as if to a foreigner or an imbecile, "is . . . a . . . bike. A . . . motorbike." There were sniggers and scattered laughter. A hand moved obscenely.

"Let's go," Sam insisted.

Lara detached herself from his arm, ignoring his suggestion, and said to the biker: "Oh, we're playing jungle games, are we?

You Tarzan, me Jane? Well, I know that game. This . . . Yamaha.'' And she traced the name etched on the glinting belly of the machine. ''Nice . . . pretty.''

The other bikers found that amusing. From inside his black leather, the owner detected an insult. The bikers gathered round Sam and Julia and the others, waiting. Something had to happen. A short distance away, several riders stood, draped casually over their bikes, behind a dark-haired, dramatically handsome man in his early thirties. He stood out from the crowd, casually dressed in gray flannel trousers and a yellow leather jacket, and was leaning against a Harley-Davidson. His velvety eyes never left Lara. She caught only a glimpse of him before she was distracted by the black-leather-clad biker cast as Tarzan.

''Nice? Pretty? Bikes like this one don't get called pretty. Go back uptown with your faggoty friends, girl. Pretty? Lady, that's pig ignorance.''

''Okay, I didn't meant to be insulting. Well, maybe I did. I know bikers can be sensitive about their machines. It's just—It's such a great-looking bike. So slick—all molded form and chrome. It's great! Nice, and pretty, too, like I said. Whereas a Harley is all classical elegance and quality. It's performance. One look at it and—well, we're talking King of the Road.''

''So you say. Molded form and chrome, is it? Harleys fucking classical? And you know shit, lady! Take her home, Charlie. Back where she belongs, with her nice and pretty Vespa scooter. That's if the lady can manage a scooter.'' He flashed his teeth at Sam, who by now was none too pleased with Lara.

''Oh, lordy.'' That was Julia, who knew what was bound to happen, and she was right.

Sam decided to terminate the bike scene. Time to quit the alley before things got out of hand. ''She's a biker, fella. Comes from a family of bikers. And she's far-gone on Harleys. Biased, I should say.''

Sam had just scratched his chance of getting away. The bikers embraced her like an old friend. Ten minutes and she had charmed her black-leathered friend into giving her a ride down the alley. At the bottom of the alley, they spoke for about five minutes. And then she was racing the machine hell-for-leather, back up the bike-lined alley. They were on first-name terms now, and Lara introduced the bikers to her friends.

The biker with the yellow jacket and the velvety eyes asked, "Still just, 'nice and pretty'?"

"Jesus, Mario, what the fuck is this 'nice and pretty' business? Ya know damn well she's beaten most of the bikes here. Ya lookin' for a three-alley race ta prove it?"

"Ya know I don't race on the saint's day."

"Oh, yeah. I forgot."

"Afraid so, Mario. 'Nice and pretty,' a good ride. A great ride as a matter of fact, Carmine, so don't be upset with me, but she just isn't my Harley-Davidson," said Lara, with all the condescension of an aficionado.

"Any Harley?" added Mario. "We have this argument between Carmine and me. We spend a lotta time proving it."

A flirtation was fizzing between Mario and Lara. If her crowd missed it, it was because they were either busy accepting short rides up and down the alley or talking to the bikers. Two guys arrived on roller skates, bearing a huge pot of steaming risotto. Some girls produced a stack of bowls and large spoons. A boy with a keg of beer called up some plastic cups.

"Now, if I had my bike here, Carmine," said Lara, "I'd prove it to you."

"We'll prove it together. Hop on," Mario suggested.

"Mario, you can see I'm okay as a rider. Lend me the bike, I won't harm it. We have a better chance with a single rider." The irresistible Lara Stanton charm, the sensuous looks used calculatingly to get her her ride, silenced the bikers. They watched and listened. Mario let anyone touch his bike? But there was an exciting tension between these two. Mario took Lara's face in his hand, raised the chin, and moved it admiringly back and forth. Silence, while his gaze probed her eyes. Then he jolted her chin to one side. "Go for it, kid. After making love, the thing I like best is winning." The surprise around them was detectable.

"All right! All right! We've got a contest!" The message lit up the alley.

Lara gave him one of her more flirtatious smiles, and then mounted the bike. It felt good. She revved the motor. Her sponsor, Mario, whispered something in her ear. Her laugh was girlish, light, and flirtatious. Someone offered her a helmet. She

declined. "I assume the law is banned from this street?" Her
mild defiance won admiring looks from the bikers.

"You catch on quick for an uptown chick. But y'll have to be
quicker to beat us." Carmine patted his bike lovingly.

The three, Lara, Mario, and Carmine, set the rules of the
three-alley race.

Sam folded his arms across his chest and watched it all. He
had no fear—she would win. But he felt the inevitable male
distaste for the way Mario looked at Lara. He knew her so well.
For her, Mario was a game. But what was she for Mario? Not
a game, he thought. Not one that stopped at racing bikes, anyway.

They were off, cheered on by the crowd lining the alley. She
won. Carmine was good-natured about being beaten. Her own
group was proud. But before they were able to get to her, Mario
had hopped on the back of the bike. Wrapping his arms around
her waist, he told her. *"Go, go, go!"* And once more Lara took
the Harley down the alley.

The crowd watched. It waited. Instead of looping for the return, Lara and Mario disappeared from sight. No one seemed
surprised. The two sets of people mingled and enjoyed the bowls
of risotto offered. Julia, looking concerned, said to one of the
bikers, "I don't know how clever it was for Lara to take off
through the crowded streets. The police are sure to stop them.
And she's been drinking since afternoon."

Carmine heard her and laughed. He went over to her. A
friendly arm around her shoulder, he assured her, "Nobody
picks up Mario Marcachetta. Who'd ya think got these alleys for
us? His father's *'the* father,' like in *The Godfather*, if you up-
towners know what I mean. Not 'the Father in heaven,' that's
for double sure!" And he crossed himself several times.

Laughter greeted the puzzled look on Julia's face. It was obvious that she had no idea that Carmine was trying to tell her
Mario was in the Mob. And not just in with the gangsters, but
his father was a capo.

Half an hour later, the bikers had lost interest, hardly paid
attention to the Harley's return. There was a change though:
Mario was driving, and Lara was sitting pillion. Sam, more
relieved to see Lara than upset with her for leaving him to the
boredom of the bikers, was wanting to get home. She kissed

him on the cheek, and he listened to her enthuse about riding through the crowds. The wonders of the Harley. What a good biker Mario was. Sam was aware that, although Lara had hopped off the back of the bike, she had not left Mario's side. Nor had he seen fit to release her. His arm was still around her waist.

"We would all like to get back to the fair."

Lara, realizing how selfish she had been to keep them all there, reacted immediately. "Of course. Sorry. I simply lost track of time." She turned to Mario. Attempting to step away from him, she said, "Thanks, Mario, it was a great ride. Meeting up with you-all has been the high point of the fair for me."

She felt him tighten his grip around her waist, and thought, How silly. He said, "The *high point* is now. I invite you to dinner. A great dinner." And turning to Sam, he added, "I'll see that she gets home."

Mario assumed too much. She told him, "Thanks, but no thanks. I have neglected my friends long enough." And this time she managed to release herself.

Sam was quick. He took her firmly by the arm. "Okay, let's go." They took only a few steps before Mario pulled Sam's hand from Lara's arm. The couple, surprised, swung round to face an enraged biker. "You can go. She stays." He grabbed Lara's hand.

There was nothing menacing in his voice. Just a tone so emphatic that everyone around them who heard it backed away, except Sam. He tried to reason,

"Mario, the lady doesn't want to stay."

"That's what she says, not what she means."

"Mario, he's right."

"Bullshit! It's this fag friend wants to take you away." Mario gave Sam a hard shove with his free hand. Not content with that, he released Lara and went after Sam with both hands, shoving him even harder, again and again, down the alley.

"What's a soft guy like you think you can do with a hot chick like her, huh? Huh? Why don'tcha say somethun'? Take her away? You're lucky I let you *get* away, fag."

Lara tried to intercede. Only then did Sam say something. "Stay out of it, Lara."

"What's that supposed to show her? Is that uptown bravery?" With that he gave Sam yet another shove, then simpered in fe-

male tones, " 'Stay out of it, Lara.' " Those were the last co-
herent words the alley heard Mario utter that afternoon. Sam hit
him with a dropkick. Mario went down, but came up fighting.

Sam amazed everyone with his brutal defense of himself. He
was destroying his opponent with karate chops and kicks. No
slouch at the martial arts, he could counterattack anything the
street fighter turned on him. And he did go after Sam now with
a vengeance. Lara and Sam's friends saw a side to Sam they had
never dreamed existed. First, the core of toughness under the
usually calm exterior was a surprise. But the brutality that surged
from him as he took on Mario, after he was visibly beaten, was
a shock. No one had dared interfere. Mario had instructed them,
"This is personal, not a gang event. Anyone muscles in on it,
he has to deal with me."

"Sam," shouted a terrified Julia. "This is barbaric." Her
words worked where Lara's had not. He bent down, picked
Mario up off the road, and sat him on an ash can. Mario leaned
against the bricks of the building. His swarthy, handsome face
was unmarked. The man held a hand over his ribs. He had
trouble breathing. Sam examined him, then told Mario, "If I'd
wanted to, I could have hurt you badly. Not my game. But you—
you would have maimed me if I'd let you. Okay, so you're right,
I *am* soft. Guys like you are why I use karate, that's all. You'll
be bruised for several days, but there's no real damage, I made
sure of that. Fag, no. Pansy, no. Gent, maybe, Mario. You
should try it sometime." Sam, more angry than he had been at
any time during that afternoon, pulled Mario to his feet and
dusted his jacket. The two men glared at each other. "We're
going to leave now, *all* of us. Are you going to be man enough
to let us leave this fair unharmed?"

Mario straightened up. No word was exchanged now. Sam's
outstretched hand demanded a handshake. Nothing happened
for several seconds. Then Mario shook Sam's hand and walked
somewhat shakily from the alley. Sam, Lara, and their friends
followed silently and melted into the crowds still clogging the
main streets.

Later that night Lara and Sam had the most passionate sexual
encounter they had had since their erotic interlude on the island.
This time Sam did not run away afterward. Instead he became

sexually obsessed with her. Now, their intimacy flourished in love *and* sex, seemed to have no bounds. They were adventurers in an erotic land, friends who had become a couple in society. For Lara, at last, her half-guilty preoccupation with her sexual life with Jamal was over. She rarely thought of him in that way anymore.

Life seemed sweeter than before. Sam and Lara appeared, at last, to have found a relationship that brought them a new intimacy, a oneness that no one and nothing could intrude on. So they made their decision: they would marry. They knew they wished never again to be parted. The passing of time made it obvious to them both that it was not enough just to be together and intimate. As a couple they craved a married existence. They wanted all the things that marriage had to offer.

If *not* being married was hard on them, actually *getting* married seemed to be even more difficult. In the end, they agreed they didn't want the complications of a large society wedding and decided to elope.

After endless discussions about the how and where of accomplishing it, finally, with the help of Julia, a plan was formulated. Not to feel cheated of a celebration, and to share their happiness with their friends, they decided to elope on the morning of the annual Cannonberry Chase summer ball. There was a Plan A, and a Plan B, and even a Plan C, as to where the wedding would take place. But all the plans contained one feature: Lara and Sam would fly to Cannonberry Chase, arriving after the ball had begun. The couple aimed to surprise everyone with the news of the wedding as their excuse for being late.

The day came. Sam looked at his watch. Everything was going according to plan, or almost. He had been far more moved by the ceremony than he had expected to be. They both had been. From the air, Cannonberry Chase looked like a tray of scattered diamonds. The copter hovered near the open French windows of the ballroom, and the guests were drawn outside by its unmistakable noise.

Lara fussed over her gown. Its skirt was voluminous: tiers of iced-green silk netting that trailed glamorously longer in the back and showed ankle in the front. The bodice of the same material was a form-fitting, off-the-shoulder affair that offered teasing glimpses of cleavage. The tiers of **netting** so cleverly designed fell from the shoulders to the elbows, making a capacious sleeve of sorts. At her waist was a bunch of fresh magnolias.

Such finery was not ideally suited to a helicopter descent, but somehow the pair, looking ravishingly grand, stepped unperturbed onto the lawn. Friends gasped and rushed up to greet them. There was applause for so spectacular an entrance. Once they felt the grass underfoot and the chopper blades no longer overhead, looks of relief lit their faces. So far so good, but here was the hard part.

Lara saw David in the crowd, walking toward them across the lawn. He was laughing, and that somehow made breaking their news to the Stantons and the Faynes a lot easier. Lara could tell by the look that passed between her and David that he had guessed what their spectacular entrance was all about. He was flanked by Emily and Henry; Max and Steven were not far behind. Only Emily seemed not amused. The two women's eyes met across the crowd of people. Lara, hand in hand with Sam, pushed her way past greeting guests toward her family. She reached up to hug her father and kiss him on the cheek, and then turned her attention to her mother. Emily smiled; it was one of those smiles she used on public-speaking occasions. She reached out and fluffed up a tier of the green silk netting clinging precariously on the edge of Lara's shoulder. Sam bent down to kiss Emily on the cheek. She looked at him. The smile returned. She reached out to touch a magnolia at Lara's waist. Then she addressed the couple: "Rather a dramatic entrance, children."

The note of disapproval in her voice was what they had expected. Lara may have expected it, but she had not counted on it silencing her. She simply could not find the words to tell Emily they had eloped. Instead she raised her hand. Emily saw the wedding band. She took her daughter's hand in hers and stroked it. "Dramatic, but not nearly dramatic enough for such a happy occasion as this." She raised Lara's hand up and waved it for the crowd to see. Then she kissed her daughter approvingly.

1981

PARIS FLORENCE
MARRAKESH

Chapter 17

Marcy was waiting for her husband Harry. Harry Cohen was always late. The late Harry Cohen, as the wags called him, while Marcy was always early. Punctuality was just about the only thing they disagreed about. To Harry it seemed a mere neurosis. Otherwise he was an angel of a husband.

Harry loved Paris, and Marcy had come to love it, too. He was a shoe manufacturer with cosmopolitan pretensions that transported them to Paris at least once a year for Harry's business and for fun. The wonderful world of Parisian footwear made a fuss over Harry. That embarrassed Marcy.

She often nagged him, "Don't you find it vulgar, all that toadying. Why do they do it? Just to get your business? How disgusting!"

And he would reply, "Don't be silly! It's because I speak impeccable French."

After years of watching the French fuss over him, she came to agree. Marcy took lessons and now spoke her own brand of French, too. She had become very possessive about Paris. Considered it *her* special place. As for the Ritz—well, she could be possessive about that, too.

This was their last day in the city, and Marcy was itching to get out into the streets. She kept pacing around the lobby, never taking her eyes off the entrance. Twice she walked out into the bright May sunshine to pace up and down the pavement there. Curious looks from the doorman made her feel foolish. She went back into the lobby and sat down, her eyes assessing the passersby from the feet upward.

Marcy got into all the muddles inverted snobs usually get into. She stayed at the Ritz, sharing the elegance and chic of the other people who stayed there, but at the same time condemning that elegance and chic. Marcy liked stylishness, but more so that she could knock it rather than because it could be pleasing to the eye and fun. She wore expensive drip-dry clothes and flat shoes. Her closet was full of designer outfits. These she would pack and unpack, but rarely wear. She enjoyed the idea of old money—and tried to behave as if she and Harry were. Old money meant conservative and plain, and worthy. She considered herself there. Harry, unfortunately, was maybe a tad too flashy to make the grade.

She forgot she was upset with him for being late. There was too much to be faulted in the parade passing through the lobby. Midday on a bright spring morning was the perfect time for people-watching at the Ritz. There was a lull at the entrance. Still no Harry. For five minutes or so no mortal darkened the doorstep of the Ritz.

Then Marcy saw two cars pull up: first a vintage Mercedes with its top down and a stylish couple in it, the backseat heaped with Louis Vuitton luggage. Behind it, was a navy blue Rolls-Royce. She guessed it was a model from the fifties or the sixties. Inside sat a chauffeur in uniform and cap. She watched alight from the backseat a child of maybe three, a nanny in gray, and another woman in dark clothes, possibly a social secretary or a maid, thought Marcy.

She saw the doorman smile and shake the hand of the man from the Mercedes. The woman, her blond hair tousled by the wind, was dressed in wide trousers of ivory flannel beneath a top of navy blue cashmere with a large sailor collar. The child ran to her, and the woman swept her up into her arms laughing, talking to the nanny and the maid at the same time.

Marcy was transfixed by the sight of the laughing woman. She could hardly believe it. She watched the group make their entrance into the lobby, several porters loaded down with the luggage from both cars following them. The woman handed the child to her husband. Marcy wanted to hide, but she was too stunned to move. The last person on earth she expected to meet in the Ritz lobby that morning was Lara Stanton.

They were coming right past her. Marcy turned her face away

from them. They mustn't see her. She saw other heads turn to look at the family. She even heard a whispered, "Who are they?" behind her.

"The Faynes. My, but they are a handsome, elegant sight. They're always like that, wherever they go. Dead stylish. Supposed to be very nice people as well. Old money, you know."

"You know them?"

"No, dear, they would consider us Eurotrash. Much too common to be worth knowing. There are limits to very niceness."

Marcy took the woman's comments personally. She felt angry to hear herself classed as inferior to Lara. Someone bumped into her as they passed. For a second their eyes met. It was Sam. He excused himself and walked on. The remainder of the Fayne entourage passed within inches of her. She had not been seen or recognized. She heaved a sigh of relief. But too soon.

A hand on her shoulder. She turned around. It was Sam.

"Marcy. So it was you!" He gave her his dazzlingly friendly smile. "Must be years since I've seen you."

"Not since Lara and I were at Smith."

"Didn't you see us come in?"

"Could hardly miss that entrance."

Sam flushed. "Why didn't you say something?"

"I thought you were the Scott Fitzgeralds reincarnated. At the very least, a bunch of his characters. The Divers, maybe. And I never knew them."

They both began to laugh, a nervous laugh, but a laugh nevertheless. "Quick as ever, Marcy. Wait here, I'll go get Lara."

"No, don't, Sam. Please."

"She'll be so happy to see you, Marcy. Maybe we can all dine together, or at least have a drink."

"We don't do that in New York, Sam. Why should we do it in Paris?"

"That's a bit harsh, Marcy."

"But true."

"Please, I insist."

His easy charm disarmed her. They turned to look for Lara, only to glimpse her as the elevator doors slid closed and she was wafted up and away.

"Come on, we'll go up to our rooms and surprise her."

"A nice idea, Sam, but honestly I can't. I'm waiting for my husband, and we have arrangements."

"Then call in on us when you get back."

"We can't. We fly home this afternoon."

An awkward silence. They stood looking at each other, each momentarily lost in memories. Finally Sam broke the silence. He placed an arm around her shoulder. "What happened to us, Marcy? All those dreams we had?"

"We grew up. And some of us, if we were lucky like you, Sam, fulfilled them, for better or for worse. All I can remember you ever wanting was to be married to Lara. You got your life's ambition. I'm still chasing mine. But there have been compensations along the way. Here he comes, forty-five minutes late. I must run, I don't want him to lose that taxi. Tell Lara I'm sorry. Maybe next time." Then she was gone.

She rushed away from Sam and through the door—just as Harry stepped from the taxi.

"Hi!" He gave a big grin. And his wife shoved him back into the taxi, and jumped in after him. He was late.

Sam watched the taxi drive away, ruefully reflecting that he had seen quite a bit of Marcy in those years while he courted Lara at Smith, yet he had never really seen her at all. She had just been there, to be tolerated because she was Lara's roommate. To be fixed up with a Yale man because she was Lara's friend. He had never considered her, or anyone else for that matter. It had been Lara, only Lara.

Instead of going up to the suite to join his wife and daughter, Sam went to the Ritz Bar. He was greeted warmly by the waiters and went directly to a table in a quiet corner next to the window. It was almost ominous that Marcy should have turned up today at the Ritz and he should have bumped into her. It had been many years since he had seen her, years since he had even heard her name mentioned. He had actually forgotten she existed. And there she was, a reminder of what they had all once been during their college years. And still with that same quick tongue. Caustic? Fresh? Yes. Irritatingly perceptive? Yes. But often only half right. At least, he liked to think that. Especially since she had so bitchily reminded him that his sole ambition in life had been to marry Lara. Why was she so angry? Had they let her down so badly? She'd expected too much.

For weeks he had been seeking the right moment to say to Lara what he now had to say. He had made up his mind they would speak in Paris in the next few days. He distracted himself from his problems with a second double extra-dry martini, known at the Ritz as a dry. And a third. He watched the bar first fill up with world travelers, chic Parisians, old-guard Americans on their annual European pilgrimage—no mere tourists—and empty again as they rushed off to lunch. He was not unhappy, far from it. Not elated, either. Rather, repressing some tingle of excitement, dampened down even further by the desire to minimize Lara's pain. He called the waiter and asked to see the cigars.

In the suite several floors above, Lara was unpacking Bonnie's toy basket. Out came the teddies, the dolls, the china toy tea set with its tiny silver teapot, creamer and sugar and tea caddies—all the accoutrements for Bonnie's favorite game, the Mad Hatter's tea party. Everywhere they traveled, Bonnie's tea set came along, too, and tea was served at some time nearly every day. Invariably Bonnie played a dual role: the hostess and a guest. That could be most anyone. The Mad Hatter, the March Hare, even the Dormouse. She expanded the guest list, inviting whomever she wanted to play with that day. Cinderella, Mr. Macaroni, her pony stabled at Cannonberry Chase, the Wicked Witch from the North, Prince Charming, any number of her playmates, her father, or her mother. Her roles varied with her mood. And her guest list was seemingly endless and always surprising. The guests, if not readily available in person, were played by Nanny, Coral, Nancy, or any adult, child, animal, alive or stuffed, and her favorite dolls. The one role that Bonnie remained consistent in was that of hostess. She did a takeoff of her grandmother, Emily, that could have gotten the three-year-old into Actor's Equity. Even Emily had been amused and entertained. Almost everyone wanted to be invited to Bonnie Fayne's tea parties.

For her second birthday David had given her a collection of all of the major characters in *Alice's Adventures in Wonderland*, in perfect proportions to a two-year-old child's size. They were as much playmates as dolls. When the Faynes traveled, the Alice people traveled with them, but not the table and chairs. There Sam had drawn the line. The very first thing Bonnie did when they arrived somewhere and her toys were unpacked was to improvise. The proper table and chairs had to be found before tea time. That was what Bonnie was doing now. She had already found a needlepoint-covered footstool and two cushions and was dragging them toward one of the windows overlooking the Place Vendôme. Leaving them there, she went to Lara, who was sitting on her haunches and leaning over the toy basket, and snuggled her way onto her mother's lap.

"What are we going to do till tea time, Mummy?" she asked, stroking Lara's hair and giving her a hug.

Lara felt herself melting. Nothing moved her more than a crushing hug from Bonnie. She gave her daughter a cuddle. "You are going to have lunch here. After lunch you go to the Bois to play with Polly and Jenna Baker. Do you remember them?"

"Polly can't swim, and Jenna is afraid of Mr. Macaroni."

"That's true."

"Can they come to tea, Mummy?"

"If you like."

"Jenna can be the Dormouse."

"I don't think she'll fit in the teapot, Bonnie."

"You are a silly, Mummy! I know that. She can make believe."

"I think she would be happier as Cinderella."

"Well, she can be Cinderella, but then she can't come to tea."

"Whyever not, Bonnie?"

"Because we already have a Cinderella."

"Who?"

"Me."

The smile she gave her mother was full of mischief. Lara stifled her amusement. She stared at the little girl, and Bonnie burst into laughter. "Oh, all right. She can be Cinderella. And I'll be—" the child hesitated for several seconds and then declared "—Minnie Mouse." Bonnie placed her hand over her mouth and lowered her eyes, a habit she had when she was thinking very hard. Then, tossing her head back and shaking it from side to side so that her very blond hair swirled back and forth over her face, she said, "No, today I will be the Sleeping Princess and Daddy can be the Prince."

"You were the Sleeping Princess yesterday."

"Oh, that doesn't count, because Coral was the Prince, and she's not a very good Prince, not like my daddy."

"That's not very nice, Bonnie. Just you wait till the next time you need a prince at your table," warned Coral, who was walking past with an armful of Lara's dresses.

"Don't be sad, Coral. I'll let you be the Mad Hatter." That was, for Bonnie, the ultimate accolade. She scrambled out of Lara's arms, and, snatching a Raggedy Ann doll from the pile of toys on the floor, ran to the maid. "Would you like to be the Mad Hatter and come for tea today, Coral? I think you could be a very good Mad Hatter."

Lara watched Bonnie. She could never remember herself or any child she had ever known being so sensitive to other people's feelings. Bonnie had a streak of caring and love in her that Lara had never had. Every day she learned more about love from her child. Coral, still pretending to be upset about being a bad prince, bent down to tell Bonnie, "Well, I don't know. Maybe. I've always wanted to be the Mad Hatter."

"Then you will?"

"Oh, yes, why not?" And the maid gave Bonnie a happy smile.

The child, clearly pleased that the maid was no longer sad, skipped away, back to her mother, the Raggedy Ann doll clutched to her chest. She flung herself into Lara's arms.

"That was a very nice thing to do, Bonnie. Coral looks very happy."

But Coral and the tea party were already has-beens. Bonnie was now engrossed in Raggedy Ann. The doll had been picked for the afternoon outing with Bonnie and the Baker children, and Bonnie was busy telling her all about Polly and Jenna. Raggedy Ann was doing her part. She was asking all sorts of questions about them. Lara listened. The child's imagination was impressive. Even a dialogue with a stuffed doll revealed Bonnie's sensitivity to the feelings of others.

And yet she showed no lack of raw courage. Lara had taught her to ride Mr. Macaroni, and Bonnie displayed the same spirit there as she had when dropped in the pool as an infant and had instantly struggled to swim. The child, already used to sailing, had had no fear of the ocean—even when Lara and Sam had first taken her on board. And, ever since she was a baby, Lara had piloted her for rides in her Cessna, and later in the seaplane kept at Cannonberry Chase. But, if Lara was teaching Bonnie, they were both learning. Life was sweet for Bonnie, but she made Lara's life even sweeter. Bonnie's birth had not changed the Faynes' life-style. It had just extended it, and the child seemed to thrive on it.

Lara and Sam were doting parents. Bonnie went with them wherever they traveled. Lara was not going to miss a day of her child's growing up. And Bonnie? For all the attention she was given by her parents, she remained a more independent child than most her age. She could read and loved books. They transported a miniature library of Bonnie's and Nanny's choosing. Before she went to bed she read herself a story, or one to Sam or Lara if they were there at bedtime. And what she couldn't read she made up as she went along. The great counter to living so much in an adult world was her many little cousins, who were always moving in and out of Cannonberry Chase. They were her friends and playmates: when the Faynes traveled, they often scooped up one or two of them as company for Bonnie.

Lara was thinking of those bedtime stories with just the three of them, Sam, Bonnie, and Lara, and what a happy family they were, how exciting a life they led, enriched by the presence of the child. Lara felt the warmth of Bonnie's body. She stroked the child's bare arm. So soft and smooth. She picked her small hand up and kissed the fingers. Bonnie gazed up into her mother's eyes. Love for Lara gleamed in them. Lara rocked her gently and placed the little fingers in her mouth and sucked them, licked them. Bonnie giggled. Lara had had a marvelous pregnancy and an easy birth, and could not stop wondering at what it had produced. She suddenly realized it was time for her and Sam to have another child. Where was he? Strange he was taking so long; he should have been with them by now. She could hardly wait to tell him. She knew how pleased he would be.

Lara kissed her child and told her, ''Mummy must get up, Bonnie. I have to bathe and change my dress.''

''Why?''

''I'm going out to lunch with Daddy.''

''And me?''

''No, not you, not today.''

Out came the Stanton pout. That was what Sam called it. A

little nibble at the lip. Was that a tear brimming at the eyes? "But you can come and wash my back, and help me to select a dress. Now how's that?"

All was forgiven. The signs of disappointment vanished, to be replaced by a smile that broadened her face and lit up her eyes. Raggedy Ann was abandoned, and Bonnie sprang out of her mother's arms, onto her feet. Taking Lara's hand in hers, the child tried to pull Lara up.

"Dress ups!" cried the three-year-old. That was Bonnie's second favorite game.

Poor Coral, thought Lara. And she was just getting the wardrobe together.

With one hand Bonnie was pulling Lara toward the bathroom, with the other she was struggling with her own buttons. Finally she dropped Lara's hand to attack the closing on her blouse with both her hands. By the time they reached the bedroom there was a trail of clothes already on the floor.

"Oh, no. Not dress ups," wailed Coral.

"Oh, yes!" shouted a now overexcited Bonnie, practically hopping from one foot to another.

"And just look at that mess you've left behind you, Bonnie."

The child stood in the bedroom in her little white cotton slip, one black patent-leather shoe on, one foot bare of even the white sock. Lara told her, "Bonnie, go back and pick up every one of the things you've left on the floor." Bonnie looked annoyed. Lara raised an eyebrow and gave her a glance the child understood. She ran back and retrieved her things and placed them neatly on the bed. Lara picked her up and swung her around, then dumped her unceremoniously on the bed, telling the child, "Don't move; not until I'm in the bath and I call you."

"How many numbers is that?" asked Bonnie, still giggling from her swingabout.

"Count to a hundred. And no cheating. No one, two, five, seven, nine, eleven, eighteen, thirty stuff, either."

Lara received the Stanton pout, but Bonnie did start counting and properly, for as far as she knew how to count. In the bath Lara relaxed in the hot water, paddling it with hands and feet, pumping up as many suds as she could. No scented bubble bath could ever generate enough bubbles for Bonnie. She called out,

"One hundred, Bonnie." The door flew open and in charged Bonnie, clad only in a red ribbon that kept her hair off her face.

"Oh, Bonnie, Nanny will be furious with us."

"Nanny *is*," came a voice from the bedroom.

Sam saw Lara coming toward him, and suddenly he could think of nothing but how much he still wanted her. She looked marvelous, more the sexy lady than ever. He could also see in her the young girl he had loved for as long as he could remember. She looked as she always looked, bewitchingly carefree and happy. She had her silvery blond hair in a snood of crisscrossed black velvet ribbons. Large canary diamond earrings he had bought her for the birth of Bonnie dazzled at her earlobes. The suit, a short jacket of woven white silk over a tight black skirt, was form-fitting. High-heeled, black patent-leather shoes, and the tiniest handbag of shiny black lizard hung from one shoulder on a fine gold chain.

He stood up and pulled a chair out for her. Then Sam bent forward and whispered, after grazing her cheek with a kiss, "I would like to fuck the ass off you. That's the way you look, as if you want to be fucked to death."

"Ah, you've had your third dry. Guaranteed to remove all inhibitions known to medical science—and take out your memory." She lowered her voice to a near whisper. "You almost did just that last night." And she gave him a teasing smile.

"I wish you looked less ravishing."

"What a strange thing to say." There was such a sober expression on his face, Lara was prompted to ask: "Sam, is something wrong?"

"I think we should go upstairs." He rose from his chair. She stopped him with a hand upon his arm.

"Lunch. Have you forgotten we're meeting the Portchesters? It's for them I'm all dolled up. And you haven't even changed."

He sat down. The waiter arrived with Lara's drink. There was something alien about Sam today. For a moment Lara had the sensation that the man opposite her was a stranger. She shrugged off the thought and became genuinely concerned for him.

"Something's wrong."

"Yes."

"You're ill?" Sam was behaving so out of character, Lara

looked genuinely frightened. It was she now who began to rise from her chair, Sam who stopped her with a hand on her arm.

"No." He knew what she was thinking, and quickly added, "And all the family is fine."

Relieved, Lara took a sip of her drink and suggested, "We don't have to go if you don't want to. We can call the restaurant. Bill and Katharine will understand. Or I could go on alone. I would rather like to see them and catch up on the gossip."

"No." It was so emphatic it took her quite by surprise.

"What *is* wrong, Sam?" She replaced her glass on the table.

"I want a divorce."

Lara said not a word, remaining calm and gazing intently at him. Sam reached out toward her. She shrank back into her chair. They remained silent for some time. Finally Lara tried to speak. There was a catch in her voice. She had to clear her throat before she could utter a sound.

"Why?"

"Does it matter why?"

Her voice was filled with shock and anger. "Of course it matters why! We spend the night with you telling me how much you love me. Our sex life is still rich and exciting. We have a child you adore, and an idyllic married life. And from out of nowhere you hit me with 'I want a divorce.' "

"Lara, *you* have an idyllic married life. I don't."

"Just what does that mean?"

"Lara, let's just leave it at that."

"I insist."

"Don't insist, Lara. I don't want to hurt you. I love you. I will always love you. But I don't want to be married to you."

"But we've been happy," she insisted, with a sinking feeling.

"No, *you've* been happy, Lara. I haven't. Not for years."

"Do you mean to tell me that you've been pretending to be happy with me for years? That we have been living a lie? I can't believe that. That's disgusting."

"Yes, it is, and I can't go on with it another day."

Lara suddenly felt as if she were going to be sick. She covered her mouth with her hand and went terribly cold. She wanted to run from the table, but her legs felt wobbly, as if they wouldn't carry her. She heard Sam say, as if from far away, "I didn't mean to tell you it like this, in the Ritz Bar. Let's go."

"No," she was quick to say. "A glass of water."

They waited in silence until she had been served the glass of water and had drunk it down. The bar was empty, except for two men at separate tables some way from where they sat. She felt strangely secure sitting there, even if beyond that room lay nothing for her but a world of desolation.

"Why didn't you say something?"

"I did. You didn't listen."

"You never gave me any indication that you were unhappy."

"That's not true."

"If you were so unhappy with our marriage, then why did you stay with me for so long? That was cruel."

"Because I was besotted with you, loved you. You enslaved me. I was sexually addicted to you. Because I got lost in you and your happiness, and forgot about my own."

"And you're not anymore?"

"No."

"But I love you," Lara said rather pathetically.

"No, you don't, you only think you do. It suits you to think you love me. What you do is use me."

That was like the thrust of a knife into her flesh. "The way you use me?" She retaliated instantly.

"Yes, if you like."

"How can you say that? It makes our whole marriage a sham. Tell me that's not true."

"It is true. Right from the beginning it was true, only we couldn't face it. We eloped because we got carried away with the romance of the moment. It was what I had always wanted to happen to us. I wanted other things in life, but none more than I wanted you. For you it was convenient to marry someone who loved you beyond all else in life, and who was already like family. We got hooked on the idea of marriage, and failed to think beyond that. Your idea of marriage is a lifetime honeymoon. And I, fool that I was, kept thinking: 'Tomorrow . . . Tomorrow she will take on the responsibilities that go with marriage.' How many times have I told you I wanted a home and a family? And how many times have you tricked me into believing that you did, too?

"In three years, I have bought five houses in various parts of the world. We've lived in none of them. You never bought a

glass for—or hung a curtain in—any of them. Cannonberry
Chase is all the home you've ever wanted. And for the first
months of our marriage, it was great. It still is great, Lara, but
it has never been *our own* home. Any more than the suite we
keep at the Sherry Netherlands, or my father's summer house in
Southampton, or my sister's house in Cap Ferrat. For three years
we've flitted around the world at our own whim and fancy like
gypsies, houseguests of our families and our friends. I conduct
my business affairs brilliantly, considering I'm always on the
hop, and I spend most of my time leaving forwarding phone
numbers. That's our livelihood, our marriage, our existence.

"When Bonnie was born, you promised we would settle in
one place. I believed you. Yet again, I offered you a place of our
own, anywhere you chose to live. You said yes, as you always
do, and nothing changed. We simply traveled with a larger entourage, and I slipped even further away from myself and what
I wanted, drawn into giving you more, always more, to keep
you happy."

"And I? I never gave you anything?"

"The most important thing in my life: Bonnie. And I will
always be grateful to you for her. But the truth of the matter is
no, not much else, except the sex."

"Which, it appears, you still find irresistible, if last night,
and this morning, and what you said when I walked into this
room are any indication," she said bitterly.

"You can't keep me any longer with just your cunt, Lara."

"That's too crude. I don't deserve that."

"Yes, I think you do. But I should be more of a gentleman
than to tell you. I'm just as much to blame for the failure of this
marriage as you are. We were a safe haven for each other. We
both took an easy way out. We were too selfish and spoiled to
realize what we were doing—I'll grant us that."

"We were the best of friends."

"We were. Still are, I hope."

"And lovers."

"More like users, satisfying our lust for each other. Users
who don't know how to love is more the truth."

"And what made you see the light?"

Sam remained silent for several seconds, then signaled to the waiter to order more drinks. After the waiter left, she insisted, "Well?"

"Let's just drop this. There really is no point. I want a divorce, and as quickly and painlessly as possible."

Sam could see that she had guessed. Her eyes showed that she knew. The shock returned, as sharp as when he first mentioned divorce. He wanted to feel sorry for her but couldn't. He had given her everything, while she had left him with nothing. There was no reserve left in him. She had used him up.

"There's another woman?"

"Yes."

"Christ, you've been deceiving me with another woman! How could you? I could never have betrayed you as you have me, Sam. You're having an affair with another woman, and you're still fucking me, playing the perfect husband and father. Another woman, that's why you are leaving me?"

"No. Get this right, Lara. I tried to spare you this, but you insisted, so get it right, goddammit! The only reason I was able to stay in our marriage at all was because I met this woman. She knows how to love and give. Her love filled the gap I felt so deeply in our marriage. It sustained me. She gave me the home I never had with you. She has been more of a wife to me than you have ever been. She has always been there, waiting in the wings, encouraging me to try harder to make our marriage work."

"You discussed our marriage with her?" Sam didn't answer. He appeared, under the hard, determined facade he was presenting to Lara, suddenly distressed. "That's despicable."

"Yes," he admitted. "I make no excuse for that. I should have discussed us with us instead. But I couldn't. You were still a love obsession that I could not live without. I was unhappy with our marriage, our life together, but not with you. For me you were always the most exciting, seductive woman in the world. You never took your claws out of me long enough for me to escape. That's why I couldn't leave you for her long ago."

"How long have we been living a lie? How long have you been keeping this woman?"

He could not answer. Little as he might want to, he felt sorry for Lara.

"Oh, no. Years? Answer me," she demanded.

He maintained his silence.

That was confirmation enough for Lara. "You, of all people, the one man I never expected would betray me." She looked away from him and fought back tears. She bit the inside of her lip, took a deep breath. Then, turning back to face him, she announced, barely above a whisper, "I will not contest a divorce."

Brave words for a young woman whose whole world was shattered over a dry at the Paris Ritz. For a young wife who had believed beyond any doubt that she had the best marriage, the right husband, that happiness was theirs and not just hers. Never once had it occurred to her to deceive her husband, or that he might be deceiving her. That bond she was so certain was love, and could never be broken between them, had given her the security to open up with her husband and be herself. She had held nothing back, and most especially the sexual side of her nature. He had reveled in it. It had counted high in their relationship, but for her no more so than some other aspects of their life together. She had never contrived to enslave her husband.

For the first time in years Lara recalled the morning when she had walked out on Jamal, for the very same reason Sam was now walking out on her: because she could not bear the idea of being sexually enslaved to him. The misery she had endured for so long under his sexual hold over her suddenly repossessed Lara, and she felt quite sick. Awareness dawned like the sting of a slap across the face. She had, though without realizing it, accomplished with Sam what Jamal had very nearly accomplished with her: total subjugation.

She had pushed her chair back and had been about to rise and leave the bar when that moment of awareness hit her. Now, not only was she unable to get up, but she could no longer hold back her sickness. She reached for her handbag. Sam saw she was in trouble and recognized the problem. He came to her rescue with a handkerchief. Gratefully she pressed it to her mouth while she fought to hold back her misery. He took her by the arm, helped her from the chair, and together they left the bar.

The walk across the lobby seemed the longest of her life. In the lift her natural instinct was to lean against Sam. She couldn't. His deceit, his cheating, his betrayal of all she had believed in, his hatred for their life together—was that something to lean on?

She straightened up and stepped a pace away from him. They stood in silence as the elevator rose laboriously through the hotel.

She tried to assemble her thoughts. Was there something to be done? Something to say to Sam? Let's wipe out the past? Can we start again? Bonnie? For Bonnie's sake? The family's? A second chance? Make an effort to save . . . To save what? Nothing there to save but the illusions they had tried to build a life on.

The elevator doors opened, and Lara stepped out into the hall. Her life was in shreds, her spirit quite broken. But from the tatters of her life rose that indomitable Stanton character. She turned to Sam. "Let's do this thing with some dignity—no acrimony—and together. For our sakes, as well as Bonnie's and the family's."

He looked relieved. He agreed, not in words, but with a nod of the head. Now, in front of the door to their suite, the key already in the lock, he turned to face her. "Lara." He reached out to touch her. She recoiled as if he were a flame about to scorch her.

She raised a hand as though shielding herself and told him, "Don't ever touch me again. I shall not forgive you for deceiving me, but the world will not know that. Only you. I can playact, put the required face on it. Now you live with that."

Chapter 18

David! There he was on the tarmac, standing with two other men next to a black Rolls-Royce. She spotted him even before the 747 rolled to a stop. David. Thanks to him a mere two hours after they called him from Paris, they were seated in the first-class section of the State Department plane returning to Washington via New York.

Lara placed the palm of her hand on the window, wanting to touch him. Seeing David waiting for them brought some sort of reality to what seemed like a dreadful dream. How can you be alive yet have no life going for you? How can you have everything going for you yet be as motiveless, selfish, and alienated as Sam intimated she was? Was her life always to be one of love and loss, of isolation within relationships? She suddenly felt weary beyond endurance. And then she saw David walking toward the plane. He waved, and she felt a spark of energy return. He smiled up at her. She sensed love, and realized how complicated a thing it was, that it had more to do with innocence and hope, betrayal even, and disappointment, than she had been prepared for.

Minutes later, the passengers were on the ramp, ready to descend the stairs. Sam and Lara gazed into each other's eyes. The sadness he saw in her face prompted him to ask, ''Are you all right?''

''Let's just say this is not the best day of my life and get on with it.''

She stepped forward and walked with Sam and Bonnie down the stairs. Once on the tarmac, Lara hung back while Sam greeted David. David took Bonnie in his arms and kissed her, but he had eyes only for Lara, eyes filled with concern. From his pocket he drew a small teddy bear with a red-and-white, polka-dot bow tie around its neck. Bonnie squealed with delight. David handed Bonnie over to her nanny and turned his attention to Sam. The two men shook hands. Sam stood aside while Lara stepped into David's arms. They greeted each other with a hug and a kiss. Lara fought back tears, and David consoled her with, "Everything will be all right, La. We're going home. Home to your beloved Cannonberry Chase."

The three adults walked toward the waiting car. Lara pictured herself riding through the entrance, past the great iron gates, and up the avenue of trees, over the rise, to that first sight of the fountain in the courtyard and the house behind. It brought a slight smile to her lips—and then she wondered when—but when would it come right for her? She wanted to believe David, but the fact was that she couldn't. She could feel sorry for herself, yes. But that was hardly the worst of it. Her sense of failure was colossal. It overwhelmed her.

The family rallied round the divorcing couple, making it very easy for Lara and Sam. That only made Lara feel an even greater failure. She played her role of forgiving Sam brilliantly.

It was all as Lara had wanted it to be: a very private divorce, friendly, with no questions asked and few explanations given. Sam and Lara left family and friends with the illusion that they remained the best of friends. It was assumed that the marriage was terminated by mutual consent.

It was a deception perpetrated by both Sam and Lara for the sake of Bonnie, and for the Fayne and Stanton families. But it was a deception that was hard for both to wear. Bonnie was a real little person, not a baby. Her mother and father had been with her day in and day out for her entire life. Suddenly to see them separated could have been traumatic for the child. Neither wanted that for her. The first morning, the child rushed into her parents' bedroom at Cannonberry Chase—to get into bed with them—and only Lara was there; the questions began.

"Where's Daddy?"

The moment Lara had dreaded. But it was here, and she was prepared for it—as was Sam. "Hop into bed, Bonnie." She flung the covers back, and the little girl bounced energetically into the bed and cuddled up to her mother. She poked her fingers through the open lacework nightdress Lara was wearing and tried to tickle her mother. Lara pretended she had, and gave the child the response she was seeking: a convincing show of giggles and begging for her to stop. That set off a chain of giggles in Bonnie. And once they had both calmed down, it began all over again, with Lara doing the serious tickling. The child could hardly catch her breath for the laughter.

"Stop, stop!" she cried.

"Have you had enough? Enough?"

"Yes, Mummy. Yes, please, stop."

Bonnie was all flailing arms and legs and uncontrollable laughter. Her nightdress of white cotton embroidered with flowers was a mass of twisted material hiked up above her knees. She kept trying to straighten it out and defend herself from her mother's tickling fingers at the same time. "What will you give me if I stop?" asked Lara.

"A kiss. A kiss and a hug."

"Oh, I can always get a kiss and a hug, it has to be something better." And she intensified her playful attack.

"I'll let you play Mummy to my doll, Lollypoulolly."

And still Lara did not stop, and the child screamed with laughter. Lara asked, "For how long?"

"One whole day."

"All right. Go and get her." And Lara stopped.

When the child had recovered herself, she scrambled off the bed and ran to her room to bring the doll. Relieved to have a few minutes of peace and quiet, Lara tried to bring herself under control. She was determined to handle this difficult interview as she and Sam had planned to.

Bonnie returned. Half reluctantly she handed over Lollypoulolly. "One whole day is a very long day, Mummy. Lollypoulolly will cry unless she can go back to the nursery for her lunch." There was not a Stanton pout, but there was a decidedly sorry little girl standing next to the bed.

"Well, we can't have that, can we?"

The child shook her head and her face began to light up. "But"—the joyful light vanished on the word—"but you did give her to me for the *whole day*," Lara continued. "And that was a promise. A promise is a promise. So she will have to stay

with me, won't she?'' There was a very sad affirmative nod of
the head. ''However . . .'' Lara put some enthusiasm into the
word: the light returned to the little face and hope glowed. ''I
repeat, however . . .'' now Bonnie was fidgeting with expectation ''. . . there is nothing to stop me from inviting you to
have lunch and spend the *whole* day with us, and Daddy, too.
What do you think of that?''

What Bonnie thought of that was to drop Lollypoulolly on the
floor and leap onto the bed and throw herself against her mother,
smothering her face in kisses. She was such a joy, so sweet and
quick, so honest and loving a child, her kisses brought tears to
Lara's eyes. Tears she did not want Bonnie to see. At that moment she hated Sam as she had never hated anyone in her life.
How could he not have been happy with them? Lara rolled Bonnie off her, leaped off the bed, and called back over her shoulder:
''Bonnie, go get Daddy. He's sleeping in the blue room. Now
when Daddy is here, you will have two rooms to wake up. What
fun! Tickles twice. I'll meet you in the nursery and we three
will have breakfast there.''

It was all a game. Another wonderful new game, so far as
Bonnie could understand it. And so Mother and Father laid
down the new ground rules. And Bonnie took the separation in
her stride, just as everyone else took it in theirs. But it had not
been all easygoing for those first days after their return from
Paris. There were lots of Bonnie questions. Seemingly endless
whys, whens, and wheres.

Once the news of the Fayne-Stanton divorce made the society
columns, the burning question for everyone was Why? Why had
this glamorous, idyllic marriage broken up? But no gossip surfaced on which to hang a scandal.

Lara retired to the seclusion of Cannonberry Chase, though
her seclusion was not total. She attended all the family's social
events, and dined with them, but spent most of her time with
Bonnie, or riding and sailing. She took to reading, spending
much of her time in the library. She even consented to see several old beaux—their calls came in as the news got out—but only
at Cannonberry Chase.

Although Sam had moved out, he came and went much as
before he and Lara were married. There was no breach between
Sam and the other Stantons, no burgeoning feud between the

Faynes and the Stantons. The two families maintained their old alliances. It was all marble-smooth and civilized. So much so that it took the family several months to realize fully that Lara had not ventured outside the estate since her return from Paris and the announcement of the divorce. Nor had she aired her feelings or future intentions. They waited, hoping she might rally herself and resume the life she had led before her marriage.

Behind closed doors they fretted. Or her brothers and Henry did. Emily and Elizabeth seethed, silent but *very* angry, believing that Lara, no matter what, should never have granted Sam a divorce. Whatever the problem, she and Sam should have made an arrangement and stayed married. They believed that Sam Fayne was unquestionably the perfect husband for Lara, and she had blown it. Condemned to silence by Henry, the two women smoldered—with much hope but little faith that Lara would ever find a better man than she had already had. But, no matter how angry they were with her, their loyalty to her overrode all else. They were there for her. The Stantons closed ranks.

Lara went through the motions of living, of being in control of her life. But the fact was she felt more lost than ever. Having to confront life as a single woman again, she only then began to understand how much she had enjoyed being married, particularly carrying a child. She relived the miracle of giving birth, the joy of rearing Bonnie. Her divorce from Sam was an incalculable loss of happiness. One thing this trauma of divorce *did* achieve for her, though: Lara became a woman, experiencing feelings and perceptions that till now had eluded her.

Solitude was her first discovery. She kept slipping into pockets of solitude, and soon consciously sought the luxury of seclusion, the healing properties of real quiet. It was a tonic that revitalized her, restored some strength with which to fight her deep sense of failure.

Julia and her other friends, more concerned than ever for her welfare, remained close to her. With infinite patience, they repeatedly tried to lure her out of her retreat and back into the bracing whirl of the social life. To little avail. Then, at last, David organized an adventure. Lara felt a touch of excitement return to her life when she agreed to fly David and Julia to Rio for a boat trip up the Orinoco.

The four-week adventure turned out to be a lifesaver for Lara.

Overwhelmed by the infinite beauty of the vast rain forests of
Brazil, on her return she consulted Harland, her trustee, and
instructed him to buy for her three hundred square miles of the
rain forest they had visited. Her intention to keep it as a natural
wildlife reserve suited her portfolio. Yet again, Harland was
impressed that she had not simply presented him the usual hare-
brained scheme of a beautiful playgirl.

The excitement of the project, and the complications of such
a purchase, sparked the barely tested business mind Lara appeared to have. She acted decisively. This was the first time
Harland had seen that side of her. Admiringly he encouraged
her to immerse herself in the development of large properties,
or the conservation of endangered parts of the world. Such projects might take her out of herself, restore her to the mainstream
of life again.

His encouragement worked to some degree. It prompted Lara
to discuss with him her interest in large working farms run on a
cooperative basis. How one day she would like to be involved
in projects like that. Listening to her own enthusiasm—and believing in what she was telling Harland—Lara felt a lift of her
spirits. She asked him to advise her of any opportunities.

On her return from Brazil, she had once again gone into retreat at Cannonberry Chase. But the holiday acted like a cathar-
sis. The epic canoe trip up the Orinoco, the danger, the primitive
people and places untouched by civilization, the emptiness and
lush jungle wilderness, were just what Lara had needed: a dramatic outlet for her sullied emotions. Part of her old self came
alive again. She suddenly felt like meeting people and attending
parties. Memories of the good times, frivolous, nonsensical fun,
came rushing back. Even sexual desire began to rekindle—one
of the impulses smothered since that morning at the Paris Ritz
by weariness and disenchantment. Lara began to wonder why
she wasn't having any fun anymore.

When she consented to attend a worthy charity ball at the
Metropolitan, and two other parties in the same week, her friends
rejoiced. Lara Stanton was back! Before long, she was once
again swept up into the life she had always led since leaving
Smith. There were several slight differences. Bonnie came first;
and a measured interest in her own personal affairs, including
the new projects she had submitted to Harland. But some habits

are hard to break. After buying an extensive working farm in Kenya and a vineyard in France, she lost interest in business and acquisitions.

Since money had never been a lure for her, she announced to Harland, "I'm shelving my involvement in business. Not for always, but for the moment. Please run things for me as you always have. I'm just not ready for so much responsibility. I feel I have a lot of living to do. I am, after all, still not thirty."

"Why am I not surprised by this?"

"Because I've done it to you before, dear Harland. But don't despair of me, I *am* trying, and I haven't lost us money yet."

"You play with your estate the way you play with your life— maybe the way you played with your toys as a child. Picking them up and dropping them the moment you're bored."

"You're irritated with me? Don't be. We're all children at heart. Even you, Harland, only you conceal the infant in you better than I do."

Her fiery charm was back. She saw him smile and went to sit on the end of his desk, leaned forward, and kissed him on the cheek. Then she said, quite seriously, "Harland, I'm just coming out of a bad time. I haven't much to show for my life, except a broken marriage that poleaxed me for a while. Unless I get out there again and find what I'm looking for, I may never have anything but Bonnie to justify having existed. And although that's a lot, it's not enough. Have faith, and take care of my affairs. Please."

That was the first time Lara had mentioned her broken marriage to Harland, or had hinted that she was not satisfied with her life. Normally he would have found it embarrassing to hear such an admission from a client. He always tried to avoid involvement in troublesome, emotional, or nonfinancial affairs. Harland had once had misgivings about Lara, but had long ago been won over by latent qualities he occasionally glimpsed in her. Now he studied her for several seconds before he spoke.

Here she was, one of America's wealthier heiresses. She had power, intelligence, a quick mind. In her late-twenties, she was more beautiful and desirable than ever. Yet lost. He felt little pity for her, but some admiration that she could recognize she was wasting herself and get on with trying to find what she was looking for. Harland's detachment didn't allow curiosity as to what that was.

He raised her hand, held it in his for several seconds, and then surprised her with his gallantry. He kissed it and said, "Taking care of your affairs is what I'm here for. Good luck."

"I wonder, does luck really have anything to do with it?"

"It does if you haven't got it, Lara."

The men came courting, and Lara was receptive. Out came a new ostrich-covered diary. Only, now there was no Emily to veto the social engagements. Marriage, divorce, and Bonnie had at least rid Lara of her mother's supervision over her life. Emily was not as relieved about it as Lara was. There was no more Missy to keep the social engagements in order, either. With Lara married, Missy had been repossessed by Emily, but only after she had trained a middle-aged friend to take over.

Nancy Clemens enjoyed her position with the Faynes. It had afforded her not the easiest, but certainly one of the most glamorous jobs, any secretary could want. When the couple divorced, she chose to stay with Lara. A pleasant surprise because Nancy had had a closer relationship with Sam than Lara. Nonetheless she kept Lara's social affairs and correspondence in perfect order. Now, several months after the divorce, Nancy, Nanny Peters, and Coral the maid were continuing to run Lara's household much as they always had, except that Sam Fayne was gone. The task was not an easy one in a household still without a house of its own.

The three servants settled down in Cannonberry Chase like a family within a family. But they were not fooled by the change in Lara during her seclusion from the world. They had been with her too long, had seen the verve for life she demonstrated in so many ways. Servants have firm views about their employers. This trio was unanimous that she would recover. They would all be on the move again.

After they had waved her off with Julia and David on the first leg of their journey to Brazil from the airfield at Cannonberry Chase, Nancy turned to Nanny Peters, who was holding Bonnie in her arms. In a voice pitched beneath the family's chattering, she said, "Now I know why I chose to stay with Mrs. Fayne. She's the one with the real spirit of adventure in her heart. When she gets back, it won't be long before we're all off again. Tomorrow I'll go into the city to Mark Cross. We'll all need new diaries.''

Now, several weeks later, Lara and her entourage were staying for a few days in the Stantons' Fifth Avenue house. Lara sat propped up against the pillows of her bed, her breakfast tray across her lap. Nancy Clemens was seated at the escritoire, going over the week's engagements with Lara. This morning was no different from any other morning, yet Nancy sensed that Lara was more restless than usual. So much so that, after half an hour, the secretary asked, ''Is something wrong, Lara?''

''No, not exactly wrong. It's just that there's a sameness about these early morning meetings we have. A repetitiveness about my life. Today, this week . . . It could have been yesterday, last week. Oh, the places I go, the people I meet, the men who come sniffing around me, they may *seem* to change—but they don't, not really.''

''That's life, Lara. I wonder how many millions of people have woken up this morning to a similar feeling?''

''But do they all feel that there must be something more out there for them, just waiting to be discovered?''

''I would venture to say yes.''

''Well, maybe you're right, and life is just one big Easter-egg hunt.''

Lara sipped her hot black coffee and noted the slight smile at the corners of Nancy's mouth. ''I know what you'd like to say: 'There's nothing special about you, Lara Stanton Fayne. Your problems are no worse than everyone else's. Get out there like us all and make the best of it.' ''

Nancy pinched her lips together. Her eyes held a smile and, though she remained silent, she nodded assent. Give or take the odd word, that was exactly what she had meant to say.

''Well, that took me down a peg or two. Oh, don't look so apologetic.''

''I wasn't.''

''Good. I'd like to get up and dress now, Nancy. Give me an hour and we'll finish.''

Lara watched her secretary leave her room. About to get up, she changed her mind and sank back down into the pillows. She wondered if those millions Nancy had evoked felt as alone as she did. It was not boredom with her life, more a sense of isolation. The lack of a romantic love affair that worked for her. She missed love, that absolute love and adoration that Sam had once felt for her. That David had once felt for her. Her father, and brothers, and sister, and, yes, even Jamal in his own strange way. That only Bonnie felt for her now.

It was her determination not to use Bonnie's love as a crutch that kept pushing Lara forward when the energy to begin again with another man was simply not there. There were so many incidents between Lara and Bonnie that tempted her to stay locked away forever at Cannonberry Chase with her daughter. But she loved the child too much to burden her with too much mother-love.

One morning when Bonnie was riding her pony, Mr. Macaroni, and Lara old Biscuit, Bonnie asked, "Who will you ride with when I go to big school, Mummy?"

"I will ride by myself or with Uncle David or Grandfather. There'll always be someone around to ride with. Why do you ask, Bonnie?"

"Daddy says the same thing."

"There, you see."

"But what little girl will be here to play with you when I'm at big school?"

"No little girl. You are my only little girl, and when you are away I play with grownups until you return."

"You won't cry?"

"No, Bonnie. I promise I won't cry."

A smile appeared on the child's face, and she said, "I was thinking maybe you would cry, and then I was thinking of crying because you were crying, and now everything's pink and we won't have to cry." Pink was the color of all-rightness in Bonnie's world. She had once heard a groom in the Cannonberry Chase stables declare he was "in the pink."

The child looked so relieved it prompted Lara to tell her, "Bonnie, when you go away with Daddy, you must not think about me all by myself. I always find people to play with, if I'm not with my little girl. It's the same as when you're away: you don't have your mummy, but you can still have a good time. And we still love each other. You do understand, wherever we are, we can still love each other, and be away from each other, and have other friends? There's no need to cry."

Children rarely waste tears on such considerations. Her answer was classic Bonnie Fayne. "Oh, good." That dispensed with, she was immediately onto something else. She told Lara, "When I grow up I want to look beautiful like Cinderella and Sleeping Beauty and you, Mummy. And I want to dress up and put all your sparkling things on my fingers and on my neck and ears, and I want to smell like you and fly a plane like you. And have everybody look at me like they look at you. And I want to have a man like Daddy in bed at night, and a little girl to love me like I love you, and a big hat with flowers on it. And shoes with very high heels. Don't you think that's a good idea?"

A low hedge loomed up, though still at some distance. Before Lara could answer, the idea of jumping it absorbed all Bonnie's attention. "May we jump it, Mummy?"

"Yes, but only if you have all your attention on the jump, and you're thinking of nothing else."

Bonnie dug her knees into Mr. Macaroni, and off they went, Lara keeping pace with them on Biscuit. The child made her jump, and it was perfect. She flung herself out of the saddle and off the pony, then kissed Mr. Macaroni, and gave him a peppermint Life Saver from her pocket. Lara was beside her and swung her up off the ground to give her a big hug and a kiss. "A jump to be proud of, Bonnie. Well done."

"That was for you, Mummy. A prize, 'cause you don't cry when I am not here with you."

It was said with such affectionate sincerity and sweetness that it actually brought a tear to Lara's eye. But not for long. Laughter took the place of sadness when Bonnie announced, as Lara was hoisting her into the saddle, "I need to put the feed bag on. I'm that hungry." The child smiled at Lara, who could not stop laughing.

"Is that funny? Nobody laughs when Tommy at the stable says it."

"Just hungry will do, Bonnie."

"Cheery pie. I'm inclined to a piece of cheery pie."

Lara did not dare to laugh again. But it did sound just like Cook.

Every day she learned more about love from Bonnie than she ever had from the men who had loved her in the past, or the men who dated her now with protestations of love. So far Bonnie, her three-year-old child, was her best teacher of the art. The way a three-year-old loves made her understand how, as the youngest of the Stanton children, all the family had fallen in love with her, and even learned about love from her as a child. Why David and Max especially were able to love her so well in return. It was hard to imagine that she had once been as innocent, as sweet, as giving and loving as Bonnie.

She still loved Bonnie, her family, and Julia that way. She could still remember having once loved Sam that way. Even Jamal. Through these terrible times, he had remained a steadfast friend. She felt more touched now by the memory of the call he had made to her, only days after her return from Paris, than she had been then. He had been honest and forthright and generous. But then, he had always been that, as well as a hard, ruthless lover to her. She could remember David calling her to the telephone, where she heard Jamal's voice: "You were always too good for him. Too special. You may not believe this, but I'm sorry. You made that choice, it didn't work out for you, and I feel for you. Come to me, here in Morocco. Bring Bonnie. My house is your house. My family and I will look after you."

She had declined the invitation. With gratitude, and in the knowledge that he was acting as a friend, not a sexual seducer. He had then made a second offer, in his alternative role in her life. "When you want me, I am here for you. You have only to call. Come to me. I have missed you more than you can know."

She recalled the marvelous sex they had had together. Perhaps only now was she ready to confront the thought of it. She had expelled it from her mind while with Sam. How she missed being married to him. She wondered if even the illusion of having simultaneously love and great sex, a happy married life, wasn't better than nothing. Because nothing was what had replaced those things. There had been so many flirtations, but she had never had another man in bed since marrying Sam. Desire had returned, yearnings for sexual release, for those sweet excursions to oblivion in the arms of a man. Several times, she came close to surrendering herself to sex with the men she was involved with. But in each case she changed her mind.

Her sexual gratification came from erotic fantasies in the darkness of her own room. She used them to resurrect in herself erotic images of experiences once shared with Sam. She achieved her orgasms by making love to herself. Jamal had taught her, and had proven an adept teacher. It was thrilling to come, with or without a man. For the moment it was enough to be able to give herself to herself. To savor the intensity in drawing out an orgasm.

Lara would work herself up to a second orgasm and a third, till at last she felt her whole body go limp, all anxiety expelled. She would feel warm and safe and happy between the smooth, white linen sheets . . .

Now she fluffed up a pillow and placed it behind her head. She felt languid and lazy. Why did she still have to submit to the ostrich-leather diary? There must be more to life than what she was getting out of hers. So what, if millions of other people felt the same way, as Nancy had suggested. Let them do something about it. She threw the covers off her, and she said aloud, "I fucking well intend to."

Lara felt a sudden surge of excitement. A plan was forming in her mind. The pieces were all there, but she could not as yet detect the pattern. She dropped her nightdress on the bed. The first shock of a cold shower hardened her resolve. Today was Day One for her. She felt full of song. The shower room echoed to the Changing of the Guard music from *Carmen*. The scent of sweet almonds from her Perlier bath cream mingled with the steam. The heady perfume transported her, in her imagination, to an almond orchard in Italy. Other orchards, too: her orange-tree rides in Florida, the apple trees at the Chase, a cherry orchard in Hungary, where once she and Jamal had made love. She stemmed the flow of water and wrapped her hair in a white towel etched in ecru lace. Another enfolded her body.

Lara returned to the bed and sat on the edge, next to the telephone. Her first call was to David. She found him in his house in Georgetown.

"Hello, La."

"How about if I fly in for lunch with you?"

"Today?"

"Sure, today."

"I've got something on." A moment's hesitation, then, "I'll cancel it."

"You are wonderful to me, David."

"One thing—I've got a friend. A girl. I'd like you to meet

her. See what you think." There was nothing unusual about that. David always had a girl, a "friend." And Lara was usually the first to veto the lady. "Stay for dinner. Stay the night if you like."

"Maybe. No promises. Let's play it by ear. But I will meet your girl."

"Shall I bring her to lunch?"

"Rather you didn't."

"Actually I'd rather not myself. Too selfish. I want you all to myself. Long time since we've had a private lunch together."

"Not since you became the up-and-coming voice in Congress. The man to watch. Isn't that what the papers say?"

"This is one time you can believe what you read in print."

"You really are doing it, aren't you? I bet you'll make the big time."

"No point in anything else, is there? See you at lunch."

"The airport," she corrected.

He laughed. He still had trouble denying Lara anything. "Okay, the airport it is."

"You're the best of cousins, David."

"Quit wooing me, La. I said I'd be there. But how about giving me a little notice next time?"

Lara laughed to herself. David knew her so well. But then, so did all the family. Since her divorce she had seen more of Steven and John than she had expected to. Steven and Lynette's marriage had begun to work well. No one had imagined it would. Steven had predicted his wife would either succumb to Emily and accept her new position in life as a Stanton, or she would suffer. Lynette had caved in. Completely awed by being a Stanton now, she had squared up to her role in society. Emily, once her challenger at every turn, was now her greatest friend and mentor. So Steven was free to pursue his career. In the years that followed, he had contributed his own useful mite to the infinite sum of human knowledge. His fieldwork—expeditions to the jungles of New Guinea, the Gobi Desert in China, digs in Polynesia—had made him a force in the world of anthropology. He used his wealth for the pursuit of knowledge and the great good of mankind.

Lara was proud of Steven's successes. She would meet him several times a week at the museum he had created on West

Fifty-third Street. Often John would join them there. Success on an even grander scale was his. It was John who had taken over the day-to-day running of the family trusts. It seemed to Lara that every year he staked a better claim to being the perfect Stanton. He had married the ideal wife, and appeared to have taken on more of Emily's and Henry's character than any of his brothers or sisters. His contribution to mankind might have been mostly monetary, but its sheer scale redeemed the lack of originality. In several years the trusts under his sharp and intelligent eye became enormously wealthy, wielding enormous power to do good. But he remained a highly social animal, like Henry and Emily, like all the family. And available especially to Steven and Lara, whenever they wanted or needed him. He was now a man to whom world leaders sent their ministers for consultations on charitable trusts. John had said many times to Lara, "Keep on saving yourself, La. When I'm burned out, it's you I'll nominate and support to take over."

Lara, still perched on the edge of the bed, felt elated by the success of her siblings, a little downcast by her own failures. She sighed. Maybe she shouldn't think about that too much. Why not remember instead where they had been in their lives at her age? She recalled her father once telling her, "Comparisons are generally odious, my dear. Not to say onerous and otiose, too." Not knowing her Shakespeare then, she had solemnly corrected her father's vocabulary.

Get on with it, girl, she told herself, toweling her damp hair vigorously. She dropped the towel on the floor and shook her hair out. She ran her fingers through it as she reached out for the telephone, anxious to make her next call.

"Sam! Oh, good, I'm glad I caught you. I'm going to travel, take Bonnie, the usual entourage. I need a change."

"If you really need a change, why don't you leave Bonnie and the entourage with me?"

"I don't think you understand. I'd like to get away for quite a long time. Go to Europe, make it my base for going anywhichway my fancy takes me. At least, that's what I think. But I know how much you love Bonnie, and she loves you. I don't mean to deprive you of each other."

"Lara, I think we should talk about this."

"We are, Sam."

"There is something else serious I want to talk to you about."

"Well, go ahead, Sam. What's on your mind?" Buoyant now about changing her life, she felt she could be generous with Sam and give him a hearing. She could take on anything. Maybe he was at last going to marry this paragon of womanhood he had left her for. Let him tell her then.

"I can't talk to you about it on the telephone."

"Of course you can. Get on with it, Sam. Be quick, I have a load of calls to make. No, maybe you're right, come and see me. What I would like to do is make an arrangement with you, so you always know where we are. Then you can fly over and see Bonnie, or I can bring her home to see you. It's not that I want to take her away from you, Sam. Believe me, it's nothing like that."

"I know. You've been fair about access. Look, you don't have to explain. Let me come and see you today."

"No, not today. I'm away today."

"Oh, then can I take Bonnie out for the day? I can move my appointments around. I'll bring her home after supper, and then we can talk."

"I may stay over in Washington with David."

"In that case I would like to keep Bonnie overnight. Is that okay?"

"Fine. Fix it with Nanny. We'll talk tomorrow, when I know more what I'm going to do. Really, I still haven't made my plans. It's just that I wanted you to be the first to know, because of Bonnie. I'm moving on for a while. Change of people and places, and all that."

Hearing her own words confirmed for her that what she was doing was right. Right for her. She was like the hamster who finally gets off the wheel. It was such a cliche that she actually winced when she told herself, New beginnings. Scouring the world in search of something. Herself? She could mock the cliche because she knew better. With a big grin she told herself: Bullshit! I know who I am, and I can live with her, and thank the Lord for that. What kept slipping in and out of her mind was Love: romantic, real. An adventuress—that's what I'm looking to be.

Sam's voice broke into her thoughts. "Why this sudden urge to move on?"

"I need to begin again, Sam. I'm sure you can understand that."

There was hesitation at the other end of the line. "Yes," he finally answered. "I can understand that. Lara, maybe we should begin again together."

The unexpected suggestion startled her, but she recovered instantly. "No way, Sam. There's as much chance of that as finding icicles in hell. Whatever made you think I would consider an idea like that?"

"We're so good together. Even divorced."

"That's for the world to see and think. I did tell you that was the way it was going to be. Play-acting, remember? You've fallen for the performance, Sam."

"Lara—"

She interrupted him, taking scant satisfaction in reminding him, in her own subtle way, that she had not forgiven him. "So what happened to this jewel of womanhood who was going to make you happy, give you a better life than we had together?"

"You. You came between us, even though you weren't there. I see you, and—"

"I don't think we should talk about this, Sam. Come and get Bonnie. When I've worked out my plans, we'll talk. You can have access when you like and wherever we are."

She replaced the phone gently. I should have guessed, she told herself, and returned to drying her hair. A few days before, while dining with the family, he had looked at her in that intimate sexual way that had always been a signal of desire for her. She had ignored it, pretended to herself that she had imagined it. Now she realized why the look had registered with her. Her immediate reaction had been to think, What a pig! That, if he could, he would resume a sexual relationship with her. Lara felt quite ill at the thought that he could have sex with her now, without love. Any kind of carnal love would have been better than sex with a man who had deceived her as he had.

Now, the right moment gone, she could think of all the smart, hurtful things she could have said to him. Just not good enough, Sam. I deserve better than you, Sam Fayne. I shall get better than you. But how pointless! Childish and pointless, even if she believed it all.

She rang for Nancy and her maid, Coral. The two women

almost collided as they entered the bedroom. Lara sat at her dressing table, still in her bath sheet, while Coral dried her hair. Above the drone of the hair dryer, Lara outlined her plans to her secretary.

"Nancy, you know that nice man who is so good with us about bookings on the QE2? Why don't you get in touch with him this morning? I would like us all to sail to England as soon as possible. We're traveling. I don't know where to, or for how long, but we have to have a jump-off place, and I think Claridge's, London, might just suit us. No Elizabeth and staying with her. And, no, I don't for the moment think I want to take up residence in the house in Gloucestershire, so forget all that.

"It's to be playtime, funtime, foot-loose-and-fancy-free time. Put-a-pin-in-the-map-and-go time. We're on an adventure. We'll just set ourselves up comfortably in a large suite at Claridge's for an indefinite stay, then see where we go from there. You make all the arrangements."

"A few firm dates might help."

"Impossible for the moment. I haven't finalized my plans yet. I just know I want a change and out of New York, like right now. Firm dates by tomorrow, maybe."

"The diary, Lara. All your engagements."

"Scrub everything from today on. Except, of course, any serious family events. Those I'll always fly back for, from wherever we are. I'm cutting loose—and, boy, does it feel good!"

Lara scrutinized the expression on the women's faces. They showed neither shock nor disapproval. Yet there was no approval, either. It wasn't indifference exactly; simply curiosity about what would come next. She gave the women the day's plan. Nanny had to be told. Then she had Coral pack her little black dress, plus accessories, in a Louis Vuitton overnight shoulder bag, together with cosmetics and a few toiletries.

She called the mechanic at Cannonberry Chase: would he load her flight bag onto her plane and taxi it onto the runway? Then she called the helicopter service she used in the city to fly her to the field in an hour's time. Nancy had already gone to her office: her first task to decommission the ostrich-covered diary and to place calls. Wheels were set in motion for Lara's open-ended journey. She was about to launch herself on the world yet again. It felt good, as if she had never done it before.

She chose from her cupboard a thinly woven, camel-hair jumpsuit, and around the waist cinched a wide, chocolate-brown suede belt. She pinned the diamond angel's wings Sam had given her over her heart and slipped into a pair of brown suede cowboy boots. Then she stretched out on the chaise longue and picked up the phone again.

Emily had to be told. Or preferably Emily and Henry together. She called Henry. "Dad?"

"Hello, Lara."

"I'm taking off. Decided to go abroad for a while. Will you tell Mother?"

"No, you tell her. When are you leaving?"

"Not sure. A few days' time, a week at the most."

"Any special reason?"

"Yes, my life isn't good enough."

"Well, that's sufficient reason. Just let us know where you are. Taking Bonnie?"

"Not sure, yet."

"Leave her with us."

"Maybe. But, if I do that, you get Sam, too."

"Whatever you think is best, La."

"Thanks, Dad."

"For what?"

"For making it easy."

There was a note of affection in her voice that meant a lot to Henry. As the years rolled by, he found himself ever more attached to Lara. She had her ups and downs, had weathered several personal traumas, and he realized she was developing into a very special lady. And Henry had always had a penchant for very special ladies. She was not the disappointment he sometimes felt his other daughter, Elizabeth, to be. He loved her, yes, but too often with her had plumbed abysses of boredom. He now saw Lara not as the failure she imagined herself, but as a late developer, who would one day blossom gloriously.

"Call your mother, Lara. And stay in touch."

She called Emily, and had to smile. Emily was incorrigible. "Have a good time, Lara, wherever you decide to go. Only no surprises, *please*!" was the upshot of that conversation. Then she sat for several minutes, trying to restrain a compulsion to make her other calls and be done with them so she could take off straightaway. To be free of family and friends within the hour seemed to be her goal. And she accomplished it.

Chapter 19

"**I**'m breaking out, you know, as in prison breakout. Not running away, don't think that."

"Never entered my mind." David smiled. "It sounds great."

"What sounds great?"

"Breaking out. Don't make any plans. Just go."

"Well, I do have to make some arrangements. Set Bonnie and the staff up somewhere."

"Not immediately. In a few weeks. Surely you can be parted from Bonnie for a few weeks."

"I don't know. I've always had her with me. Ever since the day she was born."

"More reason to leave her at home for a change. Leave everybody at home. Pack your bags and go. Send for them later. A week, ten days, a month. See how you feel."

"Mother's right about you. You're still a thrill-seeker that she can do nothing with."

"That's true." The two of them laughed. They were sitting at a table on the poop deck of a 1927 yacht moored on the Potomac, having whiskey sours before lunch. It was David's platform for entertaining guests, while avoiding the Washington social scene. "Country-hop. People-hop. Cut clear of responsibility. Arm yourself with a check-book, a pack of credit cards, a case you can carry, and your address book. Dad's got a great address book. Get a copy to stuff in your bag. He has all the right contacts, ruthlessly arranged by country. To be used as prescribed by necessity. Or is this an 'I want to be alone,' Garbo-style retreat?"

247

"Far from it. At least, I don't think it's pure Garbo. I hope it will just evolve into whatever it is. If you know what I mean? . . ."

"I do, and it sounds like a great idea to me. Something I would do myself. Just go. Have your adventure. I think that's what this is all about. That and—"

"Why does there have to be an 'and'?"

"Because I know you too well. Fess up."

She gave him a sheepish look, ignored his insinuation, and remained silent. They were lunching under a warm sun. The early October breeze bore an autumn freshness that made for perfect Washington weather. She was exactly where she wanted to be, with whom she wanted to be, and felt a sort of inner glee. She was just living in the moment and not thinking beyond that. If this was to be the pattern of her new life, she was content with it. She changed the subject.

"I always did like this boat. I was really surprised when Dad sold it to you. It holds so many memories for him. He has entertained five presidents of this country innumerable times on it, and foreign heads of state in droves. Or so he says."

"I think he sold it because he expects me to do the same. Not a bad buy for a dollar, was it?"

"Let's take her out, just for an hour or two."

David looked skeptical.

"If we do, I'll 'fess up.' "

He rose from his chair to phone an order to the captain to take them out. When he returned to the table he kissed the top of Lara's head. Lowering his voice, he told her, "I knew you would, with or without a sail down the river."

A waiter arrived with a silver tureen of hot curried parsnip soup and ladled it into their bowls. It was served with swirls of cream and crisp, crackling croutons. They finished their drinks as the crew slipped the moorings and the yacht swiftly put water between itself and the green bank. Lara took one sip of soup—which begged another—before putting the spoon down to declare: "Utterly delicious. Now you won't laugh at me?"

"Never."

She shot him a doubtful look, but spoke as she picked up her spoon again. "It all has to do with romance. I'm looking for romance." She looked closely at him to forestall his laughing at her. But there was no trace of a smile on his lips. He appeared quite serious and interested, so she continued, "I suddenly feel quite starved of real romance. You know, romantic places— Venice, Florence, Rome. Or London-in-the-blitz kind of romance: all thick fog and intense love, and danger, and living for today and the hell with tomorrow! Cairo maybe, and Alexandria. Or Paris, *but not the Ritz*. I am most definitely through with the Ritz." She managed a laugh at herself over that. David was glad to laugh with her. He adored her when she could laugh at herself.

"Island-hopping in Greece, buzzing the Dalmatian Coast by boat . . . Remember that trip, David?"

"I sure do."

"Lord, have we come a long way since then!"

A pensive "Yes."

"Well, I want more, David. You know me, I always want more. The thing is that I am going to get more."

"Good for you."

"Dare I say the word? Sure I dare! Romantic love. And a romantic man—I want him, too. And I want to get married again. I really liked being married. It was great. I'm making it sound as if I'm starved for romance."

"Maybe you are."

"I guess so. Is that pathetic?

"Truthful, I think, rather than pathetic. Wanting a unique account of the world through feminine eyes, maybe." David and Lara remained quiet while the waiter removed the soup bowls and refilled their glasses with a perfectly chilled Pouilly Fuissé. David was ever delighted by her straightforwardness and candor, the source of her strongest allure. She radiated an ardor and youthfulness that enchanted men. Then why, he wondered, were her love affairs so tragic? She was right; she did deserve better. The waiter gone, he asked, "Isn't there a man who would qualify among your current suitors? Rumors have surfaced that you don't lack offers."

"Qualify, maybe. But that's not good enough. No, I can't say any one of them has exactly rung my bell. Know what I mean? You should, you've been there enough times with women. I'm a good-time girl who's just not having a very good time. I see nothing to do but change that. A long time ago, Dad told me,

'Lara, you have something like a duty to be happy because you've got everything going for you.' I admit to slipping occasionally on that one. A bit weak-willed of me. That's not an excuse, just a face of my character. But I do bounce back, and I am now. So, I'm off. Maybe this lunch is my launch.''

He noted the change in her since her divorce. Then there had been confusion in her, malice, self-deception. But there was none of that to be detected in her now. There was about her the strange, brooding tenderness that had often touched his heart. Ever since adolescence she had been preoccupied by love and its anxieties. Love was the most compelling thing in her life. And it was going to be, until she found a man able to quench her thirst for it.

"A Russian poet, Samuel Marshak, wrote: 'Heart be intelligent and his brain be kind.' ''

"Are you trying to tell me something, David?''

"Yes. Don't live everything you read." They both laughed. "Nor does it mean—''

"Oh, David, give me credit. Not to fall recklessly in love, not to get bound in thralldom, not to allow the mess of shredded emotions over a bad love affair to flatten me—Is that what you were going to advise? Have no fear, I've been there and I'm not going back.''

"I see wisdom is not completely banned from your feelings about love.''

"Yes, on a poop deck in the sun, floating down the Potomac with a man who would never harm me, it's very easy to welcome wisdom aboard.''

Their main course arrived: fresh salmon wrapped in filo pastry with a light hollandaise sauce, served with wild rice, pureed celeriac, and a salad of Belgian endive and crispy fresh watercress dressed with the most perfect vinaigrette. While the deckhands-cum-waiters were serving, Lara abandoned herself to the cushions of her chair and watched the riverbank slowly slip by. Two joggers running along the bank waved to her, and she waved back. At a folding table an elderly couple sat on canvas chairs, reading near the edge of the sunlit bank. Further on, two children were running in and out of the tall grass. She could remember how she would once have felt isolated from all that life going on around her. No such feelings marred that afternoon. Quite the contrary. She felt in touch with all life.

David reclaimed her attention by clinking his fork against his glass. She smiled, and they both said, "To the chef."

"Stay over tonight. I have a party on at the house. And Washington is a romantic place, *if* you're interested in power politics, power climbing, power partying, power sex, all that sort of thing. Move on, though, if you think you're going to find the kind of romance you're looking for. In Washington, among this crowd, what passes for love and romance comes after the speeches, the coffee, the stiff nightcap, after the table's been cleared and the last car has quit the drive. For men, it usually arrives in the form of a thousand-dollar-a-night hooker. That's the safest, most fun form in a city where indiscretion and scandal ride shotgun with power and position. They have great hookers in Washington. And spicy, adulterous relationships. They're to be found around every corner, but even those are part of the local megalomania. They operate within a clear structure, sort of like a military operation, and with a high priority on camouflage. They are amazing, these Washington power brokers. And mostly they function on only the most crass and naive ideas about how to play power games and win . . . and stay up there. There's a high body count in Washington politics. It's a 'today you're in, tomorrow you're out' kind of town. But, I'd still say, romantic in its own way."

"Not for me, I think. Although I've always had a fun time here. All those rumpled, speedy journalists looking like they've just fallen out of bed. Intense, intelligent, aggressive—my god, but they can be aggressive when they're onto something. Newshounds is the right word. If they were in the dog world they would have to be Jack Russell terriers. And nosy? Well, I suppose that's their livelihood, snooping. But, warts and all, I've always found them the least unattractive of the Washington males."

"There will be a few at the party tonight. Make it a nice, newspaperly occasion for you. Interested yet?"

"Well, maybe. They are, in their own way, romantic figures, always looking for the big adventure."

"More like the big story."

"Oh, that's Number One priority, all else follows. But why do you have them around, David?"

"Because they're like children. Amusing, entertaining, and they do retain an odd kind of innocence."

"And they are great flirts! I always have my most fun flirting with the journalist or literary friends you have at your parties. They make a play for me as if I'm a body with no brain, and I play the airhead they expect. I rather like playing the beautiful, dumb deb role. Yes, why not? I will stay the night. For the first time since college, I'm not tied to that bloody ostrich-covered diary Mother stuck me with. I can do just what my fancy tells me. Who else will be there? No, let me guess. Your usual collection of the great and the smooth? How many foreign diplomats have you netted?"

"Now don't be cruel. They adore you, and they're very bankable, romantic figures."

"Are you laughing at me?"

"No, just teasing you, not your quest."

"Oh, well, that's all right then. I can handle them. They've been parking their limos on the family driveway for as long as I can remember."

"Confess, how many of them have made a play for you?"

"Better ask how many haven't! Another good question might be how many were single at the time! 'Diplomat' usually means 'married.' At least the more senior ones anyway. They come as couples, so to speak. If not, they're suspect. That goes for your usual smattering of senators and congressmen as well."

She caught a certain look in David's eyes. She had hit on something. Something that was bothering him—or that he wanted to talk to her about. Their meal over now, he suggested moving to the deck chairs and taking coffee there.

After only a few steps Lara's hand was on his arm. "A wild guess."

"Okay. Just one."

"You're going to get married."

He hesitated. "Thinking about it."

They sat down in the steamer chairs set next to each other, facing the riverbank. Neither of them spoke for several minutes. They overlooked a lovely garden with a late-summer rose arbor. Flowers just dropping their petals glided first into and then out of sight. The sun warmed them. Replete with fine wine and excellent food, the joy of their own company, they contemplated what David has just revealed.

At last he broke the spell. "Well, aren't you going to say something?"

"Is this a career move, or a love move?"

"A bit of both."

"Does she know that?"

"Yes, she does, actually."

Lara turned to one side, the better to see him. She held out her hand, and he took it in his. "I hadn't planned to hit you with it like this. I wanted you to know her better before I told you, but you were always too good a guesser."

"Know her better? Do I know her at all?"

"Yes, as a matter of fact, you do. Lara, this hasn't upset you, has it? That I think I want to marry?"

"Upset me? *No.* Surprised me a little, yes. But, David, I've come to the conclusion that we Stantons are the marrying kind. I told you, I loved being married. It was great until the very minute it was over. It'll be rich for you, too. You'll love being married. I just hope I like her, because I love you so much."

"Marriage to Martha won't change our relationship. No more than your marriage to Sam did, I promise."

"Why are we acting so glum? You look worried. Not on my account, please. It's going to be wonderful. Being married is great, when it works. And I'm sure you haven't waited this long to marry the wrong person. It's odd. I thought I would be jealous at the very thought of your marrying or loving someone other than me, but I'm not. I'm sort of excited."

She jumped out of the chair. "Move over." He shifted his legs, and she sat on the footrest of the steamer chair and leaned against him. With an arm around her shoulders he hugged her to him. "Tell me about her. She has to be something to have caught you. Enough women have tried."

He began to laugh. He was relieved that Lara was so happy for him. "Stop flattering me. She's wonderful."

"Well, go on. Her driver's license would tell me more about her than you have. Is she beautiful?"

"Ravishingly so. Very intelligent, very—But this is crazy. You know her."

"I do."

"Martha Winthrop."

"The Winthrop Steel family Martha?"

"That's right."

"She's Julia's first cousin. She was a Van Fleet. She's much older than we are."

"Much older than you and Julia, yes, dear. But then, I'm much older than you two."

"But she's lovely, David. I can hardly believe it. And with all that money, and all that Philadelphia mainline snob society bred into her. Mother will be delighted. Elizabeth will all but coo. Mother's delinquent will have made the best catch of all of us. A merger even better than mine."

They began to laugh. Lara had pinpointed the way Emily and Elizabeth would react to his marrying Martha. "She's even older than you are. And when I think of all those thwarted dollybirds, all those chic mannequins who have fallen by the wayside."

"Only just a little older, Lara."

"Oh, I see. It's 'who's counting?' time. You must be in love, a playboy reprobate like you marrying the older woman. But hold on, it's just beginning to sink in. She's one of those grand Washington hostesses. Her husband was Minister of Finance or something. Secretary of the Treasury under some recent administration."

"That's right."

"She's gorgeous and so chic! A great beauty. Very intelligent. I remember when they came and stayed with us in the South of France . . . Oh!" And Lara cocked an eyebrow at him.

"Oh, no, nothing like that. I never touched her till long after he died. And we have been very discreet. There are children involved. She's a wonderful woman, Lara. Really quite perfect for me."

"Is she one of those power ladies?"

"Yes, but in the nicest way. Let's just say, I don't think she would mind rearranging the furniture in the White House."

"Ah?"

"I did tell you it was a career *and* a love move."

"Who else knows about this?"

"You're the first. But we're going to have to do something about that soon."

"Oh?" The other eyebrow.

"No. She's not pregnant. But that old biological clock of hers is ticking away."

"Then there will be children?"

"As many as we can fit in."

"David, I can't believe we are having this conversation. It's so exciting. How about a bottle of champagne?"

"Why not?"

The pudding arrived: pears poached in red wine with cinnamon and cloves, and paper-thin vanilla wafers. They ate sitting on the footrests of their steamer chairs and drinking champagne. Afterward David removed the dish from her hands and placed it next to his on the polished deck. He refilled their glasses. "I'd like to raise a toast. To you, Lara. I loved you from first sight, and still cherish you. I'm devoted to you as a brother, and you're my best friend. Thanks for being so happy for me."

It was a sentimental declaration of love, made more poignant by the obvious excitement and joy they were both experiencing in their relationship—and the new phase in it which was about to begin. There was just a moment when each of them searched back through time to choose their own particular memory to reflect on. The moment passed, and they raised their glasses to drink. The last of the many ghosts haunting their affection seemed at last to have been put to rest.

It just seemed so amazingly right that he should marry Martha Winthrop. It prompted Lara to ask, "A big wedding?"

"Yes, a very big wedding. All the trimmings."

"I'll be there for it. Back from wherever I may be."

"No, La. Not that I don't want you to. There's no one I'd rather have there than you. It's more that I only want you to come back for my wedding if it fits into your plans. It's just another family wedding. Right now, it's far less important than your cutting loose. I'm really with you on that, you know."

"I know, and you're a dear about it. But, David, I am simply *not* going to miss your wedding. I'm so thrilled. I thought for years how miserable I would be when this day would come. And now, it's here, and I'm not. It's as if a part of me has found not just the rainbow but the pot of gold at the end of it. Will Martha be at your party tonight?"

"Yes."

"Then count me in. I want to get to know her. I always had

a kind of secret admiration for her, but all that beauty and sophistication warned me off. She has always been nice to me, but that cool, elegant reserve of hers always made me wonder if she did in fact like me.''

"She thinks you're very feminine. She reckons you must be the most beautiful deb in America.''

Allowing herself to be flattered, Lara said, "You don't mean it? Well, if she does, she'd better slap it into the past tense. A divorcée, a mum—hardly a deb anymore.''

"And there's something else—she knows about us. That in the family you are the most important member to me. And she understands. Knowing us all, as she has for years, she's rather in awe of the family. She was an only child, and she sees the Stantons and our closeness as something formidable, and at the same time enriching. But she wants to be as much a part of us as possible. She sees our world as much bigger than hers. The power of a family like ours is greater on all fronts than the small, closed society she's lived in all her life. She is, for all her cosmopolitan life, quite provincial in some ways. Not nearly as worldly as you are at your young age. But she has that same Van Fleet kindness. She's not unlike Julia.''

"David, enough! You're beginning to sound like a man in love. Let's just turn this tub around and go meet the future Mrs. Stanton.''

David could host a good party. The one at his house in Georgetown that evening was no exception. There had been thirty for a sit-down dinner. A table resplendent with family silver, not the Henry Stanton silver, but David's own parents' silver. It was only on rare occasions—and sometimes years could seperate them—that Lara remembered that he was not her real brother. The silver flashed that message through her mind tonight, then it was forgotten.

David watched Lara put the finishing touches to her makeup, then announced, "I've rearranged the dinner table. Sitting on your left will be a journalist from the *Washington Post*. A nice, good-looking, bright guy. Fits your idea of a journalist to perfection. On your right, my old polo-playing friend from Argentina, Jorge Mendez. Remember him? We were in college together. Still the same smooth Latin lover. Just gray-tinted now.

I chose the cream of the wifeless men at the party to grace you. So you can do your stuff. You'll wear them like a pair of ear-rings.''

And she did do her stuff. She flirted, and played amusing and charming, and was by far the most attractive and sensual-looking woman at the table. All through the meal she let her dinner companions hope. David delighted to see sidelong glances flick-ering up and down the table toward her from some of his other male guests. Veiled lusty glances. The women were too busy being charming themselves to take much notice of Lara. She was, after all, a bird of passage in Washington. Transients are important in Washington, but only as transients.

Lara favored the *Washington Post* journalist because, at one point during dinner, he leaned close to her and, in a low voice whispered, ''That upbeat personality of yours is making blithe music somewhere deep in my prematurely jaded heart. Stirring my spirit. You are rapidly becoming an object of desire.''

It was nice to think that this young man could see right to the core of who and what she was, and could express it. A few words from a near-stranger, and Lara caught a vision of herself that she had never recognized before. The journalist was right. She did have a blithe spirit. And, if others had told her that before in various ways and she had understood it, she had not till now believed it. It was like looking in a mirror for the first time. Who was that person smiling out at her? A whole person of substance. She liked what she was seeing.

Yes, she was enjoying her dinner companions, and the other guests. But Lara was also distracted. Not just by Martha, whom she had met that afternoon, but by Martha and David. As a couple they fascinated her. David with Martha was the same David she had known and loved all her life, and yet not David at all. She had rarely thought of him as powerful, charismat-ically powerful. Nor as interested in power—at least not on as serious a scale as he was emanating this evening. He and Martha were like a royal couple: dignified, solid, establishment. Still just that little bit apart from everyone around them. And all that in the nicest, most polite way!

They made the other power players at the dinner table appear much as David had described such people earlier that day: bor-derline crass, naive. From that dinner party on she would always think of David as David with Martha. It was extraordinary to her that she should love Martha so well, so immediately. She felt instinctively as if that would never change for her.

After dinner, the guests retired to the living room to be tempted with coffee and cognac. The journalist placed his cup and saucer carefully on the table and leaned toward Lara again. "You inspire the romantic knave in me. If I had a magic carpet, I would whisk us away from all this. Off to New York. Our carpet would take us to all the best jazz joints. We'd listen and get very drunk. Then there'd be a carriage ride through Central Park. I'd buy you flowers from a stand with real money, and we'd watch the sun come up, and then . . . Well, who knows about then? And what does it matter? The last magic carpet left years ago." He retrieved his coffee cup, and Lara distinctly thought she heard him sigh.

"Grab your seat belt, John. Tonight's the night. I've got the magic carpet." And she rose from her chair and seized his hand, pulling him to his feet.

Forty-five minutes later she was taxiing down the runway, one hooked journalist by her side. He laughingly told her, above the noise of the engines, "You're a heartbreaker." Then, surprisingly sweetly asked her, "Please don't break my heart."

Lara was concentrating on takeoff. She stopped the plane for a final instrument check while awaiting a signal from the tower. It came, and only then did she turn to John and tell him, "Rest easy, I don't break hearts. I only look like I break hearts. And no one has ever fallen off my magic carpet."

They exchanged broad smiles. John looked visibly relieved and sat back in the seat, relaxed and ready to go.

Chapter 20

Lara was always amused when she heard people describe her as a restless American heiress complete with a shady past. No one outside the family ever suggested that she was having the best time of her life. Or had been for the past two years. There seemed to be form and substance to her wanderings, and in many ways she continually inspired those close to her. Bonnie and the entourage traveled with her periodically during these years. But from that last morning in the New York town house, when she had decided to break out, she was out in the world, discovering it alone and for herself.

She drifted in and out of romantic attachments and places, feeling the almost casual enrichment of her experiences. She did things as the fancy took her, and her circle of friends widened to include artists, writers, and historians. People from milieus other than those she had previously been exposed to. Her own circle of friends and her familiar social life remained for her, not to be frivolously abandoned. She enjoyed it all. During this time she did several rewarding things that she could have focused on as being important, impressive work. But that was not Lara's way. She left the rewards for Harland Brent to pick up as his own. She lived every day for that day, every experience for that experience. Every morning when she awoke, she behaved as if yesterday had never been and tomorrow was unlikely to come.

As Stantons went, she was unique. The one who broke the mold. The family and her friends learned to respect her as something special in their lives. She was still in her early thirties. Who knew where her life might take her next?

The sun was quitting the sky above Florence. Slim streams of grayish clouds lay streaked across its brooding terra-cotta surface. A dark blue veil was descending, and the daytime sky slipping into the horizon. They were well into the traffic flowing into Florence. Roberto knew all the short cuts. They sped into the center of the city just as bells greeted the roseate tones of sunset on the dome of the cathedral.

They had driven in from Siena, where Lara had been for lunch with friends at a distinguished twelfth-century palazzo. She wanted to take the ring road to the Fiesole hill above the center of Florence, where she kept rooms in the Villa San Michele. She hadn't been to the hotel in several days. There might by now be letters from Sam about Bonnie. He had taken her away for a month's holiday. But Roberto insisted they stop for coffee or a drink in town.

With only minutes of color for the city left in the sun now, the narrow streets, the ochre and buff, the mocha and terra-cotta buildings were bathed in a dark, dusty pink. Coarser light from lamps was spilling from the windows. The Ponte Vecchio, over the Arno, in that theatrical light, was a perfect setting for some lurid opera Verdi neglected to write. They were driving beside the river from below the Piazza della Signoria.

"It still captures, our Florence?"

"Still. Every time I return, I think I will be disappointed. That all we visitors must by now have plucked the heart out of it. But I am always wrong."

Roberto wound his way through several side streets and pulled into one that led into the Piazza della Signoria. He abandoned the car, which was strictly forbidden. He shook the hand of a guard near the end of the street. Then, taking Lara's arm, walked her into the piazza. "Why don't you marry me? There would be advantages. In Florence, contessas get to park anywhere."

"You never stop, do you?"

"Never."

"You don't even mean it."

"I think I do."

"When you're asking?"

"Precisely."

"Then it's all a game you feel compelled to play with every woman you meet."

A wry smile. He shook his head, perhaps indicating that it might be true. Then said, "Yes."

"Why do it?"

"Ah, the ego demands it."

"But I say no every time. That surely can't be good for the ego?"

"But you are the exception to the rule. I might wear you down. And, anyway, egos are strange creatures."

Lara was laughing at Roberto and his infuriating Italian charm. They were walking among the thinning crowds of the piazza. "Just look, Lara, at this wonderful piazza. Once all the political and social bigwigs of the great Florentine Republic rubbed shoulders here. Even the hordes of tourists cannot diminish its grandeur. My ancestors saw history made here. In medieval times, and even today, all momentous meetings are held here. Only one is hard-pressed to find a noble Florentine among all those visitors paying homage to our past. Such is life. Such is progress. But I and several other friends still uphold family tradition. When I am in Florence, I come here at least several times a week. I can never remember not meeting someone else from one of the old families doing the same thing. You have to be proud to be Florentine."

Roberto gave his own twist to orthodox Italian charm. He was a clever and successful man who loved to play the fool—without being anything of the kind. He had more power than most in Florence, and he used it sparingly and wisely. At thirty-five, he had taken very seriously his obligation to his family and heritage. His efforts for the conservation of Florentine treasures bordered on the heroic. But he was a notorious cad with women. Lara listened, relishing him and his love of Florence without ever taking him seriously as a lover or suitor. To become the target for lightweight womanizing was not her goal in Italy.

"Come," he said, "we will pay our respects to *Il Biancone*." The Florentines habitually referred to the statue of Neptune in the Fountain of the Ammannati as *Il Biancone*, the big white one. A colossus of a figure, it dominated everything in the piazza, even the glorious statue of *David*. The fountain itself was magnificent. Neptune stood on a cart pulled by sea horses, in a basin surrounded by elegant bronzes representing the sea gods, with eight satyrs standing on the marble edge. It was an outrageous, breathtaking work of art that Lara never tired of looking at. Every time she saw it she found something new in the fountain that she had not seen before. And the god Neptune? He had a special kind of attraction for her. Whenever she saw *Il Biancone*, he seemed to speak to her. Draw her to him and hold her in a lustful affection she had yet to experience in real life. Like the great bronze Poseidon in Greece. These two works of art excited her love of men as no others ever did. Neptune, the huge, virile god, arising from the sea, that manufactory of myths, the mature and powerful man. He had exerted his marbly erotic power over Lara the first time she saw him. But his rude force was counteracted by the coolly poised statue of *David*, close by in front of the Palazzo Vecchio. The epitome of young male beauty. She found herself mesmerized by the handsomeness and youth of the Michelangelo masterpiece, and was often led by the copy in the piazza to approach the original that had been moved to the Academy Gallery.

Roberto and Lara drew near the fountain. A large group of chic Japanese, guidebooks in hand, cameras worn like tribal jewelery, was just dispersing. That left a clear view of the fountain. Dusk had come and night was closing in. The sky was now a bruised blue, fast taking on the color of night. Although it was warm for the early days of April, a light mist rose from the Arno and lazily wafted into the square. It skimmed across the water in the fountain and swirled ethereally around the cart and Neptune's legs. It was eerie, because mist appeared almost nowhere else in the piazza. It was the first time Lara had seen the Neptune in that light—dramatic and unnervingly mysterious. As if he were rising from his subaquatic world to cast his alien aura over their lives.

As if by divine command, the fountain lights came on. First dimly, almost imperceptibly, and then slowly becoming brighter. There were gasps of wonderment from the groups of people around the fountain. Next, the *David* sprang alight, then all the statues under the Loggia della Signoria: the Giambologna, the Sabine ladies elegantly undergoing their Rape, the Benvenuto Cellini bronze of Perseus eyeing the severed head of Medusa in his grasp. Within minutes, light played on all the other treasures, and finally the lanterns of the piazza itself glowed.

Roberto was thrilled. But, no less than Lara, remained silently enthralled by Neptune's magnetic power to draw them into a fantasy of another world. Neptune captivated them, and Lara felt dizzy with the power of such magnificence. She and Roberto stood there, arm in arm, each supporting the other. It would hardly have surprised her if Neptune's strong white marble arm had plucked her from the piazza, and plunged with her back into his miniature sea. Fanciful, yes. But the imagination working overtime is allowed to be fanciful.

"Lara."

Back to reality. She recognized the voice behind her at once. She detached herself from Roberto and swung around to face Jamal. They were in each other's arms, hugging each other, to the surprise of Roberto and the two men with Jamal.

"How long has it been?"

"David's wedding."

"And we hardly had a chance to talk then. Nearly two years?" He hugged her again. "I've missed you so much."

"What are you doing here?"

"What does anyone do in Florence? I'm a tourist and a shopper, just like everyone else."

"Jamal, how ridiculous. You've never been a tourist in your life."

"Yes, well, maybe you're right. I brought my mother to Montecatini to take the waters. Two days, and I had to escape. I find these spas wonderful for everybody else, but too healthy for me. I will tell you all about that another time. But first you must meet my friends."

Lara, momentarily forgetful of Roberto, was embarrassed. She introduced him to Jamal. The two men shook hands, and then Jamal continued introducing his friends, an American and an Italian. Roberto distracted them with details about the fountain while Jamal and Lara spoke.

"I must see more of you, now that I have stumbled upon you. Where are you staying, Lara?"

"The Villa San Michele. And you?"

"The Excelsior. They couldn't accommodate us at the

Michele. Come and have dinner with us this evening? And bring your friend.''

"Not possible.''

"But we leave Florence in the morning. It's too long. I must see you.'' Jamal, profiting by the three men's preoccupation with the fountain, propelled her by the elbow away from them. "How are you, Lara? You're lovelier than ever. I've missed you. Very much. I've always regretted our parting. Mistreating you, if that was what I did. And these last three years since my father died . . . I've been preoccupied with settling his affairs and haven't had the time to see you all as much as I used to. Don't run away. We have so much catching up to do.''

"I wasn't going to, Jamal.''

He looked relieved. Lara gazed at him more closely. Was it possible that he had become even handsomer than she remembered him? The light in the square—was it giving added fire to his normally smoldering looks? An excuse. The fact was he still stirred in her those familiar sensual feelings he had always evoked, but that she had blocked out of her life for so many years.

He grazed her cheek with the back of his hand, then raised her hand in his and lowered his lips to kiss her fingertips. Her body reacted to him as it had the first time he seduced her. She felt enlivened, filled with an urge to travel with him, once more, to that special erotic place only he seemed able to take her. Did he sense it? She would not tell him. He would have to find out for himself. "I will be dining with friends at the San Michele this evening.'' That was all she said, nothing more.

Jamal wanted her. But his desire to bed her was tempered by the ease with which she handled their meeting, the affection she showed for him. He was quite surprised at the relief he felt when she reacted to his touch. She wanted him not merely as she always had, but more, yet without desperation or absolute need. It quite thrilled him to know that she was—and had always been—no other's but his. Never mind a husband or lovers. He had been right all along: she had never replaced him.

"Meeting like this, just bumping into each other—I suppose we could only come together again if fate dealt us a good turn. We mustn't tempt the gods by wasting this coincidence, don't you think?''

"No, we mustn't."

"I'll call you this evening."

Lara hadn't realized how much a part of her life Jamal still was, even if she had excluded the memory of him for so many years. Until she had turned and found herself facing him in the piazza. She walked away from him and his friends, still standing at the Fountain of the Ammannati. On Roberto's arm now, she was aware that something momentous had indeed happened in the square, as he had airily predicted. Lara felt such inner joy, as if she and Jamal were meeting for the first time. The past was there, but very much buried. She could hardly focus it. There was something in the attitudes of both of them that was new and fresh. It appeared to lay to rest the ghosts of unhappiness that had haunted them for so long.

They were caught in the evening traffic, driving nearly bumper-to-bumper through the noisy streets, toward Fiesole. Roberto and Lara had hardly said a word since they'd left the piazza. "You are very quiet," he remarked. "Nothing unpleasant in your encounter in the piazza, I hope?"

"Oh, I doubt it, Roberto. I've been meeting that man on and off for most of my life. But I will admit he was the last person I expected to meet among the tourists of the Piazza della Signoria."

But what she didn't confide in Roberto was how good it felt to see Jamal. How she still found him the most sexually exciting man she had ever had. That in his arms, for a second, had been rekindled those same old erotic drives. And how good it felt to have those intense feelings again.

They were zigzagging up the steep, lush green of the hill of Fiesole to the Villa San Michele. Roberto drove the open black Bentley up to the subtly lit Michelangelo facade of the ancient monastery, perched among the cypress and olive trees on the hill, overlooking Florence. Lara adored staying at the Villa San Michele. With only a few rooms available for guests, it was more like an exclusive country club. Lara had a three-room suite with city-wide vistas over Florence.

Once in her rooms she threw off her shoes and lay down on the bed to read the letters from Sam. He was very good about keeping her informed while he played father to Bonnie. She was not ungrateful for that. There was a letter from Nancy and one from Nanny. Lara seemed to need to read them twice to be assured that they were all well and happy.

She turned out the lights in her room and looked down on Florence, sparkling below her. She sat there for several minutes recalling the puzzling experience she had had alongside Roberto, communing with *Il Biancone*. And Jamal. Nothing else seemed possible for her that evening but to be very rude and cancel dinner with her friends, even at this late hour. She switched on the light, found her address book, and called the three people who were to have been her guests. She told them, ''It's unforgivable, I know. You have every right to be angry with me, but I must cancel dinner. Something unexpected has happened. Nothing bad, but something I must give my full attention to.'' They were understanding and polite about it. Lara did not feel undue remorse. She knew her Florentines well. They had three hours to find another party to go to. Long enough in any city. They were a most hospitable lot, the Florentines, always ready to make room for one more at the table.

Lara called the open-air restaurant in the hotel, The Loggia. From the elegant stone loggia, with its arches and vaulted ceilings that ran along one whole side of the monastery, and with its open balustrade and the huge, arched openings above them, guests could look out over Florence—to the hills on the opposite side of the Arno—while enjoying a drink or a meal. She changed her reservation from four to two.

Then Lara called the maid and had her prepare a bath, scented with bubbles of jasmine and rose and honeysuckle. When the maid arrived, so did four page boys, olive-skinned *ragazzi* bearing bouquets of flowers: three dozen ruby-red, long-stemmed roses in a glass vase, a bowl of white tulips, another of camellias, a pot of a dozen white moth orchids, all in full bloom. No card. She smiled, pleased that he knew he hadn't needed to include a card.

The water was milky and smooth with bath oils, and Lara luxuriated in it, her mind emptied of all thoughts of past and present. The silence was like beautiful music, broken only by the trickle of water from the dipped sponge with which she gently bathed herself.

The Loggia restaurant catered to the most chic of women. When, two hours later, she walked in, every woman there turned

with admiration or envy to look at the American heiress Lara
Stanton, every man with desire.

Lara had not called Jamal. She just knew that he would come.
It was unthinkable that he might fail her. She dressed for him.
To be ravishingly beautiful and sensuous for him. She wanted
him to know, on sight, that she recognized there could be nothing else for them but to be together this night. She had taken a
long time making herself ready. Once, in Egypt, she had been
taken to a woman famous for her unguents. The most seductive
and exciting women engaged her to prepare ointments and
creams for them. The ladies rubbed their genitals with them,
applying them to their vaginas. The scent was of jasmine, the
effect to tantalize men with their sexuality.

She chose a black dress of silk jersey. It had a halter top, just
two slips of fabric that covered the breasts and plunged to the
waist in the front. It was backless, had a tight waistband and a
short skirt that was soft and cut on the bias, so that it looked
both skimpy and flared. High-heeled, black satin sandals shod
her feet. She carried a deep-violet-colored shawl of the same
material as the dress, to be used if she felt chilly.

She sat at her table, savoring the sparkle of a fine champagne.
Several people she knew stopped by to speak to her, asking her
to join them. She declined. She felt quite hungry. Since she had
no idea when Jamal might arrive, she decided to order her meal.
She chose first scallops served with a lobster sauce. Next a risotto. For a third course, veal and peppers. She postponed or-
dering dessert. She had just finished giving the maitre d' her
order when one of the page boys arrived at her table with a
folded piece of paper on the inevitable silver salver. She smiled
at the impassive boy, then looked at the note for some time. Not
in hesitation, more in pleasurable anticipation. Then she picked
it up.

Lara,
May I see you?
Jamal

She thanked the boy, rose from her chair, and draped the
shawl over the back of it. After telling the maitre d' to put an-

other bottle of champagne on ice, she left The Loggia for the reception hall. There she met Jamal.

"I am sorry about this but, quite frankly, I couldn't stay away." He took both her hands in his and kissed them in turn. There were several people in the reception hall. A clumsily discreet exit by the hall porter from behind the reception desk told them how conspicuous they were making themselves.

Lara suggested, "Let's go sit in the covered courtyard."

"Did you receive my flowers?"

"They were lovely."

"You knew they were from me?"

"Of course."

"You look ravishing. Unimaginably sexy. Every male in the reception hall thought so, too. They looked as hungry for you as I am."

"I think not. They haven't had me as you have."

That brought a smile to his lips. Although there was no tension between them, there was time and distance. Her quick retort seemed to dissolve that now.

"What happened to your friends, Jamal? I thought you were dining with them."

"They understand that, having just found you again, I can't stay away from you. They sent me here with their blessings. I know you are dining with friends, but . . . would you allow me to join you?"

"Come on, then, I'm famished."

Allowing her to pass through the door before him, he was overcome with the need to hold her in his arms. He slipped his arm around her waist and pulled her sharply back against him. "What a joy, to find you naked under your dress."

His hold on her was loose enough for her to slip round and place her arms around his neck. They were quite alone. He took advantage of that to slide his hands beneath her skirt. He was caressing her naked flesh when they heard footsteps on the stone floor. He removed his hands at once, and she released him. They walked from the inside courtyard to another room.

The look of surprise and pleasure on his face further endeared Jamal to her. "You're pleased?"

"Delighted."

"I learned my erotic lessons well from you as a young girl."

"And they have served you well, I trust."

"More than well."

She reached for his hand and together they walked up to the restaurant. They were not unaware of the sensation they were causing during their walk down that spectacular loggia, most especially to several Americans who recognized Lara. The Italians, who are such great romantics, had only to take one look to see that this was a rather special love affair going on in their midst. And, if they enjoyed a love affair, they enjoyed it tenfold if it was between two such handsome and elegant people as Jamal and Lara. They launched their commentaries in thundering whispers among themselves, before the couple had a chance even to sit down.

As they were ushered to Lara's table, and the waiter pulled the chairs back for them, Jamal saw that it had been set for only two. Lara smiled to see that she had taken him by surprise yet again.

"Your friends?"

"It was rude of me at such short notice, but what else was there to do? . . ."

And if I had not come?"

"It never crossed my mind."

He took her in his arms and kissed her with some passion; before releasing her and helping her to her seat. Unembarrassed, the waiter was still standing by attention, his hands on the back of her chair. Then Jamal took his own seat. Now half the people in The Loggia were unashamedly assessing the romance unfolding before them.

Over dinner, Lara and Jamal gossiped about family and friends. Once they started talking, they seemed to have a great deal of catching up to do. Only once did Jamal mention Sam and her marriage.

"Would it be indiscreet of me to ask what broke it up?"

"Yes, I think it might be." That was the end of that subject. They drank champagne and forgot about everything and everyone else. He moved his chair next to hers, and they watched the lights of the city in silence. A chill wind had been steadily rising. He felt Lara's hand, cold in his. Concerned, he asked, "You're cold?"

"Yes."

"Why didn't you say?"

"I didn't want this to stop."

"It's not going to stop."

"Good."

"I think it's time for bed?"

"I thought you would never notice."

Jamal pushed open the sitting room door of Lara's suite. She entered, and he followed. Just behind them was a waiter with more champagne and a tray of handmade white chocolates. Jamal closed the door as the waiter departed and double-locked it.

Lara's particular fondness for this suite of rooms at the Villa San Michele had something to do with their tranquillity. They maintained an atmosphere of immense calm, like a grain of eternity for her. Lara thought it was the effect of the soft, warm Fiesole light that filtered through the windows onto the stone walls in the daytime. At night, the shape of the rooms, with their vaulted ceilings, lent them a kind of monastic splendor.

The furniture was antique, and there was a superior elegance and pleasant lack of interior decoration. Often, when in these rooms, she would think how perfect they would be for a writer or an artist. They were rooms to inspire the imagination. This was the oldest part of the sixteenth-century monastery, and Lara was convinced that the spirit of the place lingered still in these rooms. And, after all, hadn't the Franciscan monks managed to retain possession of the building until they were suppressed by Napoléon? The monastic aura might well have clung on since 1808. She could imagine them in their brown habits, stalking the corridors and gardens.

But there was, too, something else about these rooms. Something extremely sensual. While sleeping here, she found herself always ready, yearning even, for sensual delights. For the right man to come to her and make love to her. She had never, however, imagined it would be Jamal.

Lara left him to open the wine and went into her dressing room. She sat at the dressing table and gazed at herself in the mirror. She removed the diamond earrings from her ears, the bracelets from her wrists. It seemed the most natural thing in the world that Jamal should be in the other room. That they should be there together, about to go to bed. From a drawer she selected a nightdress. White lace, finely elegant, a Parisian extravagance she had not yet worn. She brushed her hair, powdered her face. Barefoot she walked into the bedroom.

Jamal was there, waiting for her. The wine and the chocolates were forgotten.

Chapter 21

"I never thought that you could happen to me again. That such passionate love could happen to me again," Lara said.

"Why ever not, Lara?"

"Because you involve risk, more risk than I thought I would ever want to take again," she answered.

"And now?"

"And now I'm older. No less frightened perhaps, but more prepared to expose myself to new risks and the enlarged possibilities that passionate love can offer. And for the moment, what choice do I have? We're together. Fate stepped in."

Jamal looked at her pensively and then asked: "What if it was not fate but me? That I wanted you back because I miss the fire and the passion in you, and what you bring to our sex life. What then?"

"I would say then, Jamal, that you love me, pretty much the way I love you."

"Ah, then we're getting somewhere."

"No, not really. Remember, it was fate, not you, who brought us together."

He hesitated for some time before he spoke again.

"Come back to bed."

For three days they stayed at the Villa. They swam in the pool, and rode horses, and played tennis close by at the Cascine village. They dined in the hotel, in their rooms or the restaurant. By night they slaked their sensual passion for each other, with new and ever more exciting acts of lust.

Lara had once again fallen in love with Jamal. She felt the

full force of passion for him. His charm, his kindness, his intelligence, all the things the family had loved about him for years, swelled her admiration for him. She was able to give herself sexually to him, express, as he had taught her years before, every aspect of her erotic nature. They wallowed in the darker side of their sexual life together, and felt lifted to glorious heights, free to love each other as well in the light as they did in the dark.

They were in love and hid it from no one. Lara would fantasize that it would never end. That their lust would bear fruit. Children. That he would make her his wife, and parade her before the world as his only great love. He admired her and adored her, and had his own fantasies about her. The sexual fantasies: that she would never again have another man except, at his command, the men he might enlist for their mutual pleasure. She would bear him a son, many sons. He would keep her all for himself, never let her go. Their three days together gave them threads of hope that they had found love. Then there would be fleeting moments of doubt. But neither of them talked about love. They lived, for those three days, in the full flood of passion, with their hopes and their doubts. And then, in the dawn light, while lying in each other's arms and tasting their mutual lust upon the tips of Jamal's fingers, they knew they were two of the luckiest people in the world. Love had flowered between them. As lovers they were responding to the warmth and admiration throbbing through them. They knew that their fantasies would come to a fulfillment, that their wishes would be realized.

Jamal was not a man to question his emotions. Nor the two unsolved mysteries of love: why we fall in love when we do, and why we choose who we do. He knew only that he had loved and chosen. The sooner he married Lara, the happier he would be, having taken possession for always of his love object. If he did have to marry—which he did—she would at least afford him a marriage that would not sink into mere boredom. Hardly a rationalist, he could not recognize that he was excusing to himself his urgent desire to make Lara his wife. He would marry her at once. Once he had made his decision he wasted not even a minute.

He was sitting alone at the time, in the afternoon sunlight of the garden of the Villa San Michele. In the quiet, broken only by occasional bird song, he felt extremely vulnerable. Lara, through love, had power over him. It was an unwelcome feeling. He had taken on the very male role of hunting her down, captivating her with what he felt was his charm and sexual power. As with almost any man, it was the exercising of that masculinity that allowed him to fall in love. He was happier with that than actually being in love. A wedding as soon as possible would, he was certain, restore his sense of control over his emotions. Excited now, he left the garden for their rooms, to make the several phone calls that would activate his plans.

Lara was in Florence shopping, one of the things she least liked to do. But she wanted to be away from Jamal for a few hours. She needed time to gain some perspective on his reappearance in her life. Lara had matured considerably since those days when she had been obsessed with Jamal and being in love with him. Now she had no fear of being alone and facing up to her involvement with him, to having fallen in love with him again. While she wandered in and out of shops, buying beautiful things for Bonnie and herself, she was relieved to find herself capable of being in love with him and yet remaining her own person at the same time. She loved him all the more for that.

She sat in the Excelsior Bar, amid stacks of colorfully wrapped boxes with luscious satin ribbons, drinking a Cinzano and soda and eating freshly roasted salted almonds. Like most women in love she felt a newfound zest for life, yet this time without being blinded by the dazzle of love. She was well aware of everything that was happening to her, that loving Jamal was a kind of escape. And she was secure in the knowledge that she could handle it, as she had not been able to before. She was pleasantly surprised at realizing how right she had been all those years ago to want what she was now receiving from Jamal. The more he showed his love for her, the more she gave herself to loving. All inhibition had always vanished when she had been with Jamal, or so she had thought, but now . . . Well, now they were not only sexual inhibitions that vanished. All doubts were put aside. She had no fear of being made vulnerable by love. Every day she reestablished her feminine identity through loving. It embolded her. How glorious to live with all her defenses down. How lonely those years when she hadn't been in love. When no man had been in love with her.

She ordered another Cinzano and airily returned the routine flirtations of several attractive men in the bar, apparently unable to contain their admiration for her. She gazed at her purchases and smiled. How sure of herself she was. She had selected several stunningly elegant outfits. One in particular might well grace a wedding. There was no doubt in her mind that she would marry Jamal, even though he had scarcely hinted at it as yet.

It was nearly seven o'clock before Lara returned to the Villa San Michele. Jamal had been waiting for her for hours, angry to think she would stay away for so long without a call. He had tried to read. Had gone to The Loggia for a drink there. Several drinks there. Had canceled their table for the evening, reserving one for lunch on the following day instead. He ordered dinner for them in their rooms. Restless, he roamed through the public rooms of the hotel or paced around the reception area. He was there when the long, black limousine drew up at the door and she stepped out. He saw first her long, shapely legs encased in cream-colored stockings. Impatience became entangled with the erotic need to have her. He saw at once that she had indeed been shopping. She was wearing a new dress, a short skirt of chocolate-brown silk georgette, and over it a well-tailored cream jacket finished at the waist with a bright yellow lizard belt. Her small matching handbag slung over her shoulder, she took hurried strides into the hotel. Behind her the chauffeur was depositing box after box into the waiting arms of two porters.

Relief at seeing her curtailed mere speech. He rushed to meet her, swept her into his arms, and kissed her. She laughed. His own laughter was a reaction to his acute anxiety. He wanted to ask, Where have you been? Who have you been with? Why didn't you call? He asked none of those things. Instead they walked arm in arm up to their rooms, he kissing her and whispering endearments, her colorful packages being carried up behind them. At last they were alone.

"I've had a wonderful time."

"I've had a miserable time."

"Oh?"

"I've missed you terribly."

"Oh. Well, that's a good thing."

"Maybe for you, not for me. I think I will have to do something about it." He smiled. How could he help smiling? She looked so happy, so pretty, so delectable. He told her, "Your new dress is lovely."

"Valentino. And wait till you see the other things. All exciting and sexy and provocative. And all bought for the sole purpose of pleasing you." She was flirting with him, and was pleased to see by the look in his eye how much it awakened the lust he always had for her. "I'll wear one of them tonight to dinner."

"Do you mind if we dine here in our rooms?"

She sat down on the settee next to him. She leaned in toward him, and he slid an arm around her shoulders. It was her answer. He could see that she was pleased about the change of plans. He unbuttoned her jacket and felt the weight of her breasts in his hands. With the tips of his fingers he caressed the dark nimbus of her nipples with a gentle, circular motion. He talked while he fondled her. "You must let me give you all your shopping. A gift for you to surprise me with."

"That's not necessary, Jamal."

"No, but it's what I want to do. Please."

She kissed him, a sensuous kiss with parted lips. Their tongues touched and trembled with passion. Then she whispered, "Thank you."

They lay like that for a while. Quiet, with only his hands petting her. The occasional lowering of his head to her breast, where he gently sucked her nipple and licked it. His tenderness was slowly kindling her erotic needs. She tried to distract herself, wanting to hold on to this intimate state of togetherness—that was so rich and comfortable—before its momentum led them toward greater passion. To that end, she asked him, with a slight tremor in her voice, "Shall I give you a fashion show?"

He answered, "No," not unaware of what she was doing.

Her body was beginning to ache for him. But she didn't want to give in. She tried again, a little breathlessly. "A package or two, then. Just to amuse you." Before he could stop her, she reached for a parcel wrapped in shiny red paper, a pink satin bow on it, and another smaller box wrapped in yellow paper with purple spots and tied with a red bow. She dropped them onto her lap and sighed.

Now, with both hands, he reached under her jacket and caressed her breasts. Played with them, pressing them together and then pushing them apart. He removed her jacket slowly from her shoulders and laid it over the back of the settee. Once more he placed his arm around her shoulders, and she leaned against him. He caressed her arms. His tongue found the line of flesh between her breasts. Then he, too, realized he wanted to prolong this tender reunion. Grudgingly he told her, ''All right. Let's see what you have there.'' He handed her one of the parcels.

Lara pulled at the bow and it dissolved in her hands. She very carefully undid the paper and removed the lid of the box. He watched her. Her enthusiasm was so childlike, so incongruous in the bare-breasted woman lying in his arms in a Valentino silk georgette skirt, enthralling him with her sensual nature, her very special personality.

He tried to hide his surprise when she held up the red-and-white, candy-striped cotton dress. It was piped around the neck, its sleeves and the hem decorated with tiny white flowers, and it was tied with a large red organza sash, the bow to one side. The child's dress was a confection. Something he himself might have bought for Bonnie because she partly enchanted him. But here, now, she had been forgotten. That he would have to share Lara with her was something he had not counted on. For the moment it was only an irritating realization. When Lara drew from the second box a pair of suede dungarees that looked doll-size, he knew for certain that he had a very serious rival for Lara's affections. Ridiculous! A child is a child is a child, he told himself. And then aloud, he said, ''For a woman is a woman is a mother.

''They are like doll's clothes. You like playing dolls. You are still a child—part of your charm.''

''A child, playing at dolls!'' To herself she said: I am a mother, not a child, and Bonnie is a child and not a doll, and don't trivialize who and what we are! I take offense at that.

She nearly said those things to him aloud. But when she studied his face, his handsomeness, his smoldering, sensual looks, and watched him lower his head to her breasts and suck on her nipples, Bonnie was momentarily forgotten. She placed the child's things and the boxes and wrappings to one side, and took his face in her hands, raising it to her lips. Before she began kissing it, she told him, ''A child playing at dolls—hardly!''

She kissed first his lips and then his eyes, and then his lips again as she found the zipper in his trousers. Once she had him in her hands, she slid from his arms to her knees, between his legs. The weight of his penis, erect and straining for her in her hands, the feel of his large, succulent balls on her lips, in her mouth: aphrodisiacs. The dry scent of cock and sex, the taste of Jamal: aphrodisiacs. She teased him, lulled him into surrender in the ways that lead to sexual oblivion.

The telephone kept ringing. They were lying there between two worlds, unable to pull themselves back sufficiently to do anything about it. The ringing was insistent.

"Oh, god, it won't stop!"

"Don't you stop. Ignore it," he was begging.

Lara stretched past him to reach for the intrusive telephone. He grabbed her wrist. "Let it go!" he demanded. She kissed him quickly, but released his grip. He sank back among the cushions and sighed. She smiled and kissed him on the knee, then lunged for the telephone, pulling it to the floor and dragging it toward her. He watched her sprawled at his feet. She looked so feline, lewd. Half naked, the soft brown translucent silk hiked up, leaving a span of thigh exposed, a hint of bottom: voluptuous cheeks and the crack dividing them.

He listened to Lara's conversation. "Yes. Put her on the line." No need to listen further. The tone of her voice, a lilt of happiness in it; she was talking to Bonnie. Jamal stood up and walked round Lara, still stretched out on the floor, the length of the telephone cord determining her position. He stood where she could see him. She smiled up at him and continued to talk to Bonnie. Jamal stripped down in front of her. She found it difficult not to watch him. With her free hand she caressed his leg, as if to pacify him for her divided attention. He went down on his knees in front of her, his penis offering itself to her lips. She was not amused at such an inviting distraction. Rather than reject him, she gave the knob a quick kiss. Bonnie was telling Lara about the dog her father had bought her, and now that she had said everything she had to say, was quite finished talking to Lara. She managed a hurried good-bye, and Sam was back on the line.

Jamal heard Lara say, "She sounds so happy, Sam. Yes . . ." Jamal rose up from his knees. Lara reached for his hand. He squeezed hers and let it go, and walked round behind her. He pulled her up, onto her knees, and draped her skirt up around her waist. She leaned on her elbows now, trying to control herself. She found her position just as exciting as Jamal did. He caressed her bottom lovingly. She tried to stop him with a gesture and a shake of her head. But he had had enough distractions. He forced her legs wider apart, and his hands rent open the lips of her cunt. She was pink and soft. It excited him to see her thus exposed, vulnerable to his whims. He spanked her hard, just once, then found her clitoris, and heard her words falter. She placed a hand over the receiver and said quite sharply, "No. Please, Jamal."

"No!"

With one violent push he was deep inside her. His hands on her waist he fucked her, deeper, harder, more anger and violence with every thrust. He heard her lust-ridden voice tell Sam, "I must go." She dropped the telephone.

Jamal mastered her with his cock that night. The more she came, the more determined he was that her orgasms should keep coming. He used her body like a fine instrument, purpose-built for lust. By morning she was enslaved by their sexual excesses. And he more determined than ever to keep her solely for himself, for his pleasure alone. He knew no other woman who could excite passion in him, who would get down and grovel in the sexual dirt with him, and love him as she did. For that he was happy to give her everything.

In the morning they bathed together. Neither spoke about the telephone call from Sam and Bonnie. She was reluctant to look at any of the other things she had bought for her daughter. She wanted to, but she sensed that fussing about her little girl upset Jamal. Now it was she who was rationalizing: a bachelor, it would take time for him to realize he was about to become a family man. To take on Lara was to take on Bonnie as well. Surely he knew that. Instead they talked about the power of sex. How they had found love through it. How he would never let her go this time round.

There were hints, and she missed them all. When he canceled their riding that morning and charmed her out of going on her own. When he talked her out of meeting Roberto at the Uffizi, a date they had made weeks ago.

"It's a special invitation. A chance to see some of the gallery's paintings not usually seen by the public. Roberto will be disappointed. He has gone to considerable trouble to arrange things with a museum curator in order to take me."

"And what about me? The considerable trouble I have taken to escort you somewhere this afternoon? You mustn't let me down on this. Really you mustn't. Last night you told me you were mine. That submission to me was life itself. Have you forgotten so soon?"

She canceled Roberto. But she was not unaware that he was making capital out of her grand passion for him. A danger signal she chose, foolishly, to ignore. He took the edge off his demands by suggesting they send Bonnie's presents to the child air express. What fun it would be for her to have them while on holiday with Sam. They duly instructed the concierge to see to it at once. They played tennis, and during the game he was called away to see a visitor. Lara remained on the court, but finally had to relinquish it, he was away too long. She sat on a bench and watched a game between two Frenchmen. Engrossed by it, she was hardly aware of Jamal's return.

"They're good."

"No," she corrected, "they're great. But Max could beat them."

"And you?"

"Too powerful for my game."

"And mine?"

She turned from the players to look at Jamal. She didn't much like the tone of his voice. It was as if he were challenging her. That made no sense. It was fanciful for her to think that, she told herself. She wanted to tell him the truth. Those two Frenchmen would cream him. She didn't dare, but she wouldn't lie to him, either. Instead she said, "Ask them for a game."

He seemed pleased enough with her answer. Had she imagined the glint in his eyes? She must have, for it was not there now, and he was next to her, his arm around her. They walked arm in arm to the open car waiting to take them the five miles back to the Villa San Michele. In the backseat of the car he played with her hair, kept touching it. She caught him off-guard, and he was embarrassed at the tenderness he felt for her. He made an excuse. "I have always been enchanted by your hair. So silvery."

"Mother still calls it Christmas-tree angel hair."

At the Villa he stopped her before she went into the hotel. "Let's walk." There were several marked trails through the extensive parkland of the Villa. They took one and then another, uphill among the olive trees and rocks, pausing often to gaze upon the spectacular view of the Arno valley below them. They didn't talk much, absorbed by the landscape, the warm sun, the scent of spring and cypress, wild herbs and flowers. The world had stood still for them, and they were sensitive to the luxury of that.

In their rooms they bathed and changed for lunch. He never minded waiting for her, seemed to take some pleasure in her primping. He read the papers. When she finally appeared, he stood up, went to her, and raised her hands to kiss her fingers. "Perfect!"

Smiling with pleasure, she asked, "Perfect for what?"

"For me. For the occasion. For lunch."

She had chosen to wear an ivory-colored dress of the finest linen, an Armani purchased the day before. It had no collar, but a plunging neckline over a perfectly tight-fitting, well-tailored bodice, designed to emphasize the huge, balloon, accordion-pleated sleeves worn tight at the wrists. The skirt to just below her knees was slim, nearly form-fitting. Around her waist was a wide belt of black patent leather. She wore black shoes and carried a black alligator handbag: a large, flat envelope with a buckle of gold. Her long silver-blond hair was dressed in a French twist that rested low on the nape of her neck and was held in place by a band of lilies of the valley, fresh and enchanting. On one wrist she wore a pair of antique-ivory, African tribal bracelets, on the other three more. In her ears diamonds, large and square, a gift from Sam for their second anniversary.

On their way to The Loggia they passed by a large, gilt-framed mirror. Lara caught a fleeting glimpse of herself and Jamal. She saw them as a dramatically handsome and romantic couple. For a moment she thought she was being fanciful again, until she also caught the reflections of several people looking at them. It was in their faces. Everyone loves a lover, but even more so a glamorous and romantic couple in love. She raised her chin that little bit higher, and tried to suppress the glee she felt. It was impossible. She laughed aloud, bursting with happiness.

"Share it with me," he asked.

"We're like movie lovers. Perfectly inspirational. As if we had it all. The looks, romance, love. As if our message was 'We're perfect, but not unique. You, too, can have what we have. All it takes is love.' I can see it in the people watching us. The way they smile as we pass them, the guests and the staff as well."

At that moment they passed another mirror. Jamal stopped and they turned to view each other. He smiled at her in the mirror. He was mightily proud of her as she was at this time in her life. All the beautiful women he had ever had rolled into one. And it was true they were unbeatable as a couple. She would give him the sons he wanted, the life he wanted to live.

In The Loggia now, they were ushered to their table. He was not unaware of the men admiring Lara as they walked past other diners. Ordinarily it amused him. He was not amused today. It actually put him on edge. Instead of taking their chairs, they sat on the balustrade facing each other and looking down into the lush garden and across the rooftops of Florence. Faintly, almost imperceptibly, they could hear the church bells ringing out across the Duomo and the spires and towers of the city. It was the most perfect day. Sun and warmth and no breeze. Birds singing, the hum of other people's chatter, a small grand piano at the end of The Loggia, played this afternoon by a pretty young woman who had chosen Chopin Nocturnes. The music was sensitive, tender, and so very amorous. Head-in-the-clouds music. It and the place wrought magic upon Jamal and Lara, lulled them into drinking their Kir Royales in silence.

He had meant to ask her at the end of a perfect lunch, over a delicious dessert. His intention was to be very romantic. For he had never done this before, and would he ever do it again? But he could wait no longer. The waiter was refilling her glass.

"Say yes."

Lara's mind had been adrift in time and space while she gazed over the city far below. The abundant spire-shaped cypresses, the olive trees on the surrounding hills, the thread of the river Arno—a definitive Tuscan landscape. She turned away from it to face him. Puzzled, she asked, "What?"

"Say yes. Just say yes."

Lara laughed, took a sip of her wine, and smiling affection-
ately at him said, "I might. If you gave me the question."

He looked surprised. For some reason he seemed unable to
ask her. This was ridiculous. He wanted her for his wife, but
the very idea of making such a commitment suddenly stymied
him. He had been evading marriage, the appalling commitment
it entailed, for as long as that option had been open to him. And
now she had brought him to this.

"Aren't I allowed to know the question?"

"Just say yes. Why won't you say yes? Have I ever asked you
to say yes to something you didn't want?"

"That's hardly the point here."

"That is precisely the point. If you love me and trust me,
what does the question matter, when you see how much I need
you to say yes?"

His voice was rent with anxiety. She had never seen him in
such a state of nerves before. "Jamal, what matters is that you
give me a choice about saying yes or no. Without the question,
you deny me the right to choose. This is not a matter of trust or
love or loyalty. I give myself unconditionally to you, willingly,
happily, because I have the freedom to do that." She thought
she sounded as if she were on a soapbox furthering some cause,
so she stopped, remained silent for several seconds, and then
said, "This is absurd. What are we going on about?" She placed
her glass on the balustrade, reached out, and took his hands in
hers. She raised each hand in turn to kiss them.

Never had he wanted her more than he did at that moment.
She was lovelier, more his than she had ever been any man's.
He smiled back at her, all charm and seductive good looks. Back
in control. He asked her, "Would you do me the honor of marrying me?"

The maitre d' was standing in front of them, menus in hand.
He would willingly have evaporated. But, for Lara and Jamal,
it was as if he weren't there. They were locked into each
other. The poor man wanted to leave, but was reluctant to im-
peril the spell of the moment. Inching slowly backward, he
removed himself from the romantic scene.

Lara, more overcome with emotion than surprise, exclaimed:
"I don't know what to say."

"Have you any doubts?"

"None."

Jamal slid across the balustrade to sit closer to her. "Then put me out of my misery. Say yes."

He took her in his arms and kissed her lovingly on the lips. She smiled and said her simple yes.

They sat there in silence, gazing into each other's eyes. He reached up with his finger to trace the outline of her eyebrow several times, stroke the bridge of her nose, and then, with the back of his hand, graze her cheek. "The best laid plans . . . I don't know what I would have done had you not said yes. I wanted it all to be so perfect, romantic for you. Hence the Gershwin, Cole Porter, and Jerome Kern. You were playing them that first night when I decided to seduce you into my bed. I was taking you to the opera. Remember? I do, every delectable moment of the night."

"I was such an innocent then."

"And hungry. Oh, so very hungry for love, and sex."

"Nothing seems to have changed," she quipped.

It lightened the moment and brought smiles to their faces. "I've ordered a marvelous lunch for us. Some of your favorite things. Whole bowls of caviar for each of us, and thin pancakes to spread the beluga on. Dollops of sour cream, too. I know what a piggy you are for that. There are other dishes I know you find irresistible. I intended to seduce you with food, lull you with exquisite wines, then, over the chocolate soufflé, propose. But suddenly I couldn't wait. To go through that meal without knowing your answer became impossible. My dear, you have turned me into a jellyfish. A wobbly, transparent thing swimming against a tide of angst."

"I hope not! I've been stung badly by jellyfish. But it is nice to know that I have the power to make you, even for a few minutes, feel vulnerable, out of control. It's good for you, and does wonders for my ego." It was said in jest, but not entirely. And Lara was relieved to see he was really too happy to notice that she was crowing over the hold she had upon him. She teased him, "And what was to happen after dessert?"

"You were to say yes, and I was to give you this." He reached into his pocket and withdrew a Van Cleef & Arpels ring box. "While I abandoned you on the tennis courts, the jeweler flew in with a selection of baubles. I was choosing one, a gift to commemorate a momentous occasion.''

"You were very sure of me. That I would say yes.''

"True, until the very last minute, when everything was arranged, and all you had to do was agree.''

She opened the lid of the box. The ring sparkled up at her. The large, square-cut emerald, surrounded by a band of square-cut diamonds, was a riveting sight, the color of green fire surrounded by white ice. It dazzled. She was quite overcome and could find no words. He stepped in to ease a moment that was fast becoming too emotional.

"I preferred a larger stone, round, with two rows of diamonds. But I thought, Hold on. You are marrying a Stanton, Emily and Henry's daughter, and with this ring Emily might say, 'Large, but respectably elegant, certainly not vulgar, if worn on gala occasions only.' ''

They shared a laugh against Emily as the ring found its way onto Lara's finger. With Jamal holding her hand, together they looked at it. "Well?'' he asked.

The ring was such an enormous symbol. There was something in the way he held her hand, surveyed her and the jewel on her finger. She felt possessed by him as she had never felt by Sam. A kind of finality came upon their relationship. She shrugged off the feeling with a shiver. "That is exactly what Mother will say. It is very, very beautiful. I will treasure it always, Jamal. Thank you.''

During lunch he was particularly amusing, at his most seductive and winning. Replete with food and wine and love, they lingered over coffee. He lit a cigar and had the good grace to laugh before instructing her, "Say yes.''

"Oh, here we go again. Okay, yes. Yes what, Jamal?''

"Yes, it's a marvelous idea to fly to Marrakesh this afternoon.''

"It is, actually.''

"Good, then let's go.''

Chapter 22

They landed long after dark. A car awaited them. Lara's feet hardly touched the ground before she was swept into the limousine. Its headlights probed the darkness across the landing field. They raced through the night toward the city. It was much warmer than Florence. They rolled down the windows to let the strong scent of Morocco lull them into the joy of being there.

On the outskirts of the city they took secondary roads, past roadside stands lit by the sickly white light of paraffin lamps, and piled high with lemons and oranges, others with tomatoes or fat, glossy aubergines. There was a stand of flowers: Jamal prodded the driver, and they skidded to a stop. He hopped out, to return with two barefoot boys in striped burnooses, who laid long-stemmed blossoms, armfuls of them, like a carpet at Lara's feet. They sped off again, and heard snatches of Moroccan music, strange and undeniably sensuous, the beat of African drums, the sound of oboes. All from portable radios, with which groups of swarthy turbaned men in *djellabahs*, long-hooded robes, whiled away hours of their lives, squatting on the ground and smoking beautiful slender carved wooden pipes with clay bowls packed with kif. They were drinking hot sweet mint tea. Their talk and passionate gestures were their contribution to solving the world's problems.

Morocco always smelled to Lara like lemons and garlic and olive oil, oranges and saffron and cardamom, a hint of jasmine and roses. There were more pungent odors, too. She loved the color of Morocco, so brilliant under a North African sun: red, hot pink, cobalt blue, emerald green, the opulent beauty of its

old palaces and grand houses, its secret gardens of fruit trees
and bougainvillaea and plumbago hanging from raspberry-
colored walls. And from lazily working fountains, the sound of
water that glistened in the sun. All around, potted plants burst
with brightly colored blossoms, and jungly shrubs with shiny
green leaves. The embellishment of rich tiles and marbles and
mosaics, creating a style that could only be Moroccan, had always enchanted Lara. Morocco had for her that same power of
seductive magic that Jamal embodied. It also had overwhelming
hospitality, heat and dust, mountain, sea and desert, sunlight
that heightened the senses, the dark, sometimes seedy side of
life that cajoled them. Where, in secret, everything was acceptable, nothing denied. The mystery and excitement and passions,
the opulence and the poverty, could stir the dullest of senses. Its
effect upon Lara was electric.

She reached for Jamal's hand and held it. She suddenly felt
an urgency to be once again in the midst of the hubbub of Moroccan marketplaces. Who could not be fascinated by the life of
the old Arab *medinas* of Marrakesh, Rabat, and Fez, or the
Casbah of Casablanca? Winding alleys and narrow, crooked
streets; the clamor, the sights, and the smells. The crowded
passages of open-fronted shops, spice or vegetable markets, silver and brass and coppersmiths, sandalwood carvers and leather
workers. Spilling from doorways, they practiced their crafts in
the streets. One turn and then another led through the maze to
silent side streets of walled gardens, secret courtyards, and
trickling fountains. Deeper, ever deeper, into the very private
world of the *medinas*.

Lara was not naive about this bewitching country that was
about to become so much a part of her life. She had seen the
face of cruelty, harshness: it could show just as naturally as the
warmth and smiles. Through previous visits, she had come to
love this country, and could quite understand how the mélange
of foreigners that made up its large expatriate community had
lost their hearts to it. How they could so easily walk away from
lives that had given them so much less. It suddenly occurred to
her how lucky she was to be able to add this place, and the life
it might afford her, to her already rich and full existence. And
Bonnie—how visits to Morocco would enrich her child's life, all
her future children's lives. Now, speeding into Marrakesh with

Jamal, she could think of no other place in which she would rather be wed.

Well into the suburbs of the city now, she saw women standing in groups, heavily robed and veiled, with nothing showing but a tiny crescent of eye. They sat on doorsteps, leaned against the walls of their houses, or perched in open windows.

Jamal saw the enthusiasm for his country in Lara's face. Pleased, he offered, "I've always loved this country. It is mine after all. But in the last few years, since I have inherited my father's estate, it has a new hold on me, one that allows me to appreciate it even more. I've no doubt you will learn to adapt to it. Make it your own."

He was right. Here, it seemed to Lara, she might begin again. Life with Jamal, an erotic adventure, a journey of love, matching the other adventure of learning to live in a new country, a new culture. She remembered Tangiers, a city hemmed with hills and fringed by the sea. A city on the shores of Africa. Its sugary sand and undulating surf. Its seemingly endless shoreline of magnificent beach. A cosmopolitan city in an Arabian Nights' fairy-tale dream. She wondered if she would end up like the expatriates she had met there. Travelers who had landed for a brief holiday were unable ever to leave, while the years slid by. She remembered a previous visit there with Max and Jamal. The days would glide by. It was a timeless place, self-contained. It had worked its magic on Lara before.

"Remember all that time we used to spend sitting in the Petit Soko, watching the world go in and out of the Casbah in Tangiers? That square so cluttered with cafes? What crowds, what fun! I look forward to that. To being swallowed up by the mists in the Casbah. What a place! Everyone doing his thing, among the prostitutes and drug peddlers, the two-bit spies, the high-lifers and low-lifers, and all the simpler, less complicated people, just sitting and drinking their evening aperitifs. That seven o'clock hum of voices rising from the Petit Soko at the aperitif hour. Like swarming bees."

"We were a lot younger then."

"What's youth got to do with it? It's one of the special places in the world, and I expect we'll be just like everyone else in Tangiers."

"You are probably right."

"Will we live there, or in the house in Marrakesh, when we are here in Morocco?" she asked.

"Divide our time, I think."

He saw the pleasure shining in her face. It made him smile to himself. He had made the right choice. Not that he had ever doubted it. Ever since he had made that filial vow at his father's deathbed, to marry, Jamal had made spasmodic efforts to find a Moroccan girl whom he thought he could settle down with. Every eligible girl of his class had been assessed for him, vast dowries declared, near-engagements entered into. Three bargains had been struck, but each time he had finally abandoned the idea. Then had come the French aristocracy, his second hunting ground. An actress followed after that. In the end, all had been judged too dull, either in bed or out, or both. And none had been wealthy enough. He didn't want their money: he just didn't want them to want his. The woman he married would have to want him only for himself. There had been one other factor: most had been too unbending.

Then, ten days ago, he had seen a photograph of Lara with Roberto, taken at a party in Rome. It had been in the *International Herald Tribune*. It occurred to Jamal that Lara would do. More than do—was exactly right for him. He had always loved her. She was infinitely more interesting in bed than most. She had more money than he did, so would not be after his bank balance. She was fecund, and Bonnie was a beauty. And she was pliant, vulnerable, and he believed she loved him more than any man she had ever had.

He had once molded her into the sensual creature she was, and he knew he could mold her into the wife he wanted. Perfect. How to get her? For the second time in his life, many hours went into plotting the seduction of Lara Victoria Stanton Fayne. And then he called Roberto. A friend of twenty years' standing, and someone who owed him a very great favor. Fate? Well, one day, when their moods were right, he would tell Lara about fate.

They were recognized at once by the doorman at La Mamounia, who made a fuss over them. Walking through the public rooms, with their slim pillars topped by ornate capitals balancing graceful high arches encrusted with jewellike tiles, the sound of water playing its delicate music against the hum of conversation, Lara could not but think of the happy times she had had there with David and Max and Henry. It was her first pang of doubt. The second was that they had decided on a very private wedding ceremony. A civil affair, rather than religious. No fuss, no complications. Most of all, no publicity. They had agreed to tell the family after their extensive tour of the country. But Lara's doubts dissolved when she was distracted by the arrival of the manager of La Mamounia, his assistants, and several members of the staff, who handed bouquets of flowers to her.

In the suite a young girl was waiting for them. "This is Wafika. Her mother was Egyptian and her father Moroccan. She has been with the family since she was four years old. She speaks English, French, and Arabic. She was my mother's maid and companion. Now she is yours."

Lara thought it would be churlish to remind him that she had a maid of her own. Coral had not been with her in Florence only because she had given her maid and secretary two weeks off to go touring through Italy. Later perhaps. Behind Wafika loomed a hulk of a man bursting out of a gray suit.

"This is Rafik. You go nowhere without him. He's a driver-cum-bodyguard-cum-manservant. Between Wafika and Rafik you will have everything you want."

There was something in the tone of his voice, an attitude toward her since they had entered the hotel, perhaps especially since they had arrived in the suite, that she found off-putting. He was behaving so proprietorially. He had not acknowledged her ability to arrange her own domestic affairs, and she felt a loss of freedom. She turned to the half dozen men, the hotel staff, and Jamal's personal retainers, who had carried up the flowers, and thanked them generously. Then, with infinite charm and discretion, she made it quite clear that they were dismissed. Once they had left the room, she turned to face Jamal. He slipped his arm through hers and said, as he walked her toward the bedroom and opened the doors, "You were a bit obvious, darling. I think next time you just wait patiently until I dismiss them."

Start as you mean to go on. An old English nanny had instilled that in Lara when she was no more than five years old. Nanny's recipe had usually worked for her. She none too discreetly separated herself from Jamal. He sensed at once there was something on her mind, but said nothing. He waited. She walked from table to table in the marvelous room, admiring its many arrangements of flowers, the bowls of fruits and nuts and Moroccan sweets Jamal knew she was partial to. Finally she turned around and, giving him her full attention, said, "You have thought of everything. All the things I like. Don't think me ungracious, Jamal, but I expect to have everything I want, with or without Wafika and Rafik. I will of course work them into our household, but have you forgotten I have a life of my own that I am bringing into this marriage? A daughter, and a staff that keeps my life ticking. All that baggage comes along with me, Jamal. For a moment there, in the other room, I had the disturbing sensation that you had forgotten that. That you think me incapable of directing my own life. Don't make that mistake. I am very much in love with you. I think of nothing, night or day, except what a wonderful life we will have together, of all the things I want to do to make you happy. But I think you had better remember I will never again get lost in you, as I once did. I'm my own woman. Yours, yes—oh, yes—but mine, too."

Strong words, well said. Too well said. Jamal tried to hide his amusement. She was as vulnerable as ever, in spite of her bravado. If she wasn't, then why the pretty little speech? He took little notice of what she said, only pretended to. His sole reaction was, as always when he was sure he had control over Lara, sexual.

"I am already lost in you, and our life together has barely begun."

That was not what she expected. But she caught the glint in his eye. He was looking at her as if she had nothing on. It was a look that always excited her. She tried to calm herself, put from her mind erotic thoughts of how he was likely to take her. She turned away and walked to the windows that overlooked a romantic, quiet courtyard. It was subtly lit. A place of enchantment. White doves fluttered around in it. A pair settled on the rim of the fountain, one hopped in and quivered its wings in the water.

She felt him come up behind her. Caress her hair. Kiss her on the side of her neck. She was still dressed as she had been for lunch in Florence. They had gone from The Loggia in the Villa San Michele, directly to a waiting plane. He placed his arms around her waist and drew her back against him. He unbuckled the wide belt that cinched her waist and drew it slowly from around her, whispering in her ear, "You say you're mine? Show me how much you are mine." He raised the linen skirt up over her thighs, which he caressed, and then up over her bottom until he had it around her waist. He whispered again, "I have a yen to drink cum from your cunt. Fill your cunt for me so I can quench my thirst." He knew she could not resist talk like that from him. He felt her slipping under the spell of Eros. Felt the gentle pelvic gyrations beneath his touch. "Lara, you're the loveliest, most sensual lady, it's so easy to lose myself with you." Gently he pushed her away from him and leaned her over the balcony rail. There was hardly a sound but for the cooing of the doves below, the occasional flutter of their wings as they flew from ledge, to fountain, to ledge in the courtyard.

She could scarcely speak; a huskiness afflicted her voice. "Someone will see."

"Only the doves."

He had no need to ask her. She widened her stance so that her legs were as far apart as possible. He raised her bottom and gently slid his fingers along the already moist slit. She sighed, coming in gentle orgasms. He tortured her with the slowness with which he entered her, and, once deep inside her, lifted her off the balcony rail and carried her thus—back into the room and onto the floor. He withdrew slowly, then replaced his cock with his mouth, and did indeed quench his thirst for her.

He had proven to himself what he already knew to be true. It was Lara who was lost in him, not he who was lost in her. He dominated her with lust for hours. She submitted to his sexual whims without a thought of doing otherwise. She was formidable. At that moment, he made up his mind never to set her free. Always to keep her under his control, and not purely erotically. He adored her as his sexual slave, forgetting for the moment how much he himself was enslaved by her love and passion for him. It was too late to take her to the house he kept for his sexual pleasure in the *medina*. That would have to wait until they were married. But there he would introduce her to sexual delights she had never dreamed of. But would he? he wondered. After he had made her his wife, after she had given birth to their sons?

He tried to put out of his mind how he would reduce her to

no more than a decorative vessel in his hands. But visions of her being taken—not by one or two men but a dozen, a line of men— kept him crazily excited. He had done that once. Taken an amazing French nymphomaniac on safari in Africa, and as a gift had her placed naked on her knees on a camp bed, and tied comfortably down. Then he had given a whole village of men to her. He had watched them fuck Arlette in succession. It had been one of the most exciting sexual performances he had ever seen. The aftermath had been nearly fatal for the famous French beauty, but it had been an experience, which still haunted them both, as the ultimate in libertinism. Or had it? Was he simply confusing fucking with fantasy?

He looked down at the sleeping Lara, and knew the closest she would ever come to that state would be as a voyeur. However much he could control her, she had in the past always pulled back at that moment of total submission to his desire to break her spirit, annihilate her self-esteem. Was it, he wondered, that which in the end kept them, even after all these years, so besotted with each other? The game of sex and love. She was no true libertine, but a sensualist who governed her lust by sharing it with a partner, and always, so far as he knew, a love partner.

He kissed her awake. "You were dreaming. Nice dreams?"

"Dreams about us and a wedding."

He handed her a Moroccan robe, a silvery-gray, fine-woven silk, heavy with silk braid and a multitude of matching tiny buttons in a luscious plum color. She was clearly delighted with it. "There are others in the wardrobe. A lovely collection."

She fell back among the pillows, the robe draped in front of her, covering her naked breasts. She wanted more sleep. She took Jamal, who was sitting on the edge of the bed next to her, by the hand, meaning to pull him back with her. It was then that she saw he was dressed. She felt suddenly surprised and alarmed. "Why are you dressed?"

"I must go."

"What time is it?"

"Half past four in the morning."

"Where could you possibly have to go at this hour?"

"Home."

"Home?"

"That's where I'll be staying until after we're married. You will be living here."

She sat up and, tossing the robe over her head, struggled into it, and then out of the bed. "Don't be ridiculous. Give me half an hour. I'll bathe and dress and we will both go home, if that's what you prefer."

"No. What I prefer is that you stay here and I go home. Anything else is unacceptable. Unthinkable. It would ruin your reputation in Marrakesh if it were seen that we lived together before the wedding. And I cannot have a wife with a tarnished reputation."

"Well, that is rich! What about these past days at the Villa San Michele. What about my reputation then?"

"Well, *you* chose to blow it there, didn't you? You can act the high-class slut in Italy. But here in Morocco, high or low class, a slut is unacceptable. It's a role you are not allowed to play."

Lara felt as if he had slapped her. She was enraged, and raised her hand to retaliate. He grabbed her wrist and pulled her into his lap, kissing her hand once, and then again. His grip was so tight her wrist pained her. Finally she said, "You're hurting me."

He released her wrist, but pulled her tight up against him. She knew better than to struggle with one who was too strong for her. Instead she remained rigid in his arms. "Don't be angry. We are a very conservative society here, you know that. And you would be just as compromised if you were to live at my house. Forgive me, I might have put it better to you."

"You might. You should."

Her anger had barely subsided. So he sat with her cradled in his lap and rocked her gently, kissing her sweetly. He caressed her until he felt her yield to him, all anger dissolved. Then he suggested, "I've ordered hot coffee and brioches and eggs poached in a meat sauce. I'm famished and so must you be. I had meant for us to dine out, but the sex was too good to stop. Some food, and then I'll put you back to bed and go home. I'll be back before you wake. Then I'll take you out and buy you something lovely in celebration of your first day back in Marrakesh."

A table had been set up in front of the settee. It was resplendent with flowers and food. Jamal and Lara sat next to each other and held hands while Rafik poured hot black coffee for them. Waiters arrived to serve the eggs. Then, over coffee and yet another brioche, Lara asked Jamal to send everyone from the room.

Throughout the meal, Jamal had been very aware how amazingly young and innocent Lara could look. The green eyes and the naturally silver-blond hair, but especially the sensuous, puffy lips, enchanted him. He was pleased because she wore the Moroccan robe. This was the woman he would wed in three days' time, not the disturbing creature who behaved like a common whore in bed. And it was to that part of Lara that Jamal addressed himself. Or tried to. Because they both chose to speak at once.

"You go," he said, smiling at her.

"No, you say what you were going to say."

He shrugged his shoulders. "I think we've been a little hasty about—"

Lara turned very pale. "My god, you're going to jilt me."

He began to laugh, and gathered her to him for reassurance. "Far from it. In fact, quite the opposite. What I was going to say—if I am permitted to continue?" She looked relieved and nodded her consent. "We've been hasty about keeping our wedding a complete secret, as we agreed we would."

Her face lit up with enthusiasm. "I don't believe this! That is exactly what I wanted to talk to you about."

"I'm very proud to be marrying you, Lara, and of becoming a part of the Stanton family. I have been close to two of your brothers for almost all my adult life. David is still my best friend, and I would like him to be a witness at the wedding. What do you think?"

Involuntary tears filled her eyes, several trickled down her cheeks. Tears of joy. It was an emotional moment for them both. One that they had obviously avoided precisely *because* the family was so important to them that they had been unable, till now, to cope with involvement with any of the Stantons.

They called David. He called Max. And thirty-six hours later the four of them were dining together in the old courtyard of the Dar Marjana restaurant. Berber-robed, turbaned, and with Berber knife, Abdel Azziz was the perfect host, his elegant Arab palace the perfect setting for their momentous reunion.

The only other person in the family to know about the wedding was Martha. She did not accompany David because the birth of their second child was imminent.

The presence of David and Max brought a new happiness to their wedding plans. The men, who had for so long been three of the world's most eligible bachelors, had a shared past together. They also shared a longtime love of Lara. The three, a cousin, a brother, and a lover to Lara, were more like brothers than friends. And to them all she was something precious in their lives. Each of them, in his own way, knew her strengths and her weaknesses. David and Max intended that she should be protected in this marriage. They knew Jamal and the downside of his nature. No one was hiding anything. It therefore came as no surprise that they should talk openly about the coming event.

"You guys, I'd like to know we have your blessings," said Jamal.

"You do," David was quick to answer.

"And mine," chimed in Max.

"It did cross my mind that you might try to talk Lara out of marrying me."

"Talk Lara out of something? You must be kidding. Besides, she tells us she has loved you for a very long time. There is one thing, though, Jamal. If you don't make her happy, if you give her any of the shit I know you are quite capable of giving women—and mostly the ones you love—you will have the family to deal with, and most especially me." There was a look in Max's eyes that said he meant business.

"Max!"

"Sorry, La, but it had to be said. Jamal is like a brother to us. It's best we get some things straight." He then added, much to her embarrassment, "Jamal, when Lara eloped with Sam, not one of us thought about La. We were that certain that Sam was the right husband for her. This time, David and I are thinking of her."

To that end David suggested, "Why don't we all fly back to the States, to Cannonberry Chase? You could be married there, in a very private ceremony, just the four of us present—if it's secrecy you want. I can arrange that. And you could tell your friends and the family afterward." It was a loaded suggestion, and they all knew it. The marriage would then be under United

States jurisdiction. It was all about power of place. The possibility of a marriage going wrong. A court battle later. No one was surprised when Jamal declined the offer. And no one was fooled. Jamal wanted a Moroccan wedding certificate for the same reason. If there were ever to be a separation, he would want to fight the Stanton clan on his own territory.

The three men knew exactly what was going on. Her relatives were making it clear to Jamal that, until they turned Lara over to him in marriage, they were only interested in protecting her. That there was nothing personal in it. It hadn't been said, but he had understood it well. Jamal, ever the diplomat, was full of charm, but firm. He and Lara would not change their plans. He could have. He thought it would have been quite agreeable to be married at Cannonberry Chase. One of his favorite places in the world, it had always had a hold on him. He was invariably delighted to return there. It did that to people: enchanted them and never let them go. Jamal could have acquiesced, because he knew it didn't much matter where they were wed. Once the deed was done, he would never let Lara go, no matter what. There were always ways to keep her and any children in Morocco. But not to acquiesce was a matter of principle with him. Principle demanded he keep full control of Lara and their life together.

If Jamal had been taken by surprise by David's subtle demand and Max's warning, the Stanton men and Lara were equally surprised by Jamal's insistence that they accept a prenuptial agreement he had had his lawyers draw up and which he had signed. It was, in effect, a waiver on his part of all claims to any of Lara's assets—personal, family, or in trust. He asked for no such undertaking from her.

None of this went over her head. Although she was prepared to marry Jamal anywhere, she came down to earth long enough to realize that he had given her no choice as to where or how they would wed. She filed that in the back of her mind, aware that she probably would not have realized it had David not so astutely pointed it out. And now this. All three of them had been impressed when Jamal had produced the agreement he was insisting on. But once again she had not been consulted, not been offered a choice in the matter. It registered a warning that she thought to deal with later.

Walking behind David and Max, Jamal had whispered in

Lara's ear, "I think you should waive all rights to your assets, too. But I won't ask you to do that. It seems unreasonable—and unnecessary—since I will insist we live on my money, anyway. Anything you could ever want, I can afford to give you. Just think of yourself as having no money of your own, and let the interest pile up while you spend mine. You're in my hands now, I'll care for you. That's what husbands do. Promise me you'll abide by that rule. That will be enough for me."

Lara had no idea what to make of such a suggestion. All she knew was that it wasn't a good one. Rule? What rule? At the best of times she was uninterested in money, except when she had worked with Harland on her projects. Even then she got bored and bolted. For a young woman of her wealth she was hardly a spendthrift. She had always had enough for whatever she wanted. She could hardly think about it in the terms Jamal did. My money, your money. She could only think of all money as *our* money. Three years married to Sam, and she could not remember discussing anything to do with money. Not before, during, or since their divorce. Really, it was quite vulgar of Jamal to bring up the subject.

Why, she wondered, was he so insistent that she be financially dependent on him? Fortunately she had not had the chance to answer. They were interrupted by Max, who distracted them from the subject. Lara had a terrible feeling in the pit of her stomach. Had it been generosity or pride that had prompted that whisper? Or what? Whatever, it was soon lost in the excitement of the day. And cousin and brother became best man and proxy father of the bride the following day in the family house in Tangiers.

There are some women who are spoiled constantly by men. Something in their character demands it. That had been so for Lara since birth. Men were irresistibly drawn to her, they made enormous efforts to please her. No, more than that, they derived satisfaction from doting on her, spoiling her. And what was so extraordinary about Lara was that she made no demands on them for material things. In fact, she made no overt demands on men. Her need to be loved and adored by them emanated from her like a dangerous perfume.

Standing in the garden, under a cobalt-blue sky in the warmth of a morning sun, she was surrounded by three men who loved

her more than any other women in their lives. She was now the
wife of the man she had always wanted to marry and make a
life with. The man who had molded her from inexperienced
adolescent into sensuous woman. The man who had taught her
to be proud of her sexuality, her lust for life. The man she had
walked away from because he would not give her what she
wanted. What he was giving her today: a life together for all the
world to see. A marriage on which they could build something
together.

She looked past her husband to David, who was standing next
to Jamal. In David she saw again the first great love of her life.
He smiled as if to reassure her. As if she needed reminding that
he was there for her and would always be there for her. She
smiled back. And then looked at Max, who was standing next
to her. He still loved and spoiled her at every opportunity. Like
her other brothers, he was always there for her, ever offering her
another adventure, another dream to pursue. Max, who gave,
and gave, as if he gave nothing.

Lara had always taken these two men's love for granted. Now,
suddenly, she was humbled by it. In a moment of awareness she
was humbled by all the love and the loyalty they had given unstintingly. Max squeezed her hand, and she knew they, both
David and Max, had always understood that she thrived on their
love and affection. She gave her attention now to Jamal. He
seemed happier than she had ever seen him. There was a kind
of energy about these three handsome and distinguished men
who were there for her. She thought she might never experience
this surge of energy again, and took it to her heart. For at that
moment she sensed she had the romantic love that she had been
seeking, pure and perfect as she had imagined it. How had she
not understood she had been born with it? That it had always
been within her? And that she had been doubly blessed because
she had had it all her life—in all the men who had ever loved
her? She *was* romantic love.

The wedding party was ushered to a table and a chair set to
one side of the garden. There Lara took the chair while Jamal
signed the marriage certificate. The three men were standing
around her. She looked at each of them, smiled, then took the
pen in her hand. The sun struck her lavish engagement ring,
sending a rainbow of colors over the certificate. The wedding

band, a circle of square-cut diamonds, sparkled. She tried to suppress a smile brought on by thoughts of Emily. All that disapproval. Lara signed the document. A shaking of hands all around. Her men kissed her, the magistrate beamed. There was a knock on the garden gate, and David remarked, "Perfect timing."

In minutes the garden swarmed with Arab boys in striped burnooses, carrying cage upon cage of white doves. They set them free. The garden became a flutter of white wings, the sound of flapping and cooing. Several house servants dressed in their best robes and turbans arrived with champagne. A quintet of Moroccan musicians filled the garden with the thump of drums, the sound of oboes and stringed instruments. Several Arab girls pelted the party with armfuls of rose petals. After twenty minutes, the wedding party fled through the garden gate and piled into an open Rolls-Royce. The reception was being held on the streets and beaches of Tangiers, on a dhow that would sail them to a secret palace on the shoreline.

They had fled from Marrakesh because rumors of a wedding had already leaked to Jamal's family. Fled to Tangiers and then from the house there, so as not to share their happiness with anyone but the four of them. It was a crazy, wildly funny day. Lara, who had been carrying a bouquet of dozens of white moth orchids, at one point saw a couple who looked very much in love. She stood up in the car, and the couple waved and clapped, and she tossed the bouquet to the girl. It was falling short, but the boy ran for it and caught it just before the flowers hit the ground. He tossed it into the air again, and the girl caught it. They went from cafe to cafe, drinking and laughing. In the Casbah they had a wedding feast in a small restaurant at the end of a maze of narrow streets.

It was dusk when Jamal and Lara parted from David and Max. And when David kissed her good-bye, he said, "If ever you need me . . ." He pressed the amber netsuke she had given him, and from which he had never been parted, into the palm of her hand. "Just get it to me, and I will find you."

She opened the palm of her hand—the amber bead rolled around in it. She closed her fingers tight around it. "I'll be fine. Just fine. Thanks, David, for everything." And they parted.

Chapter 23

Just a few days and nights later, Lara realized that she would not be fine. That she had made a catastrophic mistake in marrying Jamal. She had not expected that he would have changed, and she had, after all, loved him in the past, in spite of the negative and sometimes evil things she knew he was capable of. What she hadn't bargained for—and it was obvious that Jamal hadn't, either—was how very much she had changed. But she had expected that their relationship would be based on truth and trust, not manipulation and deceit.

It had all started off well enough. The wedding day itself had gone marvelously, better than any bride could ask for. Alone at last on one of the African wooden sailing ships that had plied the coast of Morocco for centuries, they were thrilled to be husband and wife. Jamal could not have been more affectionate, more caring. More sentimental. It was not a perfect full moon, but it glowed silkily against a black sky studded with stars. The sea was rough, but that hardly bothered such a hardened pair of seagoers. Lara and Jamal had stood in the prow of the ship and waved to David and Max standing on the now-deserted, powdery-white beach next to several blazing bonfires, until they disappeared into the darkness of the night. Then Lara and Jamal turned their attention to the crew, scampering over the ship in burnooses and turbans to raise the sail and cut through the crashing waves to get them away from the shore and fully on course.

It was too cold for Lara, still in her champagne-colored, strapless silk dress, even with its long coat of the same material. Whereas the soft, sensuous yet casual Christian Dior outfit had been perfect for the wedding, once offshore, the wind tore at it and etched her naked figure beneath. Haute couture fell prey to raw nature. They went below, and Lara and Jamal changed into sumptuous Moroccan robes, family period pieces. Over them they wore burnooses of the finest woven cashmere, trimmed in silk embroidery. They went above once more to sit on deck, under a silk canopy stretched over the tops of narwhal tusks. The sofa they reclined on was placed on Oriental carpets of great age and beauty. They drank hot sweet mint tea and smoked kif. The wind had eventually died down, and they lay in each other's arms. She could feel his happiness, and that made her own swell. She was brimming with her newfound joy.

"This dhow and the palace where we will be staying were two of my father's favorite possessions. He would be so happy to know we are married. He always thought you lovely. Had you been his, he would have sealed you away somewhere safe. Kept you all to himself."

"He never did that to your mother."

"Ah, but he did. He only let her out of his sight when she was allowed to go to New York, and then I or my brother accompanied her everywhere. But even that was only because he didn't want his European and American friends to think him a barbarian."

"He was hardly that."

"Well, half that. There are still some seven women in residence who have never been allowed the privileges of my mother. And he was married to two of them."

"I hope it's not a case of 'Like father like son.' I don't think I could cope with that."

"Lara, they do say that of all his children I am the most like my father. One is sometimes surprised at what one can learn to cope with." His answer was less than reassuring. She turned in his arms to make her feelings clear. Candlelight fell on his face. They stared into each other's eyes. He was too quick for her. He read her expression and placed a finger over her lips, telling her, "Like a lifetime of this." He kissed her deeply.

It was dawn when they arrived at their destination, an impressive fortress on the sea, flanked by stretches of glaringly white sand beaches, empty and apparently infinite. Crashing waves beat constantly against the facade of the stone palace. The

dhow sailed through a breakwater to dock on the beach. There Jamal and Lara were met by a carriage and two horses that carried them through the gates of the palace into a courtyard lined with giant date palms rustling in the breeze. Inside, from what Lara could see, it was lavishly appointed, a treasure trove of Islamic art and artifacts. They went directly to their suite of large and sumptuous rooms that overlooked the sea on the one side, and a panorama of undulating sand dunes on the other. It was almost more a moonscape than landscape, more an erotic escape than a desert outpost. From another window were visible walled gardens of date palms and flowers, grass and pools, an oasis of lush flora and exotic birds where, Jamal insisted, a leopard and even a panther lived and roamed. Exhausted, they undressed each other and went directly to sleep.

When they awoke late the following afternoon, they remained in their rooms and made love. Sex, passion, took over, a lust in which they willingly lost themselves. And it was during one of his more violent rages of lust that, for Lara, the ending of her second marriage began.

He had inserted a line of large baroque pearls, strung several inches apart on a silk cord, into her vagina. And then he told her, ''You are to wear them all the time. Grip them as you grip me, suck them with your cunt as you suck my cock with your cunt, and you can come at anytime you choose, wherever you want to. At some boring dinner party, while shopping, in art galleries, when you're swimming, or flying, or riding. . . . Am I not the most generous of husbands?''

He was smiling, and fondling the pearls with searching fingers, kissing her lips and breasts. He told her, ''Even on demand, as now. Come for me, Lara.'' He felt the contractions, and his excitement mounted as she trembled in his arms and she came, warm and silky over his fingers and her very special string of pearls. Then again, and this time she called out in a frenzy of passion. He bit hard into her erect nipple, and then licked the tiny droplet of blood that appeared where he broke the plummy-colored skin. He had ordered, and she had obeyed.

They lay quietly, recovering from their sexual abandon, he cradling her in his arms. She had been drifting between thoughts of Jamal and how exciting it was to be a part of his life, to grant him his pleasures, to submit to one who loved as he professed to love her. To drop all the barriers, run free with her emotions. Of course she was a sexual toy that he played with, that he honed to perfection, that he flayed so that she remained sexually raw, with every nerve ending exposed. Sex with him was like a balancing act, always teetering on a dangerous edge. It was life lived and died in orgasm and rebirth and that slow climb back to life again.

That was where she was drifting when he suggested, ''When next we meet Roberto, you will be wearing your pearls. I shall demand that you come, and you will. That will be his reward, to know that you are coming for him in public. He loves that sort of thing, does our Roberto. Or should I offer you to him as a thank-you note, to do with as he chooses? Well, we know what Roberto chooses. How many times has he had you, Lara? Sodomized you with that aristocratic cock of his?''

Lara resisted his words, and yet they grew clearer, until she was hearing him plainly and not through a fog of lust and love. None of it made any sense to her. What was Jamal talking about? *Who* was Jamal talking about? The Roberto she had introduced him to when they met by chance in the piazza in Florence? Surely Jamal had never met Roberto before. But then, if that were true, how could he know Roberto's sexual preferences? She felt suddenly sick. ''Reward . . . for Roberto? A thank-you note? What could you possibly be grateful to Roberto for, Jamal?''

She was sitting up now in bed. The last play of sunshine was bright orange, and spilled through the windows to bathe the room in a pink-gold light. She could hear the sea pounding the rocks. Rage, a dying day, and a sense of danger emanating from Jamal, seemed to fill the room. She looked naked and wanton sprawled against the brocades, her long silvery hair spread over the brightly-colored intricacies of the embroidered pillows. She could see Jamal, naked and virile, on his knees now, bending over her, reflected in the huge mother-of-pearl-and-ivory mirror of Damascus work hanging opposite the bed.

Suddenly she felt real fear. A rare and unsettling experience for her. She swallowed hard, and looked away from Jamal, not wanting him to catch the expression in her eyes. There seemed to be no menace in the way he took her chin in his hands and turned her head round to face him once again. ''Don't look away from me when I'm talking to you. Where is all your Old World breeding, my dear?''

His eyes were cold as stone. But he spoke to her softly, as if coddling her. That only augmented the sense of menace. She had seen him like this in the past, when he was under the influence of some sadistic spasm. She reached for a large Chinese white silk shawl, covered in pink and peach and gold embroidered flowers, trimmed with long, silky fringes. She had an instinct to cover herself. The shawl lay on the edge of the bed. She drew it slowly over a leg, slid it gracefully up over her thigh. She tried to make it appear a casual, unimportant action. Jamal raised her hand and kissed it. The shawl slipped from her fingers and slid off her body, from the bed, onto the floor in a single frustrating slither.

He demanded, ''Just leave it there. I prefer you the way you are.'' She obeyed. He kissed her thigh and then her ankle. Then, holding her by her foot and caressing it, while staring coldly up into her eyes, he said, ''Why to Roberto? For making it so very easy for me.''

She girded herself to say, ''Tell me it's not true.''

''That what's not true? You should be more specific, less cryptic. This is not going to be a marriage, I hope, where we cannot communicate unless you are coming.''

She was cut to the quick that he should play the monster to her behind his role of Prince Charming. Where was love? She felt herself victimized by his petty stabs. She rallied, determined not to allow it, and ignored his demeaning remark.

''Fate had nothing to do with our meeting in the Piazza della Signoria, did it, Jamal?'' He remained silent. ''You stage-managed that meeting. You used Roberto to arrange it and let me believe it was fate. What a fool you and Roberto must have taken me for. For what possible reason?'' She put up her hand, as if to stop him from speaking, although he had had no intention of answering her. ''Oh!'' Pain colored her voice. ''How very stupid of me. Of course. You couldn't come to me openly and tell me you still loved me, say you wanted to marry me. You were afraid I would throw you out.''

''No, not that. Never that. I knew you would never decline an offer of marriage from me.''

''You bastard! I don't believe you. Then why the deception?

Why did you have to manipulate me into marrying you?''

''Timing. You were always easily seduced by me. I could always bend you to my will where other men never could. Deceiving you always shakes that Pilgrim stock in you. It brings out a certain vulnerability that excites my imagination. Manipulation, deceit . . . just remember it got us to the altar before the week was out.''

She tried to pull herself away from Jamal, but he held her fast by her foot. Lara felt trapped. There was no getting around the feeling that she had made a monumental mistake in undertaking marriage to him. She tried to dismiss the feeling and make the best of what she had done.

Thus began for Lara the most soul-destroying time of her life. She and Jamal lived in the palace by the sea. There were wonderful romantic days and nights when he never left her side. He showered her with gifts and spent endless time with her, teaching her the customs of his country, the history of his family. They played tennis together, they rode Arab stallions into the desert, and they sailed. He had musicians and dancers flown in from Tangiers. There were lunches for Moroccan friends to meet his bride.

He promised her she could bring her plane and her mechanic. They would fly all over North Africa, to remote architectural sites. He would build a runway for her plane. As soon as Bonnie's holiday with Sam was over, they would fly to the States to pick her up, bring her back to Morocco to live with them in the house in Marrakesh.

But none of these things happened. He kept postponing Bonnie's arrival. The excuse was flattering: he wanted Lara all to himself, for just a little longer. He refused to allow Nancy and Coral to join them in the palace by the sea. They lingered, awaiting orders, in the house in Marrakesh.

A teacher was sent for from Rabat, and Lara began her Arabic studies. Jamal seemed proud of her quickness to learn, her anxiety to please him. But, from that very afternoon she knew their marriage was a sham, his demand that she submit to him in everything became a way of life for them. And Lara's neurotic need to please Jamal, not to have another failed relationship on her hands, soul-destroying as it was, became the object of her life.

During the seven weeks that they remained in the sixty-room palace next to the sea, Lara was victimized by Jamal in a thousand petty ways. He refused to let Bonnie join them, and then called Lara a bad mother. He accused her of being attracted to his servants. She must want his Arab boys as lovers because she was starved here for rough trade. Hadn't she had American boys as secret lovers? He checked on her every movement. He countermanded her orders, read her mail, listened in on her phone calls.

It was he who spoke to Nancy in Marrakesh, who turned down the social engagements that arrived from all over. About dinner engagements, Lara was never consulted. He interrupted her when she was on the telephone, embarrassed her, insulted her intelligence. He isolated her from her child and family and friends, and then chided her for preferring her own company and his. But he never hit her. On the contrary, he made love to her every night, every day. Whenever, she realized, he felt that he had gone too far. He revived her flagging self-esteem with sex and her ability to excite his sensual passion. He flattered her as the only woman in the world he could have married. Yet he abused her emotionally on a grand scale. It was systematic, purposeful control and punishment. The effect was far more devastating than if he had punched or thrashed her.

Lara found herself living with a terrifyingly unpredictable Jekyll-and-Hyde figure who cherished and humiliated her by turns. He was like a coin flipped up in the air that might land either head or tail up. Charm or abuse, charm and abuse. He used the charm as a manipulative tool to control and confuse her. And Lara, as putty in his hands, was the excitement of Jamal's life. It inflamed the evil side of his nature. They were both locked in a game of self-destruction, glossed over by charm and a need to love each other, and fear of a failed marriage.

After seven weeks Lara knew that she was pregnant. By that time she already felt herself pulled down into the dirt of Jamal's life. It was where, seemingly, she must learn to live. But she was not unaware that he was keeping her virtually a prisoner in the palace by the sea. A place so isolated as not even to have a name. If only the joy that they were going to have a child could lift the barriers he had built around their relationship, she felt there might yet be a way to turn their marriage around.

Jamal was jubilant at the news. In a moment of passion, he told her, "I love you. You have to believe that I love you, that that's why I married you. And for this moment, to make a child with you, for you to bear my sons." And then he wept and fell asleep in her arms. He had a doctor flown in from Paris to Tangiers, and then by helicopter to the residence. When the doctor confirmed Lara's condition and that she was perfectly healthy, he was sent away. They flew to Marrakesh to take up residence there the following day.

Life changed once they settled in the house in Marrakesh. Jamal was more the Prince Charming and less the monster. He even granted some of Lara's wishes. Bonnie arrived with her nanny. Coral, Nancy, and the nanny were at last allowed to become a part of Lara's new household. Jamal treated Bonnie as if she were his own child. He soon charmed the six-year-old into an attachment to him. There was a month of euphoria, happy family played out in the house of Marrakesh. After being in Morocco for nearly three months, Lara began to meet people and make friends. There were lavish dinner parties with amusing people, an excursion nearly every day to the historic buildings and mosques of Marrakesh, or to the *medina* and cafes and tempting restaurants. There Lara discovered, between the restaurants and Jamal's cooks, that Moroccan cuisine could be as rich and varied as French or Italian.

The country, with the Sahara at its feet and both the Mediterranean and the Atlantic kissing its shores, was a land of contrasts. Like the land, its food was, too. Moroccan food in London, Paris, or New York, might mean couscous, but not for Lara in Marrakesh. For her it meant *B'stilla*. The unbelievably rich *B'stilla aux Pigeons*—translated, just plain pigeon-pie—was her favorite. But there was nothing at all plain about the dish. Encased in dozens of onion-skin-thin layers of pastry called *warkha*—so thin, in fact, that before cooking you could see through them like a piece of dusty glass—was a highly spiced, highly flavored mixture of pigeon meat and creamy, lemon-flavored eggs and almonds, spiced with cinnamon and saffron, and sweetened with pounded sugar. When baked, its crisp, golden pastry leaves were finer than any filo-pastry that Austria or France or Greece could offer.

Lara was enamored of anything cooked with the *warkha*

leaves, such as *Trid Marrakshia*, which was made with chicken.
There were other dishes and some sweets, and so many salads.
She even thought to take Jamal's cook from Marrakesh back to
Cannonberry Chase when they were in residence there. If not
for the *B'stilla*, for the *Chicken Mqualli* with olives and pre-
served lemons. She learned a great deal more about food from
her newfound friends. Lara was taken up and made a great fuss
over by the local expatriate community. She found them amusing, Jamal found them annoying. On the surface, life for her in
Marrakesh was paradise. Only she knew that it was paradise
lost.

   As the months passed, Jamal became obsessive about Lara
and the child she was carrying. Behind closed doors he began
once more to practice his destructive victimization of her. Only
this time it was far worse. If Jamal had found his wife an exciting
woman before she was pregnant, as he clearly had, now he
found it impossible to stay away from her. He had a wild passion
to possess her sexually that he could hardly explain or justify to
himself. His lust for her dominated their lives and their marriage. To counteract this grand passion and dependence upon
Lara, which he detested, Jamal would seek out ways to punish
her. He concocted excuses to justify the punishment: she was
spoiled, self-indulgent, wanton, flirtatious, lustful, insatiable.
Within months this litany of her vices had drowned out the still
small voice of Lara's self-confidence.

   On the brink of despair, she rallied and began to plot an
escape. Not an easy task. Especially since Jamal had charmed
Nancy, the nanny, and Coral and won their confidence. He was
as much their master as he was Lara's. And Bonnie, the child,
saw him as the light of her life. Lara's entourage, her little household and her daughter, had been taken over by Jamal and had
fallen under the spell of Marrakesh. They were besotted by the
city, by Morocco and its culture, its color, its people, the exotic
and glamorous life that Jamal and Lara led in that very closed
society. Only one person in that household seemed contrary and
a threat to their new paradise. Lara alone appeared ungrateful
for the life they were all living. Or so Jamal insinuated. Strangely
unappreciative of her handsome, charming husband, or his
power, social, and sometimes political standing in the country.

Jamal was the more persuasive for its being his own country of which he manipulated their vision.

So it came about that Lara became increasingly isolated from her own staff, her child, her family, and her old friends.

Nothing brought that home to her more than the day she and Bonnie were in the Marrakesh kitchen one afternoon baking cookies. Lara said, "Just look at you, Bonnie! You're almost a cookie yourself you're so covered with flour."

The child's face lit up and gleefully she told her mother, "A chocolate cookie. I'll be a chocolate cookie and you can be a gingerbread lady."

Lara pulled Bonnie onto her lap and began dusting her off with a tea towel. The child put her hand on Lara's now-rotund tummy, and then placed an ear to it. "I wish my baby brother could hear me."

"What would you tell him?"

"That Jamal is going to buy him a pony, and bring Mr. Macaroni here, and then Jamal and baby and me will ride off into the desert together."

"And what about me?"

"Oh, you have to stay home here in the house."

"Why, Bonnie? Why can't I come with you?"

"Because Jamal says you are a bad mummy. You spoil things."

Lara was appalled; she asked, "Bonnie, do you think I am a bad mummy and I spoil things?" She held her breath. What answer would her five-year-old come up with?

"No. But I have to make believe you are bad and ugly, like the Wicked Witch from the North."

"Why? What will happen if you don't?"

"Jamal won't take me with them when they go. And I want to go with them."

Lara despised herself for asking, but her insecurity dictated the question. "Bonnie, do you still love your mummy?"

No hint of hesitation. Bonnie's arms were around Lara's neck. She planted a huge kiss on her mother's mouth and held it, pressing hard. When Bonnie released Lara, she gave her a big smile and, leaning against her, whispered in her ear, "Oh, yes. But don't tell Jamal."

Even Julia, who came to visit, could see no flaw in her marriage. The three made a journey up into the Atlas Mountains, through the Berber villages. They stayed at a hunting lodge that had been in Jamal's family for three hundred years. He played the considerate host, the generous and gallant husband. Julia was fooled. She believed Lara to be happy, and Lara, not wanting to spoil the holiday, could not bring herself to admit how miserably unhappy she really was.

Lara felt herself to be dying a little every day. She imagined herself looking in the mirror one day—only to find nothing left of her own self to reflect back at her. Jamal would have absorbed all the life in her, leaving her as a mere shriveled sack of flesh and bone. Only the child she carried seemed to promise a future for her life during those months of marriage to Jamal. Lara carried easily, and her pregnancy barely showed. As with Bonnie, suddenly in the last eight weeks she began to look heavy with child. That magnified Jamal's obsessiveness, and with this came a fresh distrust. He had her watched at all times when he was not with her. At one point, after a fit of pique at some imagined peccadillo of hers, he even locked her in their rooms.

As so often before in her life, Lara was saved by the men who loved her. One day, Sam called from Paris. He was stranded there over a weekend, waiting for lawyers to draw up documents on the following Monday for him to sign. Could he drop in on them and see Bonnie? Lara almost wept with relief. There had been several lucky features to that phone call. The first was that Jamal had received it. Sam had asked him, not Lara, if he could pay them the visit. Jamal consented. Less because he wanted the company of Sam, whom he did not like, than because it would give him a chance to discuss a financial transaction with him that might be advantageous to both men. That blunted Jamal's latest obsession: that Lara craved other men to make love to her. Had she taken the call, he most assuredly would have fantasized a new liaison between them. Then he would have watched and listened incessantly. All private conversation would have been proscribed.

Lucky, too, the timing. Lara was just entering her ninth month of pregnancy. That left her enough days to get away. She was determined that she should not have her baby in Marrakesh, or anywhere in Morocco. The third real piece of luck was that a plan was already forming. She had found a way to get a call for help past Jamal and his human watchdogs. She knew she could not escape from him without some shrewd intervention from outside their circle.

For all his searching of drawers and handbags, Jamal had not found Lara's little amber netsuke. She had only to keep her nerve, get it to David, and wait. He had never failed her before. Nothing but the blackest fate could make him fail her now.

Sam arrived, and Lara worked at being very relaxed. Jamal must not sense that she was up to something. The three of them had a particularly good time together. She bided her time, waiting for the moment when she and Sam were alone. She needed only a few minutes, but Jamal never granted them even a few seconds. Only once did she nearly falter: they were having sex, and he taunted her with, "I have seen the way Sam looks at you. He wants you, fantasizes about getting you back into bed. You want him, don't you? That's why you're holding back."

"You're absurd."

"Am I? Than prove it. Let go. Give in to me."

There was too much at stake. She gave in to him. It wasn't difficult, not after she had made up her mind to save her life by submitting to his lust for her. Whatever else he might be, he was still her sexual master. There was a residue of seductiveness on which he could draw. In the morning when he woke her, he presented her with a jewel box. Inside, a necklace of rubies.

She felt sick for what she had done the night before, and the rarefied pleasure she derived from being enslaved to him in lust. Sick at not having thrown the jewels in his face, she confirmed her resolve to leave him. This stick-and-carrot kind of love! An abusive charmer! A failed marriage was better than a lifetime of that. She steeled herself to go through with what she must. Anything to find a way to catch a few minutes alone with Sam.

Jamal didn't make it easy. Still besotted with her and their night of sex, he would not leave her side. He did in fact keep her naked in their room for most of the morning. For him there was real beauty in her huge, round belly. He had her move for him around the room. He would arrange her in the most lascivious positions, study and caress her. He would suck on her now very heavy breasts. He licked her body and kissed it, and felt filled with affection and admiration for her. When finally he allowed her to dress, he sat on the bed watching her. Once she

was ready to leave the room, he slipped his arm through hers
and said, "If I ever catch you even looking at another man, I
will beat you as one whips a whore. You will be thrown to the
servants and beggars of Marrakesh to fuck."

Lara stumbled, but Jamal had her tightly by the arm. She
recovered herself quickly. She felt a blur of dizziness. Was she
about to faint? She fought that off. Then she disengaged his arm
and said, "Don't be stupid." And she unlocked the bedroom
door.

In the airport VIP lounge, Lara found her moment. Distracted
by friends who were leaving on the same plane as Sam, Jamal
turned away for only a few seconds. That gave Lara all the time
she needed. She pressed the netsuke into his hand and folded
his fingers tight over it. Then, pretending to kiss him first on
one cheek and then the other, as the French do, she whispered
in his ear: "Give this to David. Tell him it's dangerous, I'm
desperate, I want my baby born in Cannonberry Chase. No
questions, Sam. Not a word." He looked into her eyes. He
squeezed her hand. Could she be sure that he understood?

Sam shook Jamal's hand and walked away. When he turned
from the tarmac to wave good-bye to them, Lara wanted very
much to believe that her escape from Jamal had been set in
motion.

Chapter 24

Lara's second divorce did not come easy. Nor was it achieved with dignity or out of the public eye. About the only thing that did come easy was getting over being married to Jamal. Once free from his abusive treatment, she recovered her self-esteem quickly. A second failed marriage and a life alone were better than suffering with him. She was beyond his taunts, she could rebuild her life.

Now, four years later, she was in her thirties. Two divorces, the second a minor international scandal, were behind her. And she had come through her second failed marriage a stronger woman. How much more she valued freedom now. But she had had to fight hard for hers. To battle with Jamal for a divorce and custody of their son Karim. The family deplored the scandal. Once it broke, American high society would have ostracized Lara without a second thought had it not been for Emily Stanton. But she rose to the occasion—beyond it even. The first time Jamal came to Cannonberry Chase, pursuing Lara with armed heavies, reporters, and photographers, he was thrown off the estate by the sheriff. Then Emily took to the telephone. Word was put out. Ranks were closed. Jamal was to be frozen out, newshounds to be starved of comment. If folks knew what was good for their position in society, Jamal Ben El-Raisuli did not exist. Her daughter had never married him. The New York 400 would know what was required of them.

Thus had Lara's lifeline been stitched together. Because, in those early days, when she was still carrying Karim and Jamal had come after her with threats of forcibly removing her to Morocco, she knew she had family and friends rallying around her. Friends whose loyalty survived her being forced to leave them and go into hiding for a year. It was a tug-of-love story that Jamal had warned them would turn unsavory. It might ruin her reputation long before they had settled the legalities in Morocco and the States, the how and where of a divorce.

Finally, the power of the Stantons, their command of wealth and connections, overwhelmed Jamal. They reached even into the royal palace in Rabat. It was in the end Henry who talked Jamal round to some sort of sense. Henry and the palace. And even that, Henry was convinced, would never have changed Jamal's mind about a divorce, had Lara not finally been willing to allow Jamal to see his newborn son at less than an hour old. Even though she had been forced by his threats to disappear with her children, she was consistent in sending weekly photographs of Karim, to be forwarded to Jamal. It was his son who wore him down at last.

Jamal and Lara met just once, about two years after David had flown her out of Marrakesh. That was one of Jamal's conditions for a divorce. By then much acrimony had fizzed between them through the tabloids and gossip columns, a ferment of lies and distortions about their marriage. So Lara, knowing what Jamal was capable of, arrived with three bodyguards. They had been with her since the day she'd left him. He had been enraged. The men must leave. But she had obliged him to talk in their presence.

He tried one last time to win her back. He told her how much he loved her, must have her. That she had shattered his life by leaving him. Lara thought it might be true. That he did love her, as much as he was capable of loving any woman. If there was a tragedy in their marriage, it was that he could not sustain his love for Lara, or any woman. Jamal did not love women. He was not a lover. He was a charmer, a seducer.

Next he insisted that she loved him as she had never loved any other man. That was perhaps another tragic truth. But nothing worked. She remained unmoved by his pleadings, his declarations. Then he went on the attack. He ranted at her deceit. How had she managed to leave Morocco without her passport? Who had gotten her out? She revealed nothing. She gave him nothing. He faced defeat and agreed to give her up.

Lara paid dearly for her freedom, and for never having to see Jamal again. Though she had custody of Karim, she agreed to share him with Jamal, for half of each year, until the boy was thought old enough to make the harrowing choice between his parents. She felt she owed both father and son that. Her instinct told her that Jamal, however incapable of loving women, could love his son. It was an enormous sacrifice. She adored Karim greedily. Like his father, the child had a seductive charm. She could not be immune to a special kind of beauty like Jamal's, but with the sweetness of an infant, and then the innocence of a growing child. She ached to keep him close to her always.

One of the most unpardonable sins in the Stanton canon was self-pity. And no Stanton—not even Lara—needed to repent of that particular sin. The lesson read had always been to fight it constructively. Do anything that would lead them forward. Lara practiced what the family preached. That way lay her salvation. That and the family policy never to advise, never to criticize. Hired professionals were used for that. Such standards allowed the family the luxury of giving each other loyalty and support without embarrassing involvement. Therein resided their freedom to make their own mistakes, learn to live with them, pay for them, and then get on with their lives.

During the years before she was granted a divorce, Lara lived with her two children. She divided whatever time she could emerge from hiding between Cannonberry Chase and the family town house. Time that served to confirm the already strong bond she had with her immediate family, their wives and children. Her influence in the family somehow remained undiminished by her messy personal life. Perhaps it even grew. Age difference seemed to play its part. She was ten years younger than her youngest brother. As the family matured they saw her still as young and vibrant, the personification of their youthful selves.

There was something else: Cannonberry Chase had been the heart of all their lives. Now that most of the family were married with homes and families of their own, only Lara, with her overwhelming passion and love for the place, had time to devote to it. She assisted Henry and Emily in the running and preservation of the estate. Cannonberry Chase had a grip on all the family, it was still the home that governed their lives, still the center of exciting happenings, the place that bound them together. Still the world within the world that nurtured them. They were all grateful to Lara and impressed with her work there. And increasingly often John and Steven began consulting Lara on other projects the family was involved with. It was Lynette who summed it up best: "Cannonberry Chase, I am always competing with Cannonberry Chase. She's worse than 'the other woman.' A mistress I could have learned to live with."

Still the occasional trash magazine tried to rake up Lara's past, but by this time she was a minor player. It was Jamal who starred, in the handsome-playboy-of-the-Arab-world role, a semitragic figure after his broken marriage. The magazines did better than the tabloids had with Lara. They had more to work with. And where better to find it than in a scoop leaked by an irate husband? Especially since the wife involved was one of the wealthiest high-society women in the world. An American married to an Arab. A life-style that dreams are made of, that fantasies thrive on. Intimations of immorality, their bizarre sexual life, spread like mud on the title page. For a week it was horrific, then it went cold on them. The glitz wasn't there, the gloss turned to dross.

The Stantons lacked the requisite flash. Their money was too old. There was too much of it to mock. The family was too coolly conservative—if you excluded the wayward daughter—to make much muck. The ranks had closed too tight, sealed lips hid wagging tongues. Secrets were buried so deep, digging them up was an impossible task for a story withered on the grapevine before it had gotten fruity. So, ultimately, the press did better with Jamal as the star, with his escapades and love affairs, his lavish life-style and jet-set friends.

Lara had been through it all before the divorce. She could simply ignore the media gorging itself on her. There was her life to be put together. But she did it as a changed woman. She had given herself unstintingly to her two children for over two years. Now that Jamal was legally out of her life, and the fear of kidnap had receded from her and the children, she resumed a life outwardly much like that she had lived before the fatal afternoon encounter in the Piazza della Signoria.

Busy living and loving, as Lara had been doing all of her life, you tend to think of yourself as living just a day-to-day existence, like anyone else. It rarely occurred to Lara that she was constantly augmenting her life. Nor was she really aware of how she was constantly changing, or the transforming effect that life itself was having on her.

It was quite remarkable that the men in Lara's family, and her immediate circle of friends, could see something in her that they were wholly comfortable with and could depend on, though the women could not. One night, after a family dinner and perhaps too much to drink, they retreated to the library, where they sat around talking. In answer to Henry's request that David do something for him, he had said, "Ask La. She's better qualified to handle it. She's got it all. The big viewpoint. Plenty of strength, enough intelligence, and no personal ambition. She goes after things with more love and passion and courage than I do. Than any of us do, for that matter. She's the best one to hold the wheel in a storm, and you can rely on her to ride it out."

Henry took David's advice that evening. Thereafter, ever more often, he discussed projects with Lara that were of personal interest to him. She seemed to have an ability to cut to the heart of a problem. Her questions usually centered on it. With an economy of involvement she suggested creative and imaginative solutions. Henry and his committees and advisers were increasingly impressed with Lara's abilities. When Henry was going to Holland for a conference on the world's wildlife, he asked Lara to join him, wanting her feedback from the meetings. In a reception for the executive board, she charmed people with her looks and her passion for their projects. So, when a second meeting was called, Henry invited her to sit in. The committee made no objection.

Lara loathed the red tape, the inefficiency that major charitable organizations got bogged down in. She had only to catch a hint of it in any of the Stanton projects to bring it to John's or Henry's attention. She had one pat answer for any excuses from subordinates in the Stanton organizations. "You have a board of directors to answer to. As a member of the board, no matter how inactive I am, I am not satisfied. Find the angle on the problem that will solve it. If you can't, I want to know why."

It could be a tough stance to take. But her passionate interest in whatever she was dealing with, and her ready suggestions, ensured a receptive audience. Some women in her position would have been written off as interfering amateurs, and their contributions resented and rejected. That was not the case with Lara. She held no official post and was not seeking one. She had no obvious private drum to beat. Like all the Stanton men, with the exception of David, she preferred working for success behind the scenes. The limelight was for others, who worked much harder than she did. True, people did listen to her because of her money, her name. But she could radiate a straightforward honesty that added considerably to her power to influence.

Lara accompanied Henry to Helsinki. Several months later to a meeting in Geneva. That same year she made a trip with Henry and John to Japan. Always in the role of the dutiful daughter. But the fascination of the executive boardroom, the Machiavellian mire of big business, soon intrigued Lara. And trying to harness their power for a better world, for the conservation of the earth, seemed to her something that everyone could benefit from. She acted swiftly. Her successes were few but selective. Although she kept that working part of her life in perspective, she did enjoy the power she could wield in the boardroom.

Not enough, however, to accept any of the jobs Henry and John thought she should take on. The most she would do was to sit in with Harland on any Stanton trusts' business, as an interested party and in an advisory position. But, if the family had grown to respect her contributions to their affairs, their respect swelled into admiration at the next annual extraordinary general meeting and the dinner afterward. She shone for them then as never before.

Henry and Steven and Lara had gone to Japan the year before because there was a serious takeover bid from the Japanese against the Stanton Guarantee Trust of Manhattan, the family investment bank, a rival to the likes of Lazard's, Morgan Guarantee, N. M. Rothschild's, and Warburg. Billions were at stake. The board was voting on whether to accept the bid. The usual unanimous vote was needed. Every adviser around the table had recommended the family to take up the offer. Following the custom, Henry was to cast the last vote. Voting went around the table. David, Elizabeth, Max, Steven, John, all voted to sell. It was Lara's turn. She voted not to sell. A stunned silence fell at the table. A dropped pin might have created an echo. Surprise tautened the family's faces, shock froze the advisers. They all knew what Lara's veto meant. A dissenting vote from one member of the family was all it took to kill a motion. It was a family rule; they voted unanimously. Lara started to address the board.

"I can only imagine that none of you has considered what it would really mean. I mean, for us not to have the power and prestige of our bank. To have a part of our heritage taken away. For nearly two hundred and fifty years the bank has been a family business. It alone has funded us. Because of it, we have realized some of our dreams and aspirations. I want my children to inherit the opportunities that it has afforded us. If the bank goes, the Stantons go, too. It may take time, but eventually we'll just disperse, well-heeled, into the world. We will have lost an essential part of our identity. And America, incidentally, will lose an icon, one that is, in its own small way, as much a part of history as George Washington and Valley Forge. I'd hate that."

She sat down. Henry voted with her. Afterward the advisers remained poker-faced, enormously disappointed, but not the family. They gathered around Lara and thanked her for being more far-sighted than they were. Elizabeth admitted that she had been dazzled by the money offered; David that he had been thinking of himself and his ambition. He was grateful to her. Max said, "I always knew you were the best of us."

As for Lara, she had not planned it. She simply made her decision and felt she could confront the consequences. Only at the deepest, most subconscious level could she have known that what she had done in that boardroom, that morning, would one day make her the matriarch of the family, the mistress of Cannonberry Chase.

But that was far ahead. For the present, she remained content with her life, her children, her family, and friends, still living in much the manner she always had. Periods of much-savored solitude interspersed a highly charged social life. She no longer felt the deep loss she had experienced over her two failed marriages, her two loves that had gone awry. But the experiences had had their effect on her. And there was, too, something gained from such catastrophic losses. The richness of having known love—that she would never lose. Loss and gain complemented each other, were essential to each other. They became what sustained her, and what expelled all bitterness from her heart, while she waited for love to come to her again.

What sense did it make—in the darkness of her room, alone yet fulfilled by a rich and exciting life—to fantasize about a great love, something unique that probably didn't exist? It wasn't clear. Yet one thing was certain: no matter what, Lara knew that dream would go to the grave with her.

Only one thing frightened her. Romantic love might never come her way again. It wasn't just that romantic love offered the excitement of the moment, she relished the dramatic changes it brought with it. Romantic love, arch-agent of change, had visited her often enough for her to know she still needed it. Though she was content to live with the changes that it had brought in the past, she looked forward to making new ones. She still suffered that same deep loneliness that had pursued her all of her life. She missed excessive sexual love, passionate love, being the first for someone else.

But here was a wiser Lara, who understood her longings and had learned to live with them. A calmer Lara, who could accept that love comes when it chooses.

His name was Evan Harper Valentine. But she didn't know that when she met him in the Egyptian Gallery at the Metropolitan.

Theirs was to be one of those relationships that evolves out of a series of chance meetings, where a love develops that was neither looked for nor expected. The kind of *grand amour* that only fate has a hand in.

Teasingly, fate chose a snowy January afternoon. No one but the staff was in residence in the Manhattan town house. Henry was in Paris, Emily and most of the family were in the Palm Beach house. Bonnie was with Sam, and Karim with Jamal. Julia had flown to Gstaad two days before, where Lara was to join her in a week's time for some off-piste skiing. Lara had been looking forward to this prior patch of solitude, away from everyone and all the things that kept her so involved.

The snow had been coming down more than heavily. The winds and the cold approximated blizzard conditions. Crackling fires blazed in the library and the living room. Lara had a tray brought to her. She lunched in front of the fire and watched the garden turn a silent white beyond the vast oriel window. After she had put her tray aside, she went to the piano and tinkered with the keys. Finally sitting down, she played for two hours with barely a halt, and had done better than she had for years.

When she did stop, she went to stand in front of the window and was dazzled by the whiteness. It was somehow comforting, the purity of the garden under the thick blanket of white. She looked beyond that, to the gates and the buildings, all white, white, and still the snow was falling just as heavily as it had been all day. Her mind drifted back in time and lodged on the years when she was young. Little had changed in this room. Maybe it was a bit more worn, with more family photographs in silver frames, but Emily still kept it filled with spring flowers and it still smelled of potpourri. She felt warm and comfortable and so young, as if her life was just about to begin. She smiled at her own silliness, and rang for Coral.

Her maid arrived, carrying sturdy leather boots lined in fur, a coat over her arm, a hat in her hand. "Why ever would you want to go out in this, Miss Lara? It's cold out there."

"It will wake me up."

"There's hardly a car moving. No one on the streets."

"All the better. I love New York when it's like this. I won't go far." She pulled the boots on, and around her throat wrapped a terra-cotta, silk damask scarf banded with a border of black. Over her blond hair she wore a sable hat that any cossack would have been proud of. She pushed all her hair up into it and set it at a jaunty angle. Coral held the Russian sable coat that Henry had bought her for Christmas on behalf of the family, her reward for saving the bank. It covered the tops of her boots by several inches, had wide revers, and was belted with a broad band of black suede and a buckle of bronze inlaid with silver and gold. She pulled on black leather, fur-lined gloves, then checked the effect in the mirror. "Very Anna Karenina. Very Garbo." She laughed at herself and left the house, forgetful of Zhivago's Lara.

There wasn't a tire mark on the street in front of the house. Not a person, not a sound. It was a winter wonderland. Making her way against the wind to the corner, she turned up Fifth Avenue. With the wind no longer against her, she was able to walk comfortably on the deserted pavements, cushioned by inches of untrodden snow. She felt like one of those dolls in a sphere of glass, amid a shaken snowstorm that blurs the figure trapped at its center.

Lara crossed the avenue and headed for Central Park. The cold felt good, the air fresh. And it was rather mysterious, walking in a mist of snowflakes that you could only just see through. Like traversing a pointillist painting, a Seurat or a Pissaro. Her face began to sting with cold. Otherwise she was warm and comfortable wrapped in her furs. She felt somehow young and invigorated. She pushed on. A taxi appeared as if from nowhere, feeling its way. It zigzagged crazily past her and disappeared down the avenue in muffled, eerie silence, the merest ghost of a New York Yellow Cab. The wind changed direction, and the snow seemed to be intensifying. So much so that she missed the entrance to the park. She would aim for the next one.

The Metropolitan loomed out of the shadows of the gray-white afternoon. Walking was now becoming difficult. Cold was getting through to her hands and feet. She contemplated turning back, but instead found herself plodding on. Amazingly, she saw several people carefully mounting the narrow path of stairs through the snow, up to the entrance of the museum. A man and a little girl were coming down. Abandoning the idea of the park, Lara turned around to go home. She took only a few steps and stopped. Memories came flooding back of that warm September evening (or had it been October?). She took several more steps. It was so long ago, but still so vivid a memory: that night when they had all trooped into the museum as honored guests.

Recalling the erotic sights and sounds of that afternoon and evening made her smile. She stopped again and shook the snow from her coat, clapped her hands together, and stomped her feet, then resumed walking. Her emotions were stirred once again, as they had been then. Something compelled her to turn around, mount the museum stairs, and push through the entrance. She brought with her a gush of wind and cold air. And then she was in a haven of warmth.

Inside, there was hardly a soul. It was quiet, tomblike, but bright with electric lights and warmth. She heard the echo of footsteps on marble, a voice. The sounds sharpened her memory of that evening. A guard suggested she check her coat. She declined. Another passing guard recognized her. He removed his hat and greeted her. "It's Miss Stanton, isn't it?"

"Yes, hello, Joe. I won't check my coat, if you don't mind. I would just like a few minutes in the Egyptian Gallery." She removed her gloves and shook the man's hand.

On entering the gallery, she found it eerily empty and under almost exactly the same light as it had been on her last visit. She walked through the gallery, in the direction of the statue where, under a beam of light, she had seen Max fucking one of the Chinese sisters. Try as she might, she could not remember which one. She wanted to. For whatever reason, she had a compulsion to remember every detail of that evening. She yearned, if only in memory, to relive that night. To look at it objectively as a woman. To imagine herself with her innocence restored. To expunge for a few minutes the years between.

It was warm. She removed her hat and shook out her hair. Walking past a huge glass showcase, she caught sight of herself reflected in it. She stood for some time, as if surprised to see a beautiful woman dressed in furs that flared lusciously out from a cinched waist. Who was this woman? She had expected to see the girl of that other evening. She looked hard, willing the image to change. She placed her hand over her eyes and smiled, partly awed by the tricks the mind can play. She had to admire the tenacity of the subconscious. The drawn-out power of experience to shape one's life.

It was over for her. She had no need to see the statue. She turned away, to leave the gallery, then thought and said aloud, "What the hell. Why not?" She went in search of the god and was surprised to see a man standing there, admiring the colossal statue. He stood for some time, arms folded across his chest, as if transfixed by the power and beauty of the piece. He was lost in contemplation, altogether unaware of being watched. He stepped closer to the piece and touched the foot. Lara walked to his side. Her heels echoed on the floor. The spell of the moment was broken for the man. He turned round abruptly. Their eyes met. Instant attraction, but each was too surprised to recognize the fact. There was nothing to fill the intervening silence. Finally, embarrassed, Lara said, "I startled you."

"Perhaps, a little."

"Your stepping close in to the statue, touching the foot . . .

My mind was playing tricks on me, a moment of déjà vu. All very silly.''

"It doesn't matter."

Again the force of their mutual attraction silenced them. He seemed to be waiting for her to say something. She seemed unable to find the right words to get away from him gracefully. Only: "You're English." And the moment she said it, she thought, What a stupid thing to say.

"Yes."

"I must go."

"Did you want something?"

She smiled at the man. "Only to see this statue again. I was having a waltz down memory lane."

"And I didn't figure in your waltz?"

"Well, no." She could not help but laugh.

Enchanted by her, he couldn't let her go. He asked, "Is it something an Englishman might find amusing?"

"Well, maybe not so much amusing as . . ." She faltered, and smiling at him again, said, "I really must go."

She hurried from the gallery, but heard his footsteps not far behind her.

Lara stood for several minutes at the museum entrance contemplating the snowstorm. It appeared to be less violent. The flurries larger. She could actually see through them to the other side of the street. How sad that the man had been there to interrupt her memories. She would have liked to conjure up that raunchy sexiness that had excited her then, and which she could still be thrilled by now. Too bad. A little of that, and a little fantasy, did make life more fun somehow. If complicated. Just briefly she thought of the man. Why did she suddenly think she knew that face now, had seen it before? The large, bony head. Intense, fiercely intelligent eyes. The craggy but still handsome face. The dimples when he had smiled at her. With that receding hairline, he had seemed worn but strangely sexy. Yes, she did think she had seen, if not him, then certainly his photograph somewhere. She went to put her hat on, only to realize she didn't have it. She must have dropped it in the gallery. She turned round—and bumped right into the stranger.

It was her turn to be startled. "I believe you might be looking for this?" he said.

"Yes."

That smile again. It was very attractive. How old was he? In his fifties, perhaps. He might be in his sixties. She took the hat from him. He watched her put it on, tuck her hair under the fur, put on her gloves. She was giving herself time to sum up his exterior. He was wearing a sturdy camel-hair coat over a salt-and-pepper tweed suit, crimson wool challis tie, Turnbull & Asser blue shirt. He tied the belt of his coat, buttoned one of the revers over the other, and turned up his collar. From the pocket he took out a tweed cap and a pair of leather gloves.

"Shall we brave those stairs together?"

He slipped his arm though hers, and they left the museum. He took a firm grip on her arm. She felt his strength. His years had not enfeebled him. Yes, he held her firmly, but strength of character, too, was imprinted on his face, in his very presence. The stairs were more treacherous to descend than to climb. They navigated them cautiously. Once on the snow-covered pavement, she said, "Thank you," and extended a hand for him to shake.

The snow was lightly dusting his shoulders. She felt an impulse to brush it off, but resisted. There was a warmth about him, a kind of humanity that she found intoxicating. He was special, and she didn't want to walk away from him. He touched the peak of his cap as if tipping it to her and, smiling, said, "Good-bye, pretty woman."

But neither of them moved. Finally it was she who spoke. "I'm walking downtown. If that's your direction, shall we walk together?"

"That's my direction."

They passed only two people. One of them, an elderly man, slipped. They came to his aid and brushed the snow from him, and then watched him walk cautiously away, clinging to the building alongside. Otherwise they never spoke. At the curbs he would take her arm until they had crossed the road. She stopped on the corner of her street.

"Do you have far to go?" she asked.

"The Carlyle."

"This is my street."

He took her arm, and they turned into the street, off the avenue. Not many steps later, she stopped again. "And this is your house?"

"Yes," she answered.

The gates to the drive were open. It was dark by now. The wind had risen again, whipping up the snow. There were drifts against the fencing and the gate. Silence was all around them, so white, so cold: it was eerily sensual. They could have been in Russia, Sweden, Norway. Anywhere but New York. The lights streaming from the windows, the huge lantern under the portico, swinging in wind-swept snow, made the house look inviting.

He brushed some snow from her hat. It was an excuse to touch her once more: they both knew that. A little gesture, but a loaded one. He smiled at her and said, "Then this *is* good-bye."

She noticed that he kept a hand flat against the closing at the front of his coat. He had walked like that ever since the museum. "Come in, warm yourself by the fire before you go on. A whiskey? Some tea?"

She saw hesitation in his eyes and took him by the hand. And then he told her, "I can't. My wife is waiting. She'll be concerned." But he didn't move.

Lara was not surprised. She reached into her coat and slid the scarf from around her own neck. She unbuttoned his coat. The revers flopped open. He took the Gucci scarf from her hands and draped it around his neck. It was still warm from her body. "This is not necessary."

"To me it is."

"I will return it in the morning."

"No!" she said, rather too loudly. "Keep it. A memento of a brief encounter."

Chapter 25

Lara awoke the next morning to a city just coming back to life. She could hear a shovel scraping on the pavement. From her window she could see the gardener clearing the drive. A few cars moved in slow motion down Fifth Avenue. The spell of yesterday's strange afternoon, the urge to conjure up those exciting sexual scenes of that long-ago day, vanished from her thoughts. All that remained of admiration was the warm glow she had felt from an older man, a handsome stranger. How right he had been not to accept her invitation. Right for her, that is. She was not unaware that it had been one of those moments that happen to a person who is psychologically ripe, regardless of whether the man is an appropriate love object. A married man old enough to be her father, and more concerned for his wife than her, was clearly not the right man. Even if the moment had been.

During the next few days she thought about the man, a stranger whom she could not think of as such. She half expected him to return the scarf. But he did not. She tried to put him from her mind, telling herself this man was not the one to fulfill her deepest longings or oldest dreams. This was not the man who would allow her both to renew and transform herself. But where was that man? He certainly hadn't appeared in the guise of any would-be lover she had attracted since Jamal.

Several days after her encounter, a box of flowers, long-stemmed red roses, arrived at the house. On their fragrance she allowed herself to float a momentary fantasy that he might have sent them. She felt foolish when she read the card. They were from a nice enough man, but not the right one. So she put the stranger who had walked her home firmly out of her mind.

Several days later, she changed her travel plans for getting to Gstaad by Concorde and then private plane. She was packed, she was ready with time to spare to make the flight. Instead she surprised Nancy by turning her plans upside down. She had her secretary book her on the night flight to London, for two nights at the Connaught, then charter a small jet to fly her to Gstaad afterward. What particularly puzzled Nancy was that Lara then sat down in the living room and played the piano for most of the afternoon, until she left for the airport.

The steward walking her from the first-class lounge to her seat was giving her the friendly line in chatter he was trained for: the weather, the flight time, the title of the movie. "You should have a nice, quiet flight, Miss Stanton. We have only three other people booked in first class this trip." Was it to be champagne? What time should dinner be served? All that conversation was cloying, too obviously a well-intentioned professional laying on the charm.

She saw the scarf draped over the arm of an empty seat as she passed by. But it didn't register that it was hers, or at least had been, until she was being helped off with her jacket by the steward with the amiable patter. She looked back down the aisle. The scarf was still there, the seat empty. There was someone sitting in the window seat next to it, but she couldn't see who.

She buckled her seat belt and looked out at the lights of Kennedy Airport, still swathed in what was left of the snowstorm. That scarf . . . Did she think that Gucci had only made one of them? But it happened to be identical to hers . . . A coincidence? This was ridiculous. Was she going to cross the Atlantic trying to guess whether he was on board or not? Not likely.

They were airborne, so she unbuckled her seat belt. The steward was back, raising the arm of the empty seat next to her and then hers. "More room." He accorded her an on-board smile. She ran a brush through her hair and drew her fingers through it several times, then fussed with the neck of her silk blouse. She heard someone rustle some papers, a cough. Then in a dialogue with herself she thought, Funny how conveniently you've forgotten the wife. If that *is* him, than where is she? It didn't seem to matter. She had to know.

In horn-rimmed glasses, strangely, he looked younger. She could not but smile. She felt so pleased to see him again. He was completely engrossed in some papers he was reading, unaware of her. She slid the scarf from the chair and very quietly sat down. Still he was not distracted.

She was wearing a rich brown suede skirt. When she crossed her knees, its folds brushed against his trouser leg. He looked up. There was no surprise in his eyes, just pure pleasure. Then he smiled at her and removed his glasses.

"I lied. My wife was not waiting for me at the Carlyle."

"Why?" She was puzzled, concerned that he had felt the need to lie to her.

"Because to be attracted to someone is the most powerful feeling I know. And I never expected to experience that feeling again. I wanted it curtailed."

"Surely you must have known there would be no rejection from me? That I was having the very same feeling?"

"Yes. But I hoped I was wrong."

"Why? Because you sensed that, unlike you, I wanted to keep the feeling alive?"

"Maybe."

"I don't understand."

"Why should you? Physical attraction isn't simple; it's very complex, almost inexplicable. I'm a scientist, I have devoted my life to seeking out explanations of why things happen, and then finding ways for them not to happen again. And then you appeared, and I knew there could be no simple answers. That it would be folly to look for them. A quick exit was all that was possible. And now this. You. Here."

"The gods are with us." She smiled at him and placed her hand on the sleeve of his jacket.

They remained silent, looking at each other. Happy just to be able to do that. "Well, maybe one magnificent Egyptian god carved in stone thousands of years ago. I'm not so sure about any others."

"You don't believe in the gods? I thought you did, very much so, when I saw you standing in the gallery. Not them, or the afterlife their whole civilization was bound up in?"

"I would like to. But my scientific mind doesn't allow it."

"And when you stepped forward to touch the feet, I thought

you were reaching . . .'' She hesitated, and then added, "Oh, this is fanciful.''

"No, go on.''

"That you were reaching out for''—she wavered again, visibly searching for the right words—"something I'd seen happen there years ago.'' She shook her head and tried to conceal her embarrassment. "I know that makes no sense, most especially to a man of science.''

"Maybe it's not as senseless as you might think. It was a very strange afternoon.''

"Yes, I had a compulsion to go there. I was looking for something, I know that now. Then I thought it was something else. But I don't think your visit was an act of compulsion. You don't seem to me to have a compulsive nature.''

"You're quite right. I don't. I was there because the snowstorm gave me a few hours free from people and work, something that rarely happens to me. I didn't want to waste them. So I braved the storm for the museum, and specifically the Egyptian Gallery. I had always wanted to return there. To see it without the hordes of tourists. There is nothing less Egyptian than a crocodile of schoolkids being hectored by their ignorant teachers. I wanted to sense the power of the place, those works of art, get close to that civilization, in the quiet. Be alone as I could be in a public gallery. Perfect timing, I thought. Who's going to brave the weather for a museum? Not many. And I was right. You were the only person I saw among the Pharaonic artifacts that afternoon. And then only when you caught me indulging a morbid desire to touch something so rooted in death, and the belief that life after death is more valid than mere earthly existence. Something *I* cannot believe in. I wanted confirmation that the coldness of death was no different from the coldness of that stone god. That dead *is* dead. And then you startled me, stopped me.

"You were life as I had forgotten it, young and beautiful, luscious in your furs and silvery-blond hair, voluptuous with those green eyes and sensuous face. I came instantly alive just looking at you. I thought, People die without a chance to live. There hasn't been anyone to remind me of that for a very long time. Romantic love, passion, escape . . . You were living proof, to me, anyway, that life *is* more valid than death.''

The spell that he had woven around them was broken by the steward, and for once Lara was relieved to hear the young man's solicitous patter. "Will you be taking your champagne here? And will you be dining together? If that's the case, may I suggest you do so in the lady's seats? There's more leg room there, and the trays are hung from the wall." He leaned forward and lowered his voice, "Far more comfortable. By far the best place to sit in first class."

Lara could have kissed the too-well-groomed steward with BARNEY printed on his name tag. She did not give her new friend a chance to back out, but looked at him and said, "Please."

He smiled at her and stood up, towering over her. She felt such joy, a rush of pure pleasure. He thanked the young man for the suggestion and asked for a malt whiskey and soda. The steward went off smiling, pleased to have rearranged their lives for at least the duration of their flight across the Atlantic.

Lara rose from her chair and turned her back in order to step into the aisle. She felt such warmth in his presence; love, affection, a masculinity that was strong and solid, and yet gentleness, too. She could only think of him as the best, the most special of men. She hesitated, not wanting to walk away from him or to lose those feelings.

As if to reassure her, he placed a hand on her hip. She closed her eyes for a moment from the sheer need to block out the world, to feel only his hand. He raised it to clasp her waist. She placed her hand over his just briefly and then removed it, and he removed his. She placed the palm of her hand over the spot, simply to feel the warmth he left there.

Embarrassed that he might deduce how much she already felt for him, she pretended to be adjusting her antique Navaho silver belt. She toyed with the huge lumps of turquoise in the buckle, relieved she still had her back to him. More composed now, she stepped into the aisle and walked to where she had been sitting, took the window seat. He sat down next to her.

She thought she might as well get it over with. "But there is a wife and a family?"

"Yes, very much so."

"It won't make any difference, you know."

He ignored that, even though he wanted to tell her, It should. "Is there a husband?" he asked.

"There has been. Twice."

"I'm sorry."

"Yes, so am I."

"I could be your father."

"But you're not."

"You should find a young man, one you can build a life with, someone who can give you more than I can. I simply cannot ruin your life. I refuse to."

"Why are you making excuses?"

That appeared to stop him. He stroked his chin several times. He never took his eyes from hers while he told her, "You offer a mixture of hope, anxiety, and excitement. All the agitation that is part and parcel of falling in love. I don't think I can handle that at this time in my life, much as I might want to. Falling in love? It must be behind me now."

"What if I won't let you throw us away?"

"Then we will both have to be very brave, honest, and courageous. I have no doubt that you are, but I'm not so sure about myself."

"Please, don't deprive us of loving each other."

"Too much of any love affair of ours would depend on you. Not because I want it to be like that, but because life has taught me that relationships are the domain of the woman. And 'the man who shops from woman to woman, though his heart aches with idealism, with the desire for pure love, has entered the female realm.' I learned that from Saul Bellow. If a relationship between us is to work, it will be you who will make it a success."

They drank and dined, then put the overhead lights out and talked through the night, about all sorts of things. Anything but themselves and their feelings for each other. They watched the dawn. The new day gave them the notion that they might be together, maybe not all the time, but in one way or another throughout their lives. They may have felt that, but it was too big a thing to make specific. And now was much too soon. Each of them considered the other remarkable, but, strangely, not the most important thing in their lives. Simply the most important life-enhancing force in their lives. As yet they still had not exchanged names.

An hour before they landed she went to freshen up. In the

small, neon-bright compartment, she tried to come to terms
with this new phase of her life, only to realize there was little to
come to terms with. She was in love with a remarkable man,
and they were making each other happy. There had not even
been a kiss to seal the bargain.

She pushed open the door—directly into Barney the steward.
Gushing apologies, he moved aside to let her by. When she took
her seat, her friend wasn't there. "The doctor is still in the loo.
Shaving, I suppose," said Barney, while he folded blankets and
puffed up pillows before whisking them away.

Doctor. She hadn't thought of him that way. A doctor of science had every right to use the title, but still it surprised her.
Then she wondered, Is he Dr. McLeod, Dr. Voplonsky, Dr.
Jones? Dr. what? Now he would have to have a name. The
outside world was closing in on them.

"A good thing I suppose," continued Barney. "The press is
already waiting at Heathrow. Photographers and all. Even a man
from the Home Office, with his secretary and two assistants.
They radioed through to the cockpit. Suggested we take him
through another entrance to avoid the press. Seems he's a very
private guy. Hates all that folderol. The Nobel prize, and tomorrow some kind of investiture at the palace. He sure has had
quite a year. But I don't see how he can avoid them. Not with
this on the stalls." Barney pulled a *Time* magazine from the
rack. Lara Stanton's new love was fetchingly portrayed on the
cover.

She could hardly believe it. It had been there, in the rack,
directly in front of them all night. For the first time she knew
who this modest man was: Dr. Evan Harper Valentine, the brilliant biochemist. Wasn't he making amazing discoveries about
DNA or genetic engineering? Of course she had seen his photographs in the newspapers, but she had been too wrapped up
in the real man to work out why he looked familiar to her. It
had not mattered then, and astonishingly it hardly mattered now.
He was a world figure. Hadn't she heard him in a radio interview? Seen him on TV for a moment, perhaps when he was
being feted at the White House?

"Do you think he will sign it for me? It's a bit of an imposition
to ask our celebrities, and I hardly ever do. We're not supposed
to but . . . a man of his stature? I guess I'll risk it."

The celebrated scientist had made a modest return to his gang-way seat.

"Excuse me. May I?" asked Barney, handing over the magazine.

"I'd be pleased to sign this for you. But, would you mind, some coffee in about ten minutes?"

Barney took the hint. His retreat was as happy as it was hasty. But he had to return. Evan Valentine was settled in his seat next to Lara, the magazine still in his hand. "Sorry, sir, a message has come through for you that—"

Evan interrupted, "After coffee. I'll deal with it then." Barney's training equipped him to realize he was being dismissed.

Evan turned to Lara, concern evident in his expression. "I wish you need never have found out. But, now you have, are you still prepared to take me on board?"

"I wish I could say it hardly matters. But it does. The only thing that hasn't changed is my feelings, my resolve that, having just found each other, we should not give each other up merely because we have lives other than the one we can have together."

"We will have to keep them very separate."

"We can do that, so long as we let the outside world die for us when we are together."

"I don't want to drive myself to distraction thinking about what you are doing when we are not together. We will have to be strong enough to take nothing of our other lives along with us when we are together. To take a chance on love with you, I can be very strong. What about you?"

"Is that a proposal?"

"Only the second one I have ever given in my life. But, before you answer, I want to make myself clear. Ours will always have to be a secret love. I will make you my greatest love outside my work. But do you want to be an illicit love that I can flee to from fame and people? Is it enough for you to be my secret world, where only you and I and our *grand amour* exist? I am past sixty and haven't ever fallen in love at first sight, or wanted a woman as I want you. I feel alive as I have never felt before. I can't give you up without trying to make it work for us. But there have to be strict ground rules. We mustn't ever cause each other pain or disappointment."

She simply could not say yes. She could only nod her head in assent. Emotion was welling up in her. Her heart went out to him. Toward the love she saw in his eyes for her now, toward the nervous tremor in his voice. Because, against his will, he had fallen in love. Because she could see the need he felt for her—that same need she had felt all her life to be loved. To be number one in someone's life and have that feeling returned.

They said their farewells with little more intimacy than two mere acquaintances would have shown. He would call her at a specific time at the Connaught, after the investiture. That was one of the ground rules: to call each other at specific times. He would not have her waiting on the end of a telephone for him. Another rule was that they could each take one other person into their confidence, but not even to them would they divulge their lover's identity. She chose Nancy, her secretary. He chose Elspeth, his personal assistant. He was Mr. Smith, and she was to be Miss Jones.

Was this the recipe for a great love story? How was it possible? But it was. Even from the beginning they got it right. And it never went wrong. When they were together, they had no other lives. Apart, they had no life together. And their separate lives never overlapped. They worked at their love and passion for each other. And so it worked for them.

Lara had not realized how much they had wanted each other sexually until they were alone together for the first time. Oh, yes, she had wanted him, she knew that the moment she saw him in the museum. She wanted him to make love to her as she had seen Max make love to the Chinese twin. But her sexual desires had been held in check by love. Now they were alone, and he had her in his arms and kissed her. It was extraordinary that it should be their first kiss, because she felt so completely a part of his life. He was far more sensual than she expected. She had been fooled by his conservative, even straitlaced, manner; the tweed suit, the waistcoat that matched . . . Only the eyes, the sensual, passionate, smiling eyes, gave a hint of what was to come.

He held her face in his hands while he kissed her. Between kisses he kept telling her, ''I can't stop looking at you. You are so beautiful.'' Then he would touch her cheek, the bridge of her nose. He ran a finger lightly across her long, silky eyelashes. He kissed her eyes with a tenderness she had never known. She didn't dissolve under his kisses, nor did she become weak-kneed under his sensual love. Instead she found herself exhilarated. His gentle loving excited her passion. His body scent was clean and fresh, like lemons or peppermint. She felt unable to keep her hands off him, touching his face, the back of his neck, his hands. His skin was warm, not soft but smooth to the touch, and was of a pale olive tone.

When next he placed a kiss upon her lips, she slid her tongue from between them and licked his lips. She nibbled at them, and could feel him giving in to her. And the more he did, the more overwhelming was her desire to give herself to him. Everything she was, everything she had ever been, all the things she could ever be sexually, she wanted to give to this man.

She slipped out of his arms. Taking him by the hand she led him to the bedroom. Under a long, dark, rich amethyst-colored jacket of crepe de chine, she was wearing a dress of black in the same material. Soft and loose, it clung alluringly to her by the sheer magic of its cut. It was the sort of dress that was a chic prick tease, with its strapless top that just covered her breasts, and its slim slip straps over the shoulders. Around her neck was a collar of rubies, and in her ears her yellow diamonds. She looked luscious, ripe, and rich, all elegance, youth, sensuousness. Evan craved her more at that moment than life itself. She could sense his desire, the scent of his lust and love for her. His tremendous urge to multiply sexual deaths inside her.

She opened her silk jacket, and for the first time he ran the back of his hand across her skin. She let the jacket slip off her shoulders and down her arms to fall on the floor. He was as if mesmerized by her, watching her every move as she caressed her own shoulders seductively, slipping one dress strap off to fall against her upper arm and then, slowly, the other. She opened the zipper at the back. The slippery crepe de chine slid off her breasts and down around her waist, her hips, her thighs, slowly to the floor. She stepped over the silk and stood before him naked, except for the black stockings held high up around her comely thighs by a band of elasticized lace. She caressed her breasts and ran her hands down her body, to her mound of silvery silk pubic hair. Then, with arms open, she went to him, placed them around his neck, and kissed him.

He halted her kisses long enough to tell her, "You're mag-

nificent, more divine to me than any other woman. There will
be no stopping me, I want it all.'' And then he crushed her to
him with an erotic violence that amazed them both. She took
him by the hand and led him to the side of the bed. She removed
his jacket, unbuttoned his waistcoat, loosened his tie. When he
was naked, he picked her up in his arms and laid her on the bed.
He placed pillows under her bottom to raise her, wanting her at
an angle the better to view her, and where she could feel more
deeply the thrusts of his cock. He was a big man who wanted
to be between her legs. So, kneeling there, he slowly spread
them further and further apart. He needed to see her open and
ready for him. He looked at her with a kind of awe. Few men
had ever looked at her his way.

He caressed her pussy, licked it and kissed it. He was rushing
nothing, simply savoring her. With such gentleness he opened
her cunt lips and lowered his mouth to them. He sucked them;
she felt his teeth teasing them. His tongue sought out her clitoris.
She came, and he tasted her for the first time, the strange aphrodisiac that she was for him. He slipped fingers of each hand
on either side of her yearning cunt and she was open. He entered
her for the first time with his tongue. Deep as he could he probed
her, and she came for them again. He made a feast of her.

Unable to keep her silence, she allowed herself sighs of bliss,
words of lust. Her fingers dug hard into his massive shoulders.
He rubbed his face in her cunt and kissed the inside of her
thighs, then worked his way up her body to her breasts with
kissing gone wild. He bit into her flesh. He reached her breasts,
flesh as seductive and exciting as he had ever seen. The dark,
dark nipples and surrounding nimbus were rich in their
decadence. Stirring him to an animal lust he had long forgotten how to feel.

She felt his hunger. He was famished for her sex. His starving
touched her heart. She yearned to feed such erotic needs. He
raised her from the bed, placed her on her knees, and kissed the
arch of her back, licked the succulent orbs of her bottom, and
then between them, and that small, tight place. He pierced it
with his tongue till she could bear the sensations no longer. She
begged to be taken. With gentle, caressing fingers, he wrenched
apart the fleshy, deep rose inner lips of her cunt and eased himself slowly into her. He paced his fucking to give them long,

slow, tantalizing pleasure. Tears of joy trickled down her face as she came in a long, leisurely climax, soon succeeded by another.

She told him in a husky, emotion-ridden voice how much she loved him. Then she reached down to hold the soft, loose sack beneath his penis, thrilling to the weighty feel of the balls within. She cupped them in her hands and fondled them, yearning to take them in her mouth. She would suck and lick them, to give him yet more pleasure.

He felt her orgasms, warm, wet, and as slippery as silk, coat his penis and moisten his testes. Had he ever had such sex? Known a woman so ready to die in the embrace of Eros? He had hardly dreamed that a woman would want to give herself so completely. He felt her body go taut. The shudder of her ecstasy. He heard her call out in a frenzy of passion. His fingers bit into the flesh of her hips, where he held her fast and mercilessly throttled her with cock as he climaxed into a powerful orgasm.

No need for him to tell her. She sensed that this climax had been for him the end of living for years in a sexual desert. He lay for a time with her in his arms, until at last he was able to compose himself and tell her, "This is the first day of the rest of my life." And here were their beginnings.

She thanked him by making love to him that night. Kissed him as she had been kissed by him. Took him, in the full measure of his manhood, into her mouth and made love to him. He was thrilling and passionate and loving. She sucked on him until he came and she absorbed his life's force, cherishing every drop she swallowed. Before morning he had used every orifice to fill her with his seed. She was his master, he her pupil, and he obeyed her in acts of erotic love he had rarely dreamed of.

A real love and affection governed their erotic life together, allowed them to be as base as they chose to be in their sometimes fierce couplings. It allowed them to wallow in a kind of sexual depravity. She was able to draw from him his most secret sexual fantasies, and he allowed himself the luxury of passive as well as aggressive sexuality. She was a new sun in his life, and all of his hopes and dreams of a relationship with a woman. And if she was all those things for him, he was no less for her. They thought of themselves as having been given a second life when they met, and they grabbed it with both hands.

It was as if she were swimming against a tide of soft white cotton wool, that process of waking and resisting surrender to the luxury of a peaceful and oh-so-sweet sleep. She gave in and opened her eyes. But still her awakening was slow. She stretched and felt the sheer luxuriance of a body coming alive again. Her mind caught up with her body, and she remembered that this was their first morning together. She sat upright, leaning against the headboard. This was true awakening. He had opened the draperies to let grayish morning light pour through the sheer white undercurtains. The bedclothes had fallen away. She sat naked from the waist up and looked around the room. He had quite obviously straightened it up, laid his clothes out neatly over one chair, hers over the other. The bathroom door was ajar. A stream of electric light cast a stripe across the Oriental carpet.

It was a very pretty suite of rooms. The bedroom all English flowered cotton chintz, full-blown garden roses in shades of peach, red, and aquamarine, and lots of green leaves on a ground of a rich cream color, and comfortable chairs, a chaise. The chest of drawers, a dressing table, and the four-poster bed were in rich Georgian mahogany. The pictures on the walls, handsome black-and-white etchings of seventeenth-century London, were framed simply in silver leaf. A large bowl of white arum lilies adorned a round, marble-topped table. She threw the covers off and, naked, went to the dressing table; taking up the brush, she worked on her hair. She stopped and viewed in the mirror the bruises on her breasts where he had clung so hard while he had devoured her nipples and the nimbus around them. She closed her eyes to savor the memories that came flooding back of sensations he had induced in her by his appetite for her. She checked further, found another blue-black oval mark on her hip, one on the inside of her thigh. She had never known a man so hungry for her. He seemed to explode with sexual desire for her. She reached for her dressing gown. What was that promise she had extricated from him in the heat of passion? Never to hold back, but to share with her his every sexual fantasy—and for them to dwell in the house of erotica forever. It seemed melodramatic now, in the light of day, but then she was reminded of how he had told her, "Teach me. I want to experience everything with you, in a secret world we don't have to share with another soul." He needed her, she knew that, and he was worth giving herself to. She had yet another sensation she had not experienced in life before: a man who she wanted to care for, make happy.

She knocked at the bathroom door. He opened it, standing naked except for a towel wrapped around him. Remnants of lather were still on his face. The light that came into his eyes at seeing her told her all she needed to know. He loved her. The night before was not going to lapse into a fantastic one-night stand. She knew that in her heart long before she tapped on the door, but nevertheless she relished the confirmation. She wanted to say something clever, but clever seemed wrong. Then he smiled at her and bent down, kissed her lovingly on the lips and stroked her arm. That seemed enough.

"Good morning."

"Good morning, Evan." It was that simple, and simple seemed right.

He swept her off her feet and sat her down on the marble top that served as a surround for the sink he was using. With his finger he removed a stripe of shaving cream from her upper lip. Then with the corner of a white hand towel he dried the spot. The gaze that passed between them had its own wordless eloquence. It was he who finally sighed and turned his gaze toward his reflection in the mirror. He cleaned his straight razor in the bowl of still-steaming hot water and finished shaving.

Lara watched him. She felt such overpowering love and admiration for him. Her body ached for more sexual pleasure with him, and it was not for herself alone that she craved more sex. As if reading her mind, he dropped the razor in the hot water, and then, placing his hands around her waist, pushed her back on the marble shelf until her back was against the mirrored wall. He untied the cream-colored satin sash around her waist and opened the dressing gown of black lace to gaze lovingly at her body for some time—before sliding the gown off her shoulders and arms. It fell in soft folds all around her.

"That's better," he told her, and faced the mirror once again. He bent over the bowl and splashed water over his face until it was clean. Taking a fresh towel, he dried his face and his hands.

"I like watching you shave."

He placed the towel on the side of the bowl and stroked Lara's thigh. She had to close her eyes for a second, so electric was his

touch. He placed an affectionate kiss on her knee and then raised
her leg. Bending her knee back he set her foot squarely on the
marble. He kissed the top of it and repeated the gesture with the
other foot. With his hands on her knees he pushed her legs far,
far apart. She slid forward down the wall, just enough to be
sitting still upright, her genitals exposed for him to view at his
leisure.

He looked at her not in a lascivious, hungry way, but with
pure pleasure. It was a loving gaze, filled with admiration and
affection. When had a man ever looked at her like that, been
humbled by passion and love for her? The answer, of course,
was never. She, too, felt humbled by love, in the very same way
she felt humbled by the love her children had for her. Only this
was not a child's love, but that of a man for a woman. She
reached out. Her hand was inside the top of the towel he had
wrapped around his hips. She pulled and it fell to the floor. She
grazed his naked hip with the palm of her hand. They smiled at
each other. There was a declaration in that smile that made
words unnecessary.

He broke the gaze when he turned his attention back to his
ablutions. She watched him pat on an aftershave that smelled of
fresh lemons and made her think of sunshine. Then he stepped
toward her and lowered his head between her open limbs. When
finally he looked up, he told her, "I kiss you good morning, my
love." When he smiled at her and touched her cheek with the
back of his hand, she could still feel the stunning sensation of
his lips upon her cunt lips, his tongue licking between them.
Such exquisite pleasure caused her to tremble. He dressed her
once again in the black lace dressing gown and tied the sash.
Then he helped her from the black-and-gold slab of marble.

Evan had already drawn his bath. Swirls of steam were still
rising from it when he climbed in. She heard the faint sound of
a knock at the bedroom door. "I've ordered us tea and the
morning papers."

Lara felt quite dazed by her sense of contentment, the ease
with which she and Evan had become a part of each other's lives.
In his presence she had no sense of her past or thoughts of the
future, only of the present. She brought him a cup of tea and
left him to his bath. Lara poured a cup for herself and climbed
back into bed to drink it. She felt something she had rarely felt

before. It was a strange sensation, like being in limbo. She sipped her tea. She was at that special place, where all thinking stops, all desire is quiescent: contentment.

The bathroom door opened. He poured himself a second cup of tea and sat on the bed next to her to drink it.

"About last night . . ."

Was it embarrassment or shyness she saw in his face? She placed her cup and saucer on the table next to her. Sliding out from beneath the bed covers and onto her knees, she sat on her haunches behind him. She placed her arms through his and around his middle and hugged herself against him. She rested her head against his back. He felt the warmth of her body against his, her lips in an affectionate kiss. He was not unaware that she was making it easier for him. He cleared his throat and covered her caressing hands with his. "I want you to know about last night . . ." He faltered, seemed unable to put his feelings into words. She understood that he was not the sort of man to whom expressing emotion came easy. She came to his rescue.

"All morning I have been trying to find the right words to tell you what last night meant to me. How much I love you. How my life has suddenly become complete since you entered it. And I can't. And I understand if you can't, either. You don't have to tell me, Evan. I see it in the way you look at me, I can feel it in the way you touch me."

He turned on the bed to face her, pulled her roughly into his arms and across his lap. His strength had surprised her the night before, and it did again. He held her tight, and she draped her arms loosely around his neck, resting her head against his still bare chest. She could hear the beat of his heart. Overwhelming, the power of this man's presence. She could only think how much poorer her life would have been had she not met him. He released her, and she slid from his lap to sit next to him. She watched him while he dressed.

"Are you thinking, 'How old he is'?"

"No. But you must be thinking how young I am, to mention it."

"Touché. People will think you are my daughter."

"No, they won't, Evan. Have no illusions about that. The way you look at me, the way we are together, they'll know that we are lovers. They will think only one thing: that you are a sexy old rake having yet another fling. I can live with that, if you can."

He laughed. "Another reason for us to lead a very secret life. For who would believe that old, staid Evan Harper Valentine could possibly be—in your none too subtle description of me— 'an old rake.' "

"You forgot sexy."

He laughed again. "You think that? And we've only just be-gun!"

"You have also forgotten the 'Sir,' my Nobel lord."

The pun made him smile. "When I am with you I forget everything else in the world except us. I intend to keep it that way. Do you think you can manage that, too?"

"I agreed to that while flying over the Atlantic, remember? I made my commitment to you without reservation, and while that lofty Newtonian mind was still trying to come to terms with falling in love with me. I will not change my tiny, unscientific mind."

The gaze that passed between them brought a faint smile of acceptance to his mouth. He changed the subject rather quickly. Emotions were coming into play that he could not cope with. "Breakfast?"

"Oh, yes, I'm famished."

"Downstairs in the dining room?"

That surprised her. She had thought breakfast at the Con-naught too indiscreet for him. "Oh, yes, please. A huge English breakfast sounds about right to me. I won't be long."

When she came out of the bathroom, he was fully dressed and seated in the window, scanning the morning paper. She was taken aback by the stature of the man, the fierce intelligence, the formidable presence he exuded, dressed and separate from her. She would have to get used to the idea that this remarkable man she saw reading the newspaper belonged to her as to no other person on earth. She knew she could make him happy.

This was a different man than the lover of the night before, than even the man she had watched shaving. He had been so right on the airplane to tell her they should lead two separate lives, one together and one apart. There should be no overlap, or their relationship would never survive. She could but admire the measures he had taken in response to falling in love with her. He had abandoned a conservative life-style, shed a lifelong sexual reserve, and fallen in love with a young and libidinous woman. And against his will, was now coping with being in love and leading an adulterous existence. She would never let him down: that resolution came easy to her.

She nearly made a mistake that would have affected their entire future. Impressed with his eminent scientific life, of which she knew she could never be a part, she had tried to strike an attitude by her choice of dress, wanting to declare I, too, can fit into science and academia, that special world of yours—that until now has governed your life.

It was a moment of insecurity, of enforced acceptance of her isolation from the rest of his life. She caught herself just in time. That selfish impulse to have all of him, all of the time, flared up, but was extinguished. He had fallen in love with Lara Stanton and all she was, had been, and would always be. There was no need for her to create a false image of herself. She avoided the mistake.

She chose a Chanel suit of camel hair, trimmed and cuffed in chocolate-brown braid and with a half-dozen gold buttons on each sleeve, and four to close the jacket. Under it a chocolate-brown, see-through, silk chiffon blouse with a soft bow at the neck. High-heeled, brown-and-black, Chanel calfskin shoes and pale-ivory-colored stockings. The camel color, not quite beige, not quite white, was perfect to offset the long blond hair she was wearing down today, straight and combed off her face. She looked young, fresh-faced, and provocative when she presented herself to Evan while slipping her arms into the jacket. She caught his look of surprise and delight at her appearance. There was no missing the firm but heavy bare breasts under the transparent chiffon. She adjusted the jacket so that it covered her.

"You are a most seductive woman. You did that deliberately so that, over my *oeuf en cocotte* and Parma ham, I could delight in knowing you are naked and ready for me. You will make me the envy of every man breakfasting in that room this morning."

"True."

"Might I expect that you intend to seduce me one way or another every day we are together?" It was said with a twinkle in his eye.

"Yes, I think you would be safe in assuming that."

He laughed and then told her, "How delightful. Even my old heart skips a beat at the thought of what might be in store for me. I think I like being your sexual slave." He slipped his arm through hers, and they left the bedroom.

In the elevator, he whispered in her ear, "And under your skirt. . . ?"

The elevator door opened, and they walked into the sedate reception hall. She stopped and they looked at each other. She told him in a seductive voice, "Nothing. I intend never to wear anything with you. I like the idea of being naked—open and ready for you—so that you can take me when and where you like. Each other's sexual slave might be nearer the truth about us."

It was not one of those lingering romantic breakfasts women dream about, which was no bad thing, since they were parting. He to his grueling schedule that had not included time for falling in love; she to carry on with her plans for shopping and seeing old friends, having lunch with her sister Elizabeth, who was coming up from the country, a gallery visit, if time permitted, before her departure for the Alps and skiing.

It was she who found elegant sexual toys to amuse them; she who seduced him into their world of sexual depravity. It was Lara who showed him this other side of himself, and he was happier than he had ever been.

Chapter 26

Lara had had a wonderful day. Contentment can do that to you, transform the least little thing to a happy experience. They would talk, that's what they had planned, talk to each other whenever they could. She had a contact number for him. He had the number where she was staying for the next two weeks, and then home. When would they meet again? Whenever they could. It was all so tenuous, but it didn't seem to matter. They would write to each other.

The phone kept ringing. At first she thought it was a dream. Finally she gave in to the incessant sound and picked up the receiver.

"Hello."

A long silence and then, "I've woken you."

It was Evan. The sound of his voice banished sleep.

"That doesn't matter. Where are you?"

"It's six o'clock in the morning. I paced the floor for fifteen minutes thinking about waking you, but gave in to selfishness and wanting to hear your voice."

"I'd have done the same thing, worse maybe, to hear yours."

He gave a lighthearted laugh. "That makes it better, but doesn't do much to discourage me from feeling like a young buck in love. A week ago, if a man like myself had told me that, I would have thought him a senile old fool."

"Keep talking. I like to hear you declare yourself to me. But where are you?"

"I'm waiting for a car to take me to Cambridge. I'm delivering a paper at the university."

"Oh. For a minute I thought you might be in the hotel. Wishful thinking."

"Nice if I were. But it's impossible. This is the only time in the entire day I'll get a chance to hear your voice, so I grabbed it. How are you, Lara? And yesterday, after we parted, did you have a good day?"

"I had a lovely day. And you?"

"Mine was full, and periodically interrupted by thoughts of you and our first night together."

"Good."

"No, it's not. No overlapping of lives—remember? Must practice what I preach."

"Forgive yourself, Evan. These are new beginnings. Enjoy me."

"You are a corrupting influence."

"Is that good or bad?" she asked teasingly.

"A bit of both, I fear."

"And?"

"And long may it continue," he added, a sensuous warmth in the tone of his words.

"How am I corrupting you?"

"By setting me free sexually. But you know that, don't you?"

"Yes," she admitted.

"My erotic fantasies are running wild."

"How wonderful for us. How lucky we are."

"Yes, that's true. I think you may have unleashed something wild here."

She laughed, a sensuous, seductive sound. "How *very* careless of me."

"Does nothing faze you?"

"Certainly nothing about you and your sexual desires could faze me, only excite me." A new huskiness had come into his voice; she recognized it as desire. And she realized they were having their first erotic telephone conversation. "Evan, don't hold back. Let's live all your erotic fantasies."

"While racing from one meeting to another we went through Soho. I was actually looking for one of those vulgar sex shops I have looked down upon all my life. I wanted to buy erotic toys for us to play with. Things that would excite you, give you pleasure, drag you down into the darker side of sex, where my fantasies seem to be. I want to be irresistibly sexual for you. For you to want me that way all the time. See what you have done to me? You have woken the sleeping beast."

"Giant," she corrected.

Now it was he who laughed. "I am acting like a young stud. I must try to remember I am an aging man—in love with a young woman whose flesh and spirit are the most exciting thing in my life."

"A young woman who loves you, Evan. It would be good for you to remember this is no one-sided love affair."

"Lara, we will be together soon. Just to know that you're out there ready, waiting for me, is the most exciting thing in my life."

There was a click, and he was gone.

His voice had been like a caress. His desire for her very exciting. She left her warm bed to go stand by the window. She drew back the curtains and looked down into Carlos Place. The street was only just beginning to come alive. Two people were opening the front door of Bailey's, the poulterer's. A baker's van was delivering somewhere down Mount Street. Otherwise all was still and quiet on that Mayfair street. It was a gray, damp, and cold morning. With a shiver, she wrapped her arms around herself as if to protect herself from it. She searched the street again for some other signs of life. Why? She knew he wasn't there. Nor was he going to be there. But she stared into the street, looking for him anyway. Wishing he would surprise her and she could have just one more look at him. Silly woman in love, she chided herself. The warmth of her bed beckoned.

She stripped off her nightdress before slipping between the sheets and lay there quietly, on her side, for some time, using the palm of her hand to caress her skin. Over her hip, around her bottom. She ran one foot over the other, slowly, up and down her leg, again and again. Her body craved caressing, being petted. Hands cupped her own breasts. She like the feel of her skin, so satiny smooth, of her own hand upon her body.

What sexual fantasies was he having? she wondered. And which of them would he fulfill with her? And what exciting adventure could she conjure for him? There were so many ways for them to give erotic pleasure. She had seen barriers of sexual frustration break down with every sexual advance he made toward her. With every aggressive sexual move she made on him. And she realized that carnal love, combined with a yearning to possess what each of them saw in the other, was what had seduced them to take the steps they had to be together.

"When next we meet," he had told her, "I will bring you a sexual surprise." She closed her eyes and sighed at the thought of where his sexual fantasies might take them. She rubbed her legs against the silky-smooth sheets and fantasized to herself about the surprises she might offer him. Her role of sexual seductress meant something in their relationship. He relished it; she was excited by it. How thrilling it was to be a part of this distinguished man's new and secret freedom.

Lara had her skiing holiday with Julia. She and Evan spoke several times during that period. The telephone conversations, although not overtly sexual, were tense with sensuality and rife with innuendo, for both of them. She had assumed they would meet before her return to the States, but it did not happen. The circumstances of their lives kept them apart, but love and respect kept building within them, and desire held them together, if not physically, at least emotionally.

Lara was giving Bonnie a tennis lesson in the indoor court at Cannonberry Chase. It was rapidly becoming a farce, with Karim running all over the court picking up tennis balls and throwing them over the net. Nancy arrived and called Lara off the court. "Mr. Smith is on the telephone." Lara turned to tell the children she would be back, only to see Bonnie trying to teach Karim how to hold a racquet. She felt very lucky with her children, that they were so close and happy. Sad, though, to think how quickly they were growing up. "Go ahead, Mum. I'll take care of Karim," called Bonnie.

"What did I catch you doing?" asked Evan.

"Playing tennis."

"I can get away if you can. Five whole days together."

"When?"

"Tomorrow, or the next day. It's really up to you."

"Tomorrow."

He laughed. "I love you."

"Oh, good. I hate one-sided love affairs. Where?"

"Wherever you would like to go. I want to make you happy."

"Where are you?"

"Tuscany."

She knew that was home for him—somewhere near Siena—but that Tuscany was never to be on their itinerary. "And where do you have to be in five days' time?"

"Oxford."

"What will give us the most time together?"

"The least amount of travel."

"I'll take the first Concorde to London."

"A country house hotel. Or shall we rent a cottage?"

"I have a house in Gloucestershire. About an hour from Oxford."

"Is it secluded? I want you all to myself."

"Secluded and dilapidated. I've always meant to do something with it."

"Perfect."

"I'll pick you up at the airport."

After three days, Lara and Evan knew that they had found their ideal hideaway. It was a large and wonderfully beautiful house set in parkland that gave them all the privacy they could want. It was more beautiful than Lara had remembered it, while Evan took to the place at once. The caretakers, who had been there for more than thirty years, were gratified that at last Lara Stanton was taking an interest in her inherited estate. Thus inspired, they made the couple comfortable, creating for them lordly English menus, the meals of yesteryear, when the house had been famed for its hospitality. Though they had acquired a proper democratic disrespect for their lords and masters, they knew how to act like the old-time staff of a country house. During that five-day stay they were hardly seen and never heard. They disappeared into their cottage as soon as dinner had been served, and the house became a home for Lara and Evan.

By day they took long walks, exploring the estate and learning from the farmworkers and managers. The more they were together, the more they liked what they discovered in each other. At night, and not infrequently by day, they indulged themselves in sex. It was Lara who showed Evan the other side of himself, and he was happier than he had ever been, than he had ever expected to be at this late stage of his life.

He was besotted by his sexual life with her, and always amazed at how much she wanted him, at the lengths she would go to in satisfying him. How willingly she would slip with him beneath the waves of bliss he had for so long neglected. He owed her his new sexual life. And she gave and gave of herself to him, unselfishly, as she had rarely given herself to any man. He used her shamelessly to extend his sense of himself, and their intimacy. They thrived on the emotional rewards of their love affair.

Lara made her first home because of him. She found restoring the house in Gloucestershire, though a major undertaking, a worthwhile one. In time it would be a miniature Cannonberry Chase on the other side of the Atlantic. But for several years it would be home to them when they were together and wanted to play house. And playing was exactly what it was. Evan was always insistent that Lara and he be realistic about that. He always insisted there be no illusions.

But there was more to their life together than uninhibited sex and building a secret world for themselves. They learned much from each other, forcing themselves to vary their idyllic togetherness with visits to the theater, opera, and concerts. They explored each other, too, in discovering what each thought and felt about the paintings in the galleries or museums they visited. They took off to go skiing together in remote places, where they would not be recognized, and they indulged in travel whenever it was possible for Evan to get away for any length of time. They were very cautious about being discovered, more because of Lara than Evan. As he had told her the first year they were together, ''Scientists and Nobel prize winners are not movie stars. Our light fades quickly, usually long before the next prizes are awarded. But glamorous society women like you sparkle for most of their lives. Especially intelligent ones who work for the betterment of the world. After a time we will have to be cautious, more for your reputation than mine.''

And that had turned out to be true. They traveled the world together, yet still managed to keep their private lives a secret. They went to Brazil, to the rain forests. Because of him and some of his ideas about the place, she became determined to help save more of the forest and its Indians. They went to Hawaii, where together they designed a guest house, a retreat for them in that first paradise she had purchased. When they were not in residence, she allowed it to become a retreat for other recipients of the Nobel prize. If the razzmatazz of the prize didn't terminate their ability to generate ideas, maybe they'd have another world-saving thought in her very own Hawaiian think tank. It was an agreeable dream, anyway.

The years seemed to fly by. Her happiness made her life easy, and that inspired her to do more for the earth. She took a greater interest in the administration of the farm in Kenya. There she had a colonial house on the side of the mountain, and there they lived for a few weeks as husband and wife when their busy lives allowed it. They were never indiscreet, never broke their ground rules. She was not tempted to be unrealistic or greedy about their relationship.

He took great pride in the successes she had achieved since they had been together. Happiness allowed her to give herself to many more projects than she had before. And if she loved him as she did, she had good reason. He never abused her, or her love for him. He was adamant about certain things. That if he should die, mourning was out, forbidden. Let her put her grief to work. Such talk hurt, but she knew he was right. The greatest lesson she learned from the five years she was with Evan was about her own vital, erotic being: that she could give much, and love well. She had made him happier than she had ever made the other loves in her life. And she learned to appreciate herself more for it, and because his richness of spirit illuminated her own.

The family, Jamal and Sam, saw the changes in her. They never questioned, never criticized. Reticence maintains good relations. But they were all aware that there was someone in her life, someone who could give her more than any of them had been able to give her. A man of evident worth. He had presided over an impressive expansion of her life since she had been with him, and they had nothing but admiration for the way she was handling it.

Julia remained her best friend. Lara had told her, as she had told David and Max and Henry, just once, that there was someone, that she was very much in love. "It's very private, and we will never go public. There will be no marriage, no children, no friends. It is a totally selfish, passionate love affair. He makes me happy in a way I have never been happy before. That's it. I don't ever want us to talk about it again."

Though Lara's clandestine love affair did not interfere with her relationship with Julia, it did change. These were not the days of her running to her friends weeping and moaning. Nor the happy-go-lucky times of when she was married to Sam. Nor was Julia being used as the prop Lara had needed while she went through her divorces, court battles, dead-end love affairs. These were the upbeat years.

If that was true for Lara, it was doubly true for Sir Evan Harper Valentine. During the five years they maintained their affair, he and Lara averaged about three months together each year, sometimes no more than a day or two at a time. During their time apart, he did what Lara did: devoted himself to his family and his work. But not necessarily in that order. He amazed people during that period in his life. He felt a surge not only of love and spirit that he had long thought dead in him, but also of bold and creative scientific thinking. It culminated in not one but two breakthroughs in genetic research that were to be the crowning glory of his work.

Chapter 27

Lara was in Paris with Evan. They were in the oak-paneled, crimson-carpeted bar of the Raphael, their favorite hotel in the city. They enjoyed its quiet elegance. You defied death circling the Arc de Triomphe, then rode the short distance down the Avenue Kleber to the blond stone edifice of the Raphael. Then you plunged into the long paneled entrance hall, across black-and-white marble squares, softened by Oriental carpets of faded grandeur. You risked hell to stroll in heaven, French-style.

Two faded Parisian beauties of a certain age sat quite near them. Lara had been eavesdropping on them. In advanced years, they were quite obviously still playing the coquette, or so snippets of their chat indicated. Evan touched Lara's arm, seeking her attention. She placed her hand on his and smiled at him.

"I would like us to go to Tuscany together."

That came as a surprise.

"I know, I said that we would never go to Tuscany together. I've changed my mind."

"Well, maybe we should think about it some more."

"All right. We will think about it, but not for too long. Do you promise?"

"I promise," she answered.

"I must leave you now, just for an hour. What will you do?"

"I could be quite happy just waiting for you here."

He kissed her, reminding her in a quiet voice that he loved her. Another kiss and he was gone. She watched him walk away. Why, after all these years, had he suggested that they make a trip to his beloved Tuscany? He had not mentioned it since they had first made love at the Connaught in London. Their talk the following morning had been of Tuscany.

She had asked him then where he lived in England. London? And he had replied: "Some people who live in England manage not to live in London. But, darling, I don't live in England. I keep, as a pied-à-terre, rooms at my college in Oxford. It's convenient when I give seminars there, and it's close to the English laboratory I work with. But England is not my real home, only my second home. The family house is in Tuscany. And that's where I live. Where I call home.

"We are one of those English families that can boast an Italian branch, founded in the early eighteenth century, when members of the family made the grand tour. We stayed on and multiplied on both sides of the Channel. I have dual citizenship. So did my father, my grandfather, and various ancestors. My father was English and a quarter Italian, my mother wholly Italian, a Colonna. That's my other life, Lara, and I will never take you there. Much as I might like to. No overlapping of lives, we promised ourselves."

Nearly five years on he had suggested this trip. Why? He was not usually a man to break rules. The waiter arrived to refill her glass with champagne. Lara leaned back in her chair and distracted herself with a few moments of people-watching. Then his suggestion came back to her. She quickly put the questions out of her mind. It really didn't matter. She would not go. No overlapping of lives. Their rule had worked for them. In the years they had been together, they had come to know very little about each other's lives apart. They each knew something about the other's work, but she had no idea about his wife, his children—even if there were any. No more than he knew about Bonnie and Karim or any of the Stantons.

Lara marveled at the love they still felt for each other. It seemed as new and fresh as ever, the more solid for the giving and sharing, the sex life still fiercely erotic. She had seduced him into a world of erotica that suited him.

She thought about the time she had told him of her experience of being a voyeur in the museum. She had described in detail Max fucking the Chinese twin. It had excited Evan's imagination, and he had said, "All that intense sex, real life being played out beneath the petrified remnants of a culture of death."

Once imagined, hard to forget. Two years later, he had taken her, exactly the same way, in a deserted corner of an exquisite temple deep in the desert in Upper Egypt. She had found it more thrilling than she had imagined it could be. She had had to bite into her hand to subdue cries of uncontrollable passion.

She saw him coming toward her now, through the bar, still looking handsome and conservative as a man of his stature would be expected to look. A gray flannel, Savile Row suit has long been found a fair disguise for the fires of lust. She smiled, and from across the room his craggy face gave a grin in response.

"You were thinking?" he asked as he sat down.

"Hardly thinking. Wondering. How much you gave that dragoman to leave us alone in that temple in Upper Egypt?"

He began to laugh, and color came to his cheeks. "We must do that again. If I can afford it, that is."

Then, quite sheepishly, he produced a small parcel.

"That was where you went! To buy me something. Any special reason why?"

"I think you might guess. And, if you can't, it's the kind of gift that speaks for itself."

He ordered a malt whiskey. Lara began to unwrap her gift. "No, not now! Unless you want to ruin our reputations, you'd better wait. Open it upstairs in the bedroom." He was looking embarrassed.

They lunched in the dining room together. Afterward, in the plush privacy of their rooms, she opened her parcel. Wickedly sexy, black silk-and-lace lingerie, as only the French can make it. Elegant but scantily provocative, the maker's name synonymous with such garments. She dressed for Evan in this teasing undress and they made love. After a long traveling holiday together, they preferred to spend the last evening alone. Dine in their rooms and make relaxed love—unless, as sometimes, outrageously erotic, lustful sex took them over. As at the Raphael that afternoon and evening.

One of the best things about their relationship was that, when they parted, there was never sadness, just separation. Evan took Lara to Charles de Gaulle Airport to see her off to New York. Later he was to meet several colleagues and then travel with them by train to Milan—to accept yet another prize for his work on genetics.

They kissed good-bye, and when she left his arms they gazed at each other. Suddenly he changed. The sensuous smile went right out of his eyes—they looked, for a moment, quite empty. She had never seen him like that before. It wasn't sadness, nothing like that. She felt almost sick at the change in him. He seemed to pull himself together then, and shake off whatever it was. The light came back into his eyes. Relieved, Lara hurried away from him. She took but a dozen strides before she dropped the shoulder bag she was carrying onto the pavement and turned to run back to him—just in time to see him rush out of the long, black Mercedes toward her.

He picked her up in his arms and kissed her passionately, telling her, "I have no idea what all that was about. Think about Tuscany. Tuscany with me. Call me when you get home."

The following day, she tried him several times, and there was no answer. At first it didn't bother her. She went out to buy Bonnie a pair of roller skates, and to see Steven. She tried Evan again from his office. Still no answer. He and his associates obviously felt they had something to celebrate down there in Milan. She put the abortive calls out of her mind. But later, while she was walking up Madison Avenue, it occurred to her that something was wrong. In the five years they had been together, not once before had she had to "put him out of her mind." There had never been cause.

She saw a telephone booth just off the corner of Madison. She felt she could not wait until she got home but rushed into the booth. The phone, of course, was out of order. She stopped in the first shop she came to, a shop she had never been into. They sold nothing but pearls. They didn't allow customers to use the phone. She told them it was an emergency. Just saying so seemed to confirm her fear. But shop policy was shop policy. She left the pearl emporium, riled by their meanness. She was feeling quite strange, but in control. Only a few blocks from the house she saw another empty booth. Now she was obsessed with getting through to Evan. This one was working. Relieved, Lara sensed that this time she would get an answer. She dialed the number. The line clicked, and then there was Elspeth on the phone. Lara gave a sigh and thought herself foolish, behaving like a drama queen.

"Elspeth, it's Miss Jones." She smiled to herself, as she always did when she supplied her pseudonym to Elspeth. It just wasn't adult behavior, never mind the circumstances. ''May I speak to Mr. Smith? I have been calling all day. Have the phones been out or something? This is the first time since I've known him that he has not been on the other end of the telephone when he said he would be.''

Silence. She tried again. ''Elspeth? Elspeth, are you there?''

Lara heard sobbing. The sound that told her what she needed to know. But still she must hear it all. ''Elspeth, speak to me. Where is he? Elspeth, he would want you to tell me.''

At last his personal assistant spoke. ''I know. I'm so sorry. Oh, I'm so sorry.''

''He's been hurt. Where is he?''

''Paris. An accident. Mr. Smith is dead. Please, I can't talk now, Miss Jones.''

Lara could not breathe. She must get some fresh air. She couldn't step out of the booth. Her legs felt rooted. She began to shake so violently that she could not get the door open. She was struggling to stay conscious. She pounded on the glass wall of the booth. People passed her by. They ignored her. Finally she managed the door. Once she had it open she took great gulps of air. She was in a nightmare. It couldn't be real. And yet she knew that it was all happening. With clenched fists she flung her arms out and beat the glass walls of the telephone booth. She let out a horrible scream of despair. Her knees buckled and she folded, half in the booth, half out on the pavement. Blackness, nothing.

Evan's death shattered Lara physically and emotionally. Those first days after her collapse entailed round-the-clock nursing, but the drugs and intense psychotherapy she received made only small inroads in getting her back to normal. In death as in life, Evan Valentine's love for Lara reached her through the intervention of Elspeth, his personal assistant. She arrived at Cannonberry Chase after discreet arrangements had been made by Nancy. The two female guardians of the couple's secret, who had on occasion been in contact, now worked together to implement the last wishes of Evan Harper Valentine.

Although the family realized that Lara was unwell, in those first weeks of her illness only Nancy, who had been in her confidence, knew the true nature of her breakdown. By Lara's and

Nancy's request, the family was kept very much in the dark about just how ill she was. Not too difficult, with Henry and Emily having left after the tennis tournament for the house in the South of France; Elizabeth and her family, and any number of Stanton wives and children, were in England. Only David, John, and Steven, with sundry Stanton grandchildren, were drifting in and out of Cannonberry Chase. So only Lara's cousin and two brothers suspected things might be far worse than they seemed. They questioned little, nor did they interfere. But they knew Lara well. When told that she was upset over the death of an old friend, they began to assume that a friend so mourned could only have been the secret love of her life, the love who had made her so happy for several years. They stood silently by, available for her as they had always been. It was the wise David who said, "She'll heal. So long as our La is in her beloved Cannonberry Chase, she'll rally. This place is like mother's milk to her."

Who knew that better than Lara herself? She would lie on her chaise or sit in a chair looking out across the Chase, her mind a blank, all desire gone. Only the soft, warm breeze with the scent of the ocean in it, the leaves on the trees, the chirping of birds, sounds of children playing somewhere, reminded her that she was alive, that she might still love again. Only Cannonberry Chase cut through the shock and trauma of her loss.

She was sitting in a chair by the window when Nancy arrived with Coral and the nurse. The three women fussed around her, leading her from the window to her dressing table, where Coral brushed her hair. They chose a fresh dressing gown for her, some rings for her fingers, a pair of gold earrings, and a bracelet. For days they had been dressing her, hoping that she would take some interest in herself. The only time she did was when Bonnie or Karim came in for a short visit. But she was so heavily sedated they were not allowed to stay for long. Now they slipped a pair of pale gray satin slippers with pretty silk flowers of the same color on her feet. She walked on the arm of her nurse to the chaise, where she lay down. She looked up and saw Coral wipe a tear from her cheek. All she said was, "I wish I could cry."

Nancy sat down at the foot of the chaise and said, "Elspeth is here."

Lara blinked several times and rubbed her forehead, trying

to comprehend what Nancy was telling her. She looked at her and then at the nurse, who had a syringe at the ready. "Elspeth here? Are you sure, Nancy?"

The secretary felt encouraged. Lara seemed to understand, and to be taking the news well. She was coming back, albeit as though through a dense fog, but returning nevertheless. The nurse nodded, as if giving permission for Nancy to carry on.

"Yes, very sure. She would like to talk to you. Would that be all right?"

Lara felt as if her head were filled with cotton wool. She shook it in the hope that she might be able to think more clearly. She looked at the three women and said, "Well, for a start, Miss Hicks, you can put that away."

"Are you sure, Miss Stanton?"

"Quite sure." Then, turning to Nancy, "Please, I must see her at once."

When Elspeth entered the room, Lara tried to rise, but it was impossible. She fell back among the cushions, and the little color she had in her face seemed to drain away.

"No, I don't think this is a good idea," said Miss Hicks.

"For me it is. This is important to me. Please." There was something, a hint of strength in her voice, a sign that the redoubtable Miss Hicks had been looking for since she had taken the case on. Encouraged, she agreed to leave Lara alone with her visitor. Announcing, "I will be in the bedroom, if you need me," she retreated with Lara's staff.

"I never expected we would meet. We lived our affair from day to day and I just thought it would go on forever. I never thought beyond that." Lara hesitated for a few seconds and then continued. "I'm sorry. What I meant to say was . . ." She seemed confused. She hesitated once more, for some time, and then she was more under control. "Thank you for coming."

"I'm sorry you had to find out like that. I wish I could have made it easier for you, but I didn't know how. There seemed to be no other way but to tell you straight-out. I know it has been a great shock for you, for all of us. His family, his colleagues, even perhaps mankind. It is an enormous loss."

Lara listened, concentrating hard on every word Elspeth uttered. She bit nervously into the knuckle of the hand she held in a tight fist. Elspeth had been warned that Lara had been heavily sedated, and though they had been cutting the dosage, she might be sluggish of mind. Elspeth continued: "He always knew that, because of the way you had arranged your life together, yours would be, of anyone's, the greatest shock."

"He spoke to you about this?"

"No, never. But as far back as two years ago, he came to me with his will. There were letters of instruction for me to act on if he died suddenly. That's why I'm here now. He sent me to help you find a way to ease your pain. To remind you of your promise not to mourn him."

"Elspeth, is there a letter for me? Did he leave a letter with you? A note, a word, anything for me from him?"

"No."

This was clearly not what Lara had expected. For a moment, when she was asking, she seemed to rally out of her stupor. Her hopes dashed, that small flicker of life extinguished.

"He left many instructions. Mostly about his work, family, you."

"Nothing personal, no last words for me?"

"Nothing." There was a note of annoyance in Elspeth's voice that was so strong it made Lara sit up and pay attention. "Madam, you had better appreciate how much he *did* leave you," the woman continued. "That remarkable man . . . I have been his personal assistant for more than thirty years, from when you were just a child or maybe not even born. We started out still young together. Evan was a kind, humane man. A great mind, a great . . ." There was too much emotion here for Elspeth's English heart to deal with openly. She stopped.

"I shouldn't have spoken to you like that. Let's just get on with this. I'm here because Sir Evan wanted me to come here. My instructions were to tell you that he left you no note because he will not speak to you from the dead. I am here solely to remind you of the promise that you made to him that you would not mourn him. Nor did he want you to dwell on the years that you had together. I am to remind you that they are over, and that you have a duty to yourself to get on with your life. To that end I have brought with me a close friend of his. A doctor of psychiatry, nonpracticing. He's also, incidentally, a doctor of philosophy who holds a chair at Princeton University."

"It would have been different had I been prepared for this. If we had had time to say good-bye. If I could have been by his side. But this—no intimate word, not so much as a sentence or two on a scrap of paper. Am I to have nothing of him? You mean he's just gone, vanished completely from my life?''

"You lived with his vanishing for years. It was part of your deal. He wouldn't have wanted any whining, acting as if it were his fault that he was killed. No behaving like a spoiled child. . . .''

Elspeth rose from her chair and loomed over Lara, who sat nervously twisting a white lace-trimmed handkerchief in her hands. Elspeth snatched it from her. "How dare you behave like this? He gave you everything he was in a position to give. You mock his love by mourning him like this. Don't make me regret all the years I admired you and the very proper way you handled your relationship with him. You and he knew what it was, and what it wasn't. Not once when he was alive did you allow that special secret you had to interfere with your public lives. He is dead and gone. And he would want you—and you yourself should want, once you have recovered from this shock—to start again, to find someone to build a real, full-time life with. The one Sir Evan was unable to have with you.

"His instructions to me were to remind you that dead is dead, and you are not to indulge in memories of what you had together. There were many sacrifices, and they are not to be remembered lightly.

"Look, this is not a task I'm enjoying, but I have undertaken it. You are not making this easy for me, but you had better understand I intend to accomplish what I came here for. Sir Evan was the wisest man I have ever known. He would not have sent Dr. Graham here unless he was certain you needed him. I suggest you see him as often as you can, and work out your problems. I don't see how you can do that doped up, if I may say so, like a zombie!''

"You don't spare me, do you?''

"No, I don't. And you don't offend me by saying so.''

"But he left you letters?''

"Yes. And his family. But we had a different relationship with him than you did. I should have thought you would understand by now that he was too generous to do that to you. Too intelligent. He knew that sending a love letter from the dead would be like hanging an albatross around your neck. He must have loved you very much to set you free like this. You are a most fortunate woman. I will say no more. Except, do you think I might have a cup of tea?''

Lara burst into tears for the first time since she heard the news of her lover's death. She could not control them. Through them she saw the look of embarrassment on Elspeth's face, her disapproval of such weakness. The stalwart, middle-aged woman—whose emotions were cast in steel—had finally been the only one to reach Lara, and therefore had rallied her.

Lara, seeing herself through Elspeth's eyes, made a supreme effort to control herself. Nurse Hicks had entered the room at the first sound of tears. They were heartrending, but the psychiatric nurse in Miss Hicks knew that they were also, in this case, a breakthrough for her patient. She allowed Lara her cry. When the tears began to subside, she approached.

''I really think you must rest now.''

Lara ignored the nurse's suggestion. Instead she addressed Elspeth, who had by now become resigned to such an outward display of emotion. Lara's voice trembled, but she said, ''Of course you may have tea. And, if you will give me a few minutes, I will come downstairs and join you and Dr. Graham.''

''Well, that's better, Miss Stanton. We really cannot let ourselves down in this.'' Elspeth smiled for the first time, then left the room.

A few minutes ran into just over an hour. But, with the help of Coral and Nurse Hicks, Lara found the energy to get dressed and make up her face. When she walked into the library she looked to Elspeth like a different woman. The long silvery hair was neatly brushed back, and her skillfully made-up face showed off the rich beauty of the young woman. Her eyes were still sad and puffy from too many tears, but her head was held high. She looked sensuous in wide, white flannel trousers, a blouse of white cotton batiste with dropped shoulders and huge, elegant sleeves that were tight to the wrist, and glamorous jewelry. When she moved, it was evident from the outline of her breasts that she was without underclothes. And Elspeth understood the special qualities of this woman, and why Evan Valentine had fallen in love with her. Lara was still, even at her age, a child-woman. The sensuous, the vulnerable innocent who incites sexuality, demands protection and love.

Lara was surprised when introduced to Dr. Graham. She had expected to meet an older man, a contemporary of Evan's. Instead she saw a man not much older than herself. Tall, slender, and bespectacled, a lanky man, there was about him an aura of quiet intelligence. A man happier with books than people, perhaps? His first words to her were, "What a wonderful library."

"Yes."

"I'm Robert Graham. I hope you will allow me to come and talk to you for a while."

"About something in particular?"

"Life."

Lara felt there was no rejecting this man, and was surprised at how right it seemed for him to be here. "For the moment I will not leave Cannonberry Chase."

"I understand. I will come and visit with you here for as long as you will permit me."

She heard herself saying, "Is it possible for you to stay for a few days?"

"Yes, if you like."

The effort Lara was making to take command of herself was obvious. She could not quite suppress a trembling in her hands, an unsteadiness on her feet. But she did produce a modicum of charm that, though fleeting, was still effective. She also displayed to Elspeth and Robert Graham a determination to rise above her distress. Elspeth was won over by this, and by Lara's insistence that Elspeth be her guest at Cannonberry Chase for the night and, at the very least, the following day—before her return to England.

Lara remained at Cannonberry Chase for five months. Robert Graham soon had her taken off the round-the-clock nursing and intensive drug therapy, and himself became a welcome weekly guest at the Chase. And life really did, as he had suggested, become the subject of their discussions. Before long Lara was able to resume some of her activities. In the months that followed, their talks ranged freely over the story of her life. Robert had indeed been a very great friend of Evan Valentine's. From being merely her doctor and healer, he became a great friend to Lara, too.

She came to understand that, surprisingly, she had been bitter

and desperately unhappy at the time of her divorce from Jamal.
What she had needed then was professional help. Instead, she
had plunged into an unrealistic and obsessive love, a furtive affair
that was bound to end in some sort of tragedy. It had come upon
them both at what Evan called the crunch time in their lives. For
the survival of their respective souls, they had both needed something more than they were getting. Now that she could accept
that, she could also recognize that her love affair with Evan had
dominated her. Outwardly there had been no overlap between
their lives. But, inwardly, the only place it really mattered, the
overlap had been complete. So her life was shattered by Evan's
death. Emotional breakdown had been inevitable.

Lara could now see what strange compulsion had drawn her
to the museum during that snowstorm. She had lost her winning
position in the love stakes with Sam and Jamal, could only see
herself as an emotional failure, which she could no longer bear.
She had sought a love life she could make a success of. She was
trying to return to her beginnings as an adult, to the time of her
innocent surrender of her adolescence and virginity. Lara was
seeking to conjure up for herself a man who embodied the combination of qualities she had seen in that sexual act between Max
and the Chinese girl. A richly humane and loving man who was
a sexual animal as well, a man who both loved her and could
satisfy her lustful nature.

Robert Graham was instrumental in making it all fit together.
Now Lara really had herself in focus, flaws and all. She had a
clear image of who she was when she was living with Evan; and
before that, of the Lara Stanton who had chosen to become a
Fayne and then an El-Raisuli. The real weaknesses in her character and in her marriages, and why they were doomed to failure. Those talks with Robert Graham became an exercise in
rebirth. It was as if she had shed her former lives like so many
skins. She was not like some born-again Christian, but a born-
again self.

Lara began trusting everyone around her again and, most important, herself. Her confidence once restored, her natural *joie
de vivre* blossomed, too. The charm and the good life were back
on course. Once again people sought out the golden girl. She
resumed that same life that she had created for herself, that had
been so rich, full, and rewarding when Evan was alive. And he,

if not forgotten, had been laid resignedly to rest in a corner of her heart, never lightly to be disturbed. As per his instructions.

Lara had gained a new identity for herself from Evan, she could see that now. Once aware of that, she understood that she had also acquired identities from the other men in her life. And now, like a man who assumes an identity from his work, Lara realized she was reaping her reward. She had experienced that enticing combination of almost domestic affection with a thrilling sexual life, a romantic love, with Evan. And she had no intention of settling for anything less again. She had once had a quest for one great love. Now, thanks to her talks with Robert, she could see that she had encountered many. And all different. She had no doubts that she would have more—and make more mistakes—before she found the man with whom she would feel compelled to settle down. She was not afraid. She still had a rage to live.

So far hers had been a life of love and loss, of isolation within relationships—until she had met Evan. Now she had to accept that, even in that great love, there had been flaws. But it had also brought her closer than any other relationship to the love she was looking for. Lara had no intention of filling the void left by his death with another escape bid. She did not intend to replace it with anything but the love of another good man.

She had been well enough for weeks to manage her personal affairs. With Nancy and two assistants to help carry the work load, she was once again at the helm. Lara had become more like Henry in his extraordinary ability to delegate. He managed his business affairs as insouciantly as he sailed his boat or rode in a good game of polo, had tea with his wife, or advised a president. And Lara treated her work with a similar panache.

She delegated as required, and paid close day-to-day attention to people, projects, results, through specialist subordinates. She made herself mistress of the art of maintaining the unity and enthusiasm of those who worked closely with her, from senior people to workers in the field. She made the best use of her resources. People marveled at her ability to keep her eye on the smallest detail, never taking it off the progress she expected from the assembly line or the executive suite. She had learned well from her masters. Harland was still her top adviser, her trustee. She depended more on him than anyone never to squander valuable assets. Henry had taught all his children that Stanton rule. They had all lived by it and made their reputations on it. It was the banner Lara waved at international congresses on conservation, from California to Amsterdam to Ethiopia, wherever around the world her work took her.

She was a demanding boss, unafraid to fire subordinates who didn't measure up to her standards. Yet her highly engaging personal style commanded loyalty. She had become a formidable lady.

The idea occurred to her while discussing travel plans with Nancy: it was a simple thing, Nancy asking her where she wanted to stay in Paris. "The Raphael." Having said it, Lara felt no pain, no feeling of loss for Evan. Simply how pleased he would be to know she was going there again. They had traveled to so many places where she had been happy. She would like to revisit them with her friends, her children, the family. Thus did she make up her mind to retrace the journeys she had taken with Evan. It would be the exorcising of the power of their love and of her holding back from finding another.

David, Martha, their children, and Lara's children made a trip to the farm in Kenya. It was a great success. She entertained the entire family in the manor house in Gloucestershire, the first home she had made for them. There was not a trace of Evan there, which both surprised her and enabled that, too, to be a successful, happy time. Rome she visited alone. There she dated a count and forgave Roberto. Then Paris, with her usual entourage, and they all stayed again at the Raphael. Sailing around the Greek islands on a black schooner with Max and her children, she retraced a route she had taken with Evan. The past did not sail with them. With this new stability as part of her character now, she was even more happy in those places than she had been with him. No longer was there the need to lead the secret life they had somehow reconciled themselves to. There were not even ghosts to be laid to rest now. He had been right. Dead is dead.

She had fame and power, success and happiness. She still remained, as all her family had managed to, in the public eye, but lived a very private life. She was not averse to suitors, and enjoyed her flirtations, but was biding her time for love. It was during these best of times that she returned to Morocco for the first time since her dramatic escape from Jamal, simply to bring Karim to his father for Karim's birthday. A trip that she undertook for the boy's sake.

The one night she stayed at The Mamounia, Jamal paid her a visit after Karim was put to bed and proposed that she should go back to him. He made all the right sounds, was charm and kindness itself. He told her of his remorse at what he had put her through, used every ploy he could to assure her he was a changed man. Having found out the hard way how really evil he could be, she endured it as an arduous confrontation that could have no effect on her whatsoever. Lara was amazed that he should think that she still loved him.

She was surprised when he appeared at the family villa in Cap d'Antibes two days later. There he told her, "I am so proud of what you have done with your life. Of the successes you have achieved where governments have failed. I could never have believed you could be the woman you are. Take me back. I will make it up to you."

That was difficult, because she knew he was telling the truth— and because they had a wonderful son. And there was one thing about Jamal that had never died for her: the sexual attraction. It was still there.

"It must have been a time of laying ghosts to rest." That was what she was telling Julia, over lunch at the Harvard Club, on her return from Morocco. She had been recounting the surprise created by Jamal's reinvading her life after all the years that had passed, and all the acrimony. Her amazement at how a man could so distort his own perception that he could believe she loved him still. For that was what Jamal kept insisting. When Julia thanked her for the lunch, Lara said impulsively, "Let's make the next one at Harry's Bar in Venice. Just the two of us, on a long, long weekend of fun."

"No, not Venice. I have a surprise for you about Venice. But you must wait another few days before I tell you."

Chapter 28

Lara listened to the rain beating against the window. There was a clap of thunder and a flash of lightning that lit up the sky, the Grand Canal, and the other palazzos along it.

Her room was sumptuous with antique Fortuny fabrics, silk damasks of plum and coral and ruby red. On a green marble floor stood the gilt canopied bed whose four posts, in voluptuous twists and turns, displayed golden putti, naked babes with pudgy arms, rounded tums, and cherubic faces of impish disposition. The bed had held Venetian princes during its long, checkered existence. It was draped in velvets and brocades, and a bed cover with a finely embroidered field of silk flowers, faded now: daisies, roses, and honeysuckle, jasmine, and lilies; a mélange of blossoms still with some vibrant colors among them. There were cushions of silk and satin, bound in antique silk ropes, with braids, fringes, and tassels. The furniture was mostly Venetian and of venerable age, featuring marble from quarries worked out hundreds of years before. There were chairs of breathtaking elegance, sensuous in form and covered in period tapestries.

The atmosphere of this huge, beautiful room, with its twenty-foot ceilings and leaded-glass windows looking out on the Grand Canal, was made even more romantic by marble vases filled with long-stemmed roses and lilies, and by the paintings on the walls—a Donatello, a Raphael, a Caravaggio—in sumptuously carved and gilded frames. There was a nearly life-sized bronze of a naked youth, and on either side of a huge Venetian mirror stood a pair of sixteenth-century blackamoors, gilded and painted, with turbans encrusted in rose-cut diamonds. Their luminous, black faces were sculpted in shiny-smooth, flawless black marble.

Another ferocious clap of thunder and bright streaks of lightning almost directly overhead. The lights flickered. The noise hardly abated when, with a gentle knock at the door, Roberto walked in. Vivaldi floated up from the ballroom below. How handsome Roberto was, disguised in an eighteenth-century costume of ice-blue silk breeches, brocade waistcoat, and a period jacket of black and gold, topped off with a powdered wig. He wore elegant, pointed shoes, with ribbons that crossed the foot and huge diamanté buckles. A black mask covered the top half of his face. It was fashioned entirely of glass beads. A smile danced about his lips the moment he saw Lara in her costume.

"Fantastic! Really, you look amazing."

"And you."

They did a turnaround for each other. "A devil this weather, isn't it? Pity. But we did have four perfect sunny days."

"The best party ever, Roberto."

He beamed. "I've come to tell you we're going down. We must be there to receive our guests. They're just arriving. Don't rush."

"I don't know how you and Julia did it, gathering seventy people together from all over the world. And what a combination of people! Not a dud in the crowd. What organization it must have taken to give us these four days in Venice. The luxury of it all, and the thoughtful touches. The flowers and the candy, the gifts and—and!—You must have been months working it out."

"I was. I promised myself I'd give the best party ever."

"Well, you certainly have."

"And I hope this ball will be the best any of us has ever attended."

"Well, kiss us for luck," said Julia, who floated through the door, already masked. She was dressed in silver and white, with a necklace of extravagant diamonds—the only thing about the costume that was not eighteenth-century. The three abandoned themselves to a few minutes of mutual admiration. A few more kisses, then, high on the expectation of fun, Roberto and Julia were summoned by the majordomo.

Several other guests like Lara were staying in the palazzo.

Others had been put up at the Gritti Palace, only minutes away by gondola. So far it had been the most fun and glamorous party Lara had been to in years. Truly Roberto and Julia had thought of everything. From the moment they had boarded the Concorde in New York, it had been round-the-clock entertainment: food, wine, shopping trips, tours of Venice, lunch in Torcello, Murano, Burano, the Lido. The sun had beamed upon them and the nights had been soft with the warmth of the breezes. The usual hordes of tourists, as if by divine dispensation, had not materialized, even in the first days of June.

Lara jumped suddenly, surprised by another clap of thunder. The lights went out. No surprise. They had come and gone for the last hour. It posed no problem. Her room had been lit by dozens of fat white church candles placed in tall gilded wooden torches. Slimmer ivory candles glowed in wall sconces dripping with rock crystal that sparkled like diamonds. Others twinkled in silver candelabras set on tables. This time the lights did not come back on.

Lara went to the window. She could see little. Venice was seemingly under a blackout. Far down the Grand Canal, somewhere near the Piazza San Marco, there was a slash of lightning in the black sky. It glowed for a second. A dramatic night for a ball. The weather seemed to add a frisson to the event. She watched the water gushing down the windowpanes with fascination. Another flash of lightning, shooting almost through the window. It gave her a moment to see, approaching the landing of the palazzo, several gondolas. Guests huddled under canopies with side curtains, stretched over the boats to protect them from the storm. The lanterns on the gondolas cast yellowy light on the masked revelers, who were now bounding out of the boats and up the stairs. Umbrellas billowed protectively in the white-gloved hands of the bewigged, liveried footmen. The guests hurried in to the ball.

Several boys with blackened faces and dressed as blackamoors, holding red silk umbrellas in one hand and lanterns lit by candles in the other, appeared at the entrance to the palazzo to light the way for the guests. Three more gondolas arrived. Lara saw flashes of pink silk and emerald-green velvet and gold lamé, as the ladies' gowns were caught by the wind. The men, in black capes, one of white satin even, looked handsome, mysterious, dashing. It was the masks that made Lara feel truly liberated. No identity to deal with; a release from restraint. Tonight there were to be more guests, a hundred in all. What if, under their masks, they all felt as she did? It promised to be a night to remember. The very anonymity of the masks would provoke liaisons, invite sexual encounters that might throw inhibitions to the wind.

It was time to go down to the ball. Lara checked herself in the mirror for the last time. A woman knows when she looks spectacular and when she just looks good. Spectacular, declared her reflection. Her dress was modeled on an eighteenth-century Venetian ball gown. It had been painted several times by several different old masters. That gown had once adorned a famous lady of dubious reputation. Some had considered her the most perfect Venetian beauty of her time. Lara had had it copied, down to the last detail, which included a fantastic mask of egret feathers. She looked sensuous and exciting, and very risqué. The bodice was cut so low that the swell of her breasts showed nearly to the edge of the plummy-colored nimbus circling her nipples. Such a tight bodice and pinched-in waist accentuated the sweep of the voluminous skirt, billowing out over a hooped structure. From her wrist hung a black feather fan mounted on ivory. The wickedly sexy gown and mask might have wrung an invitation from the Marquis de Sade himself to partner her to the ball.

She fingered the feathered mask and laughed. She could be as provocative as she liked tonight: no one would know who she was. Lara had chosen not to wear a powdered wig, but to have her own hair dressed in the eighteenth-century style favored for such an event, a labor of some hours. But now, looking at herself, she thought it had been worth it. The dress was of black silk taffeta and nearly strapless, except for tiny drapings of silk on the shoulders. She wore diamonds, and the pearl choker Emily had given her as her first piece of serious jewelry.

Something drew her eyes to him as she was descending the grand staircase into the marble hall. He was standing at the bottom of the stairs. Waiting for someone? What a pity. Their gazes met behind the masks. They were able to lock into each other's thoughts immediately, and each recognized their immediate attraction. Was it the allure of a virtually faceless physique? Perhaps the masks themselves induced some strange compulsion.

He was tall and slim, with honey-blond hair, lots of it, and smoldering brown eyes behind the slim strip of his mask. The black eye band did little to hide the fine, sensitive, incredibly sensuous face. He emanated an erotic, even somewhat depraved masculinity, and the promise of youthful flesh. It excited her, this young flesh.

He watched her walk down the last few steps. They smiled at each other, and he was enchanted by the sensuous green eyes, the sexy pout of her upper lip. He lowered his head as if in a bow. And then, before she traversed the last step, he dropped to one knee. Raising the hem of her gown, he kissed it. That eloquent, antique gesture! Then, standing up again, he offered her his hand. She took it. He kissed it—and then spoke to her for the first time. "I think you shall be mine."

Lara was seduced by his youth, his charm, his sureness. "Have I nothing to say in the matter?"

"Oh, yes. Everything. But you are a woman, a very sexy and beautiful woman, and you will play games with me before you will consent to be mine."

She laughed, catching at once the special tone to it. It had a lilt, a note she had almost forgotten. It was the laugh of a young heart. People had commented on it when she was a girl.

He never relinquished her, not for one dance, even with his hostess. He was young, she could see it even with his mask in place, sense it by the way he moved. But she had understood that at once by his honesty, his audacity. She sensed, too, the purity of his spirit that only comes with youth.

They danced and they danced and they danced. There was something in the way he held her, the way she felt in his arms. She never wanted to leave those strong, sure, young arms. She felt the years dropping away from her. She felt she belonged to him. As if she had missed something all of her life by not having met him before. It was lunacy, but she did believe that he was right: in some way she was his. The mask was her salvation, she could hide behind it and flirt with him. She could say and do whatever foolish things the moment inspired in her. The mask gave her courage to make a fool of herself with this delicious young man.

His timing was perfect. At the very moment when her thoughts were of them, he told her, "We can tell each other everything. Or nothing. But we don't have to confess. I hate confessions. I don't want to tell you all my secrets and I don't want to know yours. Does that make sense?"

"Maybe."

"Good, then we understand each other. To have you in my arms is to ruin me for any other woman."

"Then perhaps I should tell you that I feel I fit into your arms as I have never fitted another's."

With raised eyebrows, he smiled, an expression that left her weak-kneed. Then he told her, "I know. That's because you know I love you. That you are mine and will be the great love of my life."

They were interrupted by the end of the music and the beginning of an entertainment. He was well-spoken and full of charm. He seemed to interest and amuse everyone. But he never for a moment let her drift away from him.

The ball was as Julia had wanted it to be. A glamorous and fun ball, that would be talked about for years to come. The palazzo and the costumes, the wine, the menu, the music, the dancing and good company, the timing of events, were only the basis. A group of Shakespearian actors performed scenes from *The Taming of the Shrew*, *The Two Gentlemen of Verona*, *Othello*. To offset Othello's jealousy came the jugglers and magicians. Two Russian ballet dancers out-Shakespeared the actors by dancing Prokofiev's *Romeo and Juliet*. Gypsy violinists alternated with the orchestra. Fortune-tellers roamed among the guests, shrewdly predicting what they wanted to hear. All through the night, the storm raged, to add claps of thunder and streaks of lightning. Incessant wind and rain beat dramatically against the windows.

They were dancing again, and he whispered in her ear, "I want us to go home to bed."

"Just like that?"

"Yes, just like that. You can't tell me that's not what you want."

"No. I can't tell you that."

"I'm going to marry you, if that's what you're worried about."

She could not help laughing. He, too, thought himself quite

funny, and laughed as well. "As soon as possible," he assured her.

"Oh, but you want the wedding night first? Well, I like a man who knows what he wants and goes after it."

"When I saw you at the top of the stairs you quite took my breath away, I was so attracted to you. You looked wickedly sexual to me, but you also seemed to reach out to me with love. Come to bed with me. Let's make love together. I know you are my happiness, and I think I could be yours. Can I be so wrong about that? Surely not."

He took her hand and was leading her from the ballroom. She stopped him. "And what if you're right?"

"Then the gods at last have blessed us."

"Behind this mask is an older woman."

"Behind this one is her hungry lover, her future husband."

"You assume a lot."

Walking through the reception rooms on the arm of the young man, Lara was not unaware of the wanton atmosphere. At midnight, the hour to unmask, most of the guests had chosen to keep themselves concealed behind their masks. Now, the early hours of the morning incited couples to behave rather more than flirtatiously with their semi-mysterious friends. In the upstairs hall, away from the eyes of the other guests, the young man quite gently pressed Lara against the wall. Tilting her chin up, he placed his mouth upon hers and gave her a tender, lingering kiss. His lips found the side of her neck. He removed her earring. He licked the lobe of her ear, sucked gently on it, and ran the point of his tongue behind it. She closed her eyes. Her breathing quickened with the thrill of such affection. They feasted wordlessly upon each other. His tongue licked the small hollow at the base of her neck. Passionate kisses, strong, young hands caressing her arms and bare shoulders triggered in her the urge to cry. Not out of sadness, more out of a sense of relief that he had arrived in her life, this masked stranger, able to draw from her a youthful freshness of spirit.

He took several steps back, but still held her hand. It was as if he wanted to get a better look at her, to etch her into his mind forever. He told her, "I've been wanting to do that since the moment I saw you at the top of the stairs. I will remember you always in your exotic costume and feathered mask. One day I will have your portrait painted, dressed just as I see you now, so that all our children, our grandchildren, and theirs, will know who you were, and be enriched by it and by your beauty.''

What was she to say? Overcome by his kisses and now by his words, she felt he was like no other man she had ever known, except maybe David. She reached out to trace his lips with the tip of a finger. She smiled, knowing that the love she felt for him showed. He placed an arm around her waist and together they walked slowly down the long hall with its frescoed walls, their heels clicking on the marble floor. To the distant sounds of revelry and music drifting up from the party below and rain pounding against windows, and enveloped by the scent of flowers and burning wax from the thousand candles lighting the palazzo, they each yielded to love.

She stopped in front of a door flanked by a pair of period pedestals topped by impressive white marble busts. ''Your room?'' he asked.

''Our room, I think.''

''Only *think*?'' He hesitated. ''You *think*?'' he repeated. ''This is our entrance into paradise! I don't have to *think* about it, and I don't want you to have to, either. Trust me. I'm already in love enough for both of us.''

Irresistible words for a woman. And most especially for a romantic woman looking for love and passion from a good man. It was she who opened the door. He followed her into the candlelit room. When she heard the click of the lock, something in her heart clicked, too.

He put a taper to the fire that had been laid in the massive fireplace. The flames *whooshed*, and then he gave his attention to Lara. He seemed not at all in a rush, but happy to savor every nuance of disrobing her. He caressed the feathers of her mask before he unclipped it. It was a nervous moment for them both when he removed it and Lara was revealed to him. His pleasure was obvious in his eyes. Her heart was beating fast while she watched and waited for him to untie the black ribbon that held his own mask in place. ''Someday we can wear them while we make love. But for our first time, no.''

Without his mask, her hopes were confirmed. But she was nevertheless surprised. He was very handsome, with a large head dominated by magnificent bone structure. He had a perfect

Roman nose, a face that was more sensitive than somehow she had expected, and fiercely intelligent. Unmasked there was an even greater sexuality about him. He emanated a kind of bold sensuality—that of a man who loves women and making love to them, and does quite a lot of what he likes. It was all in his face and the way he moved, but so, too, was a bold honesty and an impressive self-confidence. Here was a young man who did not deal in fantasies. He believed he could have anything he wanted, and went out and got it.

He pulled the small diamond star pins from her hair. The eighteenth-century suddenly became now. The long, silky strands fell prettily down round her shoulders and back. He ran his fingers through the silvery tresses, gathered a handful, and brought it to his lips. He removed his jacket, then his tie and waistcoat. She undid the bodice of her dress and allowed it to slip down to the floor. Their pleasure mounted as their garments fell from them.

Lara was astounded at how beautiful a body he had. His young flesh exerted its power on her. She caressed his arms and his chest. To feel his skin! The scent of him excited her. He stood before her now, naked and proud, and she in nothing but sheer black stockings and satin pumps with diamond buckles. He led her from beside the bed to in front of the fire, and threw cushions on the floor. She lay down on them, and he dropped to his knees next to her. He raised her leg and removed her shoe—then went higher, and she watched him slowly roll down the stocking. The light from the blazing fire danced and reflected on them as if they, too, were aflame. He kissed the inside of her thigh, the back of her knee, the instep of her foot.

He didn't have to ask her. She opened her legs wide and, placing her feet flat on the carpet, held her arms open for him. He knelt between her legs. She reveled in gazing at his body: the slim hips, the taut skin, the triangle of bushy pubic hair, the circumcised penis looking large and virile, lying flaccid along his thigh. His genitals looked to her sexy, perfect, the thick penis so in proportion to its length, and the sac beneath. The thighs so strong and muscular. In this young flesh and taut body, the magnificence of the genitalia, the warmth of character and virile sexuality, Leonardo would have found a perfect model.

It was as if she had been hungry for him all her life, had

missed him in her youth, and had been seeking him out ever since. She felt so young, as young as she had been when taken for the first time by Sam. She had been ready for this man then, she was ready for him now. Only this time around the desperation to be loved was thankfully gone. The need was not so pressing. What she desired was not only for herself but for him, too. To share her life with him. To give him the very pleasures she wanted. That came naturally to her, because she sensed how much he wanted to be loved by her, taken by her into erotic oblivion. That in itself was a new kind of excitement.

He pulled her up from the cushions by her hands, and, together, in front of the fire, facing each other, they took their time over their kisses and caresses. He told her how much he loved her body, the ripeness of it. The way he handled her breasts, caressed her bottom, licked her cunt—these were not the clumsy gropings of a callow boy. He was a seducer, who found lust in the very act of sexual seduction. He made love beautifully, with the dominating lust and desire of a classic Don Juan, yet she felt him yield, responsive to being made love to by a woman. That added to the already smoldering fire in her, and her erotic soul flared up.

She felt the weight of his penis in her hands and the softness of its skin, swelling with surges of lust for her. She licked the underside with pointed tongue, until she found what she wanted. Holding the sac in her hands, she fondled and licked it moist. She sucked, she came. He had no inhibitions, held nothing back. Except that crucial climax. It was for sharing with her. Hence his tempered sighs of ecstasy. Rampant now, he was more than ready to take her. She held him off until she could see his love-lust was changing to passion gone wild with desire. Only then did she give herself up to him.

Such were her new beginnings. He had been right. They belonged to each other.

Dawn arrived in streaks of pearly gray and bands of pink. The storm had blown itself out, leaving the piazzas flooded, the canals swollen. The palazzo was quiet but not silent.

"This is madness," she told him. Her happiness shone in her eyes. She was tingling with the expectations of adventure and love that being with this young man aroused.

"Love is madness."

They dressed, Lara in wide, white linen trousers, a blue-and-white-striped shirt, and a long, white linen jacket, Charles in his clothes from the night before, and padded carefully and quietly down the hall to his room, trying to avoid meeting anyone, where he changed into Levi's and a V-neck cashmere sweater. He appeared to know his way around the palazzo and found the servants' staircase easily. In the vast kitchen they seemed to know him and made him welcome. He charmed the cook and butler, teased several of the other helpers. Large cups of black coffee were produced. Chunks of newly baked bread, still warm from the ovens, were spread with thick slabs of fresh, sweet butter. They cut wedges of a semisoft, white cheese, hungrily adding it to their morning snack. A bunch of big fat black grapes was there for the taking. The cook offered them slices of luscious pink ham. They ate walking around the room, picking from platters until the butler handed them a large open wicker basket with a dramatically arched handle. A white damask napkin emblazoned with the family crest covered its contents.

Some notes were tucked in the butler's pocket, then Lara was taken by the hand and whisked out across the back garden, around the side of the palazzo, and through a gate—to where a gondola was waiting. There was a conversation and more bank notes were paid over. They boarded the gondola. He took her in his arms, she laid her head against his shoulder. The gondolier plied his oar, and they quickly left the Grand Canal for a smaller one. They wove their way quickly through the lesser waterways of Venice while the city came slowly to life.

"What did you say in your note?" he asked her.

" 'Great party. Have run off with a handsome young man. Don't worry, will be back in three days' time.' What did you say in yours?"

" 'Thanks. Have abducted the most beautiful woman at the ball.' "

Chapter 29

They spent an idyllic three days on a small island far out in the lagoon, more than an hour from the palazzo on the Grand Canal. A deserted place of tall grasses and wildflowers, and a canal that ran in from the sea. There were ruins (A temple? A church? The house of a prince?), fragments of sculptures, pillars and capitals lying broken in the grass. A marble chair cut from a single block. Blazons of carved lions mutilated and worn from centuries of wind and rain wafting across this open, flat place.

A ruined house from antique times incorporated a courtyard with a marble well at its center. An impressive arched cloister stood half in ruins.

He pulled her along after him with childlike enthusiasm, anxious for her to see it all. From under a stone, he took a large iron key. He opened the house and flung wide its shutters. One large room had windows that faced the lagoon on one side, the courtyard on the other. A wall of books and a sturdy eighteenth-century Venetian table. A doge's chair stood near a huge double bed covered in clean, crisp white linen and large square pillows, a blanket of silver fox. On a mosiac floor, as old as the ruin itself, stood a black concert grand piano and a gilded bench with shapely legs, covered in a faded tapestry depicting a wood.

Leading off that room was another, a kitchen with a large table and chairs, a great open fireplace, a wood-burning stove, and a white marble sink. Off that a bathroom dominated by a white marble bath, once a sarcophagus, and a basin of white marble.

A small motor launch visited once a day to deposit on the

bank a basket of fruit, bread and cheese, wine, cured meat, and fresh pasta, which he cooked for her, dressing it at each meal with a different succulent sauce: tomato, a perfect pesto, once something as simple as oil and fried garlic. Otherwise no one else appeared at the island. They had it all to themselves. By night, kerosene lamps and candles and love. By day, the sun and the sea. They hardly spoke. Instead, they explored the island and made love.

Lara was reminded of another time and another island, but this was not Sam. This was a young, sensitive man with a strong libido like her own. He delighted in her sexuality, did not feel threatened by it. Like Jamal, he wanted only to feed it—take it, and her along with it to even greater adventures. It was here, not at the palazzo, that they explored the wilder bounds of eroticism. Here that he took command of her sexually with his youth, vigor, and a libido that demanded adventurous sex. He knew well how to play with depravity, how to satisfy their lust and continually excite a vital relationship between them.

The days and nights seemed to drift into one and they lost track of time, as they lost themselves in each other. They were like a single being with two souls. They bathed naked in the sea, and often walked that way through the tall grasses, gathering bouquets of wildflowers. He read her poetry: Keats, Shelley, Cavafy. She played the piano for him, and often he would play Schubert and Schumann for her. This beautiful young man whom she had run away with must surely be the one she had been seeking to share a life with. Happiness, real happiness, must at last be within her grasp.

It was time to leave the island, quit one world he had created for them for another. He told her, ''We must always remember this is as much the real world as any. This is what our life is going to be, wherever we may be. It was a perfect place and time to fall in love. Repeatable wherever we are, for every day in our life.''

She could have wept. What had she done in her life to have deserved this remarkable young man? She had no doubts that there had been for him many other women, but that he had never said such words to any of them.

''Is that why you bought this place? To fall in love?''

''Maybe. I'd have bought it for that. But, really, it's been in the family always. A place no one but me ever wanted. In fact, my mother gave it to me. I am restoring it. Who knows why? Maybe it was to fall in love. Who can say? I go to a masked ball, and my life is turned upside down. In a instant I find the one piece that has been missing. Everything has changed for me. Is it the same for you?''

"Oh, yes.''

"I don't ever want you to leave me.''

"I won't. I couldn't. Nothing in this world could make me do that. To begin again with you—it's like a rebirth. It will be a wonderful life. Where shall we begin?''

He laughed from sheer happiness. "I think we have.''

"We have to leave, and I don't know where the time has gone.''

"I do. It vanished, was blown away when love and sex took over. Do you think it will be like this for the rest of our lives? What bliss.''

"There will be problems. Even greater than the difference in our ages,'' she said, matter-of-factly, but without anxiety.

"That's life. We'll solve them, or learn to live with them. We'll do what it takes.''

"There are things you should know.''

"There are things that both of us should know.''

"I've had a complex life. It has taken a great deal of living to straighten it out.''

"And I. Do you think I don't have a life behind me? And, I also have a reputation. A womanizer who has never fallen in love. Until now. I told you we don't have to tell each other all our secrets. No confessions, my darling.''

"If you take me on, you take on two children with me.''

"I love children. We'll give them little brothers and sisters.''

This was the first time they actually spoke about themselves. They had been too busy with sex and love and the sun and their island to reveal much in words, to talk about pasts or think about futures. And now the world was coming in on them, yet it was not an intrusion, but an addition to add to an already rich and beautiful love. They fell silent. "Little brothers and sisters'' sparked that sexual attraction so very much alive between them. And they wanted each other. They stopped talking and gave themselves up to Eros once more.

In those three days of sex with this young man, on his romantic island, he had taught Lara to let loose and to call out, to cry into the wind as she came. It had touched a nerve in her sexual being, and she found yet another kind of security in being able to express her lust in that way. Had he no inhibitions, this beautiful young man who had inspired her to shed what little sexual reticence she did have? Only when they heard the call of the gondolier announcing his arrival to take them back to Venice were they able to calm themselves and make ready to leave.

Lara watched him close the piano. Together they shook out the fox blanket and covered the bed with it. They shuttered the windows, and he locked the door with the heavy iron key. She watched him place it in its hideaway before they left to walk down the path to the waiting gondola.

She watched her handsome young lover greet the gondolier. The two men shook hands and spoke for several minutes before he helped Lara into the gondola. She felt like a young girl, this might have been her first love, and she was excited to think they were going out into the world together. But in the gondola, as they traversed the canal, he whispered things to her that told her his feelings were the very same as hers. Halfway down the canal, they looked back over their shoulders. They smiled, and he took her in his arms and kissed her. "I call it Aurelia."

When they arrived back at the palazzo, Julia and the other guests had gone. The party had flown back to New York. Lara had miscalculated their departure time. Roberto, kindness itself, had left the palazzo at their disposal for as long as they liked.

"Great. I'll show you a Venice you've never seen before."

That night they dined out in the Piazza San Marco, drank cognac, and walked slowly home over arched stone bridges and through a maze of dark, narrow streets. Then they returned to the bedroom where it all began.

Naked in each other's arms, bursting with happiness, they called Julia in New York. Less to apologize for running off together than to share their joy with someone. When Lara put down the telephone, she turned to her young lover and said, "Julia says your name is Charles. I didn't dare tell her I forgot to ask you your name. It suits you."

She rolled over in his arms and kissed him, and told her again that she was happy. They lay in the dark, with just a few candles lighting the sumptuous room. "Lara." He kept repeating her name. "Lara."

And then, "Lara Valentine."

She lay there quite still, and a most dreadful feeling came over her. She shook it off, refusing to allow anything to threaten her happiness. Had she misheard him? Against her better judgement, she heard herself ask, "What? What did you say?"

"Lara. Lara Valentine. It's nice. Mrs. Charles Sebastian Valentine."

The coincidence was remarkable. How strange life was.

Charles, inspired by the idea of Lara's becoming Mrs. Charles Sebastian Valentine, rolled on top of her and pinned her down by straddling her. With loving hands he caressed her hair and touched her face, fondled her breasts and maneuvered her legs apart with his. He asked her in a voice thick with passion, "Take me inside you, Mrs. Valentine."

She reached beneath him, found her pussy, and pulled the outer lips open, then parted the already moist, silky-soft inner lips. She guided the fleshy knob, pulsating in her hand, between them. He needed no more help than that. One quick, sharp thrust buried him nearly to the hilt inside her. She wrapped her legs around him. Another push and she could feel him pressing hard against the tip of her womb, his balls packed close against her body. She eased her legs down slowly. They lay on their sides, wrapped tightly in each other's arms, locked together in sex and heart to heart.

Ever since she had met him she had been moved by his young body. It had excited her. Now this man was a part of her life. It was a miracle to her to feel about him as she did. She gripped him tight inside her and made love to him that way. She was alive for him. Her cunt kisses were her way of telling him. He reveled in her passion, adored the way she kissed him. They lay that way for a long time, entwined as one, and talked to each other.

She discovered her worst fears were true: Charles Sebastian Valentine was Evan's son. He told her so casually, as no more than a point of information. "My father was Sir Evan Harper Valentine, he was a Nobel laureate. Awarded for his work on genetics. He could have won it for several other contributions he made to science. He was a very wonderful man. My hero and my friend. You would have liked him. He would have loved you.''

The shock was proving almost more than she could take. Evan! It had taken a great deal of soul-searching to forget him, to put him in her memory bank and treat him as he had wanted to be treated, as dead is dead. He was gone, and now she was in love, on the brink of a new life. One that need not be a dark, selfish love, or a secret. Lara and Charles: a life filled with adoration and love. No boundaries to hem them in. The sort of love she had been seeking all her life. How could she give him up? But how could she tell him about his father and her? It was too much to cope with. She had to set it aside. She had too much rage to love and be loved by Charles to be able to leave him.

They remained together for several more days. If Lara felt utterly unable to tell Charles she had been his father's secret love for five years, or of her own passionate love for Evan when she was first made aware of the father-and-son relationship, the passing of time only magnified her dilemma. How could it not when she was given a vision of the life she and Charles could have together?

''I'm an art historian. A visiting professor of art history at Harvard and Cambridge. But most of the time I work from home. It's a good life. I travel a great deal and see wonderful works of art, and for the most part am involved with interesting people and few fools—just so long as I avoid being frivolous and partying. At masked balls, for example,'' he teased.

''I'm impressed.''

''Oh, good. I have a house on a mountain about thirty miles from Perugia. A marvelous palazzo, twelfth century some of it. It's called Palazzo di Fontefresca. My mother's brother left it to me. I was his favorite nephew. My inheritance made me a wealthy landowner, a farmer on rather a grand scale. I should be able to feed you. I'm quite well-off, which is important for a man who has chosen to write books on Bernini, Caravaggio . . . I could name you five or six more, but I've no need to impress you. I'm only telling you now so you will know what kind of life we are in for. What about you? You're the other half of this team. Will you be happy living with me at the Fontefresca?''

''I adore Tuscany. And I think I could live with you anywhere.'' She did not miss the way he bit his lip and fell silent, the obvious need he had to calm himself, so touched was he by her words. Then he continued, spurred on by the enthusiasm he saw in her face. "It's a quite marvelous house—with lots of rooms for the children and visitors. It's surrounded by acres and acres of olive trees, a huge peach orchard, fig trees by the hundred, and vineyards. We bottle a very good wine."

Then she told him who she was, about her family, her attachment to them and her own work. She saw the admiration for her in his eyes, and the enthusiasm he had for the life she had made for herself. She knew their lives fitted together like a hand in a glove. He even understood her inordinate love for Cannonberry Chase, and responded with, "We can live in both places. It will be just a matter of timing. We can be wealthy, working gypsies, without a caravan. I have a plane. There's even a good grass field I keep in top condition at the foot of the mountain." And the more he told her, the more they had in common.

He was impressed that she had soloed across the Atlantic. There would be places to fly to together, a new plane they would buy to accommodate them, the children, their friends. He was the man she wanted to marry, a life with him all she really wanted. And she was what he had been waiting for all his young life.

They stopped in Rome on the way to Perugia, for her first visit to his mountain of olive groves dotted by thousands of cypress trees and crowned by the Palazzo di Fontefresca. There he sought out a dealer in Renaissance jewelry and bought her a ring, an engraved ruby set in gold and studded with emeralds. Once owned and worn by Catherine de Médicis. He paid a king's ransom for it and then slipped it on her finger. It was of such breathtaking beauty she wanted to weep.

It was all too perfect, too right. She was too happy. How could she keep from him such a secret as she had? She saw how women looked at him with longing, at her with envy. Two days in Rome and she understood. He was the most eligible man in Italy, adored by the demimonde, respected by the snobby Italian aristocrats.

How could she deceive this very special man? How not tell him about his father? Yet how to tell him about his father? She didn't want to deceive him. But she didn't want to reveal her secret, either. Not least because Evan would have deplored her doing so. All those years of being a back street love and now to come out with it? Impossible. But what would Charles want her to do? He had already told her, "Keep your secrets." But such a secret as this?

When, after he placed the ring on her finger, he asked her to commit herself to a date for their wedding, she kept changing the subject. He pressed on. He knew what he wanted and he was not going to let her go. He could not understand her sudden hedging. He asked her, "Do you have doubts?"

Caught off-guard, she answered him truthfully. "No doubts about you."

"You must. Or you wouldn't be hesitating about the time and place."

Her hesitation was posing more of a problem for Lara than he could have guessed. She had found in their relationship physical, spiritual, and emotional love. The very idea of living again without those things was a reminder of the past, those bleak times in her life before she had met his father. He was forcing her to push forward with her life while the secret held her back. It made Lara uneasy.

"A nine-year age difference," she told him. "I think I'm worrying about that. I think I'll be cheating you of nine more years of babies you could make with a younger woman. I saw the way those beautiful young things we met on the Via Veneto looked at you."

"You can't seriously be thinking of throwing our love away because of an age difference? You should have thought about that before I took you in my arms for our first dance. Not valid. Now that's the end of that."

"Not quite."

"Oh, you've found another excuse not to marry me? A better one, I hope, than the last."

"It isn't, it's the same one. I can live with my being older than you. But can you? You say it doesn't matter, but what about your friends, what will they think? And your mother? Oh, I just bet she will sing hosannahs to have an older woman for a daughter-in-law. Especially one with two children and a past!"

The very thought that she would have to meet his mother appalled her. How could she live with that? Facing Evan's wife and his son, with such a great secret to keep from them? How could she reveal to them that she had been the last great love of Evan's life? Evan and her secret life with him now belonged to the past. She had distanced him from her mind and her heart, but he was not forgotten. He had wanted it that way; it had been hard going, but she had accomplished it. Nothing—not even falling in love with his son, wanting to marry him and begin to build a real home with him and have children again; not even facing Evan's wife—could bring back emotions about what she once had with Evan. But it was the deceit that troubled her, panicked her even. The dilemma was eroding this love and her desire to start a new life with Charles. Lara knew that he was the love that she had never found as a girl. The young love that had eluded her. That she had been searching for and, having missed, had taken many different paths to find. Here was her future laid before her, there for the taking, and her dilemma was killing it. His voice broke into her thoughts.

"My mother? No. I suppose I didn't mention it. My mother is no longer with us. She died of cancer. I lost both my parents within the same year. First my mother and then, almost seven months to the day, my father. How they would have loved you! And they would have been so happy that I have found someone as special as you."

That news shocked her. She seemed unable to recover herself sufficiently to find words to express to Charles how sorry she was for his loss. Instead she tried to put her own thoughts out of her mind and concentrate on what he was telling her.

"It was so sad. She put up a heroic battle against her illness for a very long time, three awful years."

Lara wanted to hear no more. Evan and his family had been blocked out of her life. She didn't want to know about them now. But Charles continued, and what she heard only added to her dilemma.

"I loved my mother. She was a great lady. My father was devoted to her, and so was I. But we had a long time to get used to the idea that she was going to die, so it wasn't a shock when it came. In many ways a relief. The real shock for me was when, seven months later, my father was killed in an automobile accident in Paris."

Seven months. For the last seven months of her life with Evan, he was a widower and was free to marry her. It was too much to contemplate. Lara tried to forget what she had heard.

They had been having that conversation sitting in the late afternoon sunshine in a street cafe. The "beautiful people" of Rome were having their afternoon aperitifs. There was the usual chatter all around them, and laughter, and waiters rushing to-and-fro. Quite suddenly Charles stood up and pulled her up out of her chair with him. He kissed first her hand and then the ring he had given her only a short time before. Then he pulled her roughly into his arms and kissed her deeply, with such passion that for a few seconds she forgot everything.

Everybody loves a lover. Neighboring tables of young Romans supplied the cat calls and applause and called out in Italian, cheering him on. He released Lara, and they both smiled, and when she began to laugh, he was thrilled. It seemed obvious to him that nothing could keep them apart, no matter what excuses she made.

Pulling her into his arms once more, preparatory to kissing her again, he told her in a low voice, "You see how people react to us. They see no age difference any more than I do. They see only love and passion between a beautiful young man and woman. And what do they do? Applaud us." Then he placed his lips upon hers and kissed her again, and felt her give in to him, her lips parting. Their tongues met. Under her open jacket she felt his hands caress her breasts; the hidden, but to her obvious, bulging within his trousers rubbed against her. She felt dizzy with yearning for him. They were pelted with little bunches of spring flowers bought by the playful romantic Romans from the baskets of the two gypsies working the pavement in front of the cafe.

The lovers separated at last. Though Lara was pink with embarrassment, she was the only one. Charles was all smiles and taking bows. Clinging to Lara's hand, he told her, "I am the envy of every man here. You are mine and that's that. Do you understand?"

There could be but one answer to that. "Yes," she told him. And then, again, but louder, "Yes," for all to hear. "Yes."

A burst of applause from their now-enthralled audience. Charles, the happiness visible on his handsome young face, ignored it. He pressed on. "Since you seem incapable of setting the date, I will. Three weeks from today. You can decide the place. Now say yes, just one more time.''

A hush had suddenly fallen all around them. All that could be heard were the honking of horns and the hum of the traffic going past the cafe. Even the waiters had stopped to hear her answer. They had the dozen or so tables now involved in their romance.

Lara threw her arms out, as if to embrace the world. "Yes!"

The place erupted in convivial applause and lots of laughter. A few men rose from their chairs to shake Charles's hand and pat him on the back. One young man kissed Lara on the cheek. Everyone was chattering away among themselves or congratulating Lara and Charles. He grabbed her with one hand and the waiter with the other, thrusting some money into the waiter's hand. "Negronis for anyone who wants to drink to our happiness." Then he pulled Lara between the tables to the curb where they jumped into a taxi. Both leaned out of the same window, waving good-bye to a cafe full of strangers.

She fell back in the seat, laughing. "You are mad, Charles. What an exhibition." And then added, "And what fun."

"Not mad, just happy. Well," he conceded, "maybe mad *and* happy. Let's go back to the hotel and make love."

"Yes, please," was her answer to that.

There were moments during his passionate possession of her when she would be overcome to think that this handsome, multifaceted, very special, so sexy young man and she were going to have fun together for the rest of their lives.

He had learned so quickly the things that excited her sexually. He had found ways to give her multiple orgasms where she could hardly catch her breath. He was, among other things, a young stud in his full sexual prime. He wanted to exercise that in every way he could with her. He seemed, as once Jamal had been, obsessed with taking her down a path of sexual bliss, and reveled in her comings. He liked to rub her body and whisper the sexual delights he had in store for her that he knew would make her come. He liked to fuck her in the steamy bathwater and then, clean, lie her on a towel on the floor and massage her warm body with oil of almonds until she glistened and smelled like an orchard of almond trees in full bloom. And then he enjoyed taking her slippery-smooth body and rubbing it against his while he fucked her fiercely from the front and the back, and filled her with his sperm, and told her about all the love babies they would make.

They had dinner brought to their suite of rooms. There they dined on artichokes, pasta with cream and three cheeses, and cherry ice cream—which he rubbed inside the lips of her cunt. She writhed with the cold against her warm genitals, and laughed while it melted and he licked his ice cream from what he called his favorite vessel. Sex was fun and crazy at such times with him. He tried to insert spoonfuls of the ice cream into her and suck it out. Sated with sex, they fell asleep to the sound of a clock chiming the small hours away.

Lara slept at first the deep sleep of the exhausted, and then fitfully. She woke and tried to fall asleep again. She tossed and turned. Awake, it came rushing back to her, over and over again, that Evan had never told her his wife was dead, that they had been free to live openly. He had never given her an inkling that anything had changed in their circumstances. That they might have married and made a home together. Not a word. Only that single important hint. She should have guessed something was amiss when he told her he wanted to take her to Tuscany. And she didn't even get it. She had been so drilled into believing they could never go there together, she had crossed Tuscany out and been unable to accept Evan's suggestion.

The last thing she thought of before drifting off once again into a deep sleep was that in the morning she would tell Charles they had been hasty, she needed more time. There was too much to cope with if she married him now. She felt suddenly like a woman with too much of a past to settle on this delicious young lover, lying blissfully happy in peaceful sleep next to her.

It had been Lara's intention to sit down and talk sensibly to Charles, to make him understand that they had been acting in haste, in moments of passion, when they committed themselves to marry in three weeks' time. That in the cold light of day she had thought better of it. This seemed the only way she could solve her dilemma. Her intentions were thwarted the moment she opened her eyes to the kiss he placed upon her lips, an affectionate, gentle kiss, and saw the love he had for her shining in his eyes.

She pulled herself up against the headboard of the bed, and

he arranged the pillows behind her to make her more comfortable. She gazed at him, his youth, his handsomeness, the fierce intelligence in his face, the provocative, sensuous way he used his body. She knew by the way women turned to look at him when he was walking down a street, when he was relaxed and in conversation, that it was not just her own sexual attraction to him calling out. He was a passionately lusty young man who had had all the women he had ever wanted. There was something about his young flesh, his vigor, his passionate love for her, that told her what folly it was to run away from him. And yet . . .

She smiled at him. He removed the sheet covering her and gazed at her nakedness. He was making love to her with his eyes and his heart. He kissed her on her flat tummy, caressed her hips, and then, cupping one breast in his hands, he sucked hungrily on her dark, erect nipple. With his thumb he caressed the nimbus around it and then tongued it gently. She could not hold back her sighs of pleasure. He pulled her into his lap and said, "Good morning. It is my intention to wake you every morning of our life together with some sort of kiss. Just to remind you how extraordinarily lovely and sensuous a woman you are, and how much I appreciate your love."

She wanted to weep, so touched was she by his love for her. He found her clitoris and teased it with hungry fingers, then slipped them between the lips of the slit beneath her mound of Venus and buried them as deep inside her as his hand could reach. Then rocking her lightly in his arms he caressed her already moist, silky smooth vagina. She placed her arms around his neck and rested her head against his chest.

"I have to stop this, and you have to get dressed. But first you must call your children. A change of plans. We are not going to Perugia today, and you will not get to see Fontefresca for a while yet. We are going to have lunch with some friends in the country—my best friends, in fact. And then we are Concording to New York. The children will meet our plane, and I am whisking you all off to L.A. and a house on the beach in Malibu, where we are going to spend a few days together. It would be nice for the children to like me before they call me dad."

"I have to think about this, Charles."

"What's to think about? I have to meet them sometime."

Slowly and most reluctantly he withdrew his caresses. He

licked his fingers and laughed. "Have a taste. It's still cherry ice cream."

He carried her to the bath he had already drawn for her, placed her gently in the scented water, and handed her a sponge.

"And why L.A.?" she asked.

"I have to veto two paintings at the Getty Museum sometime this week. The fax arrived this morning. It's really important I be there. And I am not leaving you behind."

She stayed in the bath till he returned with the telephone. "Don't chicken out on me, Lara. This is important to our future." He looked at his watch. "Oh, shit! The time change. You can't call now, it's five in the morning on the East Coast. That fucks things up."

Lara hoped that she was hiding her relief. She really wanted to solve her dilemma before she brought the children into it. But she could hardly explain that to Charles. Especially since, with every gesture he made toward a future with her, Lara fell that little bit more in love with him, and her *angoisse* over telling him about herself and Evan grew greater.

"No, it doesn't. It just changes things. You and I will fly to L.A. You can get your work done, and we can send for them. Their nanny can fly out with them."

"Promise?"

"Promise."

He seemed content with that idea. Then he told her to hurry. As he was leaving the bathroom, he said, "Trousers."

"Trousers?"

"Wear trousers. You do have some in your case?"

He watched her struggle into the honey-colored, polished leather pants that fitted her like a second skin. She walked around the room bare breasted, brushing her hair. She knew very well how sexy she looked that way, in tight pants and nothing else. Jamal used to say it was because she had the raunchiest tits of any woman he had ever known. That it had all to do with the bruised, dark plum color of her nipples against the creamy-white skin, the shape and heft of them above such a narrow waist.

He picked up the polo shirt she had laid out to wear, and walking up to her, told her as he helped her into it, "Very sexy, and don't you know it!"

He was onto her, and she liked that. He was enjoying her:

she liked that even more. Now he held out the matching leather jacket. She called it the most elegant biker's jacket in the world. She slipped her arms into the Saint Laurent creation. He zipped it up. It fitted snugly and displayed her at her sexiest in clothes. It finished at the waist, and Charles gave it a tug, resisting an urge to slap her hard on her bottom. He had the feeling she was the kind of woman who would have slapped him back for doing it.

"You look sensational." He contented himself with running his hands over her body and between her legs. Teasingly he placed her hand over the fly of his tight blue jeans, and directed it so that it rubbed his swelling penis. "Sadly there's no time. But I'll get you later."

She tilted her head back and gave him that seductive, wicked little laugh of hers. "I'm hungry."

"We're having breakfast out. I have to make one stop, then we'll eat at a little place I know that you'll love. Come on, I'm late and we have to go. You may not believe this, but I am working and you're coming with me."

"The packing?"

"Nothing to pack. It's all arranged. The maids have instructions, and our luggage will be waiting for us at the airport." Seizing her hand he rushed her from the room.

Outside, in front of the Hassler, the doorman and several people were standing around the machine. He watched Lara's face. A smile broke across it. "I don't believe it."

"You had better believe it. You are not the only one mad about Harleys."

The motorbike gleamed in the sunlight. It was a perfect Roman morning in springtime. They were going to ride through Rome on his Harley-Davidson. She walked around the bike. She had a similar model back home. "I'm itching to drive it."

"No, not in the city. I know the streets better, and how to handle the mad Roman drivers. I can make better time here in town. Once we're on the outskirts of the city, you can take over."

He mounted the bike, kicked the starter, and the machine burst into life. Lara slung her leg over the bike to ride pillion. She delighted in the feel of the bike under her. They took off through the heart of Rome, to see it as she had never seen it before. It felt good to be on the bike. And he felt terrific to hold on to.

Their first stop was a museum, where the guard let them pass into the courtyard on the bike. A second guard seemed to know Charles and agreed to watch the Harley. Arm in arm, they entered the building. He introduced her to two men and then she stood aside while they spoke. They kept calling him *Dottore*. She listened to a fierce debate about how to restore, or indeed whether to risk restoring a magnificent Caravaggio, the only painting on the wall of the handsome room. On permanent loan from the Vatican, it seemed to have become the focus of a problem that centered on the museum itself. From what she could understand, the deciding factor was Charles Valentine's opinion. Lara was impressed. And then quite suddenly all the waving of arms and shouting, the thumping on the table and flipping through photographs and stacks of letters, was over. Lots of handshakes and smiles, kisses on cheeks. Everyone was relieved a decision had finally been made. Just an hour after their arrival, they were back on the bike.

They stopped for breakfast on the Piazza Navona, where Charles left the bike in the protection of three boys, Roman toughs. And they sat in the sun and ate fresh hot bread, butter and cheese, and delicious prosciutto and melon. There was hot black coffee and then irresistibly crisp, fresh-fried doughnuts, Italian-style. Then they mounted the bike and rode away from Rome.

He took her down the Appian Way, to a pine-covered hill overlooking Rome. If offered her a view of the city she would never forget. In the country they stopped in a strange wood, a forest of mingled pines and cypresses and wildflowers. There they lay among fallen pine needles and talked.

The children were on his mind. He wanted to know all about them. She had no problem about that: she adored her children. No topic was more welcome. He was quick to understand that, although she loved Bonnie no less than Karim, the boy had a charm that she found irresistible. That giving him up to Jamal for six months of the year was still a very hard thing for her to do. He asked no questions about her former husbands, and she volunteered nothing.

They dozed off in the sun. Just short catnaps. He looked like

an Adonis asleep in the wood. How many hearts had he broken
before he found her and fell in love? She hurt for all those
women, because she knew that he had found in her everything
he had ever wanted, and she was where they wanted to be. And
being there was sublime. She had already removed her jacket.
Now she pulled off her polo shirt and leaned against the trunk
of a tree, where she was certain to be the first thing he would
see when he awakened. She waited for her lover to open his
eyes.

And she was the first thing he saw. Her silvery-blond hair
shimmering in the sunlight. The sensuous green eyes smiling at
him. He leaned on his side, resting on his elbow to enjoy her.
Finally he crawled over to her and unzipped the leather pants.
They lay among the pine needles, with one of nature's stronger
perfumes luring them toward carnal lust. He took his time. He
eased himself slowly into her and took her in a long crescendo
of sexual release. They had climaxed together, and it had been
somehow more special for them. She wanted to keep him alive
inside her always, and he was intent upon her not losing a drop
of his seed. She hardly moved. She felt emotionally exhausted
by their intercourse. It was he who raised her just enough from
where she lay to pull her pants up and tenderly zip her into them.
Then he buttoned his Levis and, taking her by the hands, raised
her from the ground and held her in his arms, crushing her
breasts against him. He caressed her back with his hands. ''I
love you, Lara. The best times of our life are about to begin.''

He handed her the polo shirt, and she pulled it on. He drew
some stray pine needles from her hair and rearranged it. Then
he watched her repair her makeup till she looked perfect. They
mounted the bike, and she slipped her arms around his waist
and clung to him as they bumped their way through the wood,
onto the dirt road, and toward the rendezvous with his friends.

Lara felt wildly young, reckless, and free. She tightened her
grip around him and reveled in the idea that she held his youth
and love inside her. She was happy and very much in love,
certainly as much as he was.

She liked his friends, and they were generous and showed her
a welcoming warmth. The host couple lived in a sixteenth-
century palazzo, chock-full of marvelous things and embellished with a fine collection of Italian Renaissance paintings.

Thirty people sat down to luncheon, to be amply fed and waited upon, perhaps overly wined.

And Lara saw yet another side of her lover. He was the most structured-unstructured man she had ever had an affair with. He changed his plans with a laid-back ease, and took her along with it. They never made the Concorde. Instead they flew to London, just for one night. How, when, where had the plans changed? She had no idea. She had seen and heard nothing. But somehow he had been contacted at the luncheon party, and had arranged to be at the National Gallery in London the next morning.

After that meeting they did fly the Concorde to Washington and dashed for the connection for L.A. Lara found Charles Sebastian Valentine dizzyingly exciting to be with. Not only because she was in love, or because he was a handsome young stud as well as an intellectual with the life-style of a jet-set playboy. Or because of how impressive he was, dressed in his three-piece, gray Savile Row suit, matched by the perfect Turnbull and Asser shirt and tie, making monumental artistic decisions for those without the know-how or courage to do it themselves. He had stature and an authority she had not seen. She watched him exercise it over his slightly awed peers.

While he was waiting in the VIP lounge to board the plane, his broker and a lawyer appeared. He held one of those high-flier executive meetings calculated to impress. Was this her very own lover? She marveled at the agile mind, the ease with which he assessed a deal. For a moment she let herself believe he was and had everything. Every quality she might seek in a man. And how could she live with him, make a life that was whole and aboveboard, without confessing to him her years with his father? That dilemma still hung over their future.

The house in Malibu was his. He had bought it when he was playing the wealthy young beach bum. Or so he told her. He loved the house and the place. He talked about his plans to teach Karim to ride the surf; Bonnie, too, if she wished. Lara spoke to the children every day in long, amusing conversations. Finally she arranged for them to fly out to be with them.

His friends in L.A. were young and like him: exciting, creative, professional high fliers. They were fun and interesting. And he had been right—her age didn't matter. She didn't feel

the older woman with them. She felt, in fact, as young as they were.

On the third morning they were in the Malibu beach house, there was breakfast on the balcony overlooking the Pacific. Kiwi-fruit and strawberries, pineapple and cherries, black coffee, and wholemeal rolls drenched in butter and honey. Just a few people dotted the dazzling white sand. The stretch of multimillion-dollar houses built beside the sandy beach were bathed in California sunshine. Charles was saying how much he looked forward to the arrival of the children. What fun they would have. He was happy that in two days' time they would be here.

It was just a little thing, but it triggered something in Lara. A reminder that, beneath the surface of her happiness, she still had a past that was dogging her. She still had not come to terms with it.

There was an innocent enough start. She had said to him, "I like your friends here in L.A. They're a bit California-crazy, but great fun. I did notice a girl, Mandy. I think she's still in love with you."

His answer had been, "She's one of the things we don't have to tell each other about. She was firmly there once, but now it's in the past. Remember, we don't have to play true confessions with each other. Boring, unimportant. Who gives a shit about what's gone by? The past and its mistakes? All those bleeding hearts—whether they were mine, yours, or someone else's who once mattered. Looking back is silly—and dangerous."

He went to her and kissed her on the lips, stroking her hair. He lowered his head to lick the cleavage between her breasts. "I'll be back before four. Have a good day," he said, mocking the false bonhomie with an Americanism that he loathed. She walked him to the gray Ferrari. He climbed in, and she waved him off. As soon as he was out of sight tears filled her eyes. She had been grateful to have stemmed the flow that threatened earlier.

She did leave a note. A horrid lie. "I didn't know how to tell you. It was a wonderful fling, a holiday romance, I will never forget. Forgive me." She left the Medici ring on top of the note, the note on top of the pillow next to his.

She knew he would be devastated by what she had said and

done. She knew that it was a dreadful thing to walk out on him like that. But she couldn't help herself. She had had a chance for happiness, but her past was robbing her of it. And she seemed unable to stop looking back. That was how she fell into the abyss.

Cannonberry Chase, Karim, Bonnie . . . they were all there for her, but nothing seemed the same. Their love could not replace what she had had with Charles. How could this have happened—that fate should have dealt this final blow to her happiness? But if she thought that she could run away from Charles so easily, she was mistaken. Although she was putting on a brave front for herself, every day without him was agony.

Chapter 30

Emily was sitting on the south lawn when Lara came in from her afternoon ride. The scene was like something from a family portrait: her mother's large straw hat and pretty summer frock; the tea table dressed in a crisp, yellow silk organza embroidered cloth, rippling in the warm summer's breeze; the silver gleaming on the table; the white porcelain sparkling in the sunlight. On a perfect green lawn, with Cannonberry Chase looming in the background.

Emily was alone, and that was unusual. As Lara approached her mother, she realized that of late Emily had begun to show her years. Although she still had the looks and chic she was so famous for, still held New York high society in a tight grip, time was not on her side. Lara had really taken notice for the first time two nights before. Henry and Emily, after the three had dined together, announced to her that they had made over the deeds of Cannonberry Chase to Lara, effective upon the death of either one of them. She had as yet not quite recovered from such an accolade. It was an unexpected expression of the family's love and respect for her, a struggle hard won. She knew that such a gesture acknowledged her as the future matriarch not only of her beloved Cannonberry Chase, but of the family. Unsolicited rewards she had never set her cap for or dreamed of receiving. Lara knew what that must have cost Emily. Cannonberry Chase had been her life's work, her greatest love—and Lara her least favorite child. She wondered if Emily had been happy with her life, something she would never dream of asking.

Emily offered her daughter tea.

"This is unusual, your having tea alone, Mother."

"Hardly alone. Your father has had his tea and has gone for a sail. Sam was here with Bonnie, but they have gone off somewhere. And I have shooed everyone else away."

"Shall I stay or leave?"

"Stay. We can have one of those chats you and I never have."

"About anything special?"

Emily ignored the question. "Lara, are you contemplating another marriage?"

"Why do you ask?"

"Because it seems to me that you were never happier than when you were married to Sam. I think for all your adventurous spirit, you like the institution of marriage."

"That's true."

"In that we are alike."

That was probably the only similarity Emily had ever drawn between them. Something was amiss. Unused to any show of closeness from her mother, this conversation rather embarrassed Lara.

"I never asked then what went wrong there, and I certainly do not want to know now. But what I do know is that Sam is still waiting in the wings, wanting to marry you again. Are you going to accept?"

"I have been seriously thinking about it of late."

"Not your best choice, I think."

"Oh? There was a time when you thought he was."

"That was then. This is now. He did, after all, let us down."

The same unrelenting, unforgiving, Emily Dean Stanton speaks, thought Lara.

"No. I would choose the young man I had tea with, who left this."

Emily removed the Catherine de Médicis ring from her purse. The shock of seeing it again struck an emotional chord so strong as to make Lara feel quite queasy for a moment. Emily reached for her daughter's hand and, raising it, slid the ring on her finger.

"Just a little too loose, I think. But not dangerously so. Quite a handsome ring. Yes, Charles Sebastian Valentine would be my choice. But I think you must do something about him quite quickly, Lara. He is very angry with you. He called you a liar, actually."

"Charles, here? Where is he?"

"Gone. He came out of desperation. But, having chased across the Atlantic after you, he thought the ring could speak for him. Quite a clever move, I think."

"Did he say anything else?"

"Only that he would never chase after you again. If you want him, you will have to go to him. I suggest you get your skates on, Lara. That young man has real character, and strength of will. And he is very much in love."

"I can't believe I'm having this conversation."

The two women fell silent for some minutes. Emily poured more tea. She raised Lara's hand again, stroked her fingers, and ran her thumb over the carved ruby. Quite choked with emotion, Lara asked, "What did you tell him, Mother?"

"What would you have had me tell him, Lara? That you returned from Italy and came back home to Cannonberry Chase, where you live a life of mild unhappiness? That you are prepared to settle for that for the rest of your life? Is that what you would have had me tell him?"

Lara slid slowly from the chair, onto her knees, next to her mother. She placed her head in Emily's lap and wept. Emily hesitantly placed her hand on Lara's head and stroked her hair. "Angel's hair. Lovely hair. Like spun sugar. Christmas-tree angel's hair."

Emily handed her daughter a handkerchief. Wiping a tear from Lara's cheek, she said, "This time round, let's have a grand, proper, white wedding, here at Cannonberry Chase. You never did have one of those."

The airport was a few miles from Perugia. Lara put the plane down in a perfect landing. She got through the arrival formalities with less commotion than she had expected. Her mind was filled with nothing except getting to Charles as quickly as possible. She had made up her mind, and nothing could stop her now. Or so she thought.

At Mercatello, population about one hundred souls, she guessed, since it boasted a barber and a coffee shop, the taxi broke down. She checked her map, and tried her feet. The walk to the summit of Monte Vibiano looked none too serious a climb. It was, after all, a small mountain. When repaired, the taxi and its contents would follow. She had not counted on the heat of the sun, nor her anxiety. Nor on the fact that Monte Vibiano was the end of the road, literally. Beyond that there was nothing but a dirt track. So she began her climb up the winding road.

Her anxiety was caused by no more than wanting to be sure she had chosen the fastest route to Charles. Lara knew, when she'd left Emily at the tea table in the sun, what she must do. That it was too late to create another stopgap relationship with Sam or Jamal. Or any other man for that matter. She was returning to Charles because to have left him had been a destructive act that might have ruined both their lives. She would do what she had to for them to stay together.

Monte Vibiano was hardly a village, or even a hamlet. A magnificent Tuscan villa of stone stood behind walls and lofty, ornate iron gates that creaked open slowly into a courtyard. A few small houses overlooked the other Tuscan hills. The paved road ended there, and beyond was nothing but an empty landscape with a dirt track running through it to another steep climb. Daunted by the idea that she might get lost, Lara gave in and, from the villa, she called Charles.

"Pronto."

She had to close her eyes and take a deep breath to compose herself. It was the first time she had heard his voice since she'd left him.

"Charles, it's Lara." The line seemed to crackle and spit. He sounded a million miles away. "Charles," she shouted again into the telephone. He spoke, at last.

"Where are you?"

"Monte Vibiano. Will you come and get me?"

"You've come up the wrong side of the mountain."

"Will you come and get me?" she shouted again into the telephone.

"If you start walking now, you should be here before sunset. Just follow the track. You will come to the cypress wood. Beyond that are the olive groves. From there, just keep walking and looking up—and you will see di Fontefresca. I will be here in the house, waiting for you."

"The least you can do is meet me halfway."

"You walked out, you walk back in, Lara, all the way."

She was stunned by his harshness, but knew just how cruel

she had been, how much she must have hurt him. She had coffee with the owner of the villa, a hospitable and charming man who knew Charles. She made certain arrangements with him, so that he then drove her as far up the track as he could without a four-wheel drive. From there she followed the track.

She had seen magnificent views, a landscape that defied description. She had seen the odd shack and old lady dressed in black. One such woman gave her a bowl of cool, fresh goat's milk. The sun was at its lowest in the sky before it dropped into a glorious sunset. She was making her final approach to the palazzo. Hot and tired from her long climb, she stopped, putting up a hand to shade her eyes. She looked up through the olive trees, into the sun just dropping behind the elegant palazzo above. It was then that she saw him running down the mountain, weaving his way through the trees to her. She started running as fast as she could, and they rushed into each other's arms.

"I thought I would die without you," he told her, and kissed her with urgent passion.

"I did die a little without you. I felt only half alive from the moment I walked out on you." They kissed again.

He pushed her gently away and asked her, "How do I know you won't do this to me again? How do I know you are here to stay?"

She stepped aside. She had heard the faint sound of singing before he had. She pointed down through the gnarled olive trees—to Bonnie and Karim and their nanny, and Coral and Nancy. And then, slipping her arms beneath his shirt and around him, and caressing his flesh with adoring hands, she told him. "Because I brought the family with me."

About the Author

Roberta Latow is the author of *Tidal Wave*, *Three Rivers*, and *Cheyney Fox*. She was prominent in the New York art world during the sixties and has lived in Greece and Egypt. Ms. Latow traveled extensively in Turkey and Ethiopia and has assembled the largest private Coptic art collection in the world. She was born in Springfield, Massachusetts, and now lives in Great Britain.

Explore the darkest reaches of human desire...

with

Roberta Latow